Praise for *New York Times* bestselling author JoAnn Ross

"[JoAnn Ross has a] talent for blending vibrant characters, congenial small-town settings and pressing social issues in a heartwarming contemporary romance."
—*Booklist*

"Ross's insight into both romantic attraction and family dynamics is striking."
—*Publishers Weekly*

"A superb storyteller who always creates unforgettable characterization."
—*RT Book Reviews*

Praise for *USA TODAY* bestselling author Allison Leigh

"An emotionally moving story."
—*RT Book Reviews* on *Hard Choices*

"*Hard Choices* centers on secrets...[and] the answers unfold naturally as Leigh explores each character. I was drawn into the story right from the prologue."
—*The Romance Reader*

JoANN ROSS

New York Times and *USA TODAY* bestselling author JoAnn Ross has been published in twenty-seven countries. A member of Romance Writers of America's Honor Roll of bestselling authors, JoAnn lives with her husband and three rescued dogs—who pretty much rule the house—in the Pacific Northwest. Visit her on the web at www.joannross.com.

ALLISON LEIGH

There **is** a saying that you can never be too rich or too thin. Allison doesn't believe that, but she does believe that you can never have enough books! When her stories find a way into the hearts—and bookshelves—of others, Allison says she feels she's done something right. Making her home in Arizona with her husband, she enjoys hearing from her readers at Allison@allisonleigh.com or P.O. Box 40772, Mesa, AZ 85274-0772.

New York Times Bestselling Author

JoAnn Ross

The Return of
Caine O'Halloran

HARLEQUIN® BESTSELLING AUTHOR COLLECTION

ISBN-13: 978-0-373-18077-6

THE RETURN OF CAINE O'HALLORAN
Copyright © 2013 by Harlequin Books S.A.

The publisher acknowledges the copyright holders of the individual works as follows:

THE RETURN OF CAINE O'HALLORAN
Copyright © 1994 by JoAnn Ross

HARD CHOICES
Copyright © 2003 by Allison Lee Davidson

For questions and comments about the quality of this book, please contact us at CustomerService@Harlequin.com.

® and TM are trademarks of Harlequin Enterprises Limited or its corporate affiliates. Trademarks indicated with ® are registered in the United States Patent and Trademark Office, the Canadian Trade Marks Office and in other countries.

Printed in U.S.A.

Recycling programs
for this product may
not exist in your area.

www.Harlequin.com

CONTENTS

Dear Reader,

I've always enjoyed writing stories about reunited lovers. So much so, I drew from my own reunion romance while writing *The Return of Caine O'Halloran*, and although the book was first released in 1994, Caine and Nora remain very close to my heart.

Long ago, in a small coastal town on the Oregon coast, my high school sweetheart bought me a white paper bag of taffy, then proposed to me at the sea wall. A few months later I was a teenage bride. Nine years after our wedding, I was a divorced single mom.

Although the reasons for our breakup were not as tragic as Caine and Nora's, they were nonetheless painful.

We were apart for two years, during which time we both grew up and changed a great deal. Back then my husband's career involved a lot of traveling, but he returned to town frequently to visit our son.

It was during those visits that we realized that we each liked the person the other had become. That awareness, coupled with a very strong love that had never died, made us decide to try again.

We've never had any reason to regret that decision, and last summer, in that small coastal town we still love to visit, we celebrated our forty-seventh anniversary. And yes, that taffy store is still there!

In our case, as in Caine and Nora's, love truly is better the second time around. I hope you enjoy their story.

XO
JoAnn Ross

THE RETURN OF CAINE O'HALLORAN

New York Times Bestselling Author

JoAnn Ross

To Jay, who refused to give up on us

Chapter 1

He could have driven home blindfolded.

The two-lane road twisted like a snarled fishing line, unreeling through the sawtooth-forested mountains in sharp zigzags that defied compass reckoning. To make matters worse, the spring thaw had pitted the asphalt, creating a new season of dangerous dips and washouts. The low-slung black Ferrari, not built for back-country roads, thumped roughly over the scarred pavement.

Unfazed by the danger, Caine O'Halloran coaxed the hell-on-wheels beast around the deadly narrow switchbacks with practiced skill.

The engine behind his head whined as the revs rose and fell; blaring from the four amplified stereo speakers, Bruce Springsteen was advising "no surrender." Caine's fingers tapped out the driving rhythm of drums and acoustic guitar on the top of the steering wheel.

Towering trees—Pacific silver fir, Western hemlock and the majestic Douglas fir—screened both sides of the roadway, making it seem as if he were racing through a narrow green alley.

Those same trees were reflected in the lenses of Caine's dark glasses. Although the sky overhead was the hue of tarnished silver, a few sunbeams managed to slant through the curtain of trees, laying shimmering stripes of light across the pavement.

The sound of moving water was everywhere as streams born in melting glaciers fed the rivers running to the sea. The scent of freshly cut fir rode the brisk spring wind.

When The Boss started singing about missing Bobby Jean, Caine leaned forward and punched a button to skip the song. He damn well wasn't in any mood to reminisce about lost loves.

"Glory Days," he said approvingly when the speaker blared the familiar lyrics of the next song.

One night a few years ago, after he'd played it three times on the jukebox in a Minneapolis bar, a winsome coed from the University of Minnesota had informed him that it was really a song about faded dreams and lost opportunities.

Caine hadn't believed that then, and he sure as hell didn't now. To him it would always be The Boss's tribute to athletes who possessed blazing speedballs that made other guys look like fools. Guys like Caine O'Halloran.

He sped past a runaway-truck escape ramp that looked like a ski jump, downshifted as he approached yet another twist in the road, then punched the gas pedal. The Ferrari rocketed out of the turn like a moon shot.

Cornering in a Ferrari going top speed wasn't for the faint of heart. The speedometer shot upward and the tachometer approached the red line as the speed of the car blurred the trees. The force of over five hundred horses fully opened up pushed him back against the onyx leather seats. The engine's shriek rivaled that of a fighter jet.

When he reached one of the few straight stretches on the highway, Caine floored the accelerator; straddling the white centerline, the car streaked toward an enormous truck loaded with logs.

The Peterbilt log truck was the same green as the fir trees flashing by the Ferrari's tinted windows. Tall chrome stacks emitted billowy puffs of diesel exhaust, like smoke signals.

The strident warning of the air horn shattered the mountain stillness.

Once.

Twice.

A third time.

Smiling with grim determination, Caine refused to budge. The asphalt stretched between car and truck like a shiny black ribbon. All the time he remained as cool as if he were out for a leisurely Sunday-afternoon drive in the country, instead of barreling hell-bent-for-leather straight to his death. *No retreat; no surrender.* The rock refrain pounded in his head; adrenaline raced through his blood like a drug.

The air horn, now a steady, impatient bleat, split the air.

Time took on the strange feel of an instant slow-motion replay as Caine became vividly aware of the staccato flash of white lines disappearing beneath the

Ferrari's wide radial tires, of the sun glancing off the chrome stack of the truck, of the driver's red-and-black plaid shirt, of his orange-billed cap, of his grizzled gray beard and finally, as the truck came even closer, of the man's expression: first disbelief, then fright, finally fury.

No retreat. No surrender.

Caine waited fatalistically for the bearded man to make his move.

At the last possible second, the truck veered; its right wheels went off the road, scattering gravel. Caine got a fleeting glimpse of a stocky, raised middle finger.

A moment later, a pickup that had been following the Peterbilt passed Caine, as well. The driver stared at the Ferrari in obvious disbelief.

Caine watched the trucks disappear in his rearview mirror. When he'd been seventeen, speeding around these hairpin curves in a fire-engine-red Mustang convertible, emerging victorious from a game of chicken with the ubiquitous log trucks had always left him feeling vividly alive.

But after today's near-death encounter, he felt strangely let down. And disappointed. As Springsteen's gravelly voice began singing about "working on the highway," a hangover Caine had nearly forgotten after crossing the Oregon-Washington State border and entering the Olympic Peninsula came crashing back.

The news spread through the town of Tribulation like wildfire. Caine O'Halloran was back.

Dr. Nora Anderson was on duty in her clinic when she received the unexpected bulletin from her eight-year-old nephew, who'd become airborne after turning a corner too fast on his skateboard. The landing, not soft, had been on a gravel driveway.

"Did you hear the sick news?" Eric Anderson asked, trying with youthful bravado not to flinch as Nora picked pieces of cinder from his palm with a pair of surgical tweezers.

"Eric," his mother chided, "your aunt is trying to concentrate."

Karin Anderson's voice was edged with a stern warning tone that made Nora look up. "What news?"

"Caine got cut from the Yankees," Eric told her.

"But Jimmy Olson told me that his dad told him that Caine was comin' home to live here while he gets his arm back in shape."

"We saw his car parked outside The Log Cabin," he said. "You should see it, Aunt Nora! It looks just like the Batmobile!"

A ratmobile was more like it. And to be hanging around a bar in the middle of the afternoon! Obviously, Caine hadn't changed. "It's true," Karin said, her blue eyes offering sympathy.

"Well, I hope things work out for him," Nora said calmly. She'd sealed any feelings concerning Caine O'Halloran inside her, years ago. It was easier. Safer.

"Do you think he'll give me a ride in his car, huh, Aunt Nora?" Eric asked hopefully. "After all, we are kinda related."

Nora knew that Eric used his aunt's former marriage to the baseball star to gain points on the playground. Understanding a small boy's obsession with heroes— even ones undeserving of such loyalty—Eric's behavior had never bothered her.

But then again, Caine hadn't been living in Tribulation, either.

"I don't know," she answered. Never having been able to predict her ex-husband's behavior, she certainly wasn't going to start trying to guess what was going through his adolescent mind now. "You'll have to ask him that yourself." She tackled another piece of gravel.

"Ouch!" Eric yanked his hand back.

"Sorry." She'd used more force than necessary.

Damn Caine, anyway.

Although she'd been in the first year of medical school during their brief and stormy marriage, he hadn't believed her; it was more that he hadn't listened. By the time she'd been married a week, Nora had realized that her husband possessed the unique ability to hear only what he wanted to hear.

No, Nora corrected now. It wasn't that Caine hadn't believed her when she'd insisted that she didn't intend to let marriage or motherhood interfere with her plans to be a doctor.

"Well, I think that's all of it," she said, giving her nephew's hand one last antiseptic wash. Nora turned to her sister-in-law. "If I were you, I'd hide that skateboard."

"I'm turning it into kindling the minute we get home."

"Mom!" Color returned to Eric's cheeks, staining them as red as the raspberries that grew wild in the forest surrounding the mountain town.

"We'll discuss this later," Karin said firmly. "At home. With your father."

His shoulders slumped disconsolately. "Dad'll side with you. He always does."

Although she agreed with Karin's decision to deny Eric further skateboard privileges, Nora's heart went out to her nephew. "Hey, Eric..."

His bottom lip was thrust out over his top one. "What?"

She tossed him a couple of the silver gambling tokens Karl Mahlstrom had paid his bill with earlier that morning. The retired mill worker had returned from Reno, Nevada, with paper cups filled with coins and a stiff shoulder from eighteen hours at the slot machines. "Why don't you take your mom out for some ice cream?"

The pout wavered, a reluctant smile played at the corners of his lips. "Okay," he agreed with an outward lack of enthusiasm that Nora knew was mostly feigned. Then, remembering his manners, he said, "Thanks, Aunt Nora."

"You're welcome." Nora exchanged another long look with her sister-in-law. *We'll talk about Caine later,* Karin's look said.

Not on a bet, Nora's answered.

It was Monday, the day of the week when a steady stream of patients always showed up at the clinic, showing the effects of a weekend of recreational abuse.

On top of that, her nurse, Kirstin Lundstrom, was still on maternity leave. Nora had to serve as nurse, doctor and office clerk, which meant that she barely had time to catch her breath all day.

Not that Nora minded the hectic pace; she was grateful that she didn't have time to think about Caine O'Halloran's return. And what, if anything, that would mean to her life.

Returning to Washington's Olympic Peninsula to

practice family medicine in her hometown of two hundred and fifty residents meant that Nora saw her patients at the grocery store, or over potato salad at a church potluck social.

It also meant that she was more likely to be intimately involved with a patient, so that a serious illness or a death touched her more than it had at the big-city hospitals where she'd worked before returning home to Tribulation.

Many of her patients had lost their health insurance, along with their jobs. They were people too poor to pay for visits to the doctor, but too proud to ask for government assistance. Although the condition of the Northwest's logging and fishing industries had not been struck a fatal blow, recovery was a long time coming to this isolated forest community. In order to finance her new clinic, which she'd set up in the hundred-year-old house she'd inherited from her grandmother, Nora also made the thirty-five-mile round trip to Port Angeles to work in the hospital emergency room.

Her clinic was open on Monday, Wednesday and Friday; she worked at the emergency room on Tuesdays, Thursdays and Saturdays. Although sleep was as rare as it had been during the grueling thirty-six-hour shifts of her internship, not once had she regretted her decision.

Her work in the emergency room, while fulfilling in its own way, paid the bills and put food on the table. Her work at the clinic—caring for family, friends and neighbors—fed her soul.

The complaints today were relatively minor and she wasn't surprised that every one of her patients wanted to talk about Caine's return to Tribulation.

"Caine'll be back on the mound by the All-Star

break," Johnny Duggan informed her after she'd given him a sample package of antihistamine to soothe some yellow-jacket stings that hadn't responded to calamine lotion. "That boy always was a pistol."

Since Johnny was Caine's third cousin on his mother's side, Nora could understand the man's loyalty.

The next member of the Caine O'Halloran fan club was Ingrid Johansson, who'd run the Timberline Café since long before Nora was born. The elderly woman had strained a back muscle getting a box of steak sauce down from a too-high shelf.

"If the boy could come back from that torn rotor cuff three years ago, this new injury won't be any problem," Ingrid predicted as she paid her bill. The worn, rumpled bills, smelling faintly of chain-saw gasoline, were evidence of a clientele consisting mainly of loggers.

"Oh, I brought you something," Ingrid said. "For giving my Lars that cough medicine last week for no charge."

She handed Nora a brown paper bag from which rose an enticing scent of warm apples and brown sugar. "It's a strudel," she added unnecessarily.

"Thanks." Nora could envision the cellulite leaping to her thighs from the aroma alone. "It smells delicious."

She'd already gained ten pounds since returning to Tribulation, mostly from her patients' peach cobblers, berry pies, fresh-caught—and thankfully cleaned—fish, corn muffins and numerous other local delicacies.

It was as if everyone realized she was undercharging them for their visits, and although they were grateful, pride insisted that they augment the reduced fee with whatever they could spare.

"I figured you could use a little fattening up." Ingrid's bright eyes swept judiciously over Nora's slender frame. "You're not gonna get yourself a man unless you put a little more meat on those bones."

"Actually, I've been too busy to even think about men."

"Well, I expect that'll change, now that Caine's back in town," the older woman declared.

"My marriage to Caine ended a long time ago," Nora replied, reluctant to be discussing something so personal, but feeling that her disinterest in Caine O'Halloran needed to be put on record.

And who better to start with than Ingrid? Nora doubted that there was a person in Tribulation who didn't pop into the eatery sometime during the week. Especially on Wednesdays, for Ingrid's pot-roast special.

"Legally," Ingrid agreed, closing her pocketbook with a snap. "My experience has been that feelings are quite another kettle of fish."

Determined to get the last word in, she left the office without giving Nora an opportunity to respond.

For the rest of the day, Nora continued to smile and nod and write prescriptions and listen to yet another story depicting the life and times of Tribulation's local hero.

Twenty-one years ago, Tribulation, a timber town founded a century earlier by a Swedish logger and an Irishman who'd been laying railroad tracks up the coast, had gone through hard times.

People who could trace their roots back to those original settlers had been forced to leave their homes and seek what they hoped would be temporary employment in the Puget Sound cities of Seattle, Olympia and Tacoma.

Storefronts had been boarded up; the school established by the founding fathers had been in danger of closing, which would have forced the students to be bused to Port Angeles. Morale had been at an all-time low.

Until a cocky fourteen-year-old took the pitcher's mound during a state high school championship game between the Tribulation Loggers and the Richland Bombers and threw what Washington sportswriters the next morning were calling "the pitch heard 'round the state."

From that day on, Caine O'Halloran was known as the Golden Boy with the golden arm. His natural ability to throw a ball gained him fame and admirers and his hometown was eager to bask in the reflected glow of his popularity.

He went to college on an athletic scholarship, then on to play professional baseball. He spent some time in the minors because although his fastball flew at ballistic speed, no one, including Caine, ever had any idea exactly where it was going.

A sportswriter for the *Seattle Times* once remarked that O'Halloran, then playing for the Tacoma Athletics, didn't throw to spots, he threw to continents.

However, with time, he'd garnered control and began making headlines for his energetic play both on and off the baseball diamond as he moved from team to team, league to league, barreling into every new town like a hired gun, paid to win championships. Which he did, with almost monotonous regularity.

He was one of those rare, powerful athletes known

as a "closer"—a pitcher brought to the mound in the last innings to win the game. And like so many relief pitchers Nora had met during her brief marriage, Caine was a bit mad. Mad angry, and mad crazy.

One particular stunt she recalled vividly was during his stint at Tacoma when he'd relieved the boredom of waiting to be called to the mound by telephoning other bullpens throughout the Pacific Coast League. By imitating the voices of the other teams' coaches, he'd ordered relievers hundreds of miles away to begin warming up.

The prank had resulted in a fine and more nation-wide publicity than money ever could have purchased.

But now, according to the articles she'd read, Caine's golden arm had turned to brass and his most recent team, the New York Yankees, had put him on waivers.

Speculation ran rampant concerning his future; doc-tors who'd never examined him were interviewed on television and in the papers, their prognoses ranging from Caine's return in time for the fall playoffs, to the prediction that his career was over. The one thing every article agreed upon was that Caine refused to accept that his playing days were over.

Which wasn't surprising, since in Nora's experience, most athletes possessed a seemingly genetic inability to accept the fact that their bodies might be more fragile than their determination. Or their egos.

The afternoon was almost over when Karl Lar-strom, a rough-hewn former logger in his late seven-ties, showed up at the clinic without an appointment, his seven-year-old great-grandson in tow.

"Gunnar here got a fishhook in his ear," he advised

her laconically. "Tried to clip it off with a pair of wire cutters, but it won't budge."

Nora smiled down at the boy whose wet blue eyes suggested he'd been crying. "Hi, Gunnar," she greeted him. "Why don't you hop up here and I'll see what we can do."

"I've been teaching the boy how to cast," Karl told her while she worked on the metal fishhook firmly imbedded in the boy's earlobe. "Guess he needs a mite more practice."

"It was the damn tree," Gunnar insisted, flinching when Nora experimentally jiggled the hook. "It got in the way."

"Watch your mouth, boy," Karl advised. "Your mama's not gonna let you keep fishing with me if she thinks I'm teaching you how to cuss."

"But that's what you said when the line got tangled in the first place," Gunnar argued. "Ow!"

"Those trees are infamous for eating fishing lines," Nora assured the boy, who'd gone pale.

"I suspect you heard about Caine," Karl Larstrom offered.

A spot of bright red blood beaded where the now freed hook had entered the skin. Nora swabbed at the minuscule hole with alcohol.

"Several times. All done," she declared, hoping to forestall any more conversation concerning Caine.

"Joe Bob Carroll saw him driving toward town around noon."

"Really?" Nora asked in a tone of absolute disinterest.

"Yup." Karl had never been one to pick up on subtlety. "He was driving one of them fancy Eye-talian sports cars." He reached into his pocket and pulled out some bills.

"So Eric told me." Nora put the rumpled money in the cashbox she kept in the top drawer. Instead of gasoline, these dollar bills smelled vaguely of fish. "He said it looked like a Batmobile."

"Yup," Karl said after chewing the description over for a moment. "I reckon it does, at that. Did Eric tell you about him playing chicken with Harmon Olson's log truck?"

Despite her determination to ignore every bit of unwelcome news about her former husband, that particular tidbit earned her reluctant attention.

"He wasn't!"

"Joe Bob Carroll was right behind Harmon in his pickup." Karl's eyes brightened when he realized he'd finally hit on a piece of information Nora hadn't already heard.

"I thought you and Gunnar were out fishing all day."

"We were. But word gets around."

"Tell me about it," she murmured.

Gossip was the motherlode of small towns and in this case, Tribulation's grapevine was obviously working at warp speed.

"Caine was riding the centerline, just the way he did back when he was workin' overtime to be the town hellion, and from the way Joe Bob tells it, it looked like he wasn't gonna move, come hell or high water."

Obviously, Caine hadn't changed one little bit. Not that she would have expected him to.

Stupid reckless idiot!

Although she told herself that she didn't care what happened to Caine, Nora had spent too many years in the chaos of emergency rooms, trying to save lives, to stand for anyone foolish enough to risk throwing his life away.

"I take it Harmon gave in."

"Yup. I expect Caine'll drop in at The Log Cabin to have a drink with his old friends. In case you wanna stop by," he added slyly.

Just what she needed—another matchmaker. Nora quickly declined but after Karl and Gunner had left she couldn't stop her troubled thoughts from drifting to The Log Cabin and to Caine O'Halloran.

Chapter 2

If Tribulation, Washington, brought to mind the type of neat little New England villages that had proliferated at the turn of the century, it was because the residents preferred to keep it that way. It was a town of Nordic cleanliness, where shop owners still swept the sidewalks each morning and the streets remained as clean as a Swedish kitchen.

A traveler leaving the interstate would find no franchise restaurants in Tribulation; there were more churches—three—than taverns—one—and the movie theater was only open on weekend nights. The crack of Little League bats was heard on Saturday mornings, the chime of church bells on Sundays.

When he'd first arrived in America from his native Sweden, Olaf Anderson, one of the founders of Tribulation, had worked as a lumberjack in the forests of Maine. During those frigid winter months when logging came to a standstill, he would migrate down to Massachusetts, or Vermont, where he worked as a handyman. Eventually, he'd made his way to Washington.

Since he'd thoroughly enjoyed his time in the East, it had seemed a reasonable idea to build a replica of a New England village in this wild Western territory.

Olaf's best friend, Darcy O'Halloran, a wild Irish, hard-drinking Saturday-night brawler and jig dancer, had argued that the unruly land cloaked in a tangle of forests, steep mountains and deeply glaciated valleys bore scant resemblance to New England.

But Olaf had a very clear vision of the town he and Darcy would build together. A town that Olaf planned to name New Stockholm, while Darcy held out for New Dublin.

For a time it seemed the settlement of loggers, miners and fishermen would go nameless. Finally, after they'd been arguing for nearly a year, one frustrated citizen suggested they call the town Tribulation. The moniker, Olaf and Darcy decided, fitted nicely in a region that already boasted a Mount Despair, Mount Triumph, Torment, Forbidden, and Paradise.

More than a century later, the centerpiece of Tribulation remained a wide, grassy, green square. A fountain bubbled at one end of the green, a horseshoe pit was at the other. A clock tower, made of dark red brick that had weathered to a dusky pink over the century, could be spotted for miles in all directions.

In the middle of the green square was a lacy white Victorian bandstand, erected in the early 1900s by an O'Halloran ancestor who'd believed that every town needed a band. Beside the bandstand was a larger-than-life-size wooden statue of Olaf Anderson, erected by one of his descendants in the 1940s. A woodpecker, displaying uncanny precision, had pecked a hole in the statue's posterior.

Across from the square, between the post office and the fire station, was the gray-stone three-story city hall, the tallest structure, save for the clock tower, in town. The bronze plaque on the cornerstone revealed that the building had been erected in 1899. It also named the mayor of Tribulation at the time, Lars Anderson, and the builder, Donovan O'Halloran.

Although he'd been born into one of the town's founding families, Caine's ambition had always been to get out. Firmly believing that he was meant for life in the fast lane, he'd always found Tribulation's slow pace and old-fashioned, unchanging ways suffocating.

Slate clouds threatened in a darkening gray sky as Caine drove through the two-block downtown area, through a residential neighborhood of neat frame houses trimmed with colorful shutters, then turned onto the graded road out of town.

Drawn by emotions too complex to consider, he stopped the Ferrari in front of the wrought-iron gates of the Pioneer Cemetery, cut the engine and sat there, his hands draped over the steering wheel.

A rush of unbidden, unwanted memories flooded his mind. Memories of a little boy, plump cheeks pink from the brisk spring winds, smiling mouth stained with strawberries, a beloved green-and-yellow Oakland A's cap perched rakishly atop his blond curls, his husky legs pumping away as he ran toward the front door, eager, as always, to go anywhere with his daddy.

Daddy. The word tore at Caine, even now, years later. He pulled a pack of cigarettes from his breast pocket, shook out a cigarette, lighted it with the dashboard lighter, then slumped back into the leather seat and drew the acrid, yet soothing smoke deep into his lungs.

He sure as hell hadn't planned for Nora Anderson to get pregnant. On his way from a farm team in Montana to his new Triple A team in Tacoma, Caine had made the fatal mistake of stopping off in Tribulation the night of the Midsummer Eve festival.

Nora, a senior at the University of Washington at the time, had also been home for the weekend; at first Caine hadn't recognized his best friend's little sister.

The heavy, dark-framed glasses that had always made her look like a studious little owl had been replaced by contacts, the ugly metal braces had come off, leaving behind straight, dazzling-white teeth, and although she could never have been called voluptuous, the skinny angles he'd remembered had been replaced by slender curves in all the right places.

The young woman Nora had become had proved different from the sex-crazed baseball Annies Caine was accustomed to. Not only was she gorgeous in a quiet, understated way, she was also sweet and intelligent. And she'd smelled damn good, too.

Caine had offered to drive Nora home. When he'd taken a detour to his cabin, she hadn't offered a word of complaint.

And when he'd drawn her into his arms, she'd come. Willingly. Eagerly.

When he'd left Tribulation the following morning, Caine hadn't expected to see Nora again. After all, he had his rising career, and she'd soon be off to medical school.

Six weeks later, Caine's mother, of all people, had called him with the unwelcome news.

He'd definitely been less than thrilled when he'd learned he was going to be a father, but he'd felt the pressure of being a role model to America's youth. And as much as he'd hated the idea of giving up his carefree lifestyle, Caine had known that knocking up, and then abandoning some innocent hometown girl just wasn't who he wanted to be.

Nora had been no more eager to marry than he was. But after some painfully stilted discussion and not a little coaxing from both families, they'd reluctantly decided that marriage would be in the best interests of their unborn child. After the baby was born, they would divorce and go their separate ways.

The kicker had come when Nora had argued against allowing possible emotional entanglements to interfere with what was nothing more than a legal contrivance. And although Caine hadn't been wild about the prospect of celibate cohabitation, he'd agreed to her condition.

So he'd done his duty, albeit grudgingly. And although he hadn't exactly been husband of the year, neither had he ever—despite Nora's frequent angry accusations—been unfaithful.

Then, six months after their shotgun marriage, Dylan had come crashing into his life, all eight pounds, twelve ounces of him, and Caine had fallen head over heels in love.

Exhaling a long, weary breath, Caine leaned his head back against the car seat, closed his eyes and pressed his fingers tightly against his lids, trying to block out memories too painful to remember. But the indelible images remained, reaching out across the intervening years.

Sixteen months after Dylan's birth, Caine had been called up to the majors. He'd packed a case of beer, cold cuts from the deli and his son into the car and headed off to his cabin for a poker game with his teammates to celebrate having finally achieved his lifelong dream. He was going to The Show.

"Hot damn, Dylan," he'd said, buckling the baby into the padded car seat. "Your daddy's gonna be a big leaguer! What do you think about that?"

"Bid beader!" Dylan had clapped his hands, picking up on his father's good mood.

Caine had laughed. God, how he'd loved his son!

Two hours later, Dylan was gone—taken away by a cruel twist of fate and a drunk driver. In that one fleeting second, Caine's entire life had fallen apart.

And nine years later, he still hadn't figured out how to deal with the loss.

Cursing viciously, Caine crushed his cigarette into the ashtray, then twisted the key in the ignition; tires squealed as he slammed down on the accelerator, ignoring the posted speed limit. He needed a drink, dammit. And he needed it *now*. Less than five minutes later, he pulled the Ferrari into the parking lot of The Log Cabin, spraying gravel in all directions.

Like everything else about Tribulation, The Log Cabin hadn't changed. Oley Severson was still behind the bar, where he'd been for as long as anyone could remember.

Caine stood just inside the doorway for a moment,

allowing his eyes to adapt to the lighting that was purposefully dim to keep customers from complaining about smudges on the bar glasses. Not that any of the locals would dare, but there were more and more tourists these days and everyone knew that city folk tended to be finicky.

Neon signs advertising a variety of beers glowed in the dim haze. Mounted trophy-size steelhead trout and salmon Oley had pulled in from northwestern streams and the Pacific Ocean adorned the knotty-pine walls. Along with the fish were antique signs dating from when Oley's great-grandfather had opened the tavern designed to serve the needs of thirsty timbermen.

One hand-carved wooden sign, hearkening back to the days when a drunken logger could rent a cot in the back room to sleep it off, advised that lumberjacks must remove boots before getting into bed. Another instructed patrons to check their firearms with the bartender.

"Come on in, boy," Oley greeted Caine. "We're all waiting to hear about your tussle with Harmon Olson's new Peterbilt."

All was certainly the definitive word, Caine decided, glancing around the smoky tavern. Nearly the entire male population of Tribulation was sitting around the scarred wooden tables or perched atop the barstools.

Most of the men were wearing the traditional logger's uniform—plaid, striped or denim shirt; red suspenders; denim pants cut off midcalf to prevent snagging in the underbrush; and leather high-topped, hobnailed calk boots.

Either everyone was out of work or they'd quit early to watch Harmon Olson beat the tar out of him. Entertainment being what it was around these parts, Caine couldn't really blame them.

"News gets around fast," he said, trying not to reveal his concern to learn that it had been Olson's truck he'd been playing chicken with. Every one of the Olson boys was the size of a redwood and their tempers were legendary.

"Joe Bob, here, was followin' Harmon to Forks in his pickup." Oley nodded toward a redheaded man on a nearby stool as he filled a mug with draft beer. "When he saw you, he hightailed it back here to spread the word."

Despite the pain behind his eyes, Caine managed a lopsided grin for his old high school teammate as he crossed the sawdust-covered floor. Joe Bob Carroll had been his catcher on the Tribulation Loggers.

"I thought you looked familiar." Caine slapped his old friend on the back. "But I was goin' too fast to get a decent look at you."

And if he'd only gotten a better look at Harmon Olson, he'd be out scrounging up a thick piece of timber for self-protection.

"You were movin' like a bat outta hell," Joe Bob said, a smile splitting his face. "There sure wouldn't've been much left of you or that fancy car, if Harmon hadn't chickened out."

There were eleven rickety stools in front of the L-shaped bar. Ten were occupied; the eleventh, Caine determined, had been saved for him. He climbed up beside Joe Bob and hooked the heels of his cowboy boots over the pine rung encircling the stool.

"But he did chicken out," Caine said.

"Seems he did," Joe Bob agreed. "For now." His

tone was that of a man who'd witnessed the lighting of the fuse and was now waiting patiently for the TNT to blow sky-high.

"But I gotta warn you, Caine, Harmon does tend to think right highly of that new truck. I wouldn't want to be the guy who caused it to get all those fresh gravel dings."

There was a murmur of agreement from the other men in the bar, all of whom had had their own hassles with the Olson boys.

"No point in borrowin' trouble." Oley pushed the beer toward Caine. Foam spilled down the side of the mug, puddled on the bar and went ignored. The Log Cabin had never been the type of place to hand out cocktail napkins.

Caine took a long drink of the icy brew, then put the mug down on the bar, making a new ring. He wiped the foam off his mouth with the back of his hand.

"Real good to have you back home again," a man next to Joe Bob offered.

"Hiya, Johnny," Caine greeted his cousin. "It's good to be home." He nodded toward Dana Anderson, who'd once been his brother-in-law and had stayed his friend. "Dana."

"Caine. Good to have you back.... Heard the Yankees cut you," Dana said carefully. They'd drawn straws before Caine had arrived to see who'd broach the sensitive subject, and he had unluckily drawn the short one. "We're all sorry about that."

Caine downed the beer in thirsty swallows and pushed the empty mug toward Oley, who filled it to the brim. Just as he didn't spend money needlessly on cocktail napkins, Oley had never believed in wasting a fresh glass every time a customer wanted a refill. He took Caine's money and put it away in the King Edward cigar box he used as a cash register.

"It's not that big a deal," Caine insisted. "The feeling in my arm is coming back more every day. I figure I'll be back on the mound before the All-Star break."

"For what team?" a man in the back of the bar dared ask.

Caine shot a quick glare through the haze. "Any team that needs a championship," he retorted.

"Well," Tom Anderson, Dana's twin brother, said, "we're all rootin' for you, Caine."

A murmur of agreement went around the room.

"So," Joe Bob said, bravely forging his way deeper into dangerous conversational waters, "is it true what the papers are sayin'? That you shocked yourself with an electric drill?"

"Although it's embarrassing as hell, that's what happened," Caine said. "At first I had some weakness in my arm. But I've been working out and the strength's coming back."

He took another drink. Talking about his accident made Caine thirsty. "I'll be back to one hundred percent in no time."

"Is that what the doctors say?" Joe Bob ventured carefully.

Caine frowned down at the white foam topping his beer. "You know doctors," he said finally. "They won't commit to anything for fear of getting a malpractice suit, I guess. But I know my body better than any damn doctor and I say it's getting better."

He chugged the beer down, seeking alcohol's soothing properties. "Injuries are part of the game," he muttered. "Everyone knows that. The problem is that too many sportswriters and owners and managers—hell, even some fans—all want to be the first to predict the end of a guy's career."

A low murmur of sympathetic agreement circled the room. Caine slammed the mug down on the bar with more force than necessary. "When I retire, it's going to be because I want to. Because playing baseball isn't any fun anymore, or maybe even because I can't win."

His tone implied that he considered that alternative a major impossibility. "And no owner or manager or sportswriter or goddamn quack doctor is going to make that decision for me."

Silence descended.

"Hey, Oley," Caine called out, realizing that he was to blame for the dark mood. "How about a round of drinks to celebrate the prodigal's return?"

For the next few hours, Caine bought beer after beer for his hometown fans and congratulated himself on having the good sense to return to a place where a guy didn't have to throw a four-seam fastball ninety-five miles an hour to prove himself a man.

Much, much later, the door to the bar opened.

Bottles, glasses and mugs were slowly lowered to tables as every man in The Log Cabin stared at Harmon Olson, back from delivering his load of logs. Standing beside him was his brother Kirk.

Looking at Harmon, Caine was sorry to see that his memory hadn't been playing tricks on him. The elder Olson boy was every bit as big as he'd remembered. And Kirk, unbelievably, was even bigger.

The Olson brothers were forest-hardened males who, like so many of the men in the bar, had come into manhood wrestling with behemoths of timber twenty times their weight. Harmon's torso had thickened with age, but his muscles still bulged like boulders beneath the red-and-black plaid sleeves of his shirt, and his arms were the size of smoked hams.

His hands possessed long thick fingers that could encircle a man's throat with the same deliberate ease they circled an ax handle. Beneath a gray 1950s-style crew cut, Harmon's eyes looked like hard gray stones; his beard resembled steel wool.

His baby brother Kirk's hair was still blond and curly; his face was reddened from working outside. His beefy hands were curled at his sides into enormous loose fists and he looked every bit as dangerous as his Viking ancestors.

"That your damn Ferrari, O'Halloran?" Harmon's rough loud voice reminded Caine of the bugling of a bull elk in mating season.

"Guilty."

Caine pushed off the stool with a sigh. He'd always considered himself a lover, not a fighter, and he usually managed to talk his way out of altercations. Unfortunately, neither Harmon nor Kirk looked as if they'd dropped into The Log Cabin for afternoon conversation.

"You near caused me to roll my new truck," Harmon growled. He began rolling up his sleeves, revealing rock-hard forearms. A bluish purple tattoo had been etched into the dark flesh below his right elbow; of what, Caine couldn't quite tell.

"You know, I'm really sorry about that, Harmon," Caine said with an ingratiating smile.

The Olson brothers walked toward him, mayhem on

their minds and faces. Behind him, Caine heard chair legs scraping against the sawdust-covered floor as onlookers hurried to get out of the way.

"You made my brother get gravel dings in his new paint," Kirk said, appearing unmoved by Caine's famous smile.

"And damned impolite of me it was, too," Caine agreed.

He knew Harmon's fury had little to do with a few paint dings. What had him all uptight was the fact that he felt he'd been made to look like a coward in front of his entire town.

Caine finally saw what Harmon had tattooed on his arm. It was an amazingly accurate facsimile of a Peterbilt log truck.

Not an encouraging sign.

"So, naturally, I have every intention of paying for any damage I may have—"

He was reaching into the back pocket of his jeans for his wallet, when Harmon let out a roar, lowered his gray head and charged like an enraged buffalo, butting an unprepared Caine in the gut.

The air whooshed out of Caine's body. "D-dammit, H-H-Harmon," he gasped. "We c-c-can w-work this out."

He saw a burly fist coming and ducked just in time. Caine heard the air whiz past his ear. "I take it that's a n-no."

Someone—Kirk probably, since Harmon was standing in front of him—hit Caine a thunderous blow on the side of his head. As he lurched around on wobbly legs, Caine managed to get the heel of his hand under Harmon's pug nose and rammed upward.

When Harmon cried out in pain, Kirk grabbed a handful of Caine's hair and sent him sprawling. He skidded across the floor, coming up the way he used to pull out of a slide.

By now the entire room was in motion. Johnny Duggan left his stool as if ejected from it, with Joe Bob and Tom and Dana Anderson right behind. Other men followed.

Some, due to family loyalty along with a few others envious of Caine's fame, sided with the Olson boys. The others remained loyally in Caine O'Halloran's camp.

Caine, on the floor with his face in the sawdust, felt a steel-toed boot slam into his ribs. Flashbulbs exploded in his head behind his eyes, and his stomach roiled.

Enraged, he staggered to his feet, and while the Anderson brothers kept Kirk occupied, Caine slugged away at Harmon, resorting to the boxing techniques he'd learned in college.

Right jab, left cross. Right jab, left cross. Harmon suddenly lurched. Watching him fall to the ground, Caine had a perverse urge to call out "Timber!"

"All right, goddammit, that's enough!"

Oley took out the shotgun he kept beneath the bar for just such occasions and fired it into the air. Loaded with blank shells, it managed to silence the room without causing undue damage to the ceiling.

"You boys have had your fun. Now why don't you just sit down and get back to drinkin' before I have to start writin' out bills for broken furniture."

Harmon staggered to his feet. Caine, braced against the bar, held his fists up in front of him, Joe Sullivan-style.

To Caine's surprise, Harmon thrust out a bruised hand. "I'm willin' to call a truce if you are."

Immensely grateful for the furious giant's abrupt about-face, Caine accepted the gesture of reconciliation. As he reached out to shake Harmon's outstretched hand, Kirk hit Caine with something a great deal larger and heavier than a fist.

A red haze covered Caine's eyes, a gong reverberated inside his head. And then he went down.

When he opened his eyes again, his mouth was full of sawdust and his head was swimming.

"Caine? You okay?" The man's voice sounded as if it were coming from the bottom of the sea. "Dammit, boy, answer me," Joe Bob urged.

Caine pushed himself up onto his hands and knees. He stayed that way, his head hanging like a winded horse for a long time, trying not to embarrass himself by throwing up.

Johnny Duggan squatted down beside him. When he put his broad hand on Caine's shoulder, Caine flinched. "Want me to go for the doctor?" Johnny asked.

"No." Caine closed his eyes and took a few deep breaths. When he opened them again, he could focus a little more clearly. His shirt was wet and he reeked of whiskey. "I'm okay."

He crawled over to a nearby table, grabbed hold of a heavy oak chair and slowly pulled himself upright. The sea of faces staring at him blurred for a minute. Caine inhaled again, which cleared his vision, but made his chest feel as if it were on fire. Glancing around the bar, he saw, with relief, that the Olson boys were gone.

"What happened to the gorillas?"

"After Kirk sucker-hit you with that bottle, Oley threatened to call the sheriff. That's when they decided they had other things to do," Joe Bob explained.

The bottle explained why he smelled like a drunk coming off a three-week-long bender, Caine decided. He tentatively felt his mouth with his left hand. It was swollen and his lip was cut, but no teeth appeared to be loose. And his nose, thankfully, seemed to be okay, too.

"You know, Caine, you are whiter than new snow," Tom Anderson said.

"Not to mention your pretty face lookin' like Joe Bob's catcher's mitt," his brother Dana added. "And you're swaying on your feet like an old-growth hemlock about to fall. Come on, hotshot," he said, taking hold of Caine's arm. "Let's get you over to the clinic."

"You've got a clinic here now?" Caine was grateful for that bit of news. The way his stomach was churning, he didn't think he could take driving down those twisting mountain switchbacks to the hospital at Port Angeles. "Since when?"

"Since Nora came back from the Bronx six months ago and opened one up in Gram's old house," Tom answered.

Propped up by the Anderson brothers, Caine had been making his way, painful step by painful step, toward the door. At this latest bulletin, he stopped in his tracks. "I don't think this is a very good idea, guys."

"Try looking in a mirror and telling us that," Tom advised.

"You don't have to worry about a thing," Johnny Duggan assured Caine. "The girl turned out to be a right fine doctor. Fixed up my yella-jacket stings just fine. Should be able to patch you up without any trouble at all."

"I'm fine," Caine said, trying to ignore the flames licking at the inside of his chest. "All I need is a stiff drink and a little rest."

"You need to be checked out," Dana corrected. Under his breath, he added, "Don't worry, Caine. From what we can tell, Nora's put the past behind her."

If that was true, Caine wondered what the chances of his ex-wife passing on her secret might be. Not good. Since despite her brother's optimistic assertion, Caine couldn't forget her pale face and ice-cold eyes when she'd told him that she'd never—ever!—forgive him for their son's death.

"I still don't think…" His head fogged again; he took another breath to clear it. "Aw, hell."

Dana Anderson watched the color fade from Caine's battered face, saw the pain in his eyes and made his decision. "You're going to have to face her sometime, Caine," he said, pushing open the door. "Might as well get it over with."

Chapter 3

It had been a long day. Twenty minutes after her last patient had departed, an exhausted Nora was getting ready to close the office when the clinic door opened, and there, standing in the doorway, haloed by a blaze of light from the setting sun behind him, was Caine O'Halloran.

His handsome face had been badly battered, his upper lip was split open and his right eye was surrounded by puffy flesh the color of ripe blueberries. He was weaving in the doorway, braced on either side by two rugged blond men she knew too well.

How dare her brothers go drinking with Caine! And then, to have the unmitigated gall to bring him here, expecting her to patch him up after whatever drunken brawl he'd gotten into this time, was really pushing their luck!

Although his right eye was swollen almost completely shut, the left was as blue as a morning glory and gleamed with a devilish masculinity that long ago—in another world, at another time—had possessed the power to thrill her.

Caine's split lip curved in a boyish grin that Nora knew had coaxed more than his share of women into sharing intimate favors.

"I sure hope you weren't planning to close up shop early, Doc," he greeted her in his deep, bedroom voice.

"Because you just got yourself another patient."

It was as if time had spun backward, and Caine and her brothers were boys again. Having gone through their wild years together, the unholy trio had gotten in more than their share of fights. They'd always emerged, bloody but not bowed, grinning with the sheer satisfaction of having stuck up for one of their own.

"Dana Anderson, I thought you'd grown up," Nora turned on him, not yet prepared to confront Caine. "And exactly how do you plan to explain that black eye to Karin?" she asked Tom hotly.

He shrugged, looking sheepish. "I don't suppose you'd be willing to back me up if I told her that I got hit with the wrong end of a two-by-four."

"You're right. I wouldn't." Nora turned her back and walked into the examining room.

The three men exchanged an uneasy look, then followed.

"But it wouldn't do you any good even if I was willing to lie," she continued as she opened a small refrigerator and took out a cold pack, "since by breakfast tomorrow, everyone in town will know that the Anderson boys were out brawling with that hellion, Caine O'Halloran.

"Here." She tossed the gelled pack to her brother. "Put this on that eye. It'll be ugly as sin by morning, but that should help keep the swelling down."

She took her other brother's hands and frowned as she looked at his skinned knuckles. "This is going to hurt for at least a week," she predicted.

"You don't have to sound so pleased about it," Tom complained.

"It's only what you deserve for fighting. And at your age!"

"You saying we should have let the Olson boys kill Caine?"

"I'm saying that responsible men—intelligent adult males with wives and children—don't get into brawls in bars."

She shot Caine a cool, disapproving glance, really looking at him for the first time since the men had entered the clinic.

"I'm not surprised that you're involved in this." Her voice reminded Caine of the ice on a melting glacier— cold and dangerous. "One day back in town and you're already in trouble."

"Harmon swung the first punch, Nora," Dana said.

She arched a blond brow. "And I wonder whatever could have provoked him? Could it be, perhaps, that some hotshot jock with an IQ smaller than his neck size practically killed Harmon by playing chicken in a Ferrari in some misguided attempt to live up to his stupid macho image?"

"Ouch," Caine objected. "What the hell ever happened to Osler's creed—the part about a doctor judging not, but meting out hospitality to all alike?"

Sir William Osler had been a famous clinician in the late-nineteenth and early-twentieth centuries. Enthusiastic about his theories concerning the emotional and social responsibilities of a physician, Nora had quoted from his essays to Caine. At the time, he'd been so busy rubbing some foul-smelling grease on his damn glove, she hadn't thought he'd heard a word she'd said.

"I'm amazed you remember that." Surprise took a bit of the furious wind out of her sails.

"Oh, I remember everything about those days, Nora," Caine answered quietly.

An uncomfortable silence fell over the room. "Well," Dana said with forced enthusiasm, "now that Caine's in your expert hands, little sister, I guess I'll get back to work."

"And I promised Karin I'd stop and pick up some milk and bread on the way home," Tom said.

Caine grinned, then flinched when it hurt his split lip. "Chickens."

Dana didn't deny it. "Cluck, cluck," he said instead. "Don't be too rough on him, Nora. Those Olsons have always fought dirty."

"Kirk hit Caine on the back of the head with a whiskey bottle when he was shaking hands with Harmon," Tom added.

"I suppose that explains why you smell like a distillery," Nora said, wrinkling her nose with obvious distaste.

"Take good care of him, sis," Dana said when Caine didn't answer.

Tom seconded the request and then they were gone,

leaving Nora and Caine alone in a room that suddenly seemed too small for comfort.

"Well, I suppose we may as well get this over with," Nora said with a decided lack of enthusiasm. "Wait here while I get some ice for that eye."

"I'd rather have a cold pack like the one you gave Dana."

"Tough. We had a run on cold packs today. That was my last one."

She left the room, expecting Caine to remain where he was. Instead, he followed her to the kitchen where, in the old days, he and Tom and Dana and sometimes a young, bespectacled Nora—who'd usually had her nose stuck in a book—had sat around the table, eating cookies and drinking milk from Blossom, Anna Anderson's black-and-white cow.

Rosy red strawberries still bloomed on the cream wallpaper, shiny copper pans continued to hang from a wrought-iron rack over the island butcher-block table.

The long pine trestle table was the same, although now, instead of plates of cookies and glasses of milk, its scarred and nicked surface was covered with medical books, suggesting that Nora still read while she ate. The ladder-back chairs that he remembered being dark blue had been repainted a bright apple green; one was missing.

"I can almost smell bread and cookies baking," he said.

"Things change," Nora replied as she filled an ice pack with cubes from the double-door refrigerator-freezer.

"Tell me about it," he muttered. "I was honestly sorry when I got the letter from Dana telling me about your grandmother's stroke. She was a terrific lady. I liked her a lot."

"Gram always liked you, too." Her curt tone indicated that she couldn't imagine why.

"Dana also said something about your parents having got the travelling bug."

"The day after Dad retired and turned the mill over to Tom, he came home with a motor home. Two weeks later, he and Mom hit the road.

"That was a year ago and they haven't settled down anywhere for more than six weeks. In fact, I got a call from them last week from someplace called Tortilla Flats, Arizona. They were on their way to Yellowstone Park through Monument Valley."

"I guess they're making up for lost time. I can't remember your dad ever taking a day off, let alone a vacation." Caine rubbed his chin, dark with the stubble of several days' growth of beard, thoughtfully. "Except for the day Dylan was born." And the day he'd died, Caine recalled grimly.

It was bad enough having Caine back in Tribulation. She damn well didn't want to discuss her child with the man.

"Here." Nora shoved the ice pack at him. "If you're finished strolling down memory lane, I'd like to examine you."

Caine followed her, with uncharacteristic meekness, back down the hall to what had been her grandmother's front parlor.

Now designed for efficiency, rather than comfort, the formerly cozy room was dominated by an examining table, covered with fresh paper from a continuous roll. There was a short, wheeled, dark brown upholstered stool, a white pedestal sink and a small writing table. Beside the table was the ladder-back chair missing from the kitchen.

Instead of the fragrant potpourri Anna Anderson had made from the colorful blooms in her backyard rose garden, the room smelled vaguely of disinfectant and rubbing alcohol.

Beside the writing table, Anna's oak china cabinet, handmade by her husband, Oscar, had been turned into a supply cabinet. Behind the glass doors, the old crab-apple-decorated plates had been replaced with boxes of dressings, plastic gloves, hypodermic syringes and shiny stainless-steel instruments.

A window looked out on Anna's rose garden and the woods; between the slats of the unfamiliar mini-blinds, Caine saw a family of deer grazing, their brown and gray coats almost blending into the foliage behind them.

"Nora, look."

Surprised by his soft tone, she turned and glanced out the window. Her lips curved into a gentle, unconscious smile.

"They come every day about this time. Last Friday was the first day they brought the babies."

Caine squinted. "Where? I don't see any fawns."

"There are two of them. Beside that hemlock."

When Nora pointed, her fingers brushed against the rock-hard muscle of his upper arm. She pulled her hand back, as if burned.

Caine observed the telling gesture and decided not to comment on it. "I see them now." The creamy spots, nature's clever camouflage, had done their job well. "God, I've missed this," he said on a long deep sigh.

She glanced up at him, clearly surprised. "If you actually mean that, I'd better check out your head injury. All you ever used to talk about was how baseball was going to be your way out of Tribulation."

"I guess I did say that," Caine agreed reluctantly. Trust Nora to remember that. He ran his hand through his hair and sighed again.

"But I don't know, when everything started falling apart, I found myself drawn back home. As if somehow, I'd find the answers I've been looking for here."

"Answers to what questions?"

"That's the hell of it. I don't know." He gave her a faint embarrassed smile. "I sound like Dorothy, don't I? 'Please, Almighty Wizard of Oz, I just want to go back home, to Kansas,'" he mimicked in a falsetto.

"Hell, maybe instead of driving the Ferrari back from New York, I just should have clicked my heels together and said, 'There's no place like home. There's no place like home.'"

"If you could've gotten home by clicking your heels, there wouldn't have been any reason for the Olson boys to beat you up," Nora added briskly. "Which brings me to your examination."

She washed her hands at the sink, then dried them with a paper towel. "So where does it hurt?"

"Everywhere," he answered promptly, holding the ice pack against his eye. "But I guess my chest and the back of my head feel the worst."

Cool, measuring eyes flicked over him. "Take off your shirt and jeans and get onto the table," she instructed. "Then we'll see how much damage you've done this time."

"It was Harmon and Kirk who did the damage,"

Caine felt obliged to say. "I offered to pay for any damage to Harmon's rig, but he wasn't having it."

"Perhaps that'll teach you that you can't buy everything you want," Nora suggested dryly. "Call me when you're undressed." She left the room, closing the door with a decided click.

Caine unbuttoned the bloodstained denim shirt and shrugged out of it, grimacing when the gesture caused a sharp pain in his chest. He managed, with difficulty, to pull off his boots, then his jeans.

Finally, clad solely in white cotton briefs and crew socks, wincing and swearing under his breath, he pulled himself up onto the examination table.

"Ready," he called out in the direction of the shut door.

Although the papers were reporting that Caine O'Halloran had reached the end of his playing days, Nora's first thought, when she returned to the room, was that her ex-husband's body was definitely not that of a man past his prime. He was exactly as Nora remembered him: all lean muscle and taut sinew.

He was also, for a fleeting moment, more than a little appealing. Pressing her lips together, she blocked that thought.

"You look as if you've been kicked by a mule."

Actually, he felt as if he'd been run over by an entire mule train, but Caine would have died before admitting that. "A mule probably would have been preferable to the Olson boys."

Reminding herself that she was a physician and this near-naked man was merely her patient, Nora began her examination with his head. The whiskey bottle had broken, causing a jagged laceration.

"You're going to need stitches."

"Why do I get the impression you're just looking for an excuse to stick a sharp instrument into my flesh?"

"Don't flatter yourself. Although infected scalp wounds are admittedly rare, when they do occur they're a real mess. Medically and cosmetically."

She gave him a dry, feigned smile. "And I'm sure you wouldn't want to permanently mess up that pretty head."

"You're the doctor," Caine said.

Despite the pain, which was considerable, all the beer he'd drunk during the afternoon had created a pleasant buzz that made this meeting with Nora less stressful than he'd expected.

"If you say I need stitches, who am I to argue?"

Who indeed? She couldn't remember a time when she and Caine hadn't argued. About everything. Well, perhaps not everything. The sex, once they'd abandoned her fought-for celibacy agreement, had admittedly been good. Better than good. Unfortunately, they hadn't been able to spend all their lives in bed.

She pulled her penlight out of the pocket of her lab coat. "Keep your head straight and follow the beam with your eyes."

His dark blue eyes moved to the left, then to the right, then up and down as she checked his pupillary reactions. Although she had to lift the lid of the swollen eye to examine it, Nora found no interior damage.

Pocketing the light, she placed a hand on the back of his neck and ran her fingers over the series of bumps making up the cervical spine before going on to his chest.

"You're going to have some ugly body bruising."

So why didn't she tell him something he didn't know? "You should see the other guy."

Frowning at his flippant attitude, Nora put the bell of her stethoscope against his battered chest. The whooshing breathing sounds were a good sign that a rib hadn't punctured a lung, which was a possibility, considering the strength of the Olson boys.

"Tell me if anything hurts." She pressed his left shoulder with her fingertips, but received no response. She moved her fingers over his left nipple and pressed.

Her hands were pale and slender, her fingers long and tapered, her nails neat and unpolished. Caine remembered a time when those soft hands had moved with butterfly softness against his chest; now, her touch remained strictly professional as it probed for injuries.

When her fingers moved over his ribs, she hit a hot spot, causing Caine to suck in a quick breath. She pressed again.

"Does this hurt?"

Sadist. He decided she was probably gouging her fingers into him just to make him suffer. "It's not exactly a love pat, sweetheart," he said through gritted teeth.

"We'll need to take an X-ray. It's probably just a cracked rib, but I don't want to take a chance on it being broken and puncturing a lung."

"I don't really feel up to driving to Port Angeles, Nora."

"You don't have to. Last month I would have called an ambulance, but you're in luck, O'Halloran. My new portable X-ray machine arrived last week."

"I'm impressed."

Although he had no idea what such a piece of medical equipment cost, Caine suspected that it wasn't cheap. If she'd made such a major investment, she was obviously planning to stay in Tribulation.

Which, Caine decided, probably wasn't all that surprising. Nora had always loved it here on the peninsula; he'd been the one anxious to move on to bigger and better—meaning more exciting—things.

"I figured it would come in handy for broken arms, cracked ribs, the sort of occupational and recreational injuries I get a lot of," Nora said. "But I guess everyone's been extra careful, because not one patient has come in with a proper excuse for me to use it."

"Then I suppose that makes this all worthwhile," he declared. He brushed his hair away from his brow; as always, it fell untidily back again. "Anything to oblige a lady."

His voice was a low sexy drawl, with a hint of mockery. His eyes, dark and knowing, roamed her face with the intimate impact of a caress.

Nora's hand was still on his chest; she could feel his strong steady heartbeat beneath her fingertips. An unexpected, unbidden awareness fluttered between them.

A lull fell as they studied each other.

Her hair, which he remembered her wearing in a long braid that hung down her back like a thick piece of pale rope, had been cut to a length that just brushed her shoulders, curving inward to frame her face. The naturally blond strands glistened like sunshine on fresh snow.

Nora Anderson's eyes, unlike those of the rest of her family, whose eyes were the expected Scandinavian blue, were a soft doe brown. One of her few concessions to vanity was to darken the double layer of thick blond lashes surrounding them.

Caine's gaze drifted down to the delicately molded lips that she was still forgetting to color. Although he knew it was ridiculous, he imagined that he could taste those soft lips, even now.

Desire spread, then curled tightly, like a fist in his gut, as Caine remembered those long-ago nights, when Nora's body, rounded with child, had moved like quicksilver beneath his. He remembered her mouth—warm, soft, avid—and the way she'd murmur his name—like a prayer—after their passion had finally been spent.

As Caine silently studied her, Nora tried not to be affected by the way an unruly lock of sun-streaked sandy brown hair fell across his forehead, contrasting vividly with his dark tan. A purple bruise as dark as a pansy bloomed on his lower jaw; his square chin possessed a stubborn masculine pride that bordered on belligerence. His arms were strong, with rigid, defined tendons, his shoulders were broad, his battered chest well muscled.

His washboard-flat stomach suggested that all the drinking and carousing she'd been reading about in the papers lately was a newly acquired bad habit. Knowing how hard Caine had worked to mold his naturally athletic body to this ideal of masculine perfection, she couldn't imagine her ex-husband ever succumbing to a beer gut.

Her gaze followed the arrow of curly hair that disappeared below the waistband of his white cotton briefs with an interest that was distressingly undoctorlike.

Although she knew it was dangerous, and warned herself against it, for a long humming moment Nora, too, was remembering the fever that had once burned between them.

His head wound began to bleed again. She jammed a sterile dressing on it. "Hold this steady," she directed. "And lie down."

She continued examining him with more force than necessary, making him flinch again. "You did that on purpose."

"So file a complaint with the State Medical Board," she snapped. "I think you're going to live," she decided after more probing and poking. "Let's take some pictures of that rib."

He accompanied her into the adjoining room, where she donned a lead apron. "Stand with your chest against this plate. Hands out to your sides."

"I'll have to let go of the bandage."

"I realize that. But that wound is far from fatal." She made an adjustment to the bulky machine. "Now, when I tell you, take a deep breath and hold it."

They both knew taking such a breath was bound to be painful. "I don't remember you being so sadistic."

"That's funny—" she took hold of his shoulders and straightened his torso "—I could swear that, just a little while ago, I heard you say that you were a man who remembered everything…. Don't move."

She made another adjustment, then checked her controls. "Okay, hold absolutely still. I'm ready to shoot."

"Nora?"

"What now?"

"Do you think you could use another word? That particular one doesn't give me a great deal of confidence."

When a reluctant smile crossed her lips, Nora pressed them together. Hard.

"Shut up, O'Halloran. And don't you dare move." She stepped just outside the open doorway. "Take a deep breath. That's it. Now hold." The X-ray machine whirred, then clicked.

"Go on back to the examining room," she said briskly after she'd taken two more views. "I'll be with you in a minute."

Caine wanted to ask Nora if she'd ever thought of using the word *please*, decided that there wasn't any point in aggravating her further, and did as instructed.

He sat on the edge of the examining table, legs dangling over the side, and gazed around the room.

The walls were a soft pale green reminiscent of new fir needles in the spring. The ceiling was the color of freshly churned cream. Diplomas, framed in oak, attested to her professional competence.

It did not escape Caine's notice that the name calligraphically inscribed on all those diplomas was Dr. Nora Anderson. Not that he was surprised; neither of them had ever really thought of her as Mrs. Caine O'Halloran.

"All right," she said as she returned to the room. "Let's see what we've got here."

She snapped the X-ray film onto a light box. When she flicked on the switch, the film went from all black to shades of gray. "Just as I thought." Nora nodded with satisfaction. "You've got a cracked rib."

"You don't have to sound so pleased."

"I'm far from pleased when I get a patient who risks his health—not to mention his life—due to stupidity," she flared. "If Harmon had broken that rib instead of merely cracking it, it could have punctured a lung."

"He attacked me, Nora," Caine reminded her. "I really didn't have any choice."

"You made your choice when you decided to play chicken with him on the highway," she pointed out.

"That was an idiotic, childish thing to do."

Caine shrugged, then wished he hadn't when a lightning bolt zigzagged through his chest. "It seemed like a good idea at the time."

"If you keep up these adolescent acts of derringdo, Caine O'Halloran, you're going to end up in the morgue."

"Nice bedside manner you've got there, Dr. Anderson."

Ancient animosities, never fully dealt with, surfaced. "If you want an acquiescent female hovering at your bedside, kissing your owies to make them better, I'd suggest you get in that Ferrari and go home to your wife."

Nora examined the wound on the back of his head, then began cleansing the cut.

"I'm not married."

She tugged on a pair of surgical gloves. "That's not what I hear."

"All right, I guess we're technically married, but Tiffany—who, by the way, never let marriage interfere with her constant need for male companionship—is currently sleeping with one of my old teammates. She's also filed for divorce."

He frowned, thinking of his last conversation with his New York lawyer. Tiffany was insisting that six months of marriage entitled her to half of his last contract earnings. While Caine had been willing to pay it, writing his second marriage off as an expensive mistake, his attorney had counseled restraint.

"Apparently, an up-and-coming outfielder is socially more desirable than a relief pitcher who's been put out to pasture on waivers."

"I'm sorry," Nora said, meaning it.

"I can't really blame her," Caine said. "I knew all along that Tiffany was only along for the ride. So, I can't expect her to tag along if that ride takes a downhill turn on the way."

He didn't add that since his injury, he'd been a less-than-ideal husband. He'd been, by turns, sullen, uncommunicative, hot-tempered and angry. And those unappealing mood swings hadn't been helped by his increased drinking.

But dammit, Caine had told himself innumerable times in an attempt to justify his behavior over these past months, given the choice of sitting home and listening to his young, spoiled, self-centered bride whine about how she'd never agreed to be the wife of a washed-up old has-been, or going out to some convivial watering hole, where people still treated him like a hero, he'd choose the drinks and his newfound friends any day.

"Nice view of matrimony you've got there, O'Halloran," Nora murmured.

Caine shrugged. "Hell, Nora, you know as well as I do that marriage is nothing more than a convenient deal between two people who both have something the other wants. So long as things stay the same, the relationship putters along okay.

"But let the balance of power shift, and it's over. Finished. Kaput."

Nora thought back on the unromantic agreement she'd forged with Caine on that long-ago rainy afternoon. Their marriage had admittedly started out as a convenient deal to legitimize an unborn child's birth. But surprisingly, for a too-brief, shining time, it had blossomed into something more. And then it was gone, disappearing back into the mists of memory like the fabled Brigadoon.

"What about love?" The minute she heard the quiet words escape her lips, she wished she could take them back.

"Hell, if there's one thing life has taught me, sweetheart, it's that love is nothing more than good sex tied with pretty words."

Caine's cynical view of love and marriage, along with his wife's seeming desertion, had Nora almost feeling sorry for him.

"Well, I wouldn't worry about being alone for long, O'Halloran," she said as she drew up some lidocaine into a syringe. "If that half-nude layout in this year's *Vanity Fair* sports issue was an advertisement for wife number three, you should get a lot of applicants."

Caine felt the bite of the needle and drew in a short, painful breath. "You've seen it?"

Caine couldn't imagine, in his wildest dreams, this woman even glancing at a spread of scantily clad men. Then he remembered how, before their marriage and their lives had fallen apart, Nora had displayed a fire he'd never suspected was under all that Scandinavian ice.

"Hasn't everyone?" She put in a stitch, tied it, then moved on to the next one.

"Well?"

"Well, what?" She made another careful stitch.

"What did you think?" He pressed his hand against his stomach in a futile attempt to quiet the giant condors that were flapping their wings harder with each stitch Nora made. "Have I still got it?"

"I suppose you'll do. In a pinch."

"You always were so good for the ego," Caine muttered.

Nora scraped at the sides of the wound with a fine scalpel, straightening the jagged edge.

Caine glanced into the mirror, saw what she was doing, felt his stomach lurch and looked away. "I suppose, to be perfectly honest, I was advertising, in a way. But not for a new wife.

"Although I didn't admit it to the press until I got put on waivers," Caine said, "I knew all along that I wasn't going to be starting this season. That being the case, my agent felt we needed to keep my name in front of the public."

"I suppose I can understand keeping your name alive," Nora said, "but where does taking off your clothes and posing in your underwear with a cocker spaniel come in?"

"Hey, I sure as hell wouldn't be the first athlete to use a sexy photo shoot to show he's still in shape," Caine argued. "It's the same thing all those actresses do to prove to producers and casting directors that they're not over the hill.

"As for the spaniel, that was the photographer's idea. She said something about a cute dog making me look both tough and soft at the same time.

"Besides, at least the magazine and all the press it

generated was a helluva lot better than all those stories the sports reporters are writing about me being a washed-up, out-of-shape old wreck."

"It's fortunate you didn't get yourself beaten up before that photo shoot," Nora said. "Because right now you are anything but photogenic."

She finished the last three stitches, then pulled off the gloves and tossed them into the white enamel trash can.

"That's it?" Caine asked, not quite able to conceal his relief. Although she'd done a pretty good job of killing the pain, the sound of the silk thread pulling through his numb flesh had made him queasy.

"That's it." When she turned around, Nora caught him surreptitiously rubbing his hand. "Let me see that." She took hold of the hand that had always been so much larger and darker than her own. "Dammit, Caine, your knuckles look worse than Tom's."

"I was just grateful your brothers were there to help me."

"They always were." His knuckles were badly bruised, and skinned, but nothing was broken, Nora determined.

"The Three Musketeers," Caine remembered fondly. She turned his hand over. "You're still shaving your fingers."

"Hey, as a doctor, you use your best tools. Well, my fingers are my tools and shaving a layer of skin off my fingertips gives me an ultrasensitive touch."

She'd been three months pregnant, and a reluctant new bride, when she'd first found him using a surgical scalpel on his fingertips. She'd accused him of barbaric behavior, but months later, when they'd finally consummated the marriage neither of them had wanted, she'd been unwillingly stimulated by the idea of his heightened tactile sensitivity.

Memories, painful and evocative, hovered between them. Caine's eyes moved to the front of her white lab coat, remembering how her breasts felt like ripe plums in his hands.

Nora remembered the way his compelling midnight blue eyes seemed to darken from the pupils out when he was aroused.

Caine wondered if there was a man in Nora's life now. And if so, if they did all those things together that he'd taught her to do with him.

"I read that you've lost the feelings in your fingers," Nora ventured finally, seeking something—anything— to say.

"The feeling's come back," Caine insisted, not quite truthfully. "I just have a little control problem."

"Well, I wish you luck. Sensor-motor injuries are unpredictable. Who knows, you may actually prove all the naysayers wrong and be back on the mound by the All-Star break."

Which would, of course, result in yet another injury. Although Nora had never been a baseball fan, one of the few things she'd learned about the sport was the tradition of wearing out relief pitchers rather than starters.

The better a relief pitcher was—and Caine was undeniably one of the best—the more often a manager used him. Add to that the mental stress that came with pitching when the game was on the line, and it was no wonder relief pitchers tended to be men capable of living for the moment.

Needless to say, Nora had never been able to understand the appeal of such a life.

"I want to tape that rib. Then we'll be done." She wrapped a wide flesh-colored tape around his torso, tugging it so tightly he was forced to suck in a painful breath. "You can get dressed now," she said in the brisk, professional tone he was beginning to hate.

Without giving him a chance to answer, she left the room, closing the door behind her.

Caine braced his elbow on his bare thigh and lowered his head to his palm. The beer buzz was beginning to wear off and now, along with the pounding in his head, the ache surrounding his swollen eye, the crushing feeling in his chest and a grinding nausea, he was experiencing another all-too-familiar, almost-visceral pain.

"Damn," he muttered. "Maybe I shouldn't have come home, after all."

But he had, and now it was too late to get back in the Ferrari and drive away. One reason he couldn't leave Tribulation was that having already cracked open Pandora's box, Caine knew that all the old hurts, ancient resentments and lingering guilt would eventually have to be dealt with.

The other and more pressing reason was that as much as he hated to admit it, Caine O'Halloran, hotshot baseball star and national sports hero, had absolutely nowhere else to go.

He dressed with uncharacteristic slowness, every movement giving birth to a new pain.

Nora was standing behind the oak counter she'd had built in the foyer, waiting for him.

"You'll need another appointment." She clicked

through the appointments in her computer. "If you're still in town two weeks from today, you can come in around four-thirty. Otherwise, you'll need to find another doctor to take out those stitches."

"Sorry to disappoint you, Doc, but I'm going to stick around for a while."

"And exactly how long is 'a while'?"

"You asking for professional reasons? Or personal ones?"

"Professional." She practically flung the word in his face.

Caine started to shrug, experienced another sharp stab of pain and decided against it. "Just wondering. And to answer your solely professional question, I'm sticking around for as long as it takes."

Nora didn't quite trust the look in his eyes. "For the feeling to come back in your fingertips?"

"Yeah." Caine nodded, his gaze on hers. "That, too." When the mood threatened to become dangerously intimate once again, Nora became briskly professional, which was no less than Caine expected, and named her rock-bottom fee.

"Not exactly city rates."

"Tribulation is not exactly the city."

"Point taken."

It took a mighty effort, but he managed to pull his wallet out of his back pocket without flinching and withdrew the bills.

"You're in a hurry." He remembered this as she asked for his insurance. "I don't need a receipt."

"My accountant yells bloody murder if I don't keep accurate records," she said, taking the form from the printer and signing it with a silver ballpoint pen. Her penmanship, Caine noted, was as precise as everything else about the woman. And even as he reminded himself that such painstaking attention to detail was simply Nora's nature, there was something about the meticulous cursive script that provoked the hell out of him.

She handed him the receipt. "Where are you staying?"

"At the cabin."

"All alone?"

"That's the plan."

"You might have a concussion. It'd be better if someone kept an eye on you."

"I don't have a concussion, Nora."

Her brow arched in the frostiest look she'd given him thus far. "Now you're a doctor?"

"No. But I've had concussions before, and I think I'd recognize one."

"You've drunk a lot today," she reminded. "All the alcohol is probably numbing the pain. You really should spend the night at your folks' house."

"I'm staying at the cabin. Alone."

"Still as hardheaded as ever, I see."

"Not hard enough," he countered.

"You'll have pain."

"I'm used to that."

"I'm sure you are. However, I'm still going to prescribe something to help get you through the night and the next few days."

"I can think of something a lot better than pills to help me get through the night."

The seductive suggestion tingled in the air between them.

Nora reached for the prescription pad. "Take one

tablet, with food or a glass of water, every six hours as needed."

Her voice, Caine noted, had turned cold enough to freeze the leafy green Boston fern hanging in the front window. "Needless to say, you shouldn't drink and I wouldn't advise driving or operating heavy machinery."

"Damn. Does that mean I can't down the pills with a six-pack, then go to the mill and play Russian roulette with the ripsaw?"

She absolutely refused to smile. "Not if you want to keep that hand." She glanced at her watch as she tore off the prescription and handed it to him. "Nelson's Pharmacy should be open for another five minutes. I'll call ahead just in case his clock and mine aren't in sync."

Caine plucked the piece of white paper from her fingers and stuffed it into the pocket of his jeans without looking at it. "Thanks. I appreciate everything you've done."

"I'm a doctor, Caine. It's my job."

"True enough. But I've become painfully familiar with doctors, Nora, and believe me, none of them have as nice a touch as yours." He flashed her the bold, rakish grin that had added just the right touch to his *Vanity Fair* photo.

"If you don't behave, I'm going to call your mother to take you home."

"Why do I get the feeling you still refuse to put athletes in the same category as adults?"

"If the jockstrap fits…"

Her smile was patently false as she picked up the telephone receiver and began to dial. "You'd better get going, Caine. Ed Nelson isn't going to keep his pharmacy open all night. Even for the great local hero, Caine O'Halloran.

"Oh, hi, Ed, this is Nora. Just fine, thanks. And how are you? And Mavis? Another grandchild? Twins? You and Mavis must be thrilled. What does that make now, six? Eight? Really? Well, that's wonderful....

"The reason I called, Ed," Nora said, breaking into the pharmacist's in-depth description of the newest additions to the Nelson family, "is that I know it's near your closing time, but I'm sending a patient over."

She turned her back, studiously ignoring Caine.

Frustrated and aching practically everywhere in his body, Caine stalked to the door, then slammed it behind him with such vehemence that one of her diplomas fell off the wall in the adjoining room.

Chapter 4

Caine picked up the prescription at Nelson's Pharmacy and endured a lengthy conversation with the elderly druggist, who wanted to know all the particulars of Caine's career-threatening injury.

After finally escaping the medical interrogation, he stopped at the market, picked up cold cuts for dinner and, ignoring Nora's medical advice, purchased a couple of six-packs of beer. Just to take the edge off.

Then he drove out to the cabin—a cabin that, despite his avowal never to return to Tribulation, he'd never quite gotten around to selling.

Although he'd hired a woman from town to clean the place occasionally, the air was musty and a layer of dust covered everything. Caine neither noticed nor cared.

He turned on the television and tuned in to a game between Kansas City and Toronto on ESPN, threw himself down on the sofa, creating a dusty cloud, and pulled the tab on one of the blue metallic cans of beer. Foam spewed across the back of his hand; Caine licked it off his skin and settled back, stretching his legs out in front of him.

After swallowing two pink pills, he downed the entire can of beer in long thirsty chugs, tossed the can onto the pine coffee table, and opened another.

Three hours later, he'd made inroads on the beer and the Royals had shut out the Blue Jays at home, winning with a home run. And although the combination of pain medication and beer had created a pleasant, rather hazy buzz, he hadn't enjoyed the game.

The televised broadcast had driven home, all too painfully, the unpalatable fact that for the first time since his fourteenth summer, a new baseball season had begun without Caine O'Halloran on the mound.

That unpleasant thought kept him awake long into the night until, finally, the combination of drugs and alcohol allowed him to slip into a restless sleep.

Caine wasn't the only one who had difficulty sleeping. The following morning, Nora awoke more tired than she'd been when she went to bed and irritated with herself for letting Caine get under her skin. She'd tried to put him out of her mind, but ten-year-old memories, as vivid as if they'd occurred yesterday, had proved to be thieves of sleep.

She showered, blow-dried her hair and kept her makeup to a minimum of pink lipstick and mascara. Her clothing—pearl-gray skirt, matching blouse and low-heeled, comfortable shoes—was as subdued as her cosmetics. Although it was spring, mornings were chilly enough to require her wool coat.

As she gathered up her driving gloves, Nora cast a glance at the clock. If she left now, she could still make a stop before driving to Port Angeles.

The clouds were faint pink streaks in a pearly gray sky when Nora parked in front of the Tribulation Pioneer Cemetery. The small iron gate creaked as Nora pushed it open. The front rows of headstones, dating back to the founding of the town, were chipped and weather-pitted. An archangel guarding one resting place had been missing a wing for as long as she could remember.

Family plots were separated from the others by short white picket fences; the older stones, made of marble or granite, were elaborately carved, the words chiseled into their surfaces lengthy tributes to the deceased. The newer graves were marked by slabs laid flat on the ground with only the name, dates, and a single line to denote a life now gone.

The white picket fence surrounding the Anderson family plot was kept gleaming by a fresh coat of paint applied by her father every June. This year the task would be passed on to Tom or Dana. The names on the stones went back five generations, to her Great-great-grandfather Olaf.

Nora could have made her way to the grave blindfolded.

Dylan Kirk Anderson O'Halloran, the simple marker stated. *Beloved son.* The inscribed dates told of a young life cut tragically short.

Each time she came to the grave, Nora hoped to find

peace. The fact that she never found it never stopped her from coming.

Wildflowers were arranged in a metal cup buried in the ground beside the stone. The casual bouquet consisted of dainty purplish brown mission bells, lacy white yarrow, deep purple larkspur and cheery, nodding yellow fawn lilies. The flower petals glistened with dew.

The bouquet was silent testimony to the fact that Ellen O'Halloran had made her weekly pilgrimage to the cemetery. There were times—and this was one of them—when Nora felt slightly guilty that she'd insisted her son be buried in the Anderson family plot, especially since no one could have loved Dylan more than his paternal grandmother.

But then she would remember how Caine had arrived at the cemetery obviously drunk and had humiliated both families by punching out the workman whose job it had been to lower the small, white, flower-draped coffin into the ground.

Nora pulled off her gloves, then knelt and ran a hand over the brown grass that covered her son.

Her worst fear, after they'd put her child into that cold ground, was that she'd forget his round pink face, the sound of his bubbly laugh, his bright blue eyes, his wide, melon-slice baby smile.

But that hadn't happened.

Nine years after his death, she could see Dylan as if he were sitting right here, propped up in the maple high chair etched with teeth marks from two generations of O'Halloran boys, his bowl of oatmeal overturned on his head, laughing uproariously at this new way to win his mother's attention.

Bittersweet memories whirled through her mind—the hours spent walking the floor with Dylan at night, an anatomy text in hand, naming aloud the names of the endocrine glands.

How many babies, she'd wondered at the time, were put to sleep with an original lullaby incorporating the two hundred and six bones of the skeletal system?

Nora knelt there for a long, silent time, tasting the scent of spring in the air. The morning light was a muted rosy glow. Delicate limbs of peaceful trees, wearing their new bright green leaves, arched over the grave.

In the distance, the sawtooth peaks of the Olympic Mountains emerged from a lifting blanket of fog; the upper snowfields caught the rose light of the sky and held it.

Somewhere not far away, Nora heard the sweet morning songs of thrush and meadowlark, then the chime of the clock tower, reminding her of other responsibilities, other children who might need her.

"Mama has to go." She traced her son's name with her fingertip. The bronze marker was morning-damp and cold, but Nora imagined it was Dylan's velvety cheek she was touching. "But I'll be back, Dylan, baby. I promise."

After placing a small white pebble beside the one undoubtedly left by Dylan's paternal grandmother, Nora left the grave site. The cold ache in her heart was familiar; she always experienced it whenever she visited the cemetery. But she could no more stay away than she could stop breathing.

So immersed was she in her own thoughts, Nora

failed to notice the man who'd been watching her the entire time she'd been in the cemetery.

Caine leaned against the trunk of a tree, his arms crossed, silently observing his former wife.

A hangover was splitting his head in two, his body ached and the stitches in the back of his head had already begun to pull uncomfortably. But since he knew that he deserved the crushing pain, he wasn't about to complain.

He hadn't wanted to come to the cemetery today; indeed, he hadn't entered those gates since the day of the funeral. A day when he'd shown up drunk, causing Nora, in an uncharacteristic public display of temper, to screech at him like a banshee. Her black-gloved fists had pounded at his chest with surprising strength until her father and brothers had managed to pull her away.

It wasn't that Caine hadn't loved Dylan; on the contrary, the little boy had been the sun around which Caine's entire universe had revolved.

Which was one of the reasons he had never returned to the spot where they'd insisted on putting his son into the ground, never minding the fact that Dylan was afraid of the dark.

Caine had come to the cemetery this morning in an attempt to expunge the lingering pain, and was unsurprised when it hadn't worked. He'd been about to leave when, as if conjured up from his dark and guilty thoughts, Nora had appeared out of the morning mists, looking strangely small and heartbreakingly frail.

She was on her way back to her car when she saw Caine. He was standing half-hidden in the shadows. She stopped, but refused to approach him. If he wanted to talk, let him come to her.

They remained that way, Caine leaning against the tree, Nora standing straight and tense, like a skittish doe, poised to flee at the slightest threat of danger.

"Hello, Nora." His voice was deep and gruff and achingly familiar.

"Hello, Caine." Her voice was low and guarded. "How are you feeling this morning?"

"Like I've been run over by Harmon Olson's Peterbilt, then drawn and quartered. But, since I figure I probably deserve every ache and pain, I'm not complaining."

Caine looked, Nora considered, almost as bad as she felt. Which meant he looked absolutely terrible. His face, normally tanned, even in the dead of winter, was ashen. Lines older than his years bracketed his rigid, downturned mouth.

His eyes were red-rimmed, his jaw was grizzled by a rough beard and his clothes looked as if he'd slept in them.

"Did you take the pain pills I prescribed?"

"Not this morning." He managed a faint smile. "The way I look at it, so long as I feel the pain, I know I'm still alive."

"That's an interesting philosophy. But I'm not certain it'll catch on."

"Probably not. I hope you don't think I'm following you."

She shrugged and slipped her bare hands into her coat pockets. "Are you?"

"Actually, I've been here about an hour."

"Oh. I didn't see your car."

"I walked." He'd hoped the fresh air would clear his head. It hadn't.

"But it's at least three miles."

"My arm might be giving me a little trouble, but the day I can't walk a few measly miles is the day I hang up my glove."

A thought flickered at the back of her mind, was discarded, then returned. "You brought the flowers."

"Guilty."

Part of her wanted to go back and snatch the wildflowers from her son's grave; another part reminded her that Dylan was Caine's son, too.

"They were growing all around the cabin."

"That was very thoughtful of you."

He pushed away from the tree with a deep sigh and moved across the brown grass until he was standing in front of her.

"I came out this morning and when I saw them blooming, I thought about the time we had that picnic—one of our few summer Sunday afternoons together—and how when I went back to the car to get the portable playpen, you turned your back for a second to get the potato salad out of the cooler, and when you turned around again, Dylan was gnawing on that handful of wildflowers."

Despite her medical training, she'd been frantic, worried the blossoms might be poisonous. It had been Caine who'd calmly taken the wilting flowers from their son's grubby fist and offered a favored teething cookie in return.

"I've never been able to look at wildflowers again without thinking of how pleased he looked with himself, with yellow pollen all over his nose, his mouth ringed with dirt, and that enormous smile of his," Nora murmured.

"All four of his baby teeth gleaming like sunshine on a glacier." A reminiscent smile softened Caine's features. "That was a pretty good afternoon, wasn't it? If we'd only had a few more days like that, we might still be together."

"Caine, don't..."

She combed a hand through her silky hair in a nervous, self-conscious gesture he remembered too well; Caine caught hold of her hand on its way back to her pocket. It was, he noticed, ice-cold.

"We have to talk about it, Nora."

"No." She shook her head, sending her hair flying out like a swirling ray of sunshine in the shaft of shimmering morning light. "We said everything we had to say to one another nine years ago. There's no reason to rehash painful memories."

"We were both hurting," he reminded her, his voice as tightly controlled as hers. "And we both said things we didn't mean." His pained eyes looked directly into hers and held. "Don't you think it's time we settled things?"

She jerked her hand from his and stiffened—neck, arms, shoulders. A thin white line of tension circled her lips. "As far as I'm concerned, things were settled when you got into that new flashy red Corvette the insurance company gave you and drove away and left me all alone."

To deal with our baby's death. She hadn't said the words aloud, but they hovered in the air between them.

"You didn't ask me to stay," Caine reminded her.

"Would you have?"

For some reason he would have to think about later, Caine chose to tell the absolute truth. "No. Probably not."

"I didn't think so."

"Let me put the question another way," he said. "If I'd asked you to come with me, would you have?"

Years of controlling her expression while examining patients kept Nora from revealing how the unexpected question startled her. "And leave medical school?"

"Correct me if I'm wrong, but I believe there are medical schools in California."

He had her there. Realizing that he'd just pushed her into a very tidy corner, Nora hedged. "It's a moot point. Because you never asked me to go to California with you."

"If I had, if I had said, 'Nora, I'm so heartsick about everything that's happened, come with me to Oakland and let's try to start over again,' what would you have said?"

"I might have gone."

It was a lie; she never would have left friends and family and her lifelong ambition to go chasing after Caine's dream. But she'd blamed him for so many years that old habits died hard.

Caine's wide shoulders slumped visibly. Nora had been unrelentingly, coldly angry after the accident, after their child's death.

She'd told him so many times, in both words and actions, how much she hated him, that Caine had never suspected that he might have, with extra effort, been able to break through all her pain and fury.

But at the time, even if he'd wanted to, he wasn't sure he would have had the strength to try. Because, although he suspected she'd never believe it, he had been numb with unrelenting grief and guilt.

"I guess I really blew it, then."

When he dragged his wide bruised hand over his face, Nora felt a distant twinge of guilt for lying to him and ignored it. His dark eyes were those of a man who'd visited hell and had lived to tell about it.

"I told you, Caine, it's in the past. Let's just let it stay there."

"Life would probably be a lot easier if the past could be forgotten, Nora," he said. "But I think we both know it can't be."

Before she could answer, the clock in the village square tolled again. "I'm sorry, Caine, but I can't discuss this right now. I'm going to be late for work, as it is."

Caine glanced down at the Rolex sports watch he'd never been able to afford when he'd been married to her. "It's not even seven."

"I know, but it's a long drive to Port Angeles, and there are a lot of trucks on the road this time of morning."

"You have another clinic in Port Angeles?"

"No, I'm working in the hospital emergency room three days a week in order to fund the Tribulation clinic."

"The emergency room?"

How can you bear it? The words were unspoken, but they hung in the air between them just the same.

The memory of those hours they'd spent outside the hospital emergency room, at opposite ends of the small waiting room, anger and fear and hurtful pride keeping them from comforting one another, came flooding back.

"During my internship at New York-Presbyterian, in New York City——"

"I know where New York-Presbyterian is," Caine broke in. "I lived in New York, remember? Before the Yankees cut me."

She remembered being afraid she would run into him. She also remembered reminding herself that New York was an enormous city; the odds of seeing her former husband were astronomical. But that hadn't stopped her from getting an ulcer that had mysteriously cleared up after she'd returned to Tribulation.

"Well, anyway," she said, shaking off that uncomfortable memory, "when it came time for me to do my E.R. rotation, I was sick to my stomach all night. I'd been dreading it for weeks. In fact, I was seriously thinking of dropping out of medicine."

She fell suddenly silent and stared up at him, wondering what on earth had possessed her to tell him something she'd never admitted to another living soul.

She took a deep breath that should have calmed her but didn't. "Anyway, thirty seconds after I managed to drag myself into the E.R., an elderly woman who'd been attacked in her bed by a man with a machete was brought in. She had put her arms up to protect herself and there was blood everywhere.

"We must've pumped in a ton of blood, but eventually she stabilized enough to be sent up to surgery."

"Did she make it?"

"Oh, yes. But I didn't find that out for weeks, because all day patients just kept pouring in: knife fights, bullet wounds, heart attacks, rapes…

"The triage nurses had the patients stacked up like planes over Kennedy airport and by the time I got to stop long enough to have a cup of coffee, I'd been on the run for eighteen hours and had another eighteen to go, but—and this is hard to explain—I felt really, really good."

"Adrenaline tends to do that to you," Caine agreed absently. He was trying to come to grips with the idea of cool, calm and collected Nora covered with a stranger's blood, surrounded by the bedlam that was part and parcel of a city-hospital emergency room. Nora treating bullet wounds? Ten years ago he would have found the idea preposterous. Obviously he'd underestimated his former wife.

"I suppose so. But it was more than adrenaline. I loved being part of a team and I loved the action. It was fantastic!"

A smile as bright as a summer sun bloomed on her face and lighted her eyes. Caine tried to remember a time she'd smiled like that at him when they'd been married and came up blank.

"You should do that more often." Unable to resist touching her, he reached up and ran his palm down her hair.

It was only a hand on her hair. An unthreatening, nonintimidating touch. So why did it make her mouth go dry and her heart skip a beat?

"Do what?"

"Smile. You have a lovely smile. No wonder your patients love you."

It was happening all over again. When she felt herself falling under Caine's seductive spell, Nora took a step backward. Physically and emotionally. "I really do have to go."

"You haven't finished the story."

"What story?"

"About your first day in the emergency room."

"Oh. Well, as I said, the rush was amazing. I was hooked. I applied for a residency, got it, and I've been working in emergency departments ever since."

"I wish we'd been living together that day," Caine surprised both of them by saying. "I would have liked sharing it with you."

"Please, Caine—"

"I'd like to hear more about your work, your life. Could I take you to dinner tonight?"

"I'm sorry, Caine, but I have paperwork to catch up on tonight."

"Tomorrow night, then."

"I'm sorry, but—"

"All right, how about lunch?"

"I'm sorry, but the answer's still no."

"Breakfast?"

"No."

"I want to see you again, Nora. Just to talk. That's all."

She combed her hand through her hair again and was appalled to find it trembling visibly. "I really don't think it's a good idea, Caine," she said gently, but firmly.

"Why not?"

"Because it would be too painful." She flared suddenly, causing the birds perched on the branches overhead to take flight in a loud flurry of wings.

"Perhaps that's all the more reason to talk about it,"

Caine suggested mildly. "If we can get everything out in the open once and for all, perhaps we can put it behind us."

"Do you truly think that's possible?"

"We'll never know if we don't try."

For a brief, foolhardy moment, Nora was honestly tempted.

"No," she decided. "I don't want to see you again, Caine. Not for dinner, or lunch, or breakfast, or just to talk."

Unaccustomed to failure, but not knowing how to salvage the situation, Caine decided he had no choice but to back away. "I guess I'll just have to wait and see you in a couple of weeks."

"Really, Caine——"

"So you can take the stitches out," he reminded her.

"Unless you'd rather have me go to a doctor in Port Angeles."

"No." Her cheeks were flushed. "Of course I'll take them out. There's no reason for you to drive all that way."

"Fine. Well, I guess I'll be seein' you."

"Yes."

He knew it was the last thing she wanted, but some perverse impulse made him put his hand against the side of her cheek in a final, farewell caress.

"Goodbye, Nora."

"Goodbye, Caine."

Caine gave her one long, last look, and then he turned and walked back toward the gate.

He had only gone a few paces when she called out to him. "Caine?"

He turned back toward her. "Change your mind about breakfast?"

"No." She reached into her shoulder bag and pulled out the silver ballpoint pen and a small yellow pad. "But I thought you might like the name of a doctor in Seattle who specializes in your type of injury."

"I've gone to more damn specialists than you can shake a bat at, Nora."

"One more opinion couldn't hurt." She wrote the name on a piece of paper and held it out to him. "And Dr. Fields is really very good."

Although he wasn't at all eager, Caine took the paper and shoved it into his pocket. "Thanks. I appreciate your concern."

She searched his tone for sarcasm and found none.

"You're welcome. Good luck."

"Thanks."

A maniac was operating a chain saw behind his eyes and his stomach was roiling from the can of warm beer he'd tossed down for breakfast.

Hell, Caine thought as he crossed the cemetery. *Maybe I shouldn't have come home, after all.*

In small towns, time had a habit of standing still. When he'd made the decision to return to Tribulation, that trait had seemed a plus. With his career in shambles, he'd found himself instinctively drawn back to the one place where he was still a larger-than-life home-town hero.

But dammit, he hadn't counted on Nora having returned home, as well.

"Nothing's changed," he muttered, jamming his hands so hard into his pockets that they tore. Loose change fell to the still-brown grass underfoot and went ignored. "Not a goddamn thing."

Feeling more alone than he'd ever felt in his life, Caine walked back through the wrought-iron gates. Away from his son. And his wife.

Chapter 5

One week after her unexpected encounter with Caine in the cemetery, Nora pulled her car into her reserved parking space outside the Olympic Memorial Hospital and realized that she couldn't remember a single mile of the just-completed drive. It was not a propitious omen for the day ahead.

Ever since Caine's return, her mind had been mired in the past, rerunning old scenes from her marriage like some late-night cable-television movie.

Marrying Caine when she'd discovered she was pregnant had seemed a logical, practical solution. The problem was, she'd never planned on falling in love with the only man who had ever had the power to break her heart.

The sun had risen, the sky was as bright as a wash-tub of the Mrs. Stewart's bluing her grandmother had always favored. Walking toward the hospital, she waved at a gardener who was energetically clipping away at the rhododendron bushes flanking the sidewalk. He grinned and waved back, his own enjoyment of the perfect spring weather obvious. The double glass doors of the emergency department opened automatically at her approach. Nora took a judicial glance around the well-lighted waiting room. The only persons there this morning appeared to belong to the same family.

An exhausted-looking woman rocked a cranky baby in a stroller; at her feet, a young boy ran a toy car across the green vinyl tile while making loud roaring sounds meant to emulate a Formula race car. Beside the woman, a red-haired girl sat reading a children's book of fairy tales.

The woman and the girl didn't bother to look up as Nora passed; the boy glanced at her with a decided lack of interest, then began running the plastic car noisily up the wall.

After exchanging brief greetings with Mabel Erickson, the emergency room clerk, Nora went into the doctors' locker room, changed into a pair of unattractive but practical unpressed green scrubs, and clipped on her ID.

"You're starting out slow," Dr. Jeffrey Greene, the doctor going off the night shift, said, flipping through the aluminum clipboards. "We had a relatively quiet night. Some hotshot took a corner too fast on his Kawasaki and I spent two hours picking pieces of asphalt and gravel out of his arms and chest. His girlfriend took him home.

"EMS brought in a drug overdose." He frowned at this latest problem to have worked its way to the peninsula from the Puget Sound cities. "We stabilized him and sent him upstairs to ICU. The only patient currently in the place is a kid with night asthma who should be off the breathing machine any time. His mother's in the waiting room, waiting to take him home.

"And, for comic relief, just when the pizza guy showed up with dinner, a frantic mother brought in a three-month-old with spots. She swore he had measles." He shook his head with disgust. "I'll never figure out why people bring their kids to the emergency room at three in the morning with diaper rash."

"She was probably scared." Nora certainly remembered her own middle-of-the-night parenthood fears.

In medical school she'd been constantly reading about life-threatening diseases, then fearing that Dylan had contracted one of them whenever he became ill. One of the more embarrassing incidents had been when he'd come down with a high fever and wouldn't stop crying.

Positive that her son had meningitis, Nora had driven alone—Caine had been out of town on a road trip—through the dark streets to the hospital at two o'clock in the morning.

The doctor on call had examined the three-month-old baby, patted Nora paternalistically on the head and diagnosed an ear infection. An hour later, Nora had returned home with a bottle of antibiotic and a sense of relief mingled with an enormous dose of professional embarrassment.

"The pizza was cold by the time we got around to it," Dr. Greene complained. "At the next staff meeting I'm asking Administration about that microwave they've been promising us. What kind of E.R. doesn't have a microwave oven, this day and age?"

When Nora didn't answer what she took to be a rhetorical question, he continued. "So, there you go, Doctor. So far you're looking at a long boring day." He gathered up the pizza box and pop cans and tossed them into a nearby wastebasket. "But of course, the morning's still young so that'll undoubtedly change."

Nora knew that, only too well. For some reason no one had ever been able to figure out, emergencies invariably came in waves; things would be so quiet the medical staff would be in danger of falling asleep, then suddenly all hell would break loose.

After confirming that the asthma patient had been released, Nora returned to the office, sipped a cup of coffee and waited.

The peace was shattered twenty minutes later when the hospital speaker came to life. At the same time, the beeper in her pocket went off with the high-pitched squeal of the trauma stat code.

"All emergency personnel, trauma stat!" the wall speaker blared. "Helipad, ETA two minutes. Helipad. Two minutes."

Nora was waiting on the roof, along with a nurse and an E.R. technician, when the EVAC helicopter arrived. In order to avoid wasting critical time, the pilot brought the craft straight in, circling and descending at the same time. The moment the skids touched the ground, the pilot unpitched his rotor blades, flattening them so they no longer bit into the air.

Bending her head, Nora and the rest of the crew grabbed hold of the gurney and raced toward the side of the helicopter. The helicopter medic threw open the door, then undid the heavy web straps holding the passenger—a little boy—in place.

Four sets of hands lifted the boy, who was strapped to a fracture board, a pink plastic collar immobilizing his neck, onto the gurney. Telling him not to be afraid, the nurse put a green plastic oxygen mask over his face, then the crew pulled the gurney back across the roof at a dead run. The state police helicopter medic followed, service revolver bouncing awkwardly against his navy blue flight suit.

"This is Jason Winters," the medic informed the team as they entered the code room. "He's a four-year-old male who did a double gainer out of his two-story bedroom window and landed on a wooden deck.

"Was unconscious no more than two, maybe three minutes. He's alert, he can move all extremities, his pulse is one fifty-five, respiration twenty plus, blood pressure one ten over seventy and solid as a rock.

"His mother says there's nothing unusual in his medical history, no known allergies. She was the one who found Jason. A neighbor's driving her here. ETA twenty, thirty minutes.

"The father's a city cop. The police station was notified, but he hadn't arrived there from home yet. The desk sergeant promised to give him the message the minute he came in."

After thanking the medic for his concise report, Nora bent over the gurney and brushed the boy's hair away from his forehead with a gentle, maternal touch.

"Hello, Jason. I'm Dr. Anderson. Do you know where you are?"

"In the hospital?"

"That's right." Nora smiled. "And we're going to take very good care of you."

"I wanna go home," Jason wailed.

"I know. But first we need to check you out and make certain nothing's broken. Can you help us do that?"

"Why can't I just go home?" His face was so pale his freckles stood out in stark relief.

"You will. I promise. But not quite yet, sweetie. First we have to take a blood sample."

"I don't want no shots!" he screamed as the nurse began swabbing the crook of his slender arm.

"It'll only sting for a minute, honey," the nurse promised.

The scream escalated into high-pitched shrieks as the boy watched his blood filling the syringe. "No-o-o! I want my mommy. I wanna go ho-o-ome!"

Another nurse hooked him up to the monitor and Nora watched as the line jumped wildly on the monitor, then settled down to a rapid beat normal for a frightened child.

"If you don't untie me, I'm gonna tell my daddy on you! He's a policeman and he'll come with his gun and arrest you!"

The shrieks slid back down the scale and became racking sobs that gave Nora confidence. Every wail, every cry, said that Jason's airway was unobstructed.

"We'll take the straps off real soon, Jason," Nora promised, "but first we need to take some pictures to make certain that you didn't hurt anything when you fell."

"I didn't fall," he corrected with four-year-old pride. "I was swinging on my web."

"Your web?"

The first nurse wrapped a blood-pressure cuff around his arm and hooked it to a monitor programmed to automatically inflate the cuff and read the patient's blood pressure every two minutes.

"My Spider-Man web... Hey, what are you doing now?" Jason yelled when the nurse began cutting away at his superhero pajamas. "You can't do that! My mommy just bought me these pajamas. She'll be really mad at me!"

"We need to examine you, Jason," Nora soothed. "I promise to tell your mommy that we're the ones who tore your pajamas, but first, can you be a very big boy and tell me where it hurts?"

Fifteen minutes later, when her examination uncovered merely a sprained wrist and a nasty bump on the head, and the X-rays showed no spinal damage, Nora decided that Jason was not only a very loud little boy, he was also a very lucky one. Although children's bodies were amazingly resilient, they definitely weren't designed for two-story falls onto a solid-wood deck.

The nurse was writing his name on a plastic wristband when the E.R. clerk appeared at the door of the trauma room. "The boy's mother is here."

Through the door, Nora could see a pretty, obviously distraught young woman. She was pacing in front of the reception desk, tracks of tears staining her cheeks while her hands mangled a tissue. The stark fear and dread Nora recalled all too well were written all over her face.

Nora remembered prayers, learned in childhood, tumbling through her head on that day nine years ago. Desperate, she had made deal after deal with God: If

He'd only let Dylan live, she'd never raise her voice at him again; if He'd only allow her son to survive, she'd figure out some way to take enough time from her studies to watch cartoons with him. If only God would keep her baby from dying, she'd do anything. Anything!

Nora remembered desperately trying not to cry and strangely, succeeding. And then she remembered trying not to scream, when they'd told her that her baby had died, and failing.

After instructing Mabel to inform Mrs. Winters that she'd be right there, Nora slipped out the door and walked to the stainless-steel fountain. Water arced up in a shimmering silver stream; Nora took a long drink and an even longer breath. Then she walked back down the hall to the waiting room.

"Hello, Mrs. Winters." She offered a reassuring smile. "I'm Dr. Anderson. Jason's doctor."

"Where's Jason?" the haggard woman asked immediately. "Where's my boy?"

"He's still in the trauma room," Nora said. "With the nurses and other support staff. But he's awake and doing fine."

On cue, another scream came from the trauma room. "He's hurting! I need to be with him."

"I'm afraid it'll be a few more minutes before you can see him, Mrs. Winters."

"They wouldn't let me go in the helicopter with him, they took him away and now no one will let me see my son and I want to know why!"

Mrs. Winters's voice had the quiver and staccato rush that told Nora, who'd faced too many parents in similar circumstances, that she was on the verge of becoming hysterical.

Nora leaned forward and put her hand on the woman's arm. "I know you want the best care for Jason and that's what he's getting.

"Your son is being taken downstairs for a CT scan. It's not painful, it's merely a three-dimensional X ray that'll tell us if Jason suffered any head or internal injuries from the fall." Another wail echoed down the hall.

"Oh, God." The woman's face mirrored the anguish that Nora knew must have been on her own that day nine years ago. "Why is he screaming like that?"

"Because he's angry and frightened. And although I know how difficult it is to believe, Jason's crying is a very good sign. We've been reassured by every shriek."

Mrs. Winters dabbed her red-rimmed eyes with the shredded tissue. "Really?"

"Really. The fact that he's been talking a blue streak means that he probably didn't suffer any brain damage. He's alert and oriented and mad as hell. Which, for now, is just the way we like him."

Nora smiled reassuringly and received a wobbly one in return. "He does have a nasty bump on his head, but it doesn't seem to be bothering him and in a few days he'll probably be the star of his preschool."

"While we're waiting for your son to return from the tests, I'd like to get a bit more information. Why don't we go to my office?" she suggested. "The chairs are more comfortable than these hard plastic ones. And we'll have privacy."

The mother, appearing somewhat mollified, followed Nora meekly down the hallway.

Rather than place herself in the power spot behind her desk, Nora sat down on the suede chair adjacent to the matching sofa. "Does Jason have a regular pediatrician?"

"Yes," Mrs. Winters perched nervously on the edge of the sofa, looking prepared to bolt at any second. "Dr. Kline. His office is on Pine Street, but I can't remember the address." The tissue all but disintegrated, she began worrying the clasp of her brown suede purse with her fingers.

"No problem. We can look it up." Nora dutifully noted the information on the chart. "Is he currently taking any medication?"

"No." The purse popped open; Mrs. Winters absentmindedly snapped it shut again. As Nora questioned her about Jason's medical history, her fingers kept snapping and unsnapping, snapping and unsnapping.

Someone knocked on the door, then pushed it open. "Mr. Winters is here," Mabel informed Nora.

At that announcement, Mrs. Winters jumped. The opened purse slid off her lap; its contents scattered over the floor. The woman dropped to her knees and began frantically scooping up the collection of coins, grocery-store coupons and other items.

A man wearing the dark blue uniform of a police officer and the flushed look of a man terrified, but unable to admit it, entered the office.

"What happened?" he demanded of Nora, who noticed that he hadn't even bothered to glance at his wife. "Where's my son?"

"Your son fell out of his bedroom window. He's downstairs getting some tests done," Nora said. She held out her hand. "I'm Dr. Nora Anderson, Jason's admitting physician.

"As I was telling your wife, Jason's injuries appear

to be amazingly minor, but I ordered a CT scan to make certain that he doesn't have internal injuries my examination failed to detect."

"He fell out the window?" He turned and looked down at his wife, who'd gone the color of library paste. "The window?" Furious red spots stained his weather-roughened cheeks. "How the hell did you let that happen?"

Their eyes locked. Nora couldn't detect a hint of compassion in either gaze.

"I've been begging you to put some kind of lock on that window for weeks," Mrs. Winters said, pushing herself to her feet with more energy than she'd displayed thus far. "But you're always too busy to help around the house."

"If I'm busy it's because I'm trying to keep a roof over our heads. You think I like working two jobs so you can quit work to stay home and neglect our kid?"

Her expression turned as hostile as her husband's. "I wasn't neglecting him! I was taking a shower. If you'd only gotten around to fixing that window—"

"If you were doing your damn job—"

Nora decided the time had come to intervene. "Mrs. Winters. Officer Winters. Please, sit down. I think we need to talk about your son. And what we all can do to help him recover."

That, apparently, was the magic word. The boy's parents exchanged a long look, then in unison, they sat down, each claiming a separate corner of the couch.

"Thank you." Nora took her own seat behind the desk and folded her hands atop the clipboard. "As I said, I don't believe Jason's injuries are going to turn out to be very severe. He is obviously a very lucky boy.

Not only because it looks as if he's going to survive what could have been a fatal fall, but because he has two parents who care for him—deeply."

Mr. and Mrs. Winters nodded. "I do," they said together. It was Nora's turn to nod. "Good. Now, even if he escapes this with nothing more than a lump on his head, the entire experience, which would be frightening for you or me, is bound to be terrifying for a four-year-old child.

"And even if the CT scan shows no further injuries, I'll want Jason to stay here for observation, which means that he'll be spending the night in a strange place.

"That being the case, your son will need your reassurance and support. He also needs to know that you don't blame him for his accident. If there's tension between you, he's liable to think that it's his fault."

She paused, allowing her words to sink in. "Believe me," she said quietly, "I understand how you're feeling."

Officer Winters shot her a withering look. "Don't patronize us, Dr. Anderson. No one knows what I'm feeling."

"I do," Nora argued. "Because I've been in your shoes."

She had never told the story to anyone before, and was shocked to hear the words coming from her lips. As she viewed their startled expressions, Nora decided that having finally captured their attention, she might as well continue.

"I'm ashamed to say that I reacted with emotion rather than logic, which only succeeded in making an already horrific situation even worse," she admitted, remembering how she'd railed at Caine and blamed him for the accident that had caused their son's death.

At the time, Caine hadn't even tried to defend himself. And later, when she'd learned that the driver of the other car had been drunk and had crossed the centerline without giving Caine time to respond, she'd been too deeply immersed in her own pain to apologize.

"So," she said, "I would suggest that whatever your problems are, you manage to put them aside for now. For Jason's sake."

She paused again. The couple exchanged another long glance. "If you can't do that," Nora said quietly but firmly, "I'm going to have to ask that you visit your son separately."

Jason's father was looking down at the floor. His mother was dabbing ineffectually at her tears with the shredded, useless tissue. When the patrolman reached into a trouser pocket, took out a wide white handkerchief and began wiping at the moisture streaming down his wife's cheeks, Nora knew they'd made their decision.

She was also relieved when, caught up in their concern for their son, neither thought to ask her what the outcome of her own situation had been. Because as heartbreaking as Dylan's death had been, the still-vivid memory of how coldly she'd treated Caine, who'd been hurting himself, left Nora feeling confused. And guilty.

While Nora struggled to sort out old and painful feelings, the object of all her discomfort was sitting at a table in a weather-beaten shack on the windswept Washington coast. In contrast to the sun that had been shining in Tribulation, the sky was low and gray, the rain streaking down the window matching Caine's gloomy mood.

The bar had been dubbed The No Name by locals after the sign had blown away during a typhoon more than two decades ago. The scent of fried food, spilled beer and mildew hung over the room like an oppressive cloud.

A lone woman, wearing a rhinestone-studded T-shirt, a skin-tight denim miniskirt and black, over-the-knee suede boots, put some coins in the jukebox and pressed B7.

As Garth Brooks began singing about the damn old rodeo, the woman sauntered over to Caine's table. "Hiya, handsome. How about a little Texas two-step?" she asked, swaying enticingly to the beat.

Caine signaled the bartender for another beer. "Sorry, sweetheart, but I'm just not in the mood for dancing today."

He nodded his thanks to the bartender who placed another can of beer on the table without stopping to take away the empties. "Maybe some other time."

"That's okay. I can think of lots better things to do on a rainy afternoon." She gave him a bold, suggestive smile. "My name's Micki. What's yours?"

"Caine." He opened the can and took a long drink.

"I've always liked biblical names." She sat down and crossed her long legs. "You know, Caine——" she leaned forward and placed her hand on his thigh "——perhaps if you stopped brooding over whoever or whatever it is that put that scowl on your face, you might find that you could have some fun, after all."

She had hit just a little too close to home for comfort. "You know, Micki, you may be on to something."

Caine tossed back the rest of the beer, tossed some bills on the table and with his arm around the woman's waist, walked out of the dark bar into the slanting silver rain.

A motel was conveniently located across the gravel parking lot. Caine wasn't particularly surprised when the manager greeted the woman like an old friend. Neither was he surprised by the lecherous wink the guy gave him.

They'd no sooner entered the room when she turned, twined her bare arms around his neck and kissed him. As she pressed her mouth against his, Caine waited, with a certain fatalistic curiosity, for his body to respond. He wanted to see if this woman's scarlet lips could make him forget himself.

They couldn't.

Undeterred by his lack of response, Micki plopped down on the bed. Outside the window, a steady stream of logging trucks passed, hissing wetly down the highway.

"You know, Caine, I knew the minute you walked into The No Name that you were the kind of guy who knew how to have a good time," she said, unzipping her high-heeled suede boots.

She and Caine had gotten soaked in their dash across the parking lot and the T-shirt clung to her like a second skin. Shivering, she tugged it over her head. Her bra was black and sheer, revealing nipples that had pebbled from the chill. For some inexplicable reason, Caine found himself comparing that overtly sexy bra with a utilitarian white maternity one he remembered Nora wearing. Irritated that the seemingly safe memory made him hard, he lipped a cigarette from the pack he'd managed to keep dry.

"Those things'll kill you," Micki said with a friendly smile.

Caine shrugged. "We all gotta go some time." He lighted the cigarette and inhaled the acrid smoke into his lungs.

"True enough."

She was down to a pair of black bikini panties. Rising from the bed, she walked over to the window, drew the smoke-stained orange drapes, then stopped in front of him. Plucking the cigarette from his lips, she took a long drag.

"But why do you want to waste time smoking when we could be setting that bed on fire?"

Telling himself it was what he wanted, Caine jabbed the cigarette out in a nearby ceramic ashtray shaped like a fish and pulled her down onto the mattress.

Micki was eager and talented, and everything a man could want in a bed partner.

So why the hell did his mutinous body betray him? Caine's erection had softened like a deflated balloon and no amount of feminine coaxing could achieve success.

"That's okay," she assured him with what Caine considered inordinately good cheer a long time later. "It happens to everyone."

"Not to me." Frustrated, Caine muttered a low, pungent curse.

He told himself that it was the depressing diagnosis he'd received from that Seattle doctor Nora had referred him to that had him in such a funk. Or the fact that the baseball season was in full swing without him on the mound. The beer he'd drunk, perhaps. Or the dreary weather.

Even as he made his way through the litany of possible excuses, Caine had a nagging feeling that the reason for his uncharacteristic inability to perform was that the woman stretched out so invitingly beside him on the bed wasn't his ex-wife.

What the hell was Nora doing to his mind?

Chapter 6

For more than a week, Caine had avoided his family. Since he'd always thought of himself as the O'Halloran success story, the idea of returning home as a failure was anything but appealing.

Finally, however, knowing it was time—past time—to face them, he drove to his parents' house. He was almost relieved that no one was home. His next stop—the one he dreaded most—was his grandparents' home.

The old clapboard house was unchanged. The siding was still the faded grayish blue of a February sky, the porch railing as white as the snow that remained in patches beneath the dark green conifers surrounding the house.

Caine's grandfather, clad in a pair of dark blue overalls, a blue-and-black plaid shirt, a blue down-filled vest and a black watch cap, was sitting in a rocker on the porch, a pipestem jammed into the corner of his mouth.

Appearing unsurprised by the sight of a sleek black sports car pulling up in front of his home, he pushed himself out of the chair and came to stand by the railing.

Caine cut the engine and gazed through the tinted windows at his grandfather. When he was a boy, Caine had considered his grandfather the biggest, strongest man in the world. Even Paul Bunyan couldn't have whipped his "Pap," Caine remembered thinking.

He remembered this man's shoulders as being as straight and wide as an ax handle. And the sure, majestic way Devlin O'Halloran had reminded Caine of a ship coming into harbor.

But now, taking in his grandfather's stooped shoulders, Caine was forced, once again, to realize that the world hadn't stopped turning just because Caine O'Halloran had gone away.

Taking a deep breath, he pushed the door open and climbed out of the low-slung car.

"Hi, Pappy." Caine stood at the bottom of the porch steps.

"'Bout time you decided to pay your old Pap a visit," the deep, wonderfully familiar voice growled. "I was beginnin' to think I was gonna have to keel over to get you to come home."

When Caine was five years old, he'd run to his grandfather, seeking sanctuary after breaking Mrs. Nelson's front window with a ball that had gone higher and farther than any ball he'd ever hit before.

As he climbed the front steps on this spring morning, he breathed in the familiar scents of Old Spice aftershave, cherry tobacco, hair tonic and the distant whiff of camphor his grandmother used to prevent moths from eating holes in her husband's beloved wool shirts, and realized that once again, he'd come to his grandfather seeking refuge.

"We heard you were back," Devlin O'Halloran said. "Looks like the rumor mill was well greased this time. That car does kinda remind me of a Batmobile."

Devlin's broad hands—hands capable of the delicate task of tying a fly to the end of a fishing line—took hold of Caine's arms as he gave him a long look. "Also heard them Olson boys made mincemeat of your face." His still-bright blue eyes searched Caine's features. "Your grandmother'll be happy to see that you don't look near as bad as folks are sayin'."

"Bruises fade."

"That they do," Devlin agreed. "So, how'd she look to you?"

"Who?"

"Don't play dumb with me, boy. I was talking about your wife, the doctor."

"She's my ex-wife."

"Bull." Devlin brushed Caine's words away as if they were a pesky fly. "Unless the Pope's gone on the television this morning and changed the rules while I've been sittin' here whittlin', the Church still doesn't cotton to divorce. So, the way I see it, the woman's still your wife."

"The way the state of New York sees it, Tiffany's my wife."

"From what I hear, not for long."

Although he'd yet to find anything humorous in his second wife's defection, Caine threw back his head, looked up at the bright blue sky and laughed. "News travels fast."

"Always has, around here," the older man agreed laconically. "And I'm sorry about you and that redheaded model, but I reckon that's what you get for marryin' a woman named after a jewelry store."

"I reckon you're right, Pappy."

His grandfather had always been able to coax a smile from him, even when things looked darkest. Nearly always, Caine corrected, remembering a time when even this man hadn't been able to lift the black cloud that had settled over him like a shroud.

"Heard you were out to the cemetery. Matty Johnson was raking the leaves off his wife's restin' place when he saw you puttin' flowers on Dylan's grave. Said he was gettin' ready to go over and welcome you back to town, when Nora showed up."

There was a question in the old man's voice that Caine knew he could not ignore. "We hadn't planned to meet. I guess my showing up unexpectedly triggered some old memories for her."

"That's what your grandmother and I figured. So?"

"So, what?"

"So, you two gonna be seein' each other regular?"

"It's a small town. We're bound to run into each other. And I've got an appointment to have some stitches taken out."

"Let me see."

Caine bent his head.

"She did a right fine job," Devlin allowed with surprise. "I remember your mother trying to teach that girl how to quilt. Finally gave up when she kept stitchin' her finger and bleedin' all over the squares."

"I guess she got better."

"Seems she did," Devlin agreed. "You eat breakfast?"

"Not yet. I figured I'd stop by the Timberline for coffee and one of Ingrid's Viking omelets after visiting you and Gram."

"And break your grandmother's heart? She made flapjack batter this morning and there's a jar of rhubarb sauce waitin' on the table with your name on it."

Caine grinned. His grandfather might look older, but some things, blessedly, remained the same. "Suddenly, I'm starving."

Devlin put his arm around Caine's shoulder and ushered him through the screen door into the kitchen.

"Your grandmother must be taking a nap," Devlin said.

"So early?" Caine glanced up at the copper teakettle clock over the stove. "It's only eight o'clock."

"She was up early. Pour yourself a cup of coffee and pull up a chair, Caine. I'll go check on her."

Devlin was smiling, but Caine heard concern in his grandfather's voice. "Is everything okay?"

"Just dandy." For the first time Caine could remember, his grandfather refused to look him in the eye. "Sit yourself down. I'll be back in two shakes of a lamb's tail."

Caine poured a cup of coffee from the dented aluminum coffeepot on the stove and took a careful sip. It was hot and dark and strong with a just a hint of chicory that hearkened back to Maggie O'Halloran's New Orleans roots.

The table was covered with the oilcloth that dated back to a time before Caine was born. The kitchen radio—an ancient tube model—was tuned to a big-band station, adding to the feeling that his grandparents' house had been frozen in time.

"She just drifted off," Devlin said, returning just as the Chattanooga choo-choo left Pennsylvania station.

"I didn't think you'd want me to wake her."

"Of course not. Are you sure nothing's wrong?"

"Your grandmother's not a young woman, Caine. She gets a mite more tired these days. Same as the rest of us old codgers."

"Maybe I'd better have those flapjacks some other time."

"Don't be ridiculous," Devlin argued. "You stay put and I'll rustle them up before you can say Jack Sprat."

He moved toward the stove with the deliberate shuffle of a man of enormous energy trapped in an aging, stiff body. Caine wasn't about to sit by while a man nearly three times his age waited on him.

"How about we team up?"

"I reckon that'll be okay," Devlin replied. "But don't you dare tell your grandmother. She'd have my hide if she found out I put you to work the minute you walked in the door."

"Mum's the word," Caine agreed.

They worked in companionable silence. Caine cooked the pancakes in an iron skillet in the center of the woodstove Maggie insisted cooked better than any gas or electric one, while Devlin fried bacon in the electric frying pan.

In the background, Glenn Miller was "in the mood," followed by Erskine Hawkins swinging in the Savoy Ballroom with "Tuxedo Junction." The batter began bubbling around the edges of the silver-dollar-size cakes.

"So what're you gonna do about getting Nora back?"

"What makes you think I want her back?" Caine flipped the pancakes.

"If you don't, you're a damn fool."

"Still beating around the bush, aren't you?"

"In case you hadn't noticed, boy, I'm gettin' to be an old man. The way I figure it, I don't have time to be subtle."

The pancakes were a golden brown. Caine piled them on a plate, put the plate in the warming oven, and began spooning more batter into the pan.

"I've got too much to work out without trying to rekindle cold ashes from a failed marriage," Caine muttered. Having his grandfather bring up his love life reminded him all too vividly of the other night's humiliating sexual failure.

The old man piled the bacon onto a platter, then shuffled over to the table and placed it in the middle of the oilcloth.

"You and Nora started out kinda rocky," Devlin allowed.

Caine watched him struggling with the lid of the preserve jar and had to force himself not to rush in to help. "We ended that way, too," Caine reminded him.

Devlin shrugged. "Every marriage goes through a few rough patches. You gonna turn those or let 'em burn?"

Caine flipped the round cakes just in time.

He was relieved when his grandfather appeared willing to drop the subject while they shared a companionable breakfast.

"It's good to have you back, Caine," Devlin said, spooning the dark red rhubarb sauce over their pancakes.

"You've no idea how good it is to *be* back." Caine took a bite and remembered what heaven tasted like.

"There's been a lot of changes here on the peninsula," Devlin complained. "We're gettin' more overrun with tourists every day...the kind of folks that look like they just stepped off the pages of one of them L. L. Bean catalogs.

"Used to be you could leave your tackle in your boat—can't do that anymore. Remember the first time I took you fishing?"

"We were out for seven days, trolling for salmon." He'd been five at the time, but Caine could remember the cold winds, the churning waves and the orange floats as if it were yesterday. The memory was so vivid that when he took a bite of bacon, Caine was almost surprised that it didn't taste of fish.

"I was as sick as a dog the entire time."

"You were a mite green around the gills," Devlin confirmed. "I told your daddy that we'd better find you another occupation because it was obvious that you weren't born with the O'Halloran sea legs. Next day he bought you your first baseball."

He stabbed a piece of pancake with his fork and chewed thoughtfully. "Funny how things work out. Who would've guessed that you'd grow up to be a bigleague baseball star and end up in the Hall of Fame alongside Ruth and DiMaggio and Cobb?"

"You can't get voted into the Hall of Fame until you've been retired for five years. And I'm not ready to retire."

"Your daddy said the same thing," Devlin observed. "The fishing business has gotten so bad it looks like your daddy might have to give up *The Bountiful*."

"I went by the docks to see *The Bountiful* yesterday," Caine told him. He'd been surprised by the number of streamlined sport-fishing craft, painted red and blue and yellow, with sickeningly cute names and long whip antennae, that had taken over many of the old fishing-boat slips. "But they told me she was out to sea."

"Your daddy got himself a two-week charter. A bunch of insurance guys from Seattle won some kinda sales contest.

"That's one of those funny twists of fate. For a while, things were lookin' so bad we thought your daddy would have to turn *The Bountiful* over to the bank and go work on the beach."

"I hadn't realized he was in financial trouble. Damn! Why didn't he tell me?"

"It wasn't your problem."

"But I made seven million dollars last year."

Devlin looked up with interest. "Newspapers said ten."

"The newspapers were wrong."

"Still," Devlin mulled aloud, "seven million is a right nice piece of change."

"Enough to pay every debt my father could have racked up and buy a fleet of new boats." Caine's fingers curved tightly around the handle of his fork. "Dammit, he should have told me."

"You had your own troubles, what with your injury and your marriage problems and all," his grandfather argued patiently. "We didn't want to worry you."

Although Devlin didn't say it, Caine had the bleak

feeling that the reason his family hadn't come to him for help was that they'd never considered him all that reliable. Although he knew his parents were proud of his achievements, he also knew that they found it difficult to view baseball as a real job.

The O'Hallorans were a hardy, unpretentious, salt-of-the-earth breed who'd always worked hard for every penny; he, on the other hand, was paid a virtual fortune to play a kids' game. Add to that a press corps that loved detailing his admittedly hedonistic lifestyle, and it was no wonder his parents had opted to handle their own financial problems.

Caine shrugged. "I had a few curveballs thrown my way. Nothing I can't handle. Dad should have said something."

"'Tweren't necessary. A few months ago your daddy turned the boat into a charter and Ellen signed on as cook. Thanks to city slickers with too much time and money on their hands, he's makin' more in a month than he did all last year. Which leads me to my next point."

"What point is that?" Caine knew he sounded like a petulant twelve-year-old. Which wasn't surprising since, unfortunately, at the moment he felt like one.

"That sometimes life takes funny turns and it looks as if things are goin' downhill, but if a fella's quick on the uptake, he can turn things around to his advantage.

"Nothin' your daddy liked better than bein' out on that boat. And for a while, it looked like he was gonna have to give it up. But then he figured out this charter business and from what I can tell he's never been happier.

"And your mama. Lord, that lady never worked for

wages a day in her life, but you'd think she'd discovered heaven from the way she talks about all the pleasure she gets from those city folk gobblin' up her vittles like they'd been starving.

"So, why don't you quit feelin' sorry for yourself, Caine, and figure out how to make lemonade outta them lemons fate dealt you?"

Caine squared his shoulders. "I'm not feeling sorry for myself."

"Who's not feelin' sorry for himself?" a feminine voice asked. "Is that my Caine?" Maggie O'Halloran peered through her wire-framed glasses as she entered the kitchen.

She was wearing a scarlet sweatshirt embossed with a trio of puffins sitting atop a rock and blue jeans that hung loosely, suggesting that she'd lost a great deal of weight recently. Her hair, once a flaming red, had faded to a soft tapestry of silver-and-pink.

"Hiya, Gram."

Caine pushed himself out of his chair, crossed the room and enfolded her in his arms. She was smaller than he remembered—the top of her head barely reached the middle of his chest—and she seemed unusually frail.

"God, it's good to see you."

She tilted her head back. "Still using the Lord's name in vain, I see." There was a twinkle in her blue eyes. "What on earth are we gonna do with you, Caine O'Halloran?"

"There's always the woodshed."

She chuckled at that. "You were too big for a whupping when you were born. Guess I'll have to give you a big hug instead."

As she wrapped her arms around him, Caine couldn't help noticing that her strength wasn't what it once had been. He drank in the familiar scent of lilacs that had always surrounded her and tried to pretend that nothing had changed.

"You're sure looking good, Gram," he said. He grinned at his grandfather over the top of her pastel curls. "You'd better watch out, Pappy, or one of those big Swede loggers is gonna steal this lady right out from under your nose."

"Lars Nelson winked at her last Friday," Devlin allowed.

"That wasn't a wink," Maggie argued. "The old man just has a tic in his left eye."

"Sure looked like a wink to me," Devlin said. "I thought maybe he was lookin' for a refresher course on those flying lessons he took from you."

"That was fifty years ago," Maggie informed Caine.

"And your grandfather's still jealous."

The three of them laughed at the long-running joke.

"Besides," Maggie said as she made her way slowly and painfully, Caine noticed with alarm, to a chair, "I haven't been up in a plane for so long I probably couldn't remember how to take off."

"I doubt that, Gram," Caine said. "Everyone knows you were born to fly."

"You're right about that," Maggie agreed, smiling her thanks to her husband, who'd placed a mug of coffee liberally laced with milk in front of her. "Of course I had a heck of a time convincing others of that fact, back in the old days."

She blew on the coffee, took a sip, then gazed down into the light brown depths as if seeing herself as she'd been in those days so many years ago. As if on cue, Les Brown's "Sentimental Journey" came over the radio.

"They wouldn't let me solo, so I couldn't get my license."

Caine knew the romantic story of his grandmother's life by rote. Maggie O'Halloran, nee Margaret Rose Murphy, had been born in New Orleans in 1930. When she was fifteen years old, she'd run away from the convent school her wealthy parents had sent her to and become a singer and dancer with a travelling troupe.

It was during her days on the stage that she'd met a dashing former World War II flying ace barnstorming his way across America. He'd taken her up in his Lockheed Vega and although the pilot had moved on the following morning, Maggie's love affair with the airplane had lasted the rest of her life.

Caine had heard innumerable stories of Maggie's exploits while growing up, including how Devlin, who loved the way Maggie Murphy looked in her scandalous khaki trousers, had vowed to win the heart of the hot-tempered, flame-haired aviatrix.

Noticing the familiar warm light shining in her eyes, Caine was more than willing to sit through the story again.

"But eventually you got it," he said, on cue.

"Sure did." She chuckled, then took another sip. "Of course, it was still a man's world, and I got turned down for every airline job I applied for, but then one day I showed up at this itsy-bitsy airfield in Glendale, California, where they were having a pylon race. Won myself a trophy, which I ended up pawning to pay for fuel for my next three races."

A reminiscent smile wreathed her face, softening

the lines earned from a lifetime of working outdoors.

"Boy, I loved beating those egotistical swaggering pilots with their goggles and their baggy trousers"

"You looked better in those trousers, too," Devlin drawled.

"And you were always a silver-tongued devil, Devlin O'Halloran." A soft flush colored her cheeks, and Caine experienced a twinge of envy at this couple who, after more than fifty years of marriage, were still so much in love.

He was still considering exactly how they'd managed such a remarkable feat when his grandmother's head dropped to her chest.

"Gram?" He was on his feet and around the table like a shot.

"She's been droppin' off like that regular," his grandfather assured him. "Nora says it's normal."

"But she just woke up."

"And now she's sleepin'. Let it be, Caine."

But he couldn't. There was something wrong with Maggie. Something his grandfather wasn't saying. And if Devlin wasn't going to tell him the truth about his grandmother's condition, he had no choice but to get it from Nora.

"Thanks for the breakfast," he said. "I'll do the dishes."

"No need to worry about them. I'll stick them in the dishwasher." Devlin gave Caine a warning look. "Maggie wouldn't want you goin' off half-cocked, making a fuss about her."

"But she's old."

"She's sick."

"But she's old," his grandfather corrected. "Let it be, Caine," he said again.

Caine shrugged. "Sure, whatever you say."

They both knew it was a lie.

Caine gave his grandfather a farewell hug and walked back out to the car, feeling as if the entire weight of the world was lying heavily on his shoulders.

Johnny Baker was seven years old. His uncombed hair was the color of butterscotch candy, his bare feet were dirty and his eyes were older and more resigned than any seven-year-old's eyes had a right to be.

In a way, Johnny was lucky. His burns, which his mother alleged he'd received when he'd accidentally overturned a pot of boiling water, were no worse than a medium-harsh sunburn. If the circumstances had been different, Nora would have sent him home with a tube of analgesic ointment.

But there was something about the burns themselves that bothered her. The skin on both too-thin reddened arms had clear demarcation lines; there were none of the splash marks she would have expected above the burned area.

And there were other faint scars, on the insides of the boy's arms and buttocks. Small, round, wrinkled white scars. Nora had seen marks like that before.

When the X-rays showed what Nora had feared, she placed a call to Children's Services and began filling out the admission form that would keep the little boy in the hospital until an investigation could be launched.

She'd just finished the paperwork when her office door opened. She glanced up, then had to fight the unbidden pleasure that surged through her when she saw Caine standing there.

"Hi." She started to rise, then changed her mind,

not wanting to give up the three feet of polished desk between them. "This is a surprise."

"I need to talk to you."

"Oh, Caine. I told you——"

"It's not about us," he said quickly. "It's about Maggie."

"Oh." She folded her hands atop the manila file. "I take it you've seen her."

"This morning. And it's obvious that something's wrong with her, but my grandfather refuses to talk about it."

"I know." Nora sighed. "It's hard on him. The thought of losing her."

"My grandmother's dying?" She'd confirmed Caine's worst fears. Pain ripped through him, more brutal and severe than anything the Olson boys could have dished out.

"We're all dying, Caine," Nora reminded him quietly. "It's just that Maggie's time is getting close."

"What's wrong with her?"

She gestured toward a chair on the visitors' side of the desk. "Please, sit down. Would you like some coffee?"

"This isn't a damn tea party, Nora," Caine growled. "You don't have to play hostess. I just want to know what's wrong with my grandmother."

"Other than old age?"

He snorted in a disbelieving way. "She's not that old, dammit. Both her parents lived into their late nineties. We were talking and she fell asleep in the middle of a conversation. You can't tell me that's normal. Even at her age."

"No." His face was as dark and threatening as a

thundercloud. Nora tried to decide where to begin. "A few years ago, Maggie was diagnosed as having sideroblastic anemia."

"I remember that. Mom wrote me about it. But she said that so long as Gram received regular transfusions, she'd be fine."

"And she was. Until recently. Devlin came to me when I first opened my practice, worried because she kept falling asleep. He couldn't talk her into going to a doctor, so he wanted my help."

"Gram always did like you."

"I love her," Nora said simply. "The problem is, as you know, your grandmother's a fairly stubborn woman."

"That's putting it mildly. When Maggie Murphy O'Halloran digs in her heels, she can put a pit bull terrier to shame."

"Exactly. Finally, after a great deal of unprofessional pleading and cajoling, I managed to talk her into going to Seattle for some extensive tests."

"And?"

"She has hemochromatosis, Caine."

"What the hell is that?"

"The diagnosis is complex, but the gist of it is that the iron has built up in her heart and caused too much damage for us to treat. Which is why she can't stay awake. Her heart can only pump effectively for a short time, then it has to rest."

"So get her a new heart."

"I wish it were that simple. But it's not."

"Sure, it is. I made seven million dollars last year."

"The papers said ten."

If he weren't so worried about Maggie, Caine would

have found it interesting that Nora had bothered reading about him.

"They were wrong. It was seven. But that's still six zeros, Nora. Surely that's enough to buy Gram a new heart."

"Why not?"

"Even if you could just run to a body-parts store and pick up a new heart, which you can't, a transplant is not an option in Maggie's case."

"Why not?"

"In the first place, Maggie isn't well enough to survive the wait for a donor heart, even if we could get her on the list.

"In the second place, if a heart did become available in time, I doubt she could survive the surgery."

"It's worth a try."

"Not to her."

"What?"

"Maggie categorically refuses to consider any dramatic efforts to keep her alive."

Caine ground his teeth so hard his jaw ached. "That's ridiculous."

"It's her decision. And," Nora added softly, "one Devlin and I happen to agree with."

His face took on that familiar, stubborn expression she knew all too well. His eyes turned to flint, his jaw jutted forward.

"Gram's always listened to me. I can change her mind."

"Caine, don't do this."

Nora rose from her chair and went around the desk to stand in front of him. "Maggie's made her decision. She's comfortable with it. Please don't upset her."

Caine was on his feet, as well. "I'm trying to save her life, dammit!"

"That's just the point." Nora put her hand on his arm and felt the muscle tense beneath her fingertips. "You can't save her, Caine. No one can."

Caine muttered a litany of harsh expletives. "I am not going to let her die."

Nora remembered the paramedics trying to tell her that Caine had been shouting the same thing while the rescue team cut Dylan out of the mangled red Corvette.

"I'm sorry, Caine. Truly, I am."

"Goddamn it!" He pulled away from her and slammed his fist into the wall, punching a hole in the plasterboard. Unsatisfied, he gave the wall a vicious kick with the toe of his boot. The impact sent a jolt of lightning through his healing ribs.

"Are you all right?"

"I'm fine." He flexed his fingers. "See?" His tired gaze took in the ragged hole in the wall. "Send me the bill for your wall."

"Don't worry about it."

"I said, send me the damn bill."

"Fine, I'll send you the damn bill."

"Good." He nodded. "I'm going to get a second opinion."

"You have every right to do that," Nora told him. "But I have to warn you, Caine, all the specialists who saw Maggie agreed with the diagnosis. And she doesn't have the strength to have you dragging her all over the country."

"Shit." He threw his long frame onto the office sofa, put his head against the back cushion and covered his eyes with his hand. "Now what?"

"I suggested Maggie enter a hospice program so she can stay at home, instead of spending her last months in the hospital."

"She'd hate being stuck in some dreary hospital room," Caine said glumly. "So is she in this program?"

"She hasn't made up her mind yet. Perhaps you can help convince her."

Caine nodded. "I'll give it my best shot." He gave her a long, probing look. "What's the prognosis?"

"I told you—"

"I know." He cut the air with a swift slice of his hand. "You've convinced me that my grandmother is going to die, Nora. I want to know when. And how."

She'd seen that expression on his face before. When he'd been waiting for word of their critically injured son. Immersed in her own fear, Nora had refused to acknowledge his pain. This time, she found it impossible to ignore.

"It's hard to say," she said softly. "She could have a heart attack, or a stroke, or some other type of seizure. Or she might simply fall asleep one of these times and not wake up."

"Not a lot of nifty options, huh?"

"I'm sorry."

He looked at her, taking in her neat blond hair, her starched white jacket, the little rectangular name tag above her right breast. She seemed both familiar and foreign at the same time. Caine wondered if Nora realized that the severe tailoring of her professional clothing made her appear all the more feminine by contrast. Softer.

"I never could really think of you as a doctor."

"I know." It was one of the things they'd fought about on a regular basis.

"But you're pretty good. I'm impressed."

The faintest of smiles played at the corners of her full, serious mouth. "Thank you. I needed a kind word today."

He glanced over at the light box she'd left on. "Trouble with one of your patients?"

"A seven-year-old boy. His mother brought him in with burns she said he'd gotten from pulling a pan off the stove."

"I hope they're not too bad."

"Actually, they probably won't even blister. But I had a funny feeling about it, so I ordered some X-rays." "And?"

"See these?" Nora picked up a pencil and began pointing to various faint lines on the gray film.

Caine pushed himself off the couch and came over to stand beside her. "Those wiggly lines?"

"Those are old fractures left to heal by themselves."

"The kid was beaten?"

"Apparently. And there're more." Nora turned off the light. "There were scars about the size of a pencil eraser."

"Or a lighted cigarette." Caine felt suddenly sick.

"Or a lighted cigarette," Nora agreed flatly.

Caine wondered how it was that he and Nora, who'd loved Dylan so much, had lost him, while some other parents could deliberately hurt their child.

"Makes you wonder, doesn't it?"

She looked up into his face and read her own troubled thoughts in his pained gaze. "Yes." Her voice came out in a whisper. "It does."

They stood there, only inches apart, looking at each other, bittersweet memories swirling in the air between them.

"Nora." He ran his palm down the silk of her hair and watched the awareness rise in her eyes.

"Oh, Caine." It was little more than a whisper.

He leaned closer.

"This is a mistake," she warned.

"Probably. But no worse than any of the others I've been making lately." His knuckles caressed her cheek in a slow, seductive sweep. "And I'm willing to bet it'll be a helluva lot more enjoyable than most."

Chapter 7

As his lips touched hers, the intervening years spun away and all the reasons why this was a mistake dissolved like mist over the treetops.

Holding Nora brought not the pain of lost love he would have expected, but a rightness—almost a contentment—Caine hadn't expected to feel. How could he have forgotten how sweet she was? And how responsive.

He felt her sigh against his mouth—a slow, shuddering breath that echoed his own pleasure. Time tumbled backward, taking them past the pain to a passion that had been even more exquisite because it had been so liberally laced with love.

"God, I've missed this." Caine drew her closer, then closer still, until the rising heat threatened to fuse their bodies. "I've missed you." Although he'd never realized it, it was true.

"Don't talk," she whispered breathlessly. "Just kiss me. And hold me." Her arms wrapped possessively around him; her lips fused with his, again and again. "Tight."

Dear Lord, he was lost in her. In her touch, her taste, her scent. Nora was everything he'd been wanting, without even knowing he'd been wanting it. She was everything he'd been needing without knowing he'd been needing it. She was heaven.

She was home.

Home. The word, which once had represented unwanted strings and unwelcome commitments, now seemed like a prayer.

Caine skimmed his lips along the line of her jaw, then up her cheek to linger at her temple. Desperate to know how her body had changed during their years apart, he slipped his hands inside her lab coat. When his wide hand cupped her breast, a ragged moan escaped her parted lips.

He tugged her blouse loose, then her camisole, inching his way beneath the ivory silk. "You feel so good."

His fingers moved upward to stroke her breasts, finding them as smooth and firm and fragrant as he remembered.

He wanted to take those taut peaks in his mouth. He wanted to feel her body, hot and eager and open against his. He wanted to possess her, mind and body and soul, as he'd done on so many nights so long ago.

He was actually considering the logistics of making love to her here and now in her office, when her intercom buzzed sharply.

Like a man immersed in a sensual dream, Caine was aware of the intrusion and fought against it.

The intercom continued to buzz.

"I have to answer that." Her flat tone told him it was not her first choice.

Without removing his hands from beneath her camisole, he tugged her pearl earring off with his teeth and dropped it onto the desk before nibbling at her earlobe.

"Don't tell me this hospital will come to a halt if you don't answer your intercom?"

"No, but the E.R. clerk has a habit of just barging in."

Knowing that the idea of being caught in a heated clench with her ex-husband was more than Nora could handle, Caine reluctantly released her, then reached out to steady her when she suddenly swayed.

"You okay?"

"Of course." But her hand trembled as she fingercombed her sleek hair.

"Remind me to stop by Richie Duggan's hardware store and get a Do Not Disturb sign for your office door."

"Please, Caine." She struggled to tuck her blouse back into her waistband. "Don't do this."

They were on familiar turf again: Nora backing away, Caine pressing her for more than she wanted to give.

"I didn't do it alone."

"I know." Her eyes, her voice, revealed her regret.

There was a sharp knock on the door. A moment later, Mabel entered the office.

"Is everything all right, Dr. Anderson?"

The elderly woman's gaze reminded Caine of a curious bird's as it flicked from Nora to him and back to Nora.

"Everything's fine," Nora answered in a tone that was not nearly as strong as her usual professional voice.

"You sure?" Knowing eyes searched Nora's flushed face.

"Of course."

"You didn't answer the intercom."

"Mr. O'Halloran and I were discussing his grand-mother's case," Nora said.

Mabel turned back toward Caine, who was standing with his arms crossed over his broad chest. "I thought I recognized you."

"Mabel Erickson, Caine O'Halloran," Nora intro-duced them reluctantly. "Mabel runs the emergency room."

"No wonder everyone looks so efficient," Caine said. "Believe me, Ms. Erickson, I've been in a lot of emer-gency rooms over the years and I could tell right away that yours is one of the best."

"Call me Mabel!" She beamed. "I've got your *Van-ity Fair* issue in my locker," she surprised Nora by re-vealing. "If I go get it, will you autograph it for me?"

Caine grinned. "I'll stop by your desk on my way out."

Mabel's fleshy, smiling face was the hue of a late-July raspberry. "Don't you dare leave this hospital with-out signing it."

"I wouldn't think of it," Caine said easily.

"Mabel?" Nora called out to the receptionist's back.

The clerk stopped on her way out the door and glanced back over her shoulder. "Yes, Dr. Anderson?"

"What did you want?"

"Want?" Mabel's gaze slid back to Caine.

"The intercom," Nora reminded her. "You buzzed."

"Oh, that. The Children's Services social worker is here. About that little boy. I put her in waiting room B."

"Thank you." But Mabel had already bustled off toward the staff locker room, leaving Nora talking to air.

"You've obviously made another conquest," she snapped.

Her withdrawal was as familiar as her smoldering sexuality. Caine remembered all too well how Nora had never grown accustomed to having her husband surrounded by baseball groupies. Not that she'd ever needed to worry.

Recalling her passion that Midsummer Eve in the cabin, Caine hadn't been terribly surprised when their first encounter as man and wife six months after their marriage confirmed his long-held belief that they were a perfect sexual match.

What had come as a distinct shock that afternoon years ago, before their son was born, was the realization that somehow, when he wasn't looking, he'd fallen head over heels in love with his wife.

"I don't think this is the time or the place to get into another argument about my alleged infidelities, Nora," Caine said now. His mouth set in its grim line again; all the heated emotion he'd displayed in his kiss had disappeared from his eyes.

"It's a moot point," Nora said between clenched teeth, "since it's over between us. I gave up worrying about all your other women a very long time ago, Caine."

She brushed her hands down the front of her jacket, smoothing the wrinkles that remained as damning evidence of her uncharacteristically unprofessional behavior.

Caine rubbed his jaw. "You know, I thought it was over, too. But I'm beginning to have my doubts."

She tilted her chin. "I haven't any doubts."

"Not even one?"

"None at all."

He could have murdered her for unleashing so much raw emotion, then behaving as if that shared kiss had never happened. He could have dragged her onto the couch, her desk, hell, the floor, to prove to her how very wrong she was.

"Well, then, if that's really the case, we shouldn't have any problem getting along while you're treating Maggie."

Maggie. Caine couldn't accept the idea that his grandmother was dying. It was something he would have to think about later. When he was alone. Or better yet, with his new best friend, Jack Daniel's.

"No problem at all," Nora agreed stiffly. "I really do have to leave." Unwilling to look directly at him, Nora focused on the wall thermostat beside the door.

"Before you go, can I ask what happens next?"

"With us? I told you, Caine. Nothing."

Caine saw the lingering reluctant desire she hadn't been able to hide glowing in her eyes. That she wanted him was obvious. That she didn't want to want him was also all too apparent.

It was just as well, he decided grimly. He had enough problems right now without getting involved with the only woman he'd ever met who could make him willing to beg.

"Actually, I was referring to that little boy."

"Oh." Embarrassed that she'd misunderstood him and surprised by his obvious concern for someone other than himself, she said, "Children's Services will begin an investigation. I could release him here this afternoon, but I'd rather keep him here and avoid the risk of the social workers deciding to leave him with his mother while they conduct the investigation."

"Can you do that?" Caine asked. Concern for the unfortunate child temporarily overrode his concern for Maggie. "When there really isn't anything wrong with him?"

"You can always find something wrong with a kid if you're creative."

"Sounds as if you've had some experience with this."

"More than I'd like." She picked up the file, prepared to leave the office. "I really do have to leave."

"Sure." Caine stepped aside. "Do you think it'd be okay if I dropped in on the kid?"

"That would be terrific. I don't know why I didn't think of it myself." She rewarded him with a faint, appreciative smile. "He's upstairs on the pediatric ward. Perhaps you could go up now while I talk with the social worker."

"Great." He frowned. "I just wish I had a baseball or something for him."

"I think meeting you will be tonic enough." The smile reached her eyes as she put her hand on his arm. "Thank you."

"No thanks necessary, Doc." Caine covered her hand with his own. "I'm just happy to be able to help out."

He decided, for discretion's sake, not to admit that if he were to go home to that lonely cabin to think about Maggie, and face his undeniable role in the failure of his and Nora's marriage, he'd give in to the need to get very, very drunk.

Her soft smile—a portent that perhaps things might be looking up—stayed with Caine as he took the elevator to the second-floor pediatric wing.

For a man who'd been seeking something—someone—to make him feel like a hero again, Johnny Baker proved the perfect prescription.

But it was more than just being put atop his lofty pedestal again, which, Caine considered, wasn't all that bad. After drowning in self-pity for months, one look at those small bandaged hands went a long way to putting things back into perspective. If what Nora suspected was true, fate had certainly dealt this kid more than his share of rotten luck.

Although Johnny had surrounded himself with protective walls even Nora might have envied, after a few minutes of regaling the seven-year-old with tales of games past, Caine began to breach those parapets.

Enough so that Johnny had actually begun to relax when Nora entered the room with the social worker.

"Look who came to see me, Dr. Anderson," Johnny greeted her. "Caine O'Halloran." He breathed the name in the way a religious zealot might whisper the name of his god. Johnny's eyes, which had been so flat and lifeless during her examination, gleamed with youthful enthusiasm.

"Dr. Anderson and I are old friends," Caine said.

"Wow!" The boy's gaze went back and forth between them. "You're really lucky, Dr. Anderson."

"I guess I am at that," Nora said.

"You know what?"

"What?"

"He's gonna bring me an autographed baseball."

"And a Yankees cap," Caine reminded him.

"Yeah." Johnny Baker's expression was that of a boy for whom Christmas had come seven months early. "A real Yankees cap. Autographed by Billy Martin and Mickey Mantle!"

Knowing how he had revered that particular piece of baseball memorabilia, Nora looked up at Caine in surprise and received an embarrassed grin in return.

"That's wonderful," she said with a smile. "Johnny, this is Mrs. Langley. She'd like to have a little chat with you."

The light left his eyes, like a candle snuffed out by an icy wind. "You're from Social Services, aren't you?" He said the words without emotion, but his flat, older-than-his-years tone touched Caine more deeply than his earlier hero worship.

A little pool of silence settled over the room. "Yes, I am," the social worker agreed quietly.

Thin shoulders, clad in a pair of the superhero pajamas given to all the little boys on the ward, lifted and fell in a resigned shrug. "I figured you were."

"Have you talked with social workers before, Johnny?" Nora asked.

"Yeah. In Portland. And a couple times in L.A. And every time, Mama'd get mad afterward and we'd have to move again." He sighed. "I'm gettin' awful tired of moving."

"Perhaps you won't have to," Mrs. Langley suggested. She pulled a chair up to the side of the bed. When she sat down, she was at eye level with the boy. "Perhaps this time, things will be different."

He stiffened slightly, as if bracing for the worst.

"That's what they all say."

He was retreating, back behind those self-protective walls. Feeling the boy's pain and experiencing a strange sort of kinship with this child whose life had started out on such a different path from his own, Caine squeezed Johnny's shoulder.

"Listen, sport. I've got a feeling that between the four of us in this room, we can make a difference. But you've got to help."

"How?" A glimmer of hope cut through the shadows as Johnny looked up at his hero.

"You've got to tell the truth." When the seven-year-old didn't immediately answer, Caine leaned closer and whispered in his ear.

"I'll think about it," Johnny replied. "But only if you promise."

"Scout's honor."

Johnny Baker looked into Caine's face for a long time. "I guess I can trust you."

"I wouldn't let you down, Johnny. You can count on it."

Apparently making his decision, the boy turned back to the social worker. "So, what do you want to know?"

"What did you say to make him change his mind?" Nora asked, as she and Caine left the room.

She'd seen similar cases where there were obvious signs of abuse and the children, whether from fear or misplaced loyalty, absolutely refused to say a single accusing word against their parents.

"Not that much." Caine pushed the elevator button. "I simply told him that I wouldn't let Social Services send him back to his mother."

"Caine!" Nora stared up at him. "You had no right to tell him any such thing!"

"Why not?"

"Because you have no control over the situation."

"Of course I do."

The elevator reached the floor; the green metal doors opened. Caine stood aside and gestured for Nora to enter first.

"If Social Services drops the ball and lets his mother take him back home again," Caine said as he followed her into the elevator and pushed the button for the first floor, "I'll call a press conference and tell everyone in the state what she's done. That should get the bureaucrats off their behinds."

"You can't do that!"

"Why not?"

"Because the mother could turn around and sue you for libel, or slander."

"Let her sue," Caine said. "I'll just hire the best attorney in the country and keep her tied up in court until the kid's an adult and safely out of her control."

He meant it, Nora realized, stunned by this man she'd thought she knew so well. "Why would you go out on a limb for a child you don't even know?"

"Why would you?" he countered. "Obviously filing a suspected abuse form is not something a doctor does without weighing all the options."

"He's a child at risk. I had no choice."

"Exactly." Caine nodded, satisfied. The car reached their floor. "And believe it or not, for once in our lives, we're in perfect agreement." He followed her out of the elevator. "And there's something else."

"What?"

"Dylan probably would have looked a lot like Johnny Baker," Caine said in a hushed, pained voice. "If he'd lived."

"Dammit, Caine..."

Tears began to well in Nora's eyes and she turned away. She felt his hand on her shoulder.

"Don't you think it's finally time we dealt with it, Nora?"

She could have wept with relief when the speaker above her head began to blare a code. "I've got to go," she said. "I'm on duty."

He dropped his hand to his side. "What time do you get off?"

"Three-thirty, but—"

"I'll be waiting."

"But, Caine..." The code continued to blare. "Oh, hell. Do whatever you want. You always have." Welcoming the irritation that steamrolled over her earlier emotional turmoil, she took off running to the ambulance entrance.

Caine watched her talking to the paramedics as they pulled a gurney from the back of the red-and-white vehicle. She was no longer the young woman he'd seduced in front of a crackling fire on Midsummer Eve so many years ago. Nor was she the exhausted, surprisingly insecure, angry bride he'd alternately fought with, shared terrific sex with, and ultimately abandoned.

A late bloomer, Dr. Nora Anderson had definitely come into her own. That she was satisfied—even happy—with her life was obvious.

Not for the first time since returning to Tribulation, Caine wished he could learn her secret.

*   *   *

Nora was not surprised to find Caine waiting for her when she left the hospital that afternoon. Nor was she all that surprised that he'd ignored all the posted signs and parked in the staff parking lot.

"Eric was right," she said as she approached the man who was leaning against the gleaming black car. "That Ferrari does look like the Batmobile."

"I know." Caine grinned. "It's a ridiculously juvenile car for a grown man, but I couldn't help myself. Think I'm going through male menopause, Doc?"

Her mind, so calm and deliberate earlier in the emergency room, sprang to fevered life at his cocky grin. Her body followed at an alarming pace.

"That would be a little difficult," she said in a dry tone meant to conceal the havoc going on inside her, "since emotionally, you still haven't gotten out of your teens."

The smile in her eyes took the sting out of her words. "Ouch. You really know how to hurt a guy, don't you? And here I thought we were becoming friends."

"Fine. As your friend, I feel it's my duty to point out that you're parked in a reserved spot."

"It was empty."

"It belongs to the chief of staff."

"If the guy worked a full day like he was supposed to, his spot wouldn't have been vacant, so I couldn't have taken it," Caine argued. "So, what was your big emergency?"

"A sixteen-year-old girl was kicked in the abdomen by a horse."

"Is she going to be okay?"

"It's touch and go. The surgeon repaired her lacerated liver and removed a ruptured kidney, but it's still iffy," Nora frowned. "Here's a kid who could very well die and you know what she's worried about?"

"That her parents are going to get rid of her horse?"

"Exactly. How did you know?"

Caine shrugged. "You're the one who pointed out that I still haven't outgrown my teenage stage. I guess I can identify with a sixteen-year-old kid."

"I'm sorry about that. I was out of line. Especially after the way you jumped to Johnny Baker's defense." Nora managed a weak smile. "I suppose I could use the excuse that I'm exhausted, but I think the truth is that snapping at you is a leftover knee-jerk reaction."

"Makes sense to me," Caine said agreeably. "Since I'm suffering from a few old knee-jerk responses myself."

"Really?"

"Really. Except in my case, the feelings are a bit different."

Nora saw the devil in his eye and turned away to unlock her car door.

"Don't you want to know what they are?"

"Not really," she said with pretended indifference, struggling to turn a key in the lock.

"I think I'll tell you anyway." He plucked the keys from her hand, located the correct one and unlocked the door. "I can't seem to resist the urge to taste you whenever those ridiculously kissable lips come within puckering distance."

Before she could get into the car, he cupped her chin, lifted her frowning lips to his and gave her a long, deep kiss that left them both breathless.

"We still set off sparks, Nora," he murmured when they finally came up for air.

He brushed the pad of his ultrasensitized thumb against the flesh of her bottom lip. Caine's heart was pounding with a rhythm he usually associated with spring-training wind sprints. He'd never met another woman who could make him suffer so, and relish the pain.

"You can't deny it, babe."

"It's only sex. Nothing more."

"You were always good for my ego."

"And you always had sex on the brain."

Amusement flickered in his eyes as he skimmed a slow, sensual glance over her. "I don't remember you complaining."

Once again the atmosphere between them had become intensely charged. "Dammit, Caine—"

"Besides," he said, "I think we were wrong."

"About what?"

"About the only thing we had going for us in those days, besides Dylan, was sex. Oh, I know that's what we always used to say," he said when she opened her mouth to argue. "But you've no idea how many women I've gone to bed with over the past nine years trying to forget you, Nora."

"I don't want to hear about all your other women."

"That's fine with me, since I don't want to talk about them." He ran his palm down her hair. "Your hair has always reminded me of corn silk." Memories of it draped across his naked chest, after making love, made his already aroused body hard.

"I suppose you tell that to all your women."

"I thought we'd agreed not to talk about other women."

"Although what you do and who you do it with isn't any of my business, as a doctor I have to point out that casual sex is dangerous, Caine. Especially these days."

"True enough. But you know, Nora, sex was never casual with you." His fingers curled around the back of her neck, his warm dark blue eyes captured her wary ones.

"Don't you think I know how uncomfortable this is for you?" he said in a low rough voice. "But it's not exactly a picnic for me, either, babe. Because right now my life is really messed up, and I have this feeling that if you and I could at least try to put the past to rest, maybe I'll be able to handle whatever the future brings.

"Besides—" he took hold of her hand, brought it to his lips and kissed her fingertips, one at a time "— we're still emotionally linked, Nora, whether we want to be or not."

"That's ridiculous."

"Why don't you kiss me again and try telling me that?"

She might be reckless whenever Caine was around, but Nora wasn't a complete idiot. "You've always been a good kisser, Caine. But then, practice makes perfect."

"It helps," he said easily. "Want to practice some more?"

"I just want to go home. I've had a long day."

"Come out to the cabin and I'll massage your feet. You used to like that."

Too much, Nora agreed silently. During their ill-fated marriage she'd reluctantly come to like far too many things about this man.

"You may be right about putting the past behind us," she agreed. "You're also probably right about us leaving a lot of things unsaid and saying a lot of things we didn't mean. But so help me God, if you so much as touch my feet, or any other part of my anatomy, Caine O'Halloran, I'll walk away and never speak to you again."

"You drive a hard bargain, Doc."

She lifted her chin. "Take it or leave it."

Caine rubbed his jaw thoughtfully, considering her ultimatum. Nora would come to him, he vowed. And not because of any past sexual memory and not because of any shared grief. She would come because of the same aching need he'd been suffering since that suspended, sensual moment in her examining room.

"You're on," he said. "I promise, on my word as a former Eagle Scout and New York Yankee, not to pounce on Dr. Nora Anderson O'Halloran."

His words were carefully chosen to remind her that they'd once shared the same name. Along with the same apartment, and more important, the same warm double bed.

Caine watched the awareness rise in her eyes again; he was not all that surprised when it was just as quickly banked.

"I haven't been Nora O'Halloran for nine years, Caine." She glanced at his car. "You go ahead in the Batmobile. I'll follow you out to the cabin."

"You know," Caine said casually, as if the thought had just occurred to him, "Dana dropped by the cabin with some Dungeness crab. Why don't you stay for dinner? We'll have them with rice pilaf. And a tomato-mozzarella salad with honey vinaigrette, topped off by a nice, unpretentious little bottle of Fumé Blanc."

"Rice pilaf? And honey vinaigrette? Is this the same man who had trouble boiling a hot dog?"

"I bought a cookbook especially written for the kitchen-impaired this afternoon." He didn't add that he'd purchased it specifically in the hopes of persuading Nora to have an intimate dinner with him. "It's got full-color photographs and everything. How about helping me to try it out?"

Nora thought about the frozen dinner waiting to be nuked in the microwave. "All right. Fresh crab sounds delicious. And I can't pass up the opportunity to see you in an apron."

"I'll do my best not to disappoint." He dug into his pocket, pulled out his keys and slid one brass key off the ring. "Here's the front door key. I'll just stop at the store for the wine, rice and tomatoes and be right behind you."

"Just remember," she warned as she took the key from his outstretched hand, "we're only going to talk. You promised not to pounce."

"Scout's honor." He lifted his fingers in the same pledge he'd given Johnny Baker earlier. "Although I refuse to be held responsible for any naughty ideas you might come up with once you get me alone."

Refusing to dignify that remark with a response, Nora climbed into her car and slammed the door.

Unrepentant, Caine began whistling "My Girl" as he sauntered over to his own black beast parked two spaces away.

Chapter 8

Caine's chalet-style cabin was situated in a remote forest clearing, on the bank of a stream in a grove of silver-trunked aspen, nestled up against the slope of the Olympic Mountains. Behind the cabin was a small, unnamed glacial lake.

Much more than a typical rustic structure, the chalet had a soaring cathedral ceiling and an open balustrade leading to the upstairs loft. Adding to the sense of spaciousness was a panoramic wall of glass that thrust outward toward the forest like the prow of an ancient sailing ship.

From the outside, surrounded by a dazzling carpet of the same yellow, blue and white wildflowers Caine had brought to the cemetery, the cabin appeared warm and welcoming.

The inside, however, looked as if a hurricane had

swept through it. Clothes were strewn over every available piece of furniture, and although he'd been home nearly two weeks, other clothing remained in open suitcases on the floor. The rest of the plank flooring was littered with newspapers—all opened to the sports pages.

Empty beer cans littered the tops of the tables along with glasses that had etched white rings into the pine. Nora was surprised and disappointed to see an oversize plastic ashtray overflowing with cigarette butts. Cobwebs hung in the ceiling corners; dust covered everything.

She went into the kitchen, where she found more empty beer cans and a distressing number of bourbon bottles. The only time she'd ever seen Caine drink hard liquor was after the accident that had taken their son's life. His drinking, which had begun the night Dylan died, had escalated daily, culminating in that horrid, drunken scene at the cemetery.

A pizza box was open on the counter, the two remaining pieces of pepperoni pizza cold and forgotten. In the refrigerator were three additional six-packs of beer, the crab her brother had given Caine, a taco wrapped in bright yellow waxed paper, a handful of individual plastic hot-sauce containers and a bowl of guacamole that looked like an organic-chemistry lab experiment gone awry.

This was a mistake, Nora thought. The one thing she'd always admired about Caine O'Halloran was his absolute, unwavering self-confidence. To think of him, hiding away out here, drinking too much, destroying his lungs, and clogging his arteries with fat and cholesterol as he ate his solitary meals from TV trays, was surprisingly painful.

She had just decided to leave when the unmistakable whine of the Ferrari's engine cut through the mountain silence. A moment later, she heard the car door slam and Caine burst into the cabin, his arms filled with brown paper bags.

"Sorry it took longer than I'd planned," he greeted with a cheerfulness that was at distinct odds with the bleakness of their surroundings. "But I figured I might as well pick up a few basics while I was at it."

"That's a good idea. Since you don't have enough food around here to feed a starving gerbil."

"Old Mother Hubbard's cupboard has gotten a bit bare."

"Unfortunately, you can't say the same thing about the bar," she countered. "It seems to be more than adequately stocked. And when did you start smoking?"

"A few weeks ago. And for the record, I don't know why the hell people do it. The stuff tastes like shit."

"Not to mention the little fact that cigarettes cause heart disease, lung cancer, emphysema——"

"And may result in fetal injury, premature birth and low birth weight," he cut in. He tried to make room on the cluttered counter for the grocery bags, then, giving up, put them on the floor instead. "I read all the labels, Doc."

"But you smoked them anyway."

"I'm probably the only guy my age who never tried smoking when he was a kid. I thought I might enjoy it. I didn't. So I quit. Okay?"

"Too bad you didn't quit the booze while you were at it," she retorted. "I should take you into the hospital morgue and show you what an alcoholic's liver looks like."

A stony expression came over his face. "I'm not an alcoholic. And I damn well don't need a show-and-tell lecture from you, Dr. Anderson."

"You need something. Because in case you haven't noticed, Caine, this place looks like a pigsty." She wrinkled her nose. "And it smells like a saloon!"

"I happen to like saloons." Caine knew he'd been spending far too much time in them lately, but he'd throw himself off the top of nearby Mount Olympus before admitting that to Nora.

They were standing toe-to-toe. "Well, *I* don't."

"If you don't like the way the place smells, why don't you open a damn window?"

"I'd rather leave!"

"Fine. Go ahead and leave. I'm used to eating alone."

"No wonder, the way you've been acting. And a woman had better be current on her vaccinations before she risks walking in the front door, because this place is a toxic-waste dump. I'm surprised the county health inspector hasn't condemned it."

Caine raked his hand through his hair. "Christ, I'd forgotten what a shrew you could be."

"Shrew?" Her voice rose. "You invited me all the way out here to call me a shrew?" Nora was trembling with a temper only this man had ever been able to ignite. "You're insufferable."

"And you're still absolutely gorgeous when you're furious."

She would not let him get away with this again. "You really need to work on your pickup lines, O'Halloran. Because that one went out with 'What's your sign?'"

"I do okay," he growled. "Besides, if I *were* in the market to pick up a woman, I sure as hell wouldn't waste my time with some flat-chested, acid-tongued nag."

A lesser woman would have been intimidated by his glare, but Nora threw up her chin and met his blistering look with a furious one of her own.

"Then we're even. Because the last thing I want in my life is some out-of-control, self-pitying over-the-hill jock with a Peter Pan complex!"

Her words reverberated around the kitchen like an unwelcome echo. Caine was looming over her, forcing her to tilt her head back to see his eyes. He was angry—more than angry. He was as furious as Nora had ever seen him.

Caine felt a fresh surge of fury and welcomed it. He'd been going through the motions since realizing he was going to be put on waivers. How long had it been since he'd allowed himself to experience pure, unadulterated emotion? Too long.

A muscle jerked in his jaw. They glared at one another, each daring the other to make the next move.

"You know, your aim has gotten a helluva lot more accurate," Caine said finally. "Because you definitely scored a direct hit with that one, Nora."

They'd had too many of these fights in the past. And although they'd eventually made up in bed, each argument, every cruel word, had succeeded in straining the already tenuous bonds of their marriage. Until finally, those ties had snapped.

"I didn't want to score any hit," she murmured, looking down at the floor. "I thought that's what this dinner was all about. To put the past behind us, not relive it, word by hurtful word."

His hands were far from steady as he brushed Nora's bangs off her forehead. Caine wanted to try to make her understand the desperation that had led to his recent, admittedly less-than-ideal lifestyle. But how could he make her understand? When he still didn't understand himself?

"Hell. I'm sorry. Things have been a little rough lately. What with Maggie. And this damn arm and getting put on waivers. But I had no right to take my problems out on you."

"You just need to give it a bit more time," she advised. "Try a little patience."

"You know patience has never been my long suit."

"Would it be the end of the world," she asked quietly, "if you had to quit playing ball?"

"That's a moot point. Since I'm not finished."

A nagging doubt had been nibbling at the edges of his mind. Thus far, Caine had successfully ignored it. "If Nolan Ryan can pitch a no-hitter at forty-four, I'm damned if I'm going to admit to being washed up at thirty-five."

"You'll be thirty-six next month."

"Okay, thirty-six. So who's counting?"

Everyone. And they both knew it.

Caine had been a ballplayer for as long as he could remember, and the one thing he refused to admit to Nora was that he didn't know how to separate the man from the athlete, even if he wanted to. Which he damn well didn't.

"Look, Nora," he said, trying to explain once again the one thing he'd never been able to make her understand, "I've spent my entire adult life, standing on a mound in front of a stadium of thousands and a television audience in the millions, expecting them to take me seriously for throwing a little piece of white cowhide at a stick.

"I know that to you, with your education and lofty profession, that seems like a ridiculous way to earn a living.

"But I throw that ball nearly a hundred miles an hour and I make a helluva lot of money for embarrassing some of the league's best hitters. I'm Caine the Giant Killer, and I love it. I love the competition. And I love to win."

"But your injury——"

He cut her off with an impatient wave of his hand. "Injuries are part of the game. And dammit, I refuse to allow a bit of bad luck to sidetrack me from a lifelong quest."

"I remember you were always questing after glory," she murmured. At the same time, she'd been in her first year of medical school and struggling with morning sickness.

"It's more than glory. I feel I have something left to achieve."

"So you're going to hang in there and keep swinging at the curveballs."

That earned a smile. "And if you swing at enough of them," he agreed, "eventually you'll hit a few out of the park. I hadn't realized you'd been listening in those days."

Just as she hadn't realized he'd been listening to her go on and on about medical school. Nora wondered if perhaps she'd misjudged him back then. Perhaps, she considered now, they'd misjudged one another.

"But I didn't ask you here to talk about baseball——" Caine's low voice broke into her thoughts "——or my injury." He slid his hand beneath her hair to cup her neck and hold her to his darkening gaze, making her nerve endings sizzle.

"How about a temporary truce?" he asked quietly.

The brief hot argument had left her drained. Nora wanted to lean her head against his broad shoulder; she wanted to wrap her arms around his waist and feel his strong arms around her, reassuring her that they could put this fight behind them, as they had so many others.

In the end, she released a slow, ragged breath and nodded. "Truce," she whispered.

She reached up and traced the planes of his face with her fingertips. Frowning at the yellowish bruise around his eye, she said, "Your eye still looks horrendous."

"It'll heal. They always do."

She shook her head in mute frustration. "You really haven't changed." Her faint smile took the sting out of her words.

Her stroking touch was beginning to drive him crazy. Unable to keep from touching her, Caine ran his palms up and down her arms. "Ah, we're back to my Peter Pan complex."

"I shouldn't have said that."

He shrugged. "I shouldn't have called you a shrew." Lightly he traced her ear and played with her pearl earring.

"Don't forget the 'flat-chested, acid-tongued nag.'" Caine had the good grace to flush at that one. "Definitely uncalled-for." His finger trailed down her throat. "Your chest is just right."

The finger crossed her collarbone. "In fact, I remember thinking, that first time here in the cabin, how perfectly your breasts fit my palms and wondering if everything between us would be such a close and perfect fit."

With deliberate leisure, the treacherous finger glided over her breast. "And it was." Just as she felt herself slipping under his seductive spell, the beeper in her coat pocket buzzed; its screen displayed the emergency-code number. Saved by the bell. Again.

She called the hospital from the kitchen phone, then turned back to Caine. He was leaning against the counter, his long legs crossed at the ankles, watching her with unwavering intensity.

"I have to go."

He wasn't surprised; her relief at the untimely interruption had been palpable. With uncommon self-control, Caine managed not to complain as he followed Nora out to her car.

"How about coming back after you're finished with your emergency?" Behind her, the rays of the sunset spread out over the Olympic Mountains like an enormous scarlet fan.

"I don't think that would be a very good idea."

"Why not?"

"Because I have no idea how long I'll be." Her hand remained firmly on the car door handle, as if to anchor herself against the storm of emotions swirling inside her.

"I don't mind waiting." Uncurling her fingers from the door handle, he took her hand in his.

"I wouldn't want you to have to do that. Especially when it could take all night." She forced a smile. "But there will be other chances to talk before you leave town."

"You know I want to do more than talk, Nora."

"Yes." Her eyes were painfully grave. "And to tell you the truth, back in there——" she tossed her head in the direction of the cabin "——I was tempted. But I think what's happening here doesn't really have anything to do with us, Caine.

"I think deep inside you there's a voice saying that if you could only turn the clock back to when you were younger, to those days when you and I were married and you first got called up to the majors, perhaps you could start pitching the way you once did again, too."

He lifted a challenging brow. "Now you're a shrink?"

"No. But it doesn't take a psychology degree to see that you're dealing with a lot of difficult issues, Caine. As your doctor, and your friend, I'd suggest you try to take things more slowly."

With that, she pulled her hand free, climbed into the driver's seat, closed the door, fastened her seat belt and drove away from the cabin.

Caine stood at the end of the driveway, hands shoved into his pockets, and watched Nora leave. Timing, he considered grimly, as he trudged back up to the cabin, was everything.

He went back into the cabin, swore as he glanced at the bags of groceries, then picked up a bottle of bourbon and walked down to the dock.

The night grew cool. A gentle mist that wasn't quite rain began to fall. Caine sat alone, on the end of his dock, drinking his way through the Jack Daniel's.

He'd told himself that he'd come down here to think, but that was a lie. He'd come down here to get roaring drunk.

The problem was, Caine realized, holding the bottle up toward the crescent moon to determine the level of the remaining bourbon, it wasn't working.

Oh, he knew that if he suddenly stood his legs wouldn't be all that steady, that the dock would undoubtedly appear to be swaying. But while the alcohol was undoubtedly having its effect on his body, his mind was, unfortunately, distressingly clear.

He tipped the bottle to his lips. Flames slid down his throat and spread thickly, soothingly, in his stomach as he thought back to the afternoon when he'd finally made love to Nora for the second time.

They'd been married for six months that week, but neither had thought to celebrate the anniversary. After all, theirs had not been a conventional marriage. It had been a practical arrangement, a contract entered into by both parties for their mutual benefit. Nothing more.

At least that was what he'd been telling himself.

Until that fateful day when his life had inexorably changed. He'd been eating a pizza and drinking beer while watching television when Nora burst into the apartment, her eyes red from crying. She ran past him into the bedroom as if he were invisible, slamming the door behind her. A moment later, Caine heard the sound of water running in the bathroom, the buzz of her electric toothbrush, then the unmistakable sound of weeping.

He lowered the beer can to the coffee table and sat there, debating what to do next. Part of him opted for ignoring the incident.

But another, stronger part of him couldn't overlook the fact that something was definitely wrong. When he thought that it might have something to do with the baby, his blood chilled.

He'd pointed the remote control at the screen; the screen went black. Realizing that his breath undoubtedly reeked of beer and pepperoni, and remembering how she'd looked a little queasy this morning, Caine dug a lint-covered peppermint out of his jeans pocket and popped it into his mouth.

Then he crossed the living room and opened the bedroom door.

"Nora?" The room was dark but he could see her, curled up in a fetal position on the bed. "What's wrong?"

"Go away." She was hugging a pillow against her; her words were muffled by the foam.

"Not until I find out if anything's wrong with the baby."

"The baby's fine."

But she wasn't. And that disturbed the hell out of him. Caine crossed the room. The mattress sank under his weight as he sat down beside her. "You want to tell me what happened?"

"No."

He could feel her trembling. "Come on, Nora." Feeling awkward, he smoothed her hair with his palm. "Whatever it is, it can't be all that bad."

To his surprise, Nora Anderson O'Halloran, the same woman who'd taken extra pains to avoid so much as accidentally brushing against him in their cramped apartment, had suddenly sat up, flung her arms around his neck and pressed her wet face into his shirt.

"Oh, Caine!" She lifted her doe brown eyes that were dark and heartbreakingly bleak. "I'm never going to be a doctor!"

"Of course you are."

"Not after what I did in gross anatomy class today."

"What did you do? Make a slip with the scalpel and emasculate Irving?"

Irving was the cadaver her anatomy study group had been laboring over.

When he'd first heard about the class, Caine had thought the term "gross anatomy" a perfect description. Eventually, he'd become accustomed to the fact that his wife spent her mornings with a dead body the same way he'd grown used to the faint odor of formaldehyde lingering in her blond hair.

"It's n-n-not funny," she insisted on a tortured breath.

"I'm sorry." Caine tried to understand. "What happened?"

"My morning sickness came back today."

"I thought you looked a little under the weather at breakfast," Caine remembered. "But didn't Dr. Palmer tell you that might happen if you got too tired?"

"Yes. But, oh, y-y-you don't understand." Her shoulders slumped defeatedly.

"I'm trying." Caine lifted her chin on a finger and looked into her red-rimmed eyes. "But you're not exactly a font of information, Nora."

"It's s-s-so embarrassing." She dashed at the moisture stinging her eyes and shook her head in a violent gesture.

Comprehension dawned. "You threw up in class."

Nora gave him a weary look. "All over Irving's inferior v-v-vena c-cava."

Caine had absolutely no idea what an inferior vena cava was and decided that it probably didn't really matter. Not to Irving anymore, anyway.

"Is that all?" Caine gave Nora an encouraging smile.

"I seem to recall you telling me about three students who tossed their cookies the first week of class."

"That was the first week," Nora explained soberly. "By now we're all supposed to be used to it."

Personally, Caine thought he could probably spend the rest of his life with Irving and not get used to the idea of cutting into human organs—dead or alive—but he knew that was not the point of this conversation.

If he were to be perfectly fair, he'd have to acknowledge that Nora probably couldn't imagine the pure pleasure of watching a batter hit a pop fly off your curveball, either. "You're pregnant. I'm sure your professor will take that into consideration."

"Dr. Eugene Fairfield is an antiquated old fossil who doesn't believe women belong in medicine, period," she muttered. "As for pregnant women..." She sighed. "And it gets worse. After I got sick, I fainted."

"Fainted?" Fear raced through him as his hand dropped to her belly, rounded with his child. "Are you sure you're okay?"

"Yes. I was only out for a second, and the only person who got hurt was Irving."

"How the hell could Irving get hurt?"

"I pulled the table over when I fell and the next thing I knew, Irving was sprawled on the floor, with his gall bladder and his liver lying beside him."

Nora drew in a deep, shuddering breath. "I know Dr.

Fairfield's going to flunk me and I'll get kicked out of medical school and I'll never be a doctor!"

Moisture flooded her eyes again and she clung to him, sobbing harshly into his shoulder.

If he hadn't been so genuinely distressed, Caine would have laughed at the idea of quiet, studious Nora, of all people, causing such havoc in class.

But she was more distraught than he'd ever seen her. And, staggered by her misery, Caine rocked her in his arms and murmured inarticulate words of comfort into her ear.

His hands moved up and down her back, the gesture meant to comfort, rather than arouse. His lips pressed against her hair and caught the soft scent of flowers beneath the aroma of formaldeyhde she'd brought with her from the lab.

After an immeasurable time, Caine could tell by Nora's slow steady breathing that her pain had run its course.

"Feeling better?"

"Yes." Her soft eyes mirrored her surprise as she tilted her head back and looked up at him. "I am. Thank you."

Her quiet formality along with the lingering pain in her eyes had tugged at something elemental deep inside him. Looking down into her pale and unusually open face, Caine was engulfed with a tenderness like nothing he'd ever known.

And with that tenderness, he realized, came love.

"You don't have to thank me, Nora." His gaze moved over her pale, uplifted face. "I'm your husband. And although I'll admit to being a little vague about husbandly duties, I think a shoulder to cry on comes with the job."

"But we agreed—"

"I don't give a damn what we agreed." She'd pointed out the terms of their agreement innumerable times over the past six months and Caine was sick of hearing it. "Would it be against the rules if I kissed you?"

Surprise warred with unwilling desire on her lovely features. "I think it would."

"Too bad." Bending his head, he kissed her face where salty tears were still drying.

"Caine—"

"What, Nora?" His lips skimmed along the slanted line of her cheekbone.

"I don't think this is a very good idea."

"You might be right." His teeth closed around the tender skin of her earlobe and Nora drew in a quick breath but did not pull away. "But I can't come up with a logical reason why I shouldn't make love to my wife."

With a sensitivity neither had been aware of him possessing, his hand moved slowly, possessively, from her shoulder to her belly. "How about you?"

"No." Nora's soft breathless voice was a whisper of surrender. "I can't." With a sigh, she closed her eyes, relaxed and let him guide her into the mists.

His hands slipped under her maternity top, unhooked the front clasp of her bra with ease and cupped her breasts. When his thumb brushed against her nipple, Nora gasped and would have pulled away. But before she could move, Caine's lips fused to hers.

Caine felt the last vestiges of her resistance ebb. He felt it in the softening of her lips and the strength of her fingers as she clutched his upper arms. Heat simmered at the base of his spine, making him ache.

He pulled off her oversize blouse and tossed it onto

the floor. Her nipples, which he remembered as being a rosy pink, had darkened to the hue of the cranberries that grew wild in bogs along the coast. And they were just as hard, Caine discovered as he brushed his hand over one dusky bud. The intimate touch made Nora stiffen in his arms. "Don't worry," he soothed. "I promise not to take you anywhere you don't want to go, Nora."

Passively, she relaxed again. Sensing her trust, Caine took pains not to abuse it. Slowly, banking the rising desire born of six long and lonely months of celibacy, he ran whisper-soft kisses across her lips, from one corner of her mouth to the other, before going on to kiss her cheeks, her forehead, her temple, the bridge of her nose.

All the time, his fingers circled her breasts, caressing, stroking. Caine could feel her pulse beginning to thunder; still he took his time, determined not to succumb to any quick burst of pleasure.

"I've been going crazy, thinking about this." His tongue traced a line from her throat down to her breasts. "Remembering the sweet, sexy taste of your skin." When he took a nipple between his teeth and tugged, she gasped, then arched against him. "How you turn to liquid silk in my arms."

"Oh, Caine." The softly spoken name seemed to echo off the wall, surrounding them. Embracing them. "Tell me," she whispered. "Tell me everything you've been thinking."

"Everything?" He wove his fingers into her hair, holding her gaze with his. "Are you sure a woman in your delicate condition is up to some of my more graphic fantasies?"

"Why don't you try me and see?" she suggested with

a smile that managed to be both shy and seductive at the same time.

"All right." He coaxed her onto her back and skimmed a trail of wet, openmouthed kisses down her rib cage. "But don't say I didn't warn you."

Her maternity jeans had an elastic insert to allow room for her expanding belly. The jeans were, Caine considered, highly practical and decidedly unsexy. After unbuttoning them at the waist, he began pulling them slowly down her legs.

What he found beneath the durable denim came as a distinct surprise. "Black silk?"

"They were a wedding present from Karin." Nora's cheeks flamed.

"I think I like these a lot better than the pots and pans my parents gave us." Caine smoothed his hands over her stomach, where the child—their child, he thought wonderingly—had been growing all these months. Imbued with tenderness, he pressed his lips against her flesh.

Then, moving on, Caine slipped his fingers beneath the lace-trimmed legs and inched upward to secret pleasures. "Remind me to thank your sister-in-law, first chance I get."

"Don't you dare!"

"It won't do any good to pretend to be scandalized, my dear wife." He lowered his mouth and drew a wet swath just above the waistband of the low-rise panties with his tongue. "Because any woman who'd wear panties like this in your condition is a wild woman at heart."

"I must be." Nora combed her hands through Caine's hair and writhed beneath his increasingly intimate touch. "Because this is just about all I've been thinking about lately."

"Really?" The admission brought a burst of male pride.

"Really. My obstetrician says it's raging hormones, but I'm not so sure she's right."

He dipped his tongue into her navel. "Then what do you think has been making you all hot and bothered lately?"

"I don't know."

She was lying. Caine could read it in her eyes. Apparently he wasn't the only one who'd found forced celibacy a burden.

"Perhaps you've been reading my mind." He lay down beside her and cupped her breast. "Perhaps you tuned in on how much I wanted to taste you again." He took the hardened nipple into his mouth, causing a moan of pleasure to slip past her lips.

The soft moan brought a fresh surge of arousal— one Caine managed, with effort, to bank.

"Maybe you knew how I've been imagining the feel of your body against mine." He yanked his T-shirt over his head and pulled her against him, heated flesh against heated flesh. "And how the thought of you, hot and wet, makes me hard."

He took her hand and pressed it against the placket of his jeans, letting her feel the full extent of his need. "See how much I want you?"

"I've tried to understand," she murmured with reluctant wonder. Her fingers began stroking his burgeoning flesh through the thick material. "I've lain awake nights trying to analyze why everything's so different with you, but I can't come up with a logical answer."

"Then don't think." With fingers that were not as steady as she would have liked, Caine unfastened the five-button jeans, vowing to go out and buy a pair with a zipper as soon as the stores opened in the morning. "Don't analyze. Just feel."

The room was washed in shadows. A full moon rose in the sky outside the bedroom, bathing the lovers in a soft silvery light. But still Caine refused to rush.

Even when they were laying together, naked, he kept his own flaming hunger tightly reined as his hands continued to stroke and his lips took long, leisurely tours over her body—her rounded stomach, the small of her back, her shoulders, that sensitive spot he'd discovered on her ankle—always to return again and again to her soft, pliant lips.

When he finally slipped into her, a deep current of love flowed through him, like a river, and he realized how fulfilling tenderness could be.

Very soon after that day, Nora's obstetrician had cautioned against engaging in intercourse. But that hadn't stopped them from exploring myriad other imaginative ways to pleasure one another. Nora was the only woman Caine had ever met who could actually be brought to orgasm by nibbling on the tendon at the back of her knee.

And he was positive that she was one of the few women who'd ever climaxed during labor. At the time, he'd only been trying to take her mind off her pain. But when his stroking hand had moved under the hospital sheet, beyond her undulating belly and between her legs, to recklessly toy with the hard pink nubbin of flesh, Nora had cried out, not in pain, but in absolute, stunned pleasure. Her noisy response had brought the nurse, who, after examining her, had found her not fully dilated. The nurse had patted Nora's head in a maternal way, and told her to go ahead and yell whenever she felt the urge.

The moment she'd left the room in a rustle of starched cotton, Nora and Caine had collapsed in gales of shared laughter.

The memories made Caine's body throb. He tipped the bottle back, only to discover it was empty. "Damn."

Cursing inarticulately, he flung it into the lake, struggled to his feet and wove his way back to the cabin.

He staggered across the living room and crashed onto the newspaper-strewn sofa. The painkillers were on the coffee table where he'd left them that first night. Caine picked up the plastic bottle, shook a handful of the pink pills into his palm and stared blearily down at them.

What would happen if he just said the hell with everything and swallowed them all? It would, he considered for a fleeting second, solve a hell of a lot of problems.

Except he couldn't do it. He might be nothing but a drunk, washed-up ballplayer with two failed marriages behind him, but he damn well didn't want his fans to remember him as a coward.

Cursing, he flung the tablets away. They scattered over the clothes-covered floor and were immediately forgotten.

Then, exhausted by the too-vivid memories and numbed by too much alcohol, Caine fell instantly into a deep sleep.

Chapter 9

"What in the blazes do you think you're doing, Caine O'Halloran?"

Maggie crossed her arms over her chest, where a trio of pilot whales swam against the bright blue background of today's sweatshirt. "Chasing after Nora Anderson when you've already got yourself a wife back in New York City."

"Now, Maggie," Devlin soothed as he put a cup of coffee down in front of her. "Don't you think you're bein' a little hard on the boy?"

"That's just my point," Maggie snapped. "Caine is not a boy. He's a grown man with a wife."

"Tiffany and I are getting a divorce."

Caine took a bite of one of the glazed doughnuts Devlin had brought to the table along with the coffee.

He'd come to turn over his grandmother's garden, a spring ritual Maggie was definitely not up to this year.

Maggie frowned at Caine over the rim of her mug.

"Even if that's the case, like it or not, the law still says you're a married man, Caine. Which means you have no business chasing after Nora."

"I wasn't chasing after her," Caine argued. "Hell, after Harmon beat me up, Dana and Tom took me to the clinic to have her patch me up."

"You're not going to try to tell me that you invited her to your cabin the other night for medical reasons, are you? I may be old, but I'm not senile. Least, not yet," Maggie muttered.

Caine silently cursed Trudy down at the market. The woman had the biggest mouth in town. Second biggest, he amended, remembering Ingrid Johansson.

"I invited her to the cabin for dinner. And to talk."

"It's still not right, Caine," Maggie said. "It isn't fair to your wife. And it damn well isn't fair to Nora."

"But—"

"Better hear your grandmother out, Caine," Devlin said in a quiet but firm tone.

"All right." Feeling like he had when he was nine years old and had accidentally driven Maggie's Cessna twin engine through the side of the hangar, Caine tilted the kitchen chair back on its rear legs, crossed his out-stretched legs at the ankle and waited. "Fire away."

Maggie nodded, satisfied that she had his undivided attention. "Now, I'm not saying there's anything wrong with your feelings for Nora. Everyone in town can see that you and that girl are ripe for a second chance. And the way things ended the last time, Lord knows you both deserve one.

"But you were brought up to do the right thing, Caine. And courtin' your second one just isn't the right thing married to your first wife while you're still to do."

"Even if it feels right?" he couldn't help asking.

Maggie's stern gaze softened for a moment. "If everybody did what felt right at the time, Caine, the world would be in an even worse pickle than it is now."

"You gotta choose, Caine," Devlin advised. "One wife or the other."

"Hell, there's no choice." Caine dropped the chair back on all four legs. "I want Nora." The moment he heard himself say the words out loud, Caine knew they were true.

"Then take care of your problem with the other one," Maggie instructed. "This Tiffany. And then, when you're free, you can do whatever it takes to get Nora back."

"Speaking about doing the right thing," Caine ventured carefully, "I've been talking to Nora about you." Maggie's expressive face instantly closed. "You had no right doin' that, Caine."

"I've every right. I love you and I can't stand by and watch you..."

"Die?" Maggie finished matter-of-factly, when Caine couldn't say it.

"Don't you see," Caine said, leaning forward, his own problems momentarily forgotten, "you don't have to give up, Gram. I've got more money than I can count—"

"I told her about the seven million," Devlin broke in.

"And it's a right nice piece of change," Maggie allowed. "Your pappy and I are real proud of you, Caine."

"Thank you. But the point is that all the money doesn't mean a damn thing if I can't make life better for my family."

"Our lives are pretty good the way they are, boy," Devlin said quietly.

"But if you had a new heart, Gram..."

"I like the heart I've got just fine," she told him briskly. "It's served me right well for all these years."

Maggie pushed herself up from the table and came over to stand beside him. Her always-wiry frame looked heartbreakingly frail. But the feisty determination gleaming in her blue eyes reminded Caine of a bantam rooster.

He rose and gathered the small woman into his arms. "Nora told me she'd talked to you about a hospice program. Will you at least take her advice about that?"

Maggie tilted her head back to meet his entreating gaze. "I'll think about it."

Well, it wasn't the answer he'd wanted, but, Caine told himself, it was a start.

"On one condition," Maggie warned.

"I figured there'd be a catch."

"There usually is with your grandmother," Devlin murmured knowingly.

"I want you to stop actin' like a crazy damn fool," Maggie insisted. "It's time you stopped drinking and drivin' too fast and gettin' into fistfights and whorin' around."

She poked a bony finger into his chest—a vivid reminder that she hadn't always been so weak. "Nora Anderson is a nice, sensible girl. She deserves a whole lot better than the idiot you've been since you came back to town. So it's high time you straightened up and flew right."

She wasn't telling him anything he hadn't been telling himself. Truthfully, Caine had been finding his recent lifestyle depressing.

There'd been a time, in his admittedly reckless youth, when he could party like a wild man all night, then show up at the ballpark and blaze that little white ball a hundred miles an hour past a stunned batter. But no more.

Maybe, he considered, he really was getting old. Lord, that was a depressing thought.

Refusing to consider such a negative idea when he already had enough problems to work out, Caine reached down and ruffled Maggie's pink-and-silver hair affectionately.

"Okay, Gram," he said, flashing her the bold smile that had brightened the cover of *Sports Illustrated* on three separate occasions. "You've got yourself a deal."

Later that afternoon, seeking companionship, Caine drove to the hospital to visit Johnny Baker. He dumped his purchases—an enormous bag of buttered popcorn, a six-pack of cola and a red-and-white-striped peanut bag—on the rollaway table. Then, making himself comfortable, he sprawled out on the vacant bed.

They were watching television when Nora entered the room.

"Hi, Dr. Anderson," Johnny greeted her. "The Yankees are playing the Twins," he explained, his enthusiasm a vast contrast to the dispirited little boy who'd shown up at her emergency room. "And boy, are they gettin' stomped. They need Caine real bad."

"I'm sure they do," she murmured absently. "How are you feeling, Johnny?" She crossed the room, picked up the remote control from the rumpled sheet, pointed it at the screen and muted the audio.

"I've been kinda lonely. This is a big place and the nurses are too busy with all the sick little kids to come visit me. But I'm feelin' a lot better," Johnny assured her. "Now that Caine's here."

"I'm surprised you don't have a major stomachache," Nora said, looking pointedly at the peanut shells scattered over the table and the bed.

"Can't watch a baseball game without the proper food, Doc," Caine said easily. "It's downright un-American."

"The hospital dietician would have a heart attack if she walked into this room right now."

"Caine just wanted to cheer me up," Johnny argued. The color drained from his face as if he feared she might send his hero away. "Please don't get mad at him, Dr. Anderson."

"I'm not angry at Caine." She flashed the seven-year-old an encouraging smile. "I hear we're losing you this afternoon."

"Yeah." He didn't sound very eager. "The social-worker lady found me a foster home."

"I know. She told me they were nice people."

"Yeah, that's what she told me, too." He sighed. "Worried?"

"Kinda." He looked up at her, a tense white line around his mouth. "What if they don't like me?"

"Of course they'll like you. You're a terrific kid, Johnny," Caine assured him.

"Caine's right. All the nurses say you're one of the best they've ever had on the ward," Nora added.

"Really?"

"Really. And I agree," she said. "One hundred percent."

There was a little silence as Johnny thought about that.

"Besides," Nora continued, "you don't think an important ballplayer like Caine O'Halloran would spend so much time with a kid who wasn't terrific, do you?" Johnny chewed his bottom lip as he considered that. Apparently satisfied, he announced, "Caine's going to Canada."

Nora shot Caine a surprised glance. "Oh?"

"I was going to stop by your office and change my appointment to get the stitches out." Caine wondered if it was disappointment he saw in her guarded gaze and hoped like hell it was. "I'm flying some guys up for a few days of fishing so Gram won't lose her charter fee."

"His grandmother's sick," Johnny offered.

"I know." Nora knew Maggie had started Caine flying young. He'd earned his private pilot's license before he was old enough for a driver's permit. "That's a nice thing to do."

He shrugged. "It's not as if I'm real busy these days. Besides, it's an excuse to go fishing and get paid for it."

"When Caine gets back, he's takin' me flying."

A light gleamed in Johnny's eyes and Nora knew that Caine was responsible for putting it there. She'd seen that same pleasure in Dylan's eyes, in what seemed like a lifetime ago.

That her son had adored his father had always been

obvious. And it had been just as obvious that Caine had loved his little boy.

"Caine, may I speak with you? Outside?"

"Sure." He slid off the bed, rumpling the sheets even more. "I'll be back in a flash, sport." He tugged on the brim of the autographed Yankees cap, then turned it around backward.

It was only a casual gesture, but it made Johnny's eyes turn as adoring as a cocker spaniel's. "Don't be too long. The seventh-inning stretch'll be over in a minute."

Nora returned the remote to Johnny, who immediately turned on the sound.

"I'm really sorry about the popcorn, Nora," Caine said when they were alone in the waiting room at the end of the hallway. "It seemed like a good idea at the time."

"This isn't a playground, Caine. It's a hospital. And Johnny's my patient."

"But you're the one who said that there wasn't really anything physically wrong with the kid. I figured a little TLC never hurt anyone."

"TLC? Is that what you call it?"

"Okay, how about attention? Is that a better word?"

"That child has been through hell. I will not let you hurt him."

"Hurt him?" Caine's brows climbed his tanned forehead. "I was trying to help, Nora."

"Right now Johnny's proving a pleasant enough little diversion for you. But what about if you get called back to the majors——"

"When."

"What?" She dragged a frustrated hand through her hair.

"You said, *if* I get called back. I was merely clarifying that the proper phrasing was *when* I return to major-league ball."

"When, if—the words don't matter," she said, brushing his correction away with a furious wave of her hand. "The point is that Johnny's going to start to care for you, and count on you, and maybe even love you, and you're going to abandon him, just like—"

She cut her words off in midsentence, but the damage had already been done. Caine would have had to be dense as a stump not to get her drift.

"Like I abandoned you?" he asked quietly.

"That's not what I was going to say." It was a lie and they both knew it.

"Look, I'll be the first to admit that marriage wasn't high on my list of priorities ten years ago, Nora.

"But that day you embarrassed yourself in anatomy class by tossing your cookies all over Irving, I realized that somehow, when I wasn't looking, you'd become much, much more."

"What happened between us is in the past, Caine."

"Now why can't I believe that?"

"Believe it." She turned to leave, then stopped long enough to give him a warning. "And don't you dare hurt Johnny Baker."

With that, she marched away.

Caine wanted to go after her. But remembering his pledge to Maggie, he sighed and returned to watch the rest of the game with the one person in Tribulation who wasn't asking more than he could deliver.

Five days later, Caine was back in Tribulation, sitting in a window booth in the Timberline Café, watching the rain streak down the glass, when Nora walked in.

"Hi." She stopped beside the table.

"Hi, yourself."

"So how was the fishing?"

"Terrific. Of course, Fortress Lake is easy; you could catch a boatful of Eastern brook trout on peanut-butter-and-jelly sandwiches."

"You probably stocked your freezer, then."

"Naw. Except for the fish we cooked each night for dinner, and one mounted trophy per paying guest, we put the rest back."

"Oh. That's nice."

The polite conversation trailed off, but neither one moved. Caine sat looking up at her while Nora looked down at him; both were oblivious to the interested quiet that had settled over the café.

"I heard from Social Services that Johnny's settling into his foster home," she said.

"I know. I stopped by to see him on the way home from the airport."

"How's he getting along?"

"Great. When I left, he was rolling on the lawn with a litter of six-week-old golden retriever puppies." His lips curved into a reminiscent smile. "You should have seen him, Nora. He looked just like any other kid."

"You've had a lot to do with that," she said. "I'm not sure he ever would have opened up to that social worker if you hadn't encouraged him."

Caine shrugged. "It wasn't that big a deal."

"It was to Johnny." She combed her fingers through her hair in a nervous gesture he remembered too well.

"I owe you an apology. For what I said the other day. About you hurting him."

"You were only thinking of Johnny," Caine said without rancor. "Did you know his mother is putting him up for adoption?"

"I heard this morning."

Caine shook his head. "Helluva thing, giving up your own child. But I suppose it's for the best. For Johnny."

"I think it probably is," Nora agreed.

There was another poignant silence as they studied each other.

Nora searched for something, anything, to say. "I see you're working on your second five gallons," she said finally, looking down at his mug.

The white mug, which bore Caine's name in black block print, proclaimed that he was a member of Ingrid's five-gallon club.

It took one hundred cups of coffee to make five gallons, and once a customer made the quota, he got his own mug. The mugs stayed on a shelf on the back wall; the fact that Caine's had been waiting for him all these years was additional proof that some things never changed.

"Every man needs a goal," Caine answered easily. "Pappy comes here every morning. Says that if his mug's on the shelf, he knows he's still alive."

Nora laughed even as she felt a bittersweet pain. "I was by their house yesterday. Maggie was looking well."

Caine's jaw tensed. "For someone who's now bedridden."

"Oh, Caine." Feeling his frustration, she put a comforting hand on his shoulder. Refusing to consider whether or not it was a wise or safe thing to do, he raised his own to cover hers.

They exchanged another long, heartfelt look. Somewhere in the background, Nora heard the sound of bells.

"Caine…"

"Nora…"

They spoke at the same time, then laughed uneasily.

"Ladies first," Caine said.

Before Nora could respond, Ingrid, who'd been watching the exchange along with the others, called out to her. "Nora, telephone."

Forgetting that they had an audience, forgetting that such unruly feelings were inordinately risky, Nora struggled against breaking the spell. "Could you please take a message, Ingrid," she asked softly, not taking her eyes from Caine's face.

"I think you'd better take this one, Nora," Ingrid insisted.

Hearing the strain in the elderly woman's voice, Nora dragged her gaze from Caine's. Concern was etched into every deep line of Ingrid Johansson's face.

When she took the receiver from Ingrid, a foreboding chill ran up Nora's spine. "Hello?"

"Thank God I found you. Your cells off." Her brother's voice, ragged and hurried, came over the wire.

"What's wrong?"

"Tom called. Eric is missing," Dana said.

"Missing?" She sagged against Caine, who, having seen the color leave her face, had come up behind her. "How? Where?"

"According to Tom, he was on a Scout hike at Lake Crescent. He got separated from the group and then a squall came up. All the other kids got back to the cabins safe and sound. The sheriff and the Park Service are organizing a search party."

"Are they at the lodge?"

"Yeah. The troop rented a couple of the cabins, but the command post is being set up in the lodge lobby. I'll meet you there."

"I'm leaving now." She thrust the phone toward Ingrid and turned, prepared to run toward the door.

Caine took hold of Nora's elbow and felt her tremors. "Let's go."

Set dramatically among the lushly forested northern ridges of the Olympic Mountains, Lake Crescent had long been considered the gem of the peninsula's many scenic attractions.

Although Native American legend taught that Lake Crescent was created when Mountain Storm King, angered by a fight that had broke out in Peaceful Valley, hurled part of his crest and dammed the river, geologists insisted on the more mundane explanation that a slow-moving glacier, gnawing at bedrock, had created the incredible blue-green lake.

The lake had been drawing tourists since the early 1890s; the two-story, shingled lodge had been constructed in 1915. Caine had enjoyed many weekend outings at the lake; today, however, the mood was anything but festive.

When he and Nora entered the lodge, Karin, who'd been standing by the stone fireplace, surrounded by a protective circle of friends, ran toward them.

"Thank God you're here!"

"You know there's nowhere else I'd be." Nora hugged her. "Everything's going to be all right. Eric's going to be found."

"I wish I could believe that." Karin turned to Caine.

"Hello, Caine," she said with a formal politeness that was so ill-suited to the occasion, Caine suspected that it was the only way she could keep from breaking into torrents of weeping. "Thank you for coming."

Caine gathered her into his arms, bent his head and brushed his lips against her temple. "How could I not?"

Tilting her head back, Karin bit her lip as new tears threatened. "Please find my little boy, Caine."

"We will," he promised roughly. "I promise." He handed her gently back to Nora, squeezed his former wife's shoulder comfortingly, then strode across the room to join the search team.

What had been a dreary drizzle in Tribulation was a full-fledged squall at the lake. The cold wind howled off the steep slopes of the mountains; icy rain intermittently turned to sleet. The sky over the lake was as thick and dark as a wet wool blanket.

The searchers, working in teams of four, had been assigned sections: each section led in a different direction from the trail from which Eric had disappeared. As darkness descended on the mountains, the temperature dropped.

An icy rain dripped off the hood of his poncho as Caine searched; the yellow beam of his flashlight disappeared into the fog and mist.

The look of absolute fear in Karin's eyes had sliced at him like a sharp knife. It had been the same look he'd seen in Nora's eyes when she'd arrived at the emergency room that fateful day. The day Dylan...

No! Caine shook his head, spattering rain the way

Ranger, his old springer spaniel, used to do when he'd gotten wet waiting with his master in a duck blind.

Never again would he listen to the sound of a human heart shattering. He was going to find Eric, dammit! He was.

It was then he heard a faint sound that could have been the wind whistling.

Caine stopped and gestured for the rest of his team to do the same. The sound grew more distinct. It was, Caine realized with a burst of relief, the unmistakable sobbing of a child.

They found Eric lying on a bed of needles beneath the spreading dark green arms of a towering Douglas fir. He was filthy and scared and exhausted. But, Caine determined as he ran his hands over the young body, unharmed.

"Uncle Caine? Is that really you?"

"It's me, all right." Caine scooped the eight-year-old into his arms. "Come on, sport," he said. "We're taking you home."

Two wet, dirty arms crept around Caine's neck. "I saw a fawn. I was following it when I got lost."

"That'll teach you to stick to the trail," Caine advised with a calm that belied the runaway pounding of his heart.

"I'm probably going to be in trouble, huh?"

"Your mom's real worried."

"Was she crying?"

"A little. When she sees you safe and sound, she'll probably cry a lot more."

"And then she'll ground me."

"I'd say that's a distinct possibility," Caine agreed.

"But my grandpappy taught me, when I was about your

age, that it's best just to take your medicine and get it over with."

"Yeah. That's what Dad always says," Eric said glumly.

"Of course, my gram taught me something else about medicine," Caine said.

"What?"

"That it always goes down smoother if you follow it with a spoonful of honey. So how about, after you get ungrounded, you and I go to Seattle and take in a Mariners game?"

"Really?"

"Really."

They entered the lodge with a gust of rain and wind. Caine, carrying Eric, was flanked by Dana and Joe Bob Carroll. Bring up the rear was Harmon Olson. Which wasn't all that unbelievable, Nora decided. Tribulation's citizens were the type of people who always pulled together in times of trouble. And a missing child was enough to make even the most long-term adversaries put aside their personal differences.

Tears of joy coursing down her face, Karin ran toward Caine and flung her arms around both of them. "I was so worried." Her hands trembled as they moved over her son's dirt-caked face. "Are you all right?"

"I think he's fine," Caine answered. "Nora can confirm that, for sure."

"So worried," Karin repeated shakily. "I'm so happy to see you." She combed her hands through his tousled hair, dislodging fir needles. "You're grounded for a week."

Heaving a deep sigh, Eric exchanged an I-told-you-so look with his uncle over the top of his mother's pale blond head.

Feeling better than he had in ages, Caine threw back his head and laughed.

Chapter 10

Caine and Nora drove back to Tribulation in weary, but comfortable silence.

"My car's at the Timberline," she remembered when he turned down the street toward her house.

"I'll bring it by tomorrow," he suggested. "You look beat. I thought you'd rather go straight home."

"I am tired." Nora glanced over his strong profile silhouetted in the slanting silver moonlight. "But I wasn't trudging around in the rain all night. You must be exhausted."

Caine pulled up in front of her grandmother's house and cut the engine. "Actually, I'm still a little wired."

They went up the front walk in silence, side by side, shoulders almost touching. The boards creaked underfoot as they climbed the five wooden steps to the porch. They stood there, facing one another in front of her door. "Would you like to come in?" Nora asked. "I can make tea. Or decaf?"

A prudent man would go. A wise man would avoid a situation rife with dangerous possibilities. The problem was that Caine had never thought of himself as either a wise or prudent man.

"Decaf sounds great. But you're tired and—"

"It's instant."

His last excuse gone, Caine said, "Perfect."

He followed her into the kitchen and sat at the table, watching her fill the kettle with water.

The trestle table was piled high with books and papers. One particular stack of typed pages caught his attention.

"What's this?"

When she saw what he was holding in his hands, she flushed. "Oh, just an article I've been working on."

He scanned the opening paragraphs. "It's about treating children in emergency rooms?"

"Trauma centers," Nora corrected. "Emergency rooms are overwhelmed with nonsurgical emergencies, like asthma, dehydration, stomach pumping, things like that. This causes delays, but they're mostly not life-threatening.

"Until a trauma victim shows up. And things become even more complicated when the victim is a child."

"Like Dylan."

He lifted his gaze from the paper; his eyes met hers, asking her to finally share the most tragic experience of their lives with him.

Knowing what he needed and needing it, too, Nora didn't take her eyes away. "Yes," she said softly. "Like Dylan." She took a deep breath. "There's something

I've been wanting to say." The teakettle began to whistle shrilly. Caine watched and waited as she poured the water over the dark crystals. She sat down across from him.

"When I stopped by to check on Maggie yesterday," she said quietly, "Devlin told me that you still blame yourself for Dylan's death."

When Caine's grandfather had divulged that particular piece of intimate information, Nora had been shocked.

"I think that's when I finally realized that it was time for me to stop blaming you. And for you to stop blaming yourself."

"Oh, hell, Nora, if Dylan hadn't been in the car—"

"You're being too hard on yourself." How strange that after all the years of blaming Caine for the death of their child, she now wanted so desperately to convince him of the contrary.

"I had a teammate in Detroit," Caine said slowly, painfully. "A shortstop. He dabbled in a lot of Eastern religions. When I knew him, he was into Zen.

"Used to drive us crazy, sitting stark-naked in front of his locker before every game, chanting his mantra. But I have to admit, he was the best player under pressure I've ever seen.

"One time, on a road trip, he told me something I've never forgotten."

"What's that?"

"He said that there is no such thing as coincidence, that life is only a response to Karma. That every word we utter, every breath we take, stirs the cosmos around us. That around every corner is a consequence, under every rock a repercussion."

Nora rose abruptly from the table and began to open a box of cookies. "I refuse to believe that Dylan's death was part of some enormous cosmic plan."

"But how do you know he's not right? What if it was a consequence of my ambition?" Caine asked. "How else can you explain that he died the day after I learned I was finally getting called up to the majors?"

"Coincidence, dammit!" Her hands were trembling as she overturned the box, scattering cookies all over the table. "I was just as ambitious as you, Caine. We were both obsessed by our own goals.

"But that doesn't mean that we didn't love our son. And it certainly doesn't mean that either of us caused his death. It was an accident. A stupid, tragic, senseless accident."

The words were meant to comfort Caine. What Nora hadn't expected was, that for the first time in nine years, she could truly believe them.

"You sound awfully sure of that."

Nora drew in a long, shuddering breath. "I've seen too many children die since that day. I've had a great deal of time to think about how that could happen and why."

"Which brings us back to this paper."

"Yes." She took another breath, clearing her mind. "There are so many things people need to know about the treatment of children who've suffered accidents. So many ways they're different from adults."

"Such as?"

"Well, a child's head is much larger, in relation to the rest of his body, than an adult's. Which makes him more vulnerable to head injuries.

"And then there's his spleen. When an injured adult

comes into the emergency room with a bleeding spleen, it's standard procedure to remove it. An adult will never miss it. But to a child, the spleen is vital to the immune system.

"If you take it out, the patient will seem to recover. Until he catches a cold or the flu, and since his body can't handle the infection, he dies from what should have been a simple case of the sniffles."

She frowned, remembering the first time she'd encountered such a case. A light case of flu that should have been cured with chicken soup, fluids and a few days spent in bed watching cartoons had killed a six-year-old former accident victim.

"And bones," she said. "Children's bones have a remarkable ability to heal themselves, but the problem is that broken bones grow faster than unbroken ones, so if you set a child's leg the same way you do an adult's, the broken leg will grow longer than the other.

"So many things," she murmured, glancing down at the papers he was still holding.

"Sounds like too many for a mere paper," Caine observed. "Perhaps you ought to write a book."

"And while I'm at it, I might as well shoot for the moon and establish a pediatric trauma center in my spare time," she said. "All I'd have to do is give up sleep."

Having watched her grueling schedule, Caine knew she was right. "Too bad. It sounds like a book that needs to be written."

Nora nodded an agreement.

When the grandfather clock in the foyer struck the hour, Caine glanced down at his watch in surprise. "It'll be daylight soon. You're going to be beat."

"It's my monthly Saturday off," Nora reminded him.

Caine found the idea of spending a rainy Saturday in bed with this woman infinitely appealing.

"Well, I'd better get going and let you get some rest." Even as he pushed himself away from the table, Caine wished she would ask him to stay.

A very strong part of Nora did not want Caine to leave. Telling herself that it was for the best, she stood, as well.

"Thanks again," she said, walking him to the door.

"For everything."

"Thank you," he replied. "For the coffee, and the cookies and, well, everything."

Knowing Nora no longer blamed him for Dylan's death had taken a very heavy load from Caine's shoulders. If she could forgive him, perhaps he could learn to forgive himself.

They stood in the foyer, inches apart, looking at each other. Caine brushed his knuckles down her cheek. It felt too damn good for comfort.

"Sleep tight." Caine watched the desire rise in her remarkable eyes and knew he should go. Now, before it was too late.

"You, too. Give Maggie my love."

"I'll do that. See you on Monday. So you can take out my stitches," he said, reminding her of his new appointment date.

Because he wanted to kiss her, wanted to drag her upstairs to the bedroom and discover exactly how much of her elusive scent remained on her warm skin, Caine turned and trotted down the steps to the car parked at the curb.

Nora opened her mouth to call him back, then closed it. But she did remain standing in the open doorway until the Ferrari's taillights had disappeared around the corner.

Later that day, Caine flew a pair of tourists from California to Orcas Island. Since the honeymooning couple was clearly besotted with one another, he doubted they fully appreciated the magnificent scenery.

Sunday he spent up to his elbows in soapsuds. Imbued with a new sense of purpose, he scrubbed the cabin floor, scoured the countertops and evicted the spiders that had taken up residence in the high ceiling corners. While washing the front window, he watched a robin weave a scarlet ribbon into the nest the robin was energetically building in a nearby tree and felt a strange sort of kinship with the red-breasted bird.

On Monday morning, the cabin was clean enough for his mother to visit. After a trip to the dump, where the circling seagulls seemed delighted with his nearly three weeks' collection of trash, Caine returned home, sat down at the kitchen table with a pot of coffee and a legal pad and began making telephone calls to friends and sports contacts around the country.

By the time he left for his appointment with Nora, Caine felt, for the first time in a very long while, that he finally had his life back on track.

Spring light latticed the landscape with shifting shades of green: the goldish green of early willows bent along the streams, the reddish green of maple leaves unfolding from their burst buds, the delicate green of bracken fern uncurling slender fronds, and always, the deep blue-green of water.

Caine had long ago decided that there were probably more shades of green on Washington's Olympic Peninsula than his Irish ancestors could have counted in Eire. During his years away from the peninsula, he'd grown increasingly homesick for such sights.

But as he drove to the clinic, the willows, the maple leaves, the ferns and the water all went unnoticed. Because the only thing he could see was Nora's exquisite face.

As was usual on Mondays, a continuous stream of patients filed into Nora's clinic. Fortunately Kirstin, her nurse, had returned from maternity leave and things were running a great deal more smoothly.

Nora finished wrapping Eva Nelson's sprained ankle. The teenager had stumbled while backpacking. Warning Eva to keep any stress off the ankle until the sprain was healed, to keep the leg elevated as much as possible, and to take aspirin as needed, Nora walked her to the reception area. That's when she saw Caine, sprawled in her grandmother's Queen Anne chair as if he belonged there. With his long legs stretched out in front of him, he seemed to take up half the narrow foyer.

"Good afternoon, Mr. O'Halloran," she greeted him formally.

"Afternoon, Doc."

"I can see you now."

It did not escape Nora's notice that her very efficient nurse, who was watching Caine surreptitiously as she filled out an insurance receipt for the injured teenager, made an uncharacteristic mistake, and with a murmured apology to the patient, had to begin again.

"You've no idea how much I appreciate your making

time for me in your busy schedule," he drawled, rising to follow her back into the room in his easy, loose-hipped athlete's gait.

"Get up on the table——"

"I know the drill, Nora." He grinned. "Want me to take off my clothes again?"

"That isn't necessary." She turned and reached into the cabinet for surgical scissors and gloves.

Her sharp tone pleased him. Caine had noticed long ago that very few things got under Nora's skin. He decided the fact that he was one of them was definitely an encouraging sign.

When Nora turned around he was standing behind her, closer than she'd thought.

"Did you have a nice weekend?" he asked.

"Lovely," she replied. "And you?"

"Actually I did. I flew another one of Maggie's charters to the islands. It felt funny being paid to do something I'd do for free. Funny, but nice."

"You always said you'd play ball for free."

"Got me there," Caine said agreeably. Not quite ready to fill her in on what else he'd been doing, he pulled himself up onto the table, dangled his legs and said, "Snip away, Doc. I'm ready."

"I received a call from the hospice coordinator today about Maggie," she said conversationally as she clipped the first stitch with deft hands.

"I know." Caine felt a slight tug against his scalp. "We made a deal."

"What kind of deal?" *Clip.* Another stitch gone.

"In return for her entering the hospice program, I promised to quit drinking too much, stop speeding, and turn celibate."

"I can't imagine Maggie holding you to that last one." *Clip. Clip. Snip. Snip.*

"You're right." There was a sudden charge in the air as his gaze met hers. "She pointed out, in her inimitably direct way, that it wasn't right, my courting one woman while I was technically married to another. So I promised to stay away from you until my divorce is final. Which makes celibacy a given."

His stormy eyes lowered slowly, purposefully to her lips, the look as physical as a kiss, and lingered there for a long, heartfelt moment. "Since you're the only woman I want."

Her lovely face was a contradiction of emotions. Caine saw anxiety, fear, irritation, and most encouraging of all, need. "Back off, Caine."

"I told you, that's exactly what I'm going to do," he agreed with an easy smile. "For now."

He wanted to draw her into his arms and resisted the urge. "Haven't you noticed that I've been in your office for at least ten minutes without giving in to the impulse to kiss you?"

"Dammit, Caine——"

"May I ask a question?"

She peeled off the thin gloves. "I suppose that depends on the question."

"Are we done?"

"Taking out the stitches? Yes."

"Then the professional part of this visit is over?"

"Yes." Her voice wasn't quite as strong as before.

"Good."

With a silent apology to his grandmother, Caine slid off the table, put his arms around Nora, lowered his mouth to hers and kissed her with all the pent-up passion he'd been feeling.

"We can't keep doing this," she complained weakly when the long, hot kiss finally ended.

His lips plucked enticingly at hers. "Give me one good reason to stop."

"How about your wife?"

"Bull's-eye." Sighing, Caine reluctantly released her.

"I hate it when you insist on acting like a grown-up."

"One of us has to." Her cheeks were still flushed, her lips swollen, and her eyes were laced with desire. "Perhaps it'd be better if we just stayed away from one another."

"In this town?" Caine knew that no matter where they were living, things had gone too far to back away now.

"You have a point," Nora conceded reluctantly. "I suppose I'll be seeing you next Friday night."

Midsummer's Eve was an annual festival dating back to the days of Swedish pagan worship, a celebration of the summer solstice. Years ago someone had gotten the idea to add a contest of lumbering skills to the festivities, which resulted in loggers coming from all over the country to try to win the purse that had grown larger each year. Neither Caine nor Nora had attended since the night Dylan had been conceived.

"I suppose. If I'm in town."

"Oh. Are you taking another charter for Maggie?" she asked with more casualness than she was feeling.

"No." He'd been trying to think of a way to break the news. "I got a call from the Tigers."

"Oh? I hadn't realized you'd recovered well enough to pitch again."

Caine watched her shutting up, like a wildflower closing its petals prior to a storm. "I haven't. They're about to fire their pitching coach and I'm on the short list to be his replacement."

"I see." She did, all too well. "Does that mean you've given up the idea of playing again?"

"For the time being." He flexed his fingers. "Hell, there's no point in trying to fool myself any longer, Nora. I've still got the moves, but I've lost the feeling necessary for absolute control."

"Well, then, I certainly wish you luck with this new offer."

The intimacy between them was gone, replaced by that cold formality Caine had always hated. Only the knowledge that Nora was iciest when she was experiencing the greatest inner turmoil kept him from pushing.

"Thanks. These days I need all the luck I can get."

He decided to leave before they got into an argument regarding what she'd always considered his self-centered career choices. "You don't have to see me out." He bent his head, stealing another quick kiss. "I know the way."

Frustrated by the way he could still cause such havoc to her emotional equilibrium, Nora curved her fingers around the handle of the surgical scissors. She was unreasonably tempted to throw them at his cocky, sun-streaked head.

Instead, she deliberately put them down on the table, closed her eyes and struggled for calm—something that was difficult to achieve when she heard Caine's deep voice, followed by an all-too-familiar rumbling chuckle coming from the foyer.

If she was upset by the way Caine had left her shaken—and, dammit, wanting—Nora was appalled at the surge of dark jealousy caused by the sound of Kirstin's appreciative, answering laugh.

Chapter 11

As if ancient pagan gods had benevolently conspired with Mother Nature, Midsummer Eve was warm and clear. A full moon hung like a silver dollar in the sky, bathing the town in a light that was nearly as bright as day, only softer.

Japanese lanterns had been strung around the square; white lights twinkled in the broad leaves of maple trees planted by some long-ago town council. At one end of the square, men drank beer from a keg and slung horseshoes. The plink of forged iron shoes against the iron stakes joined with the sound of crickets.

Tables were covered with food: cold fruit soups, a variety of local clams and oysters, *pyttipanna*—a traditional late-supper hash—and platters of salmon topped with *senapssås*, a cold mustard-dill sauce.

On the dessert table, delicate *pålattar*—traditional

Swedish pancakes topped with lingonberries—shared space with blueberry filled tortes topped with a frothy meringue and *mazarintsarta*—a raspberry torte topped with lemon icing. At the end of the dessert table was hot *punsch*, a lethal brandy-and-rum drink. If all that weren't enough to satiate appetites, people stood in line, paper plates in hand, waiting for one of the flame-broiled Olympic burgers Ingrid Johansson was cooking on an enormous charcoal grill.

The opposite end of the square had been turned into a modern-day Highland games, where loggers competed to win the coveted purse that this year had grown to five thousand dollars. There was the angry, beelike drone of chain saws, the thwack of an ax landing on target, raucous laughter and wild splashing whenever a hapless logger tumbled off a rolling log into the fishpond.

On her way across the green, Nora paused to watch the women's ax-throwing contest.

"Now that's a magnificent, if admittedly frightening sight," a deep voice murmured in her ear. "A beautiful woman swinging a double-headed ax."

She turned around, struggled to keep the smile off her face, and failed. "Hi."

Caine would have had to be deaf not to hear the uncensored pleasure in her voice. "Hi, yourself."

She was wearing something floaty and flowery and very feminine. She smelled like a spring garden. He reached out and fingered a dangling earring crafted from pastel shells. "You look absolutely gorgeous."

Color stained her cheeks. "Thank you."

The billowy skirt ended well below her knees; until

tonight, Caine had never realized exactly how sexy a woman's calves could be.

"The town council made a big mistake." He was looking down at her as if he wanted to grab her by the hair and drag her off to his cave. Nora looked up at him as if she hoped he would.

"A mistake?" She glanced around at the festival that was an obvious success. "About what?"

"They should have voted you Queen. Instead of Britta Nelson."

Nora followed his gaze to the *majstång*—the flower-decked pole that a circle of young girls were currently dancing around. Fifteen-year-old Britta Nelson was wearing her crown, a circlet of fresh flowers, perched atop her silvery blond hair.

"I brought you something," Caine pulled a bouquet of wildflowers from behind his back.

"Oh, they're lovely." In spite of her better judgment, Nora buried her nose in the fragrant blooms.

"There are seven different kinds."

The significance of that number did not escape her. Swedish folklore decreed any maiden who placed seven different wildflowers beneath her pillow on Midsummer Eve would dream of the man she would marry.

"Really, Caine…"

When she would have backed away, he captured her hand and lifted it to his lips. "Don't tell me you're afraid you'll dream about me?"

"Of course not."

"I've been dreaming about you." Smiling, he began to kiss her fingers. "Every night. Want to hear a few of the more interesting ones?"

When his lips moved to the soft skin at the center

of her palm, although Nora the doctor knew it was impossible, Nora the woman could have sworn that every muscle in her body began to melt. Knowing that nothing in Tribulation went unnoticed, she yanked her hand free.

"No." She put her hands behind her back to keep them out of Caine's range. Unfortunately, such defensive behavior made it impossible to push him away when he proceeded to back her up against the trunk of the maple tree behind her. "I don't."

"Too bad." He put his hands on either side of her head, effectively holding her hostage. "My favorite is the one where we're flying over the ocean in Maggie's Learjet—"

"Maggie doesn't have a Learjet—"

"It's a dream," Caine argued easily. "Anyway, we're over the ocean, and all we can see for miles in all directions, is the blue-green of the sea and the blue of the sky. It's as if we're the only two people in the world.

"Just you and me and the wild blue yonder. And here's where the good part begins: I put the plane on autopilot, and—"

There was the sound of a throat clearing behind them.

"Ah, excuse me, Caine. Hi, Nora," Joe Bob Carroll said apologetically. "Sorry to interrupt. But your grandpappy's lookin' for the both of you, Caine. Since he looked a little ragged around the edges, I told him to wait over by the horseshoe pits while I went and found you."

Caine dropped his hands to his sides. He gave Nora a worried look. "Devlin stayed home with Maggie tonight. If he left her to come here..."

Nora wanted to cover his grimly set lips with her own, to press kisses all over that dark, tortured face. She longed to tell him that there was no need to worry, that his grandmother would live to be a hundred.

In the end, she merely lifted a palm to his cheek.

"We'd better go see what he wants," she said in the quiet, reassuring tone she'd adopted during her years of medical practice.

Nora took her ex-husband's hand in hers and led him, atypically meek as a lamb, across the crowded green, through the throng of merrymakers, toward Devlin O'Halloran.

When they reached the house, Ellen and Mike O'Halloran were waiting. Mike, Caine's father, had always been a taciturn man, more comfortable with his lures and lines than with people. A crisis did not change his nature.

After murmuring a vague, inarticulate greeting to Nora, he gave her an awkward hug. Although he might not be as talkative as either Devlin or Caine, the painful prospect of losing his mother had made his dark eyes moist.

Ellen O'Halloran's face, still remarkably unlined for a woman nearing sixty, was tanned to a deep hazelnut color from the lifestyle change that now had her spending so much of her time outdoors. Her short hair was the color of autumn leaves, laced with random streaks of sun-lightened auburn and silver.

As she embraced her former mother-in-law, Nora experienced a moment's confusion over whether she was here in her role as doctor or family.

As a doctor, although she continually fought against

it, death had become a fellow traveler, at times welcome, most often not. As a family member—at the moment, her divorce from Caine seemed inconsequential—Nora shared everyone's feelings of helplessness and sorrow.

The hospice nurse came out of the bedroom and drew Nora aside. "I informed Maggie's family that she won't last the night," she murmured. "But, of course, I've been wrong before."

Nora knew only too well the futility of second-guessing death. "I'd better examine her."

Maggie was asleep when Nora entered the bedroom. She was wearing an old-fashioned ivory cotton gown with long sleeves trimmed with hand-tatted lace. Her thinning red hair was spread across the embroidered pillow like strands of silver touched by a setting sun. Her face, in repose, was calm.

Nora reached down and lifted a frail wrist. Her pulse was thin and thready. Nora had just lowered the elderly woman's hand to the sheet again when Maggie's blue eyes popped open.

"I figured that was you," she said. "Caine always said you smelled like wildflowers after a spring rain."

Maggie laced their fingers together. "He's right."

"Speaking of Caine," Nora said, "he's waiting to see you."

"I know. I've already said my goodbyes to Michael and Ellen and was just hangin' on until you and Caine got here." Her eyes fluttered shut. Nora slid her thumb to Maggie's wrist and was relieved to find her pulse unchanged. A few moments later, Maggie's eyes opened again. "So how was the festival?"

"Nice." Nora knew Maggie wanted particulars so she

filled her in on the sawdust competition, the dancing, the Japanese lanterns, and the smorgasbord.

"Did Eva Magnuson bring her apple torte?"

"Of course."

"Her apples are never tart enough," Maggie complained. "And her crust is like concrete. But she's been makin' the damn thing forever, so no one has the heart to tell her.

"I remember Midsummer Eve during Vietnam," Maggie mused. "We couldn't have the lanterns because of the blackouts. Never knew when an enemy submarine was going to come steaming up the strait to the shipyards."

She closed her eyes again. The corners of her mouth twitched upward. "A lot of smooching went on in the shadows behind those old maples, let me tell you. Especially with all the boys shippin' out. Nothin' like a war to steam up a romance."

The smile faded. "Michael's hurtin' bad," Maggie continued. "Not that he'd ever admit it. If I lived another eighty-two years, I'd probably never figure out how a magpie like me could've given birth to such a closemouthed boy.

"But he's got Ellen, so I'm not worried about him. Of course, poor Caine's probably gonna carry on something awful because he couldn't keep his grandmother alive."

She sighed, pressed a hand against her failing heart and took a ragged breath. "Caine always did take too much on his own shoulders. But it's the boy's nature, so what can you do?"

Maggie's lashes drifted down again, but she didn't fall asleep. "Caine's been telling me about this teammate of his. Some Buddhist fella. They believe in reincarnation."

"The Detroit shortstop," Nora remembered.

"I've been thinking about that a lot, lately," Maggie admitted. "I kinda like the idea of comin' back again. Maybe this time as an astronaut."

"The first woman to pilot a spaceship to Mars," Nora suggested with a smile.

Maggie smiled, as well. "I'd like that. Devlin wouldn't. He gets airsick." She chuckled again. "Imagine, a man who's spent most of his life on the water getting airsick. I never have been able to figure that one out."

She drifted off again. Nora had just about decided that it was time to bring the family in when Maggie opened her eyes, fixed her with her bright blue gaze and said, "If there does turn out to be a heaven, I'll tell Dylan his mama says hello."

Nora had to swallow past the lump in her throat. "Thank you."

"If we do get to come back again, I reckon your paths will cross one of these days and you can tell him yourself," Maggie decided.

Tears were burning at the backs of her lids. Nora could only nod.

"You'd better send Caine in now, Nora. After you give me a kiss."

Nora bent her head and brushed her lips against the older woman's cheek. Her skin was as thin and dry as old parchment.

"I love you, Maggie." All right, perhaps it wasn't the most professional thing to say, but it was the truth.

"And I love you, girl." It took an obvious effort, but

Maggie managed to lift her hand from the sheet to pat Nora's cheek. "Take good care of my grandson," she whispered. "I know he can be a bit of a hotshot from time to time, Nora, but he's a good boy. Deep down."

"I know." That, too, was the truth.

It was with a heavy heart that Nora went to the door and gestured toward Caine. When he entered the bedroom, she brushed her fingers against his rigid jaw, then left him alone with his grandmother.

He'd been watching Maggie's decline for weeks, but in the back of his mind, Caine had refused to accept the fact that his grandmother was dying. Even now, looking at her ivory complexion and her frail frame, he couldn't face the sad truth.

"You're missing the dancing."

"I know. And that really gets my goat. Your pappy's a good dancer." A faint reminiscent light flickered in Maggie's eyes.

"The first time we danced together was on Midsummer Eve. I'd landed in town as part of a five-girl flying exhibition team. The town council hired us thinkin' we might bring some tourists in from the cities. Your pappy was mayor. It was his idea."

Caine sat down in the straight-backed chair beside the bed. "Did you? Bring in more tourists?"

Maggie shrugged her frail shoulders. "Don't remember. Only thing I recollect about that night is dancin' the rumba with Devlin. After that, everything kinda passed in a blur. The next day, when the sun came up, the rest of the girls moved on."

"But you stayed." It was one of Caine's favorite stories.

"And never regretted a single day. What your pappy

and I had was special. We both knew that right off the bat." Maggie's eyes closed, but her hand reached across the sheets to pat his.

"It's taken you and Nora a little longer, but you'll get there. Eventually. Like that Buddhist friend of yours says, a man can't escape his Karma…. Would you do me a favor?"

"You've got it," Caine said without hesitation.

"Would you help me brush my hair?"

She was as light as a feather; Caine lifted her with ease and propped her up against the plump goose-down pillows. Retrieving a silver-handled hairbrush, he began stroking the brush over her scalp, smoothing out the once-fiery strands.

"Mmm," Maggie murmured. "That feels good." Just when Caine thought she'd fallen asleep, Maggie said, "Love's a powerful thing, Caine. Even more powerful than fate. And you and Nora have got both goin' for you."

He'd come to that same realization himself. Now all he had to do was convince Nora. "I know, Gram. And that's why you have to stay well enough to stick around for the wedding."

"There's nothin' I'd like better. But don't you worry, boy, I'll be there in spirit." Caine watched her struggle to lift her lids. "How do I look?"

"Beautiful." On impulse, he spritzed her with the lilac cologne she'd always worn. "You smell pretty good, too. If you weren't my grandmother, I'd probably have to give pappy a run for his money."

She dimpled at that, looking remarkably, for one fleeting second, like a girl of sixteen. "You and Devlin," she murmured. "Two peas in a pod. Both of you must've kissed the blarney stone in some past life."

She smoothed her hair with a trembling hand and pinched her cheeks. "Speakin' of your pappy," she said, "I think you'd better send him in."

"Gram...."

"It's my time, Caine," Maggie said soothingly. "And as much as I do truly love you, I still need to say goodbye to the best rumba dancer in Tribulation."

Caine no longer attempted to check his tears. They flowed down his face, onto the sheets, and splashed on his grandmother's blue-veined hand. He wanted to drag her into his arms and beg her not to die, but since she looked as breakable as a piece of fine porcelain, he forced himself to simply press a kiss against the top of her freshly brushed hair.

"God, I love you," he said in a choked voice. Then, before he lost it completely, he turned and walked toward the door that his grandfather had already opened, as if answering some unspoken call.

Devlin patted Caine on the shoulder, then squared his own broad shoulders and crossed the room, forgoing the chair to sit on the edge of the bed.

"You are still the most gorgeous girl in Tribulation," he said, running a hand down her hair.

Rather than accuse him of exaggerating, as she had Caine, Maggie turned her head and pressed her dry lips against his palm. "And you're still the handsomest man."

He stretched out beside her, drew her close and knew he'd never see a lilac bush without thinking of Maggie. They stayed that way for a long, silent time, her head on his shoulder, his lips against the top of her head.

"I love you, Margaret Rose Murphy O'Halloran," Devlin whispered after a time.

"And I love you, Devlin Patrick O'Halloran." She tilted her head to smile up at him, but her eyes were earnest. "I want you to promise me something."

"Anything."

"Just in case that shortstop friend of Caine's is right, and some other life, you meet a woman—maybe an aviatrix or even an astronaut—who asks you to rumba, promise me that you'll say yes."

"I promise." He touched his lips to hers and covered her breast with his broad hand. "Yes. Always."

Devlin felt the quick flutter of her heart, like that of a wounded sparrow, against his fingertips. Then it was still. The light outside the window turned from ebony to gray to a pale, misty silver. Pink fingers of dawn began creeping into the room.

And still Devlin remained, with his bride, the light of his life for more than half a century, in his arms.

Remembering.

Chapter 12

The memorial service for Maggie was held, at her request, at the airport. Hundreds came to pay tribute to the woman who'd brought so much life and laughter and spirit to Tribulation.

The mourners who overflowed the tent stood beneath black umbrellas, until finally, when the drizzle escalated into a downpour, the services were moved inside the hangar.

When the rain stopped and the pewter clouds parted, Caine and Devlin—the older man fortified by the Dramamine tablet Nora had given him—took off in Maggie's beloved Cessna to spread her ashes over the mountain meadows she'd loved.

The others retired to Mike and Ellen's, where they shared a potluck supper and swapped Maggie stories, each more outrageous than the last, all of them true.

It was late when Nora returned home, but she wasn't surprised to see Caine sitting on the porch in the wicker swing, waiting for her. Neither was she surprised by the surge of pure pleasure that flowed through her.

"Hi." She slipped her hands into the skirt pockets of her black dress. "How's Devlin?"

"About as well as can be expected," Caine replied. "I offered to take him back to the cabin with me, but he wanted to stay at the house. He says he can feel Maggie's spirit there."

"I suppose that's not surprising."

"I guess not." Caine raked his hands through his hair. "He feels she's hanging around to make sure he's okay with all this."

"That's not surprising, either. Are you?"

"Am I what?"

"Okay with all this?"

Caine shrugged. "I suppose. As much as I can be.... By the way, I got a call today from my lawyer. By this time tomorrow, I'll be a free man."

Her heart soared, even as Nora attempted to bank her joy. "I guess congratulations are in order." Wicker creaked as she sat down beside him.

"Thanks. The entire process looked like it was going to last until the next century, so I decided to make an end run around the legal eagles and wrote out a generous enough check to send her to the Dominican Republic."

"That's football," Nora murmured.

"What?"

"An end run. That's football."

He chuckled. "I can remember when you thought a tight end was a groupie in too-snug jeans."

"You can't escape sports talk in the doctors' lounge."

"I thought doctors only talked about golf."

"I suppose they do, mostly."

"Did you ever take it up so you'd have something to do on Wednesday afternoons?"

"Golf? No." Nora shook her head. "I never could figure out whether to hit the ball when the dragon's mouth was open or closed."

He laughed and put his arm around her. Nora didn't move away. For a while there was only the soft sigh of the night breeze in the trees and a swish-swish sound as they swung gently.

"Was it hard?" she asked finally. "Scattering Maggie's ashes?"

"I thought it would be," Caine admitted. "But the meadows were in full bloom and while we were circling, looking for a space, a ray of sun came out of the clouds, and gilded this one spot on the mountainside pure gold. I looked at Devlin and he looked at me, and we both knew that somehow, Maggie was guiding us."

"She probably was," Nora said quietly. "I worried when you didn't show up at the potluck."

"Devlin just wanted to go home. After I dropped him off, I drove to Port Angeles and played a little catch with Johnny."

"That was nice of you."

"I did it more for myself than for him. I like the kid. A lot."

"And he idolizes you. How's he doing?"

"Okay." Caine shrugged. "He's worried that no one will adopt him because people would rather have a new baby."

"Most people would, I suppose. But Johnny's a wonderful little boy. He'll find a family."

"That's what I told him," Caine agreed.

They fell silent again. Somewhere in a distant treetop an owl hooted.

"I brought you something," Caine said.

When he reached into his pocket, Nora thought he was going to give her some small memento of his grandmother, but instead, he handed her a legal-size white envelope.

Slanting him a questioning look, she slid her fingernail under the flap and opened it. "A check?"

The moon was riding high above the horizon, the cool white light bright enough to enable Nora to read the amount. "I don't understand."

Stunned, unable to believe what her eyes were telling her, she slowly counted all the zeros again. "It's made out to the Dylan Anderson O'Halloran Memorial Pediatric Trauma Center."

Caine nodded. "That's right."

"But there isn't any such center."

"Not now. But there will be."

She couldn't believe he was serious. Her first thought was that this was some sort of grandstand play to win her approval. Her second thought was that Caine was not the type of man to indulge in such subterfuge.

She stood and began to pace. "But a trauma center is so very expensive."

"Tiffany didn't get all my money, Nora."

"But even you can't fund it by yourself."

"I know that. But I'm a helluva fund-raiser. You should hear my after-dinner speeches. Besides, I'm going to have help."

She stopped in her tracks. "What kind of help?"

"There's going to be an All-Star baseball game in October, after the World Series and before winter ball begins in South America," he informed her. "All proceeds going to the center. ESPN has committed to broadcasting the game and here's a list of people who've signed up to play. I expect more when the word gets out."

Nora scanned the list he'd pulled from his pocket. The names represented the top stars, past and present, of the game.

"You've been busy."

Caine shrugged. "I spent the past few weeks making some phone calls. It kept me out of the pool halls."

He'd done more than make phone calls. It was obvious that he'd spent a great deal of time and effort on the project. Not to mention money. "I can't let you do this."

"It's too late to stop me, Nora. Besides, I'm not doing it for you," Caine argued calmly. "I'm doing it for all the little kids like Dylan who need a fighting chance."

Caine's incredible plans left Nora feeling drained. She sat back in the swing and stared up at the starspangled sky.

"After all these years, I didn't think there was anything you could do to surprise me," she said finally.

"But you've succeeded."

"I'm glad to hear that. But I didn't do it as some elaborate scheme to get you back in my life, Nora."

"I know."

They resumed swinging.

Need was a fist, twisting at Caine's gut, crawling beneath his skin, burning him from the inside out. With effort, he pushed it down.

As if reading his mind, Nora turned her head so that her face was inches from Caine's. His arm was stretched along the top of the swing; the slightest movement would have it around her shoulders.

"I guess I'd better go home," he said quietly. "Before I stoop to begging."

When he began to rise—fully, honorably, intending to leave—she placed her hand on his arm. Her eyes, more gold than brown in the streaming moonlight, revealed her own desire.

"You wouldn't have to beg."

He couldn't resist. He had to touch her, if only to cup her face with his hand. "I want you to be sure about this, Nora. Very sure."

"I am." Her answering laugh was as quick and shaky as her pulse. "In fact, I don't think I've ever been so sure about anything in my life."

She slid her arms around his neck, her smile a seduction in itself. If Scheherazade had flashed that fatal, womanly smile at the Sultan, Caine mused, she definitely wouldn't have needed to tell the guy stories to keep him interested during those thousand and one nights.

"Kiss me, Caine." Nora's soft voice curled around him like smoke. "Kiss me the way you were going to kiss me at the festival."

He combed his hands through her hair, gathering it into a knot at the nape of her neck, and held her gaze to his. "If I do," he warned, "it won't stop with a kiss."

"Good." Her fingers were playing with the curls at the back of his collar. "Because I want you to make love to me." Her eyes were open and fixed on his. "Nobody has ever made me fly so high."

Caine hadn't come to Nora's house to take her to bed. He'd only wanted to be with her, to tell her about the center, and, perhaps, ease the pain of losing his grandmother just a little.

He thought of his promise to Maggie, to stay away from Nora until he was free.

But dammit, Tiffany was on her way to the Dominican Republic—along with a cashier's check—and in a matter of hours a marriage that should have been declared dead at the altar would be legally dissolved.

Reminding himself that he'd never been bucking for sainthood, Caine tangled his hands in her hair and kissed her—a deep, drugging kiss that had heat pouring out of him and into her.

Kissing Nora was like partaking of a feast after a long fast. Hunger. Greed. Need. They rose like ancient demons, battering at his insides.

Fighting for patience, Caine buried his lips in the soft scent of her hair. Every ragged breath he took was an agony of effort.

"I want to make love with you, too, sweetheart." He ran his palms down her arms and struggled valiantly for some semblance of control. "But let's try to keep this flight from being over too fast."

"I'll try if you will. But I've never had a great deal of self-control where you're concerned, Caine."

"I know the feeling." Caine laced their fingers together and stood, bringing her to her feet with him.

When he led her into the house and up the stairs, Nora experienced a moment's hesitation—one that did not go unnoticed by Caine.

He stopped on the landing and framed her face between his hands. "If this isn't what you want—"

"It is." She pressed her lips against his quickly, cutting him off. Although she was thirty-two years old, there was no artifice in her kiss, no clever experience; only honest, feminine need.

"I've never wanted anyone the way I want you right now, Caine," she whispered when the brief flare ended. "I've never needed anyone the way I need you at this moment."

It was all he needed to hear. Holding hands again, they walked the rest of the way up the stairs and into her bedroom.

The room was a direct contrast to the proper, professional image Nora showed the world. It was pretty and feminine and smelled of flowers. It was the kind of room a man would only feel comfortable in if invited.

Antique perfume bottles stood atop her dresser along with a trio of fat white candles and a dish of potpourri made from the petals of the scarlet roses Nora's grandmother had planted behind the house.

Framed photos, of friends and family, covered most of the rest of the dresser top.

Caine smiled when he saw a picture of Maggie, standing in front of a red Stinson four-seater she'd owned back in the 1950s. She was grinning with the sheer confidence of a woman who had never let any obstacle stand in her way.

Caine's gaze moved to an open sandalwood box where a strand of polite pearls was hopelessly entangled with gold hoops, and a pair of discreet silver stud earrings rested on velvet beside a funky ceramic pin shaped like a gray whale.

Caine remembered the pin well; he'd bought it for Nora on impulse one April day when they'd taken a cranky, teething Dylan on a ferryboat ride to Orcas Island. He was moved and vastly encouraged by the fact that she'd kept it all these years.

The hand-carved bed was wide and tall; the four posters reached almost to the ceiling. The mattress was covered with a wedding-ring quilt from some Anderson bride's hope chest. Piled atop the quilt were dozens of pillows—too small to be useful for anything other than feminine ornamentation—covered in lace and satin and pretty floral-chintz prints.

Beside the bed, he was pleased to see, his wildflowers sat in a white china pitcher he remembered Anna Anderson pouring milk from. He plucked a petal and rubbed it between his thumb and forefinger, releasing a burst of sweet fragrance.

"I dreamed of you that night," Nora murmured. "On Midsummer Eve."

He'd known she would. Just as he had dreamed of her.

Centuries of folklore hovered in the perfumed air between them. "But I don't think it counts," she whispered, "because I've been dreaming of you every night since you came back to Tribulation."

The soft admission was more than he'd dared to hope for. "Every night?"

"Yes." The single word shuddered from between her lips on a soft sigh. "Every single one."

A fierce burst of primitive satisfaction surged through his veins. "Although I've never been a man to worry about setting the scene for romance, I wanted to do this right." His gaze moved lingeringly over her face; he was making love to her with his eyes. "I had it all planned: champagne and red roses and music."

"I don't need champagne. Or roses. Or music." He was standing so close to her, Nora couldn't tell if it was Caine's heart beating so wildly, or her own. "All I need is you."

His eyes didn't waver from hers as he slowly traced the exquisite shape of her mouth with his thumb. His fingers explored the planes of her face and found her perfect. His mouth drank from hers with a gentleness he hadn't known he possessed.

When his tongue slipped between her parted lips to touch the tip of hers, Nora wondered how it was that her body could be so thrillingly alive while her mind remained so clouded.

Refusing to dwell on it, she let herself slide effortlessly into this seductive, misty world. She lifted her arms, entwined them around Caine's neck and pulled him to her. Their bodies fit just as she remembered. Perfectly. Wonderfully.

The more she gave, the more Caine wanted. He ached for her—body, mind and soul.

"All these years," he told her, "I've tried to forget the way you felt in my arms when we made love. And the incredible, terrifying way you make me feel."

"I know." She ran her fingers over his dark face. "I've tried to forget, too. And I've tried to pretend that it wasn't real—that it had been only a fantasy, a trick of memory."

The wonder of her admission shimmered in her voice. "But it was real." Her fingers moved down his neck, to the open collar of his shirt.

Something about Caine had always had Nora wanting to give him more than she'd given to any other man.

Something about him always had her wanting more from him than any man had ever given her.

She pressed her lips against his warm skin, drinking in his mysterious male taste. "It's only ever been that way with you, Caine." Very slowly, he unbuttoned her dress. Caine O'Halloran had always made love the way he played baseball: with a skill that made every move seem eminently natural.

Yet, as his fingers fumbled with the small pearl buttons running down the front of her dress, he wondered why it was that this act, which he'd performed so many times before, could suddenly seem so different. So new. So frightening.

The buttons went all the way to the hem. Breathing a sigh of relief as he released the final one, Caine folded back the material. She was wearing a silk teddy with a low-cut lace-trimmed bodice and a pair of black, lace-topped thigh-high stockings that had looked appropriately somber with the dress, but now were incredibly sexy contrasted with the pale skin above them.

The fact that the teddy was as scarlet as sin made him smile, reminding him of the first time he'd discovered her penchant for sexy lingerie.

When Caine slid the dress from her shoulders, Nora reached for him, but he caught her hands.

"No, let me." He brushed his lips against hers again, tempting, tantalizing, tormenting. "Let me see if I can make you float."

"You always could."

The crimson teddy smelled like her. Caine could have drowned in her scent. But since the temptation of her silky skin was even more irresistible, Caine dispensed with the sensual barrier. Slowly, thoroughly, he seduced her solely with his mouth. Her blood warmed, her pulse hummed. And then, as impossible as it sounded, Nora began to float.

She found herself lying on the bed without knowing how she'd gotten there. When Caine's lips closed around the rosy tip of her breast and tugged, Nora gasped; they moved on, scattering hot kisses over her stomach, the inside of her thigh, the back of her thigh, the back of her knee. His teeth nibbled at the ultrasensitive tendon that only he had ever discovered, creating a flash of heat that spiraled outward to her fingertips.

But she wasn't allowed to dwell on that riveting feeling. His mouth was everywhere, tasting, tempting its way along a seductive path from her tingling lips to her bare toes. Everywhere his lips touched, they left tormenting trails of heat. Her blood was molten, flowing hot and thick through her veins, then deeper still, to the bone.

Caine was a tender, but ruthless lover—driving her toward delirium as he turned her in his arms, bending her to his will, tasting every fragrant bit of exposed flesh. And just when Nora didn't think she could take any more, he drove her higher, to where the air grew thin and it became hard to breathe.

Dazzled, dazed, desperate, she closed her eyes and clung to him as the years peeled away. And then she was tumbling over the rocky precipice, shuddering as climax after impossible, breath-stealing climax slammed through her.

Caine watched Nora's dazed eyes fly open. He heard her astonishment as she gasped his name. Strangely, the absolute trust she'd shown him had made him feel like a hero again—for the first time in a very long while.

He held her until the wild, aching tremors passed. "Lord, I've missed this," he murmured against her mouth. "I've missed you."

For what seemed like an eternity, Nora lay limp in his arms, her mind spinning, her heated skin drenched. How could she have forgotten that it was possible to feel so much?

Sometime during the heady lovemaking, Caine's clothes had vanished. But how could that be? When she couldn't remember a single instant when his lips or his hands had not been warming her body.

Outside the window, the large white moon rising in the sky made Caine's dark skin gleam. Nora touched his chest. His flesh under her stroking fingers was soft and smooth. But the muscle beneath was hard and wiretaut. She pressed her lips against that warm moist flesh, drinking in the texture, the taste, his earthy male scent.

She ran her hands over his body, delighting in the way his muscles rippled and clenched beneath her palm. She pressed her open mouth against his flat stomach and felt him shudder. She flicked her tongue over his pebbly dark nipple and heard him groan.

The idea that she could cause such a primitive response was thrilling. Abandoning caution, she rose to her knees and ran her palms down his legs, her fingers exploring the corded muscles of his thighs, his calves. Testing, she touched her lips to the flesh her hands had warmed.

How had the tables turned so devastatingly? Caine wondered dizzily. Just moments ago, he'd been the one in absolute control. He'd been the one creating havoc with Nora's stunned senses.

But now, with just the delicate glide of her hands,

the feel of her mouth against his skin, the scrape of her teeth against the aching flesh at the inside of his thigh, she was driving him beyond reason. Her daring touch was like a flame; his flesh burned with it.

Overcome with a heady feminine power, Nora laughed and trailed her tongue wetly down his chest. The throaty sound tolled in his head as his body throbbed. Frustration warred with passion. Caine wanted her to stop; he wanted her never to stop.

He ached to take her now, quickly, before she succeeded in making him mad, but his power was gone. Somehow, when he wasn't looking, Nora had stolen it; it had flowed from him into her and for the first time in his life, Caine was experiencing true helplessness.

Moaning her name between short ragged breaths, he reached for her, but his touch was vague, almost dreamlike.

"Not yet," she whispered silkily.

He knew what she was going to do; every atom in his body was poised for that incredible moment when she would take his swollen sex into her soft wet mouth.

As if determined to torment him as he had tormented her, Nora drew the moment out. Her tongue slid hotly along his length, making him groan as he thrust his lean hips off the mattress in a mute plea for fulfillment. But still she made him wait. When her tongue encircled the plum-hued tip, Caine thought he was going to explode.

"No more." Need made his tone raw.

He grabbed hold of Nora's shoulders, turned her onto her back and levered himself over her. His eyes locked with hers. A promise, felt by both, sizzled between them.

He gripped her hips to pull her close, but Nora was already rising to meet him, to draw him in.

Caine slid into her, steel into silk. His hands linked with hers. Their fingers tightened.

Outside the window the white moon rose higher.

And so did they.

"That," Caine said when he could talk again, "was definitely worth waiting for."

"Mmm." Nora's head was on his chest; she pressed a kiss against his cooling flesh.

She was basking in a warm and satisfied glow and would have been more than happy to spend the rest of her days just lying in Caine's arms.

Even as common sense told her that that would be a remarkably impractical way to spend her life, the romantic side of her that this man had always been able to tap could think of nothing that would bring more pleasure. Caine ran a lazy finger down her spine. "Have I mentioned that you're still the most incredibly beautiful woman I've ever known?"

"Flatterer." His touch created a new flare of arousal that was as sharp as it was sweet.

"It's true." Smiling, he wound a thick strand of her hair around his hand. "And even now, after all we've shared, I still want you more than I've ever wanted any other woman."

"I want you, too," she admitted with a soft sigh.

He glanced down at her. "You don't sound very happy about that."

"It's just that nothing has changed." She was trembling. Caine felt an ominous feeling of foreboding and ignored it.

"Everything's changed." After brushing a kiss against the top of her head, he untangled himself from their embrace, left the bed and found his jeans.

"I have something for you."

"You've already given me so much," Nora protested, thinking of the generous check, not to mention all the work he'd been doing to establish her dream clinic. She sat up against the pillows.

"That was business. This is strictly personal."

Nora froze when he handed her the familiar blue sapphire set in antique gold filigree. "It's Maggie's engagement ring."

"Got it on the first try. She wanted you to have it."

"Me?"

Nora stared down at the ring, remembering that Devlin had bought his bride-to-be a sapphire, rather than a more traditional diamond, because it was the color of the sky she loved so well.

She ran her finger over the intricate gold weave. "You'd think Devlin would want to keep it."

"He and Maggie decided that it didn't make any sense to have it stashed away in some forgotten drawer."

"But—"

"They figured, and I agreed, that you might like it. And since we didn't exactly have a traditional wedding the first time around, I never got you a proper engagement ring."

"The first time?"

The mattress sighed as Caine sat down on the edge of the bed beside her. "You know how I feel, Nora. I love you. And, unless every instinct I've got has gone on the blink, you love me, too."

She couldn't lie any longer. Not to herself. Not to Caine. "I do."

"So the next logical thing to do is to get married."

"Caine——"

"In fact, the cabin's all ready for you to move in. I shoveled out the trash, washed the windows, changed the sheets and dusted. Even beneath the couch." He was more than a little pleased with himself about that. "And the refrigerator's filled with those healthy green vegetables you like."

"I'm sorry. But I can't marry you, Caine."

"Can't? Or won't?" Nora thought she detected a note of vulnerability in his tired tone.

"You have to understand."

"That's what I'm trying to do." Although Caine's voice remained calm, his eyes were not. "But you have to remember that I'm just a dumb jock. So perhaps you'd better try speaking slowly. And stick to words with no more than two syllables."

Caine's passion had always simmered just below the surface. Such intensity had always been exciting to Nora. At this moment, she was discovering that it could also be frightening.

Her nerves in a tangle, she pulled the rumpled sheet up to cover her breasts. "What we shared was wonderful, Caine. It always was. But it's not enough."

How could such an intelligent woman not see that after such intense lovemaking, she belonged to him? The same way he belonged to her.

"It's not enough because you won't let it be," he argued. "We both finally came home tonight, Nora. Where we belong. I want to spend all the rest of my nights with you, for fifty—hell, if we're lucky—even sixty or seventy-five years.

"I want to go to sleep every night with my arms wrapped around you and I want to wake up every morning knowing that you're beside me. I want to grow old with you, Nora."

Dear Lord, that's what she wanted, too. But there was something else. Something she knew he was leaving out.

"What about children?"

Don't let me mess this up, he begged whatever unforeseen fates had taken control of their lives.

Caine took a deep breath and chose his words very carefully.

"I know you've always considered me selfish. And perhaps I am. Because since coming back to Tribulation, I've discovered I want it all, sweetheart.

"I want to marry you and live in a house with a white picket fence. I want a stupid, friendly mutt who'll track mud in on the freshly washed floors, steal the steaks off the backyard barbecue and dig up the tulip bulbs every spring.

"And yes, I want children."

This was probably one of the longest speeches he'd ever made in his life. Reminding himself that it was also the most important, Caine took a deep breath.

"The best thing we ever did, in spite of ourselves, was create Dylan," he said, his voice gruff with emotion. "I love you, Nora. I want to have a family with you. Kids, Mom, Pop, a dog, the works."

Nora went ice-cold. Hands, feet, heart. "And where is this dream house going to be located? Detroit? And for how long?"

He flinched, knowing she had a point. There had been a time when he'd been so caught up in chasing his own dream, he would have thought nothing of dragging his family across the country, from town to town, wherever there was a baseball stadium.

"I didn't realize that the word had already gotten out."

"What word?"

"That I'd been offered the coaching job in Detroit."

"Oh." Amazingly, she hadn't known. Maggie's death had definitely put a crimp in Tribulation's rapid-fire gossip line. "Congratulations."

Caine shrugged. "I turned it down."

It was one more surprise in a night of surprises. "Why?"

Caine stared down at her in disbelief. Hadn't she been listening to a single word he'd said? "So I could stay in Tribulation. With you."

"I can't let you turn down an opportunity to stay in baseball for me."

"I'm not turning it down entirely because of you, Nora. I'd already decided to take over Maggie's charter business. It was what Gram wanted and the more I thought about it, the more I found myself liking the idea."

The decision had proven surprisingly easy. In the beginning, before Maggie's death, he'd suspected that the odds of Nora being willing to leave Tribulation and follow him to Detroit were slim to none. But, dammit, he'd told himself over and over again, he wasn't asking her to give up medicine; she could practice in Detroit. Perhaps, he'd considered, if he couched things carefully, he could make her understand that baseball had always been, aside from her and Dylan, the most important thing in his life.

But by the time he'd finished polishing the cabin windows he'd realized that he didn't really want to return to living out of a suitcase, never having any sense of belonging.

What he wanted was for him and Nora to sink their own family roots into the forest soil of a town that had been home to so many generations of Andersons and O'Hallorans.

"So you're staying?" She'd be seeing him almost every day. On the street, in the market, perhaps even here at the clinic. The idea was as terrifying as it was wonderful.

"For good."

"Well...if it's what you really want to do..."

"It is." Sighing, he linked their fingers together and brought them to his lips. "I told you, downstairs, that I was going to leave before I stooped to begging, but dammit, if that's what it takes—"

"No." She pressed the fingers of her free hand against his mouth, silencing him. "There's nothing you can say that'll change my mind, Caine."

"Nothing? Are you sure about that?"

"Positive."

Instead of moving away, as she had expected him to, Caine drew her close. He pressed his lips against her temple. "You're far too passionate a woman to give up what we have together." He kissed her eyelids. Her cheek. Her chin.

"You said I could always make you fly," he murmured, his lips gently brushing against her mouth. "But

I only ever felt that way with you. Let's fly together, Nora. You and me. Forever."

His words and his kisses caused a renewed flare of warmth. Against all common sense, Nora tilted her head back, giving his mouth access to her throat.

A soft silvery mist was fogging her senses, her body began to yearn. "I want to," she told him in a shuddering whisper.

"I know." His mouth skimmed down her throat, along her collarbone. Caine tugged the sheet free. "So why not marry me?"

When his tongue stroked wetly along the aching slope of her breasts, Nora realized that she was teetering once again on the very edge of seduction.

"Because," she managed, "you want a family." Caine was already imagining her hot and hungry beneath him. He was already remembering the soft little sounds she made when he made her rise, the look of astonished pleasure in her eyes when he took her over the edge. But Nora's unexpected words sliced through his erotic fantasy like a sharp knife.

"Are you telling me that you don't?" That idea had never occurred to him.

"No." Her skin, which had been warm and prettily flushed from their lovemaking, had turned as cold as ice and as pale as sleet. "I don't."

Moisture pooled in her distressed brown eyes.

Comprehension, when it dawned, was staggering. "It's because of Dylan, isn't it?" A single tear escaped, Caine reached out and brushed it away. "Nora, sweetheart, what happened to Dylan was an accident. It could never happen again."

Didn't he think she knew that? She was an intelligent woman. She had a wall downstairs covered with degrees to prove it. But that didn't expunge the absolute fear she felt whenever she thought about having another baby.

Loving a child was the greatest treasure any woman could ever know. And the greatest peril. And although she'd never considered herself a coward, Nora didn't think she had the strength to ever face such risk again.

"I don't want to talk about Dylan." Her hands pushed ineffectually at his chest.

Caine tightened his hold. "Dammit, Nora. I can understand what you're feeling. I can understand why you're afraid. But although life doesn't come with guarantees, I love you and you love me and that should be enough to get us through any storms that might come along."

"I can't handle it, Caine," Nora insisted, her voice rising unnaturally high. "Losing Dylan almost destroyed me. I won't risk that pain again. Not even for you."

"Not even for us?"

"No." The tears were flowing freely now. Nora dashed at them with the backs of her hands. "Not even for us."

"All right."

Caine dropped his hands to his sides although he wanted to go on holding her. Nearly as quickly as he'd dispensed with them in the first place, he located his scattered clothes and dressed while Nora watched silently, not trusting his sudden acquiescence.

"I'm going to leave now," he said, after he'd finished buttoning his shirt. "But there's something you need to know."

"What now?"

"Loving someone doesn't necessarily mean losing them."

He bent down, captured her chin in his fingers and held her wary gaze to his. "This time, I'm not going to get in my car and drive away, just because things have gotten a little rough."

A little rough? Her heart was lying in tatters all over the floor and he was calling things a little rough?

"I love you, Nora Anderson O'Halloran," he said, feeling an ache deep inside when his words and his use of her married name made her flinch. "Fully, totally, irrevocably. With every fiber of my being.

"And being an admittedly greedy man, I intend to spend the rest of my life making love with you here in this bed, or in front of a roaring fire, or even in the lake behind my cabin."

"We'd drown," Nora couldn't resist saying.

He smiled at that and she knew she was in major trouble when the sight warmed her to the core. "Not if we're careful." He ran his finger down the slope of her nose. "How long can you hold your breath?"

Before she could respond, he gave her a quick, hard kiss. "What do you think about an August wedding? The weather should be warm and sunny and your grandmother's flowers will be in full bloom, so we can hold the ceremony in her garden."

He was doing it again—refusing to listen to a word she said. Nora welcomed the burst of irritation; it overrode her pain.

"Caine, we're not going to get married."

"Wanna bet? Or are you afraid to put your money where that luscious mouth of yours is?"

She'd never been able to resist that challenge in his eyes. "All right, dammit. Fifty dollars."

"That's chicken feed. Five hundred says you'll be Mrs. Nora O'Halloran before the summer's over."

It was more than she could safely risk. But frustration at the way some things never changed made Nora rash. "You're on."

"Terrific." He brushed a hand down her hair and followed the corn-silk strands around her jaw. "Remind me to remind you of this conversation on our fiftieth anniversary. When we're sitting on the porch in our rocking chairs, holding hands and watching our grandchildren splashing around in the lake behind the cabin."

"For the last time—"

He bent his head and touched his mouth to hers. "See you around, sweetheart," he said when the brief, possessive kiss ended. "Call me when you've changed your mind."

And then, to her astonishment, he was gone.

Nora sat there in the middle of the rumpled sheets still redolent of their lovemaking, and listened to Caine take the stairs two at a time.

Downstairs, the grandfather clock struck the hour with a flurry of Westminster chimes. She heard the front door open, then close. And then there was only silence.

Dark, lonely silence.

Chapter 13

Although Caine spoke with Nora on the phone almost daily, filling her in on the progress of the trauma center, he managed, with Herculean effort, to keep his promise to stay away for four long and lonely weeks.

Despite the fact that the charter business was booming, he made time to talk public-relations firms in New York, Washington, D.C., and Seattle into donating their services. In addition, he'd convinced the governor to agree to declare the first week in September Children's Safety Week.

And if that wasn't enough to make his ex-wife sit up and take notice, an Academy Award-winning movie director Caine had once met at a New York premier was traveling around the country, filming a documentary about children in the emergency room. The Dylan Anderson O'Halloran Memorial Foundation was only paying the director's expenses; when contacted by Caine, the woman had agreed to donate her time and equipment.

Although Nora knew it took more than PR and governmental declarations and films to build a hospital, all the proclamations and public relations had already brought in a stunning amount of money.

As she watched Caine's unflagging devotion to this cause, which was so important not only to her, personally, but to all the children of the state, Nora was forced to admit how badly she'd misjudged him.

And with that realization came a long hard look at her own life. It wasn't that she'd purposely shied away from marriage since her divorce. In the beginning, work had required all her energy. Then, once she'd begun to date, she'd quickly discovered that although men might not be imbued with a woman's biological clock, they all definitely seemed to possess a strong sense of dynasty.

After Dylan's death, Nora had vowed never to give birth to another child. The risk was too great, the pain of loss too overwhelming. Whenever the man she was dating realized that she had no intention of bearing his child, he would drift on in quest of some woman who would, leaving Nora alone. Again.

The truth was, Nora was tired of being alone. The even greater truth was that there was only one man she wanted to share her life with. A month ago, Nora had been trying to convince herself that marrying Caine would be impossible. Now she knew that the impossibility would be *not* marrying him.

More nervous than she'd ever been in her life, and more determined, Nora left the hospital at the end of her shift and headed for the airstrip. Toward her future.

Caine had just landed a red-and-white six-seater aircraft and was taxiing to the hangar when he saw Nora's car headed down the road toward the tarmac.

"It's about time." He was on the ground, but his heart was suddenly back in the air.

"Handles like a dream, doesn't she?" the enthusiastic salesman beside him said, misunderstanding Caine's murmured statement. "And the club seating in the back is perfect for your kind of recreational charter work."

"She's a sweetheart, all right," Caine agreed, trying to keep his mind on bringing the turbocharged plane to a gradual stop when what he wanted to do was jump out of the cockpit, run across the tarmac, sweep Nora into his arms like some crazed guy in a shampoo commercial and never let her go again. She was parking next to his new blue Jeep.

"And the price is right," the man added.

"I said, I like the plane," Caine interrupted impatiently. He cut the engine, unfastened his seat belt and opened the pilot's door. "But something's come up. I've got your card. Why don't I call you tomorrow morning?"

Nora was getting out of her car. Caine saw a flash of thigh. "Make that tomorrow afternoon," he decided.

Business taken care of, he began briskly striding across the tarmac as Nora walked toward him.

They met halfway.

"Hi," she said softly.

"Hi, yourself."

"Nice plane. Is it new?"

"I'm thinking about buying it."

"Nice truck, too. Where's the Ferrari?"

He grinned. "I sold it. Figured it was time I bought a halfway grown-up car."

"It still suits you," Nora decided. Caine saw the flash of blue as she combed her left hand nervously through her hair. He caught her hand on its way down.

"I like your ring. It looks familiar."

"I like it, too." Breathless, Nora smiled up at him.

"In fact, I was thinking about keeping it."

It was going to be all right, Caine realized. They were going to be all right. "Oh? For how long?"

"How does fifty or sixty years sound?"

"Not bad. For starters." He pulled her close and gave her a long, heartfelt kiss.

Nora threw her arms around his neck and kissed him back, earning a rousing cheer from the ground crew.

"Come on, sweetheart," Caine murmured huskily. "Let's get out of here. Before we have to start selling tickets."

"Which house?"

"For now, yours, because it's closer. But later, why don't we live in the cabin and save your place for your clinic?" he suggested. "Until we get you pregnant. Then we can build that house with the picket fence."

The minute he heard himself say the words, Caine realized he was pushing again. He held his breath, waiting for Nora to stiffen in his arms.

Surprisingly, the decision to have children, once Nora had accepted her feelings for Caine, hadn't proved as difficult as she'd feared. She had no doubt that Caine loved her. And she loved him.

And it was that love which made the risk worthwhile.

"That sounds like a wonderful solution," she agreed.

Relief came in cooling waves. With his arm wrapped around her waist, Caine began walking with her back to her car.

"By the way, Dr. Anderson, you owe me five hundred bucks."

She'd forgotten all about their ridiculous bet.

Happier than she could ever remember being, Nora threw back her head and laughed. "Luckily for me, I'm going to have a rich husband to pay off my gambling debts."

The room looked and smelled like an explosion at a Rose Bowl Parade. Flowers were everywhere; on the utilitarian pine dresser, the metal dining tray, the windowsill, the floor.

"Wow! Look at this!"

Eight-year-old Johnny O'Halloran, wearing a blue Little League uniform with O'Halloran Air Charters stenciled on the back in bright red letters, plucked a white card from an enormous white wicker basket overflowing with tiger lilies, creamy orchids, purple gladioli and trailing jasmine vines.

"Miguel Cabrera," he breathed with wonder.

"How soon they forget," Caine grumbled good-naturedly to Nora. "I can remember a time not all that long ago, when the kid had me up on that lofty pedestal."

"That was before you put him to work painting all those pickets," Nora reminded with an answering grin as she packed a box of fragrant dusting powder into her red overnight case.

Caine had surprised her with the scented powder while she'd been in labor. Using a soft, crystal-handled brush, with unerring accuracy he'd smoothed it over all her sensitive spots, making her forget, albeit for a short time, all about the pain.

"I didn't mind helping Dad out with the painting," Johnny said dismissively. "It was cleaning up those brushes and things that was such a drag."

"I remember feeling the same way when my dad put me to work scraping barnacles off the hull of *The Bountiful*," Caine said.

"That sounds a lot worse than cleaning paintbrushes," Johnny decided. "At least Eric helped."

"You boys were both a big help," Caine assured him. He refrained from bringing up the slight argument over territory that had ended with both boys looking like snowmen, covered head to foot in Glacier White ten-year-guaranteed outdoor latex.

"I know." Johnny roamed the room, scanning each card in turn, reading off the names that sounded like an All-Star roster.

He wove his way back through the colorful profusion of flowers and stood looking down at eight-pound, six-ounce Margaret Caitlin O'Halloran.

"You must be pretty special. To get all this stuff," he said to the baby, who looked up at him with bright blue eyes and made a soft cooing sound. "Even if you are a girl."

Sensing a possible sibling rivalry beginning to brew, Nora ran her hand down his arm. "You're special, too, Johnny."

"I know. Because you picked me out."

"That's right," Caine added, ruffling the blond hair that was only slightly darker than the fuzz atop his daughter's head.

Now that Johnny had put on some much-needed weight and his face had lost that worried, pinched expression, he looked like any other eight-year-old boy. He looked, Caine and Nora had agreed, as if he could have been their natural son.

"And you've no idea how glad we are that we did."

Last year, while flying to Hawaii for a honeymoon, Nora had tried to come up with some way to broach the idea of Johnny becoming part of their family. She needn't have worried. They'd no sooner arrived at their Kauai hotel when Caine suggested adopting the boy they'd both come to care for so deeply.

"I'm glad, too," Johnny said.

He reached out a finger and touched one of Caitlin's tiny pink hands; the baby closed a pudgy fist around his finger and held it with surprising strength. "And I guess I'm glad I've got a little sister. Even if I was kinda hoping for a boy."

"I didn't know that," Nora said.

"So I'd have someone to play ball with," Johnny explained. "Girls like dolls better than baseball."

"Don't say that too loudly around your mother," Caine suggested mildly, "or you'll have to listen to yet another lecture on women's equality."

"It sounds as if one is definitely in order," Nora told them. "But we'll save it for another day."

She glanced around the room, checking to see if she'd forgotten anything. "I think that's it," She frowned at the wheelchair beside the hospital bed. "I hate that thing."

"As a doctor, you should know it's hospital rules," Caine reminded. "Have a seat, sweetheart. Your chariot awaits."

After Nora reluctantly sat down in the chair, Caine took their daughter out of the bassinet and placed her in her mother's arms.

Feeling a surge of emotion so strong it rocked him, he brushed a quick kiss atop Caitlin's head, then kissed his wife, lingering for a moment over the sweet taste he knew he'd never tire of if he lived to be a hundred.

"Ugh. More mushy stuff," Johnny groaned.

"One of these days, you and I are going to have a long father-and-son talk," Caine said with a laugh.

"About girls and kissing and all that other mushy stuff?"

"I'd rather talk about batting averages," Johnny replied.

Putting his arm around his son's shoulder, Caine said, "Come on, gang, let's go home."

Nora smiled up at her husband of ten months. "Yes," she agreed. Her heart was shining in her eyes. "Let's all go home."

Home. As he walked out of the hospital into the bright sunshine with his family, Caine decided there was no more wonderful word in the entire English language.

* * * * *

Dear Reader,

As a writer, I am often asked how I come up with new story ideas. And in the years since my first book was published, I still don't have a hard and fast answer for them. The spark of a story can come from anywhere—a news story, a situation of which I'm personally aware, a song on the radio, even a television commercial. But what has always held true from the first time I put a sheet of paper into my typewriter (yes, I *have* been trying to be a writer for that long!) is that it isn't the plot that is so interesting to me but the people themselves. What makes them tick? What makes them laugh and cry and love?

I first introduced the island of Turnabout and its residents in 2003. Some of the individuals living there are escaping their pasts; some are seeking their future. Annie Hess is just trying to survive. As a girl, she preferred walking on the wild side of life—her version of it, at least—as a defense against situations in her real life. She wore the mask of "bad girl" because it was safer than exposing her true self to more hurt. But now Annie is an adult, and even though she's left her wild side long behind, her life is still ruled by it. Logan Drake was never the "bad boy" in his youth. But the career he's chosen has him convinced he's not exactly a good man. They've both made hard choices in their lives. Now they're together again, and linked in a way that neither expects. The choices they make now matter more than ever before.

I hope you enjoy your journey to Turnabout with Annie and Logan as they come to understand that a mask is just that. A mask. It can be set aside. Particularly when the person who loves you knows that the mask never did quite fit.

Best wishes and happy reading,

Allison Leigh

HARD CHOICES

USA TODAY Bestselling Author

Allison Leigh

For my daughters, Amanda and Anna Claire.
Always a joy, continually challenging
and the greatest of blessings.

Prologue

"Don't."

She nearly sagged with relief at the deep voice that came out of the darkness. But she didn't sag too long; she took advantage of Drago's momentary surprise and twisted out of his loosened grip. The whitewashed stucco snagged at her dress as she pushed away from where he'd pinned her into the corner outside the boathouse.

Drago's surprise didn't last long, though. His hand shot out and sank into her hair, yanking her back toward him. She cried out, twisting her ankle as she tipped back, scrabbling at his hold on her. Tears stung her eyes. Her skin crawled as his mouth touched her cheek.

"I said, *don't.*" The voice came again.

It was all she could do not to whimper—in pain at the agonizing pull of Drago's hand on her hair, in relief that maybe her own stupidity wasn't going to be the end of her, after all.

The moment seemed excruciatingly clear. Drago's breath on her cheek. Her own whistling between her clenched teeth. And the faint scrape of a shoe on the damp walkway.

Her rescuer.

She shifted, trying to alleviate the pressure on her scalp. "Let go of me, Drago. I warned you to leave me alone."

He laughed softly, and slid one hand over her hip. "We had a deal, baby doll. Remember?"

She wriggled against his grip. "And the deal's off. You're dealing dr——ah!" She fell back against him at another vicious pull on her hair. She opened her mouth to scream, but suddenly, she was free. She stumbled, tried to right herself, but failed. She threw her hands backward to catch herself, but the sidewalk still met her rear with teeth-jarring force, and fresh tears clogged her throat, stung her nose.

Her hair streamed across her face. The curls she'd painstakingly ironed smooth were springing back to life in the damp air and she watched through them as Drago scrambled up from where he, too, had hit the sidewalk.

The man who stood over Drago was tall. Taller, even, than her brother, Will, who topped six feet. And he was dark. She didn't need the golden light cast by the iron lampposts to tell her that his dark hair was just shy of ebony, or that he was tanned. Not a cultivated tan like that her father maintained to complement his tennis whites, either. But the hard, bronzed kind. The kind worn by a man who could drop a thug to the ground without so much as creasing the classic black tux he wore.

"Don't move." Despite the laughter and music floating on the night air from the wedding reception, his quiet voice could still be heard.

She held her breath and looked at Drago, not wanting to acknowledge her own fear of what he might do. But he subsided, sitting on the ground, glaring at her, as if the entire situation were her fault.

It probably was, of course. Most things that went wrong in the sphere Annie Hess occupied *were* her fault.

And now, she had Logan Drake—her big brother's friend—to deal with as well.

"Are you all right?"

She gingerly brushed her hands together. Her palms stung like mad. She'd been trying to get Logan's attention for the past two days, ever since he'd arrived for Will's wedding. She hadn't intended him to notice her in this manner, though.

"Annie." Logan's voice was a little sharper. "Are you all right?"

She pushed her hair out of her face and nodded. He was watching her, his expression neutral. "Go back to the house," he said evenly. "Call 911. And get your brother or your father."

Her stomach clenched. "No."

Logan raised his eyebrows. "No?"

Drago smirked with satisfaction.

Annie wanted to kick herself. She'd been working like a dog to convince Drago that their relationship was over, that she didn't care what happened to him as long as he left her alone. "I don't want to cause a scene at Will's wedding," she said.

His gaze drifted over her and she shivered. "Then you shouldn't have invited your boyfriend, here."

"I didn't." She eyed Drago. He'd been the last person she'd wanted to see. And though she'd threatened him with the combined wrath of her father and brother, she'd failed to get rid of him on her own. "And he's not my boyfriend."

Logan's lip curled. "Right."

"Ah, baby doll, don't lie to the dude."

"Shut up, Drago." She wasn't going to sit there on the ground like a schoolgirl beneath Logan's censorious look. But rising was hardly an easy task, given the tight fit of her thigh-length dress. And she'd be damned if she'd hike the thing up to her hips just to stand.

Not with the way Drago was leering at her. She was nearly positive he was high. Why else would he have been so intent on getting her alone? Despite the appearance she'd fostered to others, he'd known the terms of their deal, and it hadn't included *her*.

Logan finally made an impatient sound and reached down, sliding his hands under her arms and lifting her to her feet as if she were some toddler who couldn't find her balance on her own. But when his hands slid away from her again, her heart thudded and her skin prickled in an entirely adult way.

His gaze traveled downward from her face, and it took every speck of nonchalance she possessed not to shiver visibly.

Logan Drake was her brother's friend. He was also her best friend's older brother. Yet she could probably count on her hand the number of times she'd actually *seen* him, and those incidents had left their impression. This time was no exception. He was dressed in the same sedate black tux that all the groomsmen wore, yet Logan possessed an edge the others did not.

And there was nothing Annie Hess liked better than walking on the edge.

"Get out of here, Drago, or I really will turn you in to the cops myself." She didn't look away from Logan as she spoke. She'd warned Drago that she'd turn him in, that she'd sic her father, the venerable judge George Hess, on him if he continued bugging her. He didn't need to know what an empty threat it was. She'd already sought out her father—and her mother—during the reception, when she'd realized Drago wasn't going to be so easily shaken.

Neither George nor Lucia—that's Loo-sha, dear—had been remotely interested in setting aside their champagne or their friends' company to assist their wayward daughter.

Again, her own fault. She'd taken up with Drago in the first place to annoy her parents. But that was before she'd realized he was into a whole scene she wanted no part of.

Annie walked the wild edge, but she wasn't a fool, and she had no desire to acquaint herself with a jail cell; which was definitely where Drago was headed if Will's warnings were to be believed. Since her brother was already ensconced in the prosecutor's office, believing him wasn't difficult.

"You're not going to turn me in, baby doll." Drago rose, flipping back his shock of gold-brown hair. He smiled, as cocky as he'd ever been. "You and me are two of a kind, remember?"

That uneasiness she didn't want to acknowledge coiled in her stomach again. "Hardly."

"Annie, go and do what I said." Logan's voice was inflexible.

She looked from him to Drago. Going to her father would be useless. And Will—well, Will was already annoyed with her. They'd always been a team. But now her brother had married the dazzling Noelle and Annie's one claim to any semblance of family who mattered was gone. He'd chosen Noelle, and that was that. Just like Lucia had warned. Will would have a new life and the troublesome Annie would have no place in it. He had a golden career ahead of him with Noelle-the-perfect right beside him. "Fine," she bluffed, and headed up the walkway. Her painfully high heels clicked on the stone.

The last place she wanted to go was back into the fray of the reception. Yet, if she hadn't cut off her own nose to spite her face and flatly refused to be one of Noelle's bridesmaids, Annie would be dressed in elegantly tasteful salmon silk and standing up there with the rest of the wedding party while Will and Noelle shoved raspberry-cream-filled wedding cake into one another's mouths and Drago wouldn't have had an opportunity to get near her.

"All right, all right, I'm going."

She stopped and looked back. Drago was shaking his head, backing away from Logan.

"Stay away from Annie. Permanently," Logan said. Her heart stuttered.

Drago's lips curled. "Wanting a little jailbait yourself?"

Annie winced as Logan's fist shot out, clipping Drago's jaw. Drago stumbled back, but didn't go down. His smile was oily as he turned and jogged away, disappearing into the thick stand of trees that bordered the palatial Hess estate.

Logan looked ready to pursue him and Annie hastily darted back to him, grabbing his arm. "He's an idiot. Let him go."

"So he can get away with assaulting you?"

"He didn't—". She exhaled. The truth was, she wasn't entirely sure what Drago would have done if Logan hadn't come along when he had. Before now, Drago had seemed content with the bargain they'd struck—she'd get him an in at her private school so he could pick up mechanic work on all the rich kids' cars, and though in public he'd portray the totally inappropriate boyfriend, in private he'd keep his hands off her. "Look, I'm glad you came when you did. But I meant it when I said I didn't want to cause a scene during the reception."

"I don't think you've ever walked away from creating a scene. What did your parents do? Threaten to disown you if something happened today?"

"My parents threaten to disown me every other week," she assured blandly. The truth was, she hadn't wanted to disappoint Will any more than she already had with her refusal to accept Noelle's efforts at friendship. "Believe me, they'll probably be disappointed when the day ends without me doing something to embarrass them in front of their guests."

From the other side of the boathouse, where the enormous awning had been erected on the richly groomed grounds, applause and cheering broke out from the revelers.

"Is that why you wouldn't go ask for their help?"

Annie kept her smile in place, but it took an effort.

"As it happens, I did ask."

He drew his eyebrows together. "And?"

She shrugged. "Well, Drago didn't leave until just now, did he?" She didn't like the look in his eyes. The one that seemed a little too close to pitying. "You should be back there." She tilted her head in the direction of the party. "Will's probably tossing the garter or something about now."

"Why aren't *you* back there?"

"What? To catch the bouquet?" She managed an uncaring shrug. "Not my style."

His eyebrow lifted. "You're seventeen years old. You don't have a style yet."

She nearly laughed. "I'll be eighteen in a few months, and you know better than that. Annie's style is to go wherever there is trouble, and if there isn't trouble yet, there soon will be once she arrives."

"Is that what you really think or are you just quoting your parents?"

Her smile faltered a little. "What's the difference?"

Another burst of clapping and laughter sprang through the night. Logan's steady, silent look made her feel positively itchy. "If you don't like something, Annie, you're the one who has the power to change it."

"Annie'll never change," she assured. "My parents say that all the time." She hated the way her throat felt, all tight. She focused hard on the empty champagne bottle lying in the grass beside the walkway until her vision cleared.

Then she nudged the bottle with the pointed toe of

her red pump. "Pity about the champagne. It spilled out when I tried to hit Drago with the bottle. Such a waste."

"I think you've already had plenty."

"Me? I'm underage, Logan, remember? You don't think I meant to drink it myself, do you?"

The corner of his lips tilted. "I'm well aware of your age, and yes, I do think you meant to drink it." His voice was as dry as the imported bubbly.

The man was intoxicating. More so than any amount of champagne she might have consumed on the sly.

"That's why you snuck down here by the boathouse, I suspect. To drink your little heart out."

"How nice of you to notice." She'd perfected that bored tone when she was knee-high to a grasshopper. But, when she languidly brushed her hair back from her shoulder and his gaze tracked the movement, she hid another little shudder.

"Oh, you're noticeable, all right. Somebody should put you on a leash."

Despite his wholly overwhelming appeal, she was more comfortable with this sort of exchange with him than any other. She didn't want his pity. She wanted his hands on her. Simple.

Her lips curved. "Why, Logan. Is there a bit of kink hiding beneath your straight-arrow exterior?"

He didn't look amused.

She exhaled, pouting a little, and walked closer to him. Her heels were so ungodly high that the top of her head nearly reached his chin. She tilted her head back a little, leaning toward him. Her heart was beating so hard that she wondered hazily if he could see it right through the wedge of skin revealed by the plunging V of her dress.

"What the hell do you think you're doing?"

"Giving you a proper thank-you." She pressed her lips to his jaw, settling her hand against his chest when her knees seemed too shaky to hold her.

"Fine." His voice was clipped. "You're welcome."

He hadn't moved, and she felt the heady beat of his heart right through the shirt he wore. Her palm still hurt, but the white silk felt unreasonably soft as she moved her hand down over his hard abdomen. Her lips tingled as she drew them along the hard, raspy line of his jaw. She rose on her toes, her mouth slowly, agonizingly nearing his. For an altogether too brief moment, his hand slid behind her neck, tangling in her hair. His lips hovered enticingly close to hers.

Then he suddenly set her from him, dragging her hand away from his belt as he pushed her back. "Dammit, Annie. You don't have to behave this way, just for the sake of getting some attention from your worthless parents."

Her defenses closed around her again like a vise. "You want me, Logan. I know you do." She leaned toward him once more.

His hands held her off. "Grow up." His voice was hard. "You're a beautiful, selfish little girl who doesn't think about anything other than what she wants."

His words stung. Not because it was the first time she'd heard such accusations, but because they came from *him*. "And you're saying you don't want to kiss me? Touch me? Believe me, Logan, I know when a guy's interested." Her gaze ran over him.

"Is this what you do back at that expensive boarding school you and my sister go to? Convince yourself that any guy you throw yourself at is interested just because you've gotten a physical reaction out of him?"

The truth was, she hadn't thrown herself at *any* man, until now. Everything up to then—the scores of boy-friends, Drago, the alcohol, the failed tests—had been just a front. A futile attempt to get kicked out of a school she'd loathed every minute of the three years she'd been there, to go back to parents who didn't have time or interest in her, anyway. The only reason she'd been allowed home from Bendlemaier now was because of Will's wedding.

"Don't worry about Sara," she said smoothly. Her roommate was at the exclusive school on scholarship, and despite the differences between them, they'd be-come good friends. "Your sister's still as pure as the driven snow," Annie went on. "And in a few short months, we'll graduate from that godforsaken prison and be out of there altogether." She smiled. "I'll be eigh-teen and you'll be, what? Twenty-three? Twenty-four? Come on, Logan. It's only a few months away. Weeks, really. Don't be so uptight."

His eyes narrowed. "So what do you propose here, Annie? Go into the boathouse? We'll just pull that ex-cuse for a dress you're wearing up another three inches and go at it, just because you think I *want* you? You're my friend's kid sister and I don't care what you think I do or don't want. If you want to get laid, go find that sleaze, Drago. He's probably still hiding out there in the woods. I'm not interested."

Without a second glance, he strode up the walk.

Annie leaned back against the stucco again, his words ringing in her head. There was truth in Logan's words. She *was* selfish. She wanted what she wanted when she wanted it.

She looked out over the narrow gleam of water beyond the end of the dock. More laughter and cheering echoed on the night air.

If it hadn't been for Logan, who knew what Drago might have done? Logan was the only one who'd noticed her absence, the only one who'd thought to investigate, and he didn't even like her.

It was pathetic.

She should have just stayed at Bendlemaier.

She swallowed past the knot in her throat and pushed away from the boathouse. She kicked off her shoes and they disappeared into the night to land silently somewhere in the thick green grass.

Then she walked around to the front of the boathouse and went inside where the catering crew had stored the cases of champagne.

Nobody would miss another bottle.

Chapter 1

There was no mistaking the sound of breaking glass.

Annie closed her eyes at the latest shatter and ordered her nerves to stop jumping all over the place. She didn't even really need to open her eyes to move to the rear portion of the shop, though she did. She knew every corner, every surface, inside and out. But considering how edgy she'd been for the past two days, it wouldn't have surprised her greatly if she *did* run into one of the chrome-and-glass display racks as she moved.

She stepped through the doorway that separated the stock- and workroom from the retail front of Island Botanica and took in the scene with a glance.

Bunches of lavender, rosemary and California poppy hung drying from the large grid-shaped rack suspended from the ceiling. And below the colorful, fragrant display a teenaged girl stood in the midst of broken dark-green glassware. "Are you hurt?"

Her niece looked down at the mess around her heavy leather boots. "That's the third bottle I've broken." Riley's voice sounded thick, as if she were near tears.

There were no signs of blood and Annie's heart began to settle again. She shrugged and plucked the broom from the hook on the wall and began sweeping up the shards. "It happens," she said calmly. "Particularly with a concrete floor." She realized her hands were trembling and tightened them around the broom handle. "Sara and I have joked about having the floor in here because we've broken so many things." She smiled a little. "Too impractical. At least concrete's easy to sweep."

The dozen bracelets around Riley's slender wrist jangled as she tucked her waving blond hair behind her ears. She stepped out of the way as Annie swept. "Dad'll pay for whatever I damage."

Annie's heart clutched a little at that. Since she'd unexpectedly shown up on Annie's doorstep two days ago, Riley had not voluntarily mentioned either one of her parents. Annie had been the one to insist on calling Will and Noelle to let them know their daughter was safe.

As safe as she could be given that she was in Annie's company.

She stopped sweeping for a moment. Started to reach out and touch Riley's arm, but stopped.

Instead, she bent over the broken glass and swept the broken glass into it. Riley hadn't been thrilled when Annie had insisted on calling her parents, but she hadn't bolted, at least. "Don't be silly. Nobody has to pay for anything."

"Except you and Sara, cause now you can't sell that." The girl jerked her chin at the rain of glass that tumbled from the dustpan when Annie tipped it over the large garbage can. "Dad said you guys are barely keeping your heads above water."

"Well, a broken bottle or two isn't going to ruin us," she said dryly. "It's all right, Riley. Truly." She began sweeping over the floor once more for good measure. "Why don't you finish unpacking that crate of bottles and then we'll break for lunch."

Riley's blue gaze flicked above Annie's head and she knew the girl was looking at the plain round clock on the wall. "A little early for lunch, isn't it?"

Annie shook the dustpan over the garbage can again before putting it and the broom back. "One of the perks of being an owner. Lunch whenever we want. I'll take you over to Maisy's Place. The cook there does a great lunch, and maybe we can still sit outside if the rain holds off." She managed a smile, feeling lighter at the prospect. Trying to keep Riley occupied in the shop all morning had been harder than she'd expected. But the shop needed tending, even on a stormy day, and she hadn't wanted to leave Riley alone. "Let me know when you're finished with that crate."

Threat of tears apparently gone, Riley nodded and reached again into the packing material that surrounded each bottle in the wooden crate. After a moment, Annie made herself go back out to the front of the shop. Riley didn't need her looking over her shoulder.

It was quiet that morning, much as she'd expect it to be in the middle of the week. Turnabout's small tourist trade picked up around the weekends, and the herbal shop, Island Botanica, Annie owned with her friend Sara Drake, picked up business then as a result.

Thank goodness for their mail-order trade, she thought faintly. If not for that exceptionally successful portion of their business, Will's opinion would have been borne out, and there would probably be no shop at all. Which was an unbearable thought.

She picked up a dusting cloth and moved across the light pine floor to the display cases at the window. The shop was small but still had an airy, simple and clean feel to it that Annie loved as much now as she had when she and Sara had opened it five years earlier.

Sitting atop the clear glass shelves were their trademark green glass bottles, jars and matching tubes. A person could get almost everything from tonics to perfume at Island Botanica, and all of it was made right there on Turnabout Island. She turned a bottle so the silver print on the narrow ivory label could be seen more clearly and dashed her rag over a fingerprint smudging the shelf.

She glanced through the windows lining the front of the shop, glad to see the sidewalk was still dry, then looked up at the dark clouds in the sky. If it hadn't been the middle of the week, she suspected that the threatening weather would have chased off any prospective customers, anyway. There was a storm moving in, no doubt about it.

Turnabout Island often had drizzly days, and the climate was ideal for the fertile fields that supplied the shop. But it wasn't all that often they had such threatening clouds hovering overhead as they'd had for the past several days.

The clouds had rolled in the same day Riley had arrived. Annie had been a mess of nerves, dread and euphoria ever since. Her niece had run away from home, but instead of disappearing completely, she'd come to Annie.

Annie still didn't really know why.

She twisted the cloth in her hands, turning toward the door as she heard the soft, tinkling bell that signaled someone entering. Her gaze had barely caught a glimpse of height and gleaming brown hair when Riley came in from the back.

"Auntie Annie, I'm finished with the—" Riley's voice stopped cold.

Annie glanced at her. "Great, Riley. Thanks. Just sit tight for a minute while I take care of—" Her own voice broke off at the sight of their visitor. Her foot fell back a step and she bumped into one of the display cases after all. Bottles jangled ominously but she was so rooted in shock she didn't even reach back to steady them. "Logan?"

"I warned them," her niece said, lips tight. "I *warned* them not to come after me. So he sent *you* instead. I'm not stupid, you know. I recognize you from Mom and Dad's wedding pictures."

The man drew his eyebrows together as he continued watching Riley. "Excuse me?"

Riley didn't lose her mutinous expression.

Annie felt as though her jaw must be near the floor as she gaped at the incomer. "Logan," she said again. "Logan *Drake?*" It had been years since she'd seen him in the flesh. *Years.* She'd believed that he'd lost touch with Will shortly after Will and Noelle got married. And even though Sara had spoken of him from time to time, the sight of him was still like a flashback to another life. Another time.

Another Annie.

Finally, the man looked from Riley to her. "Hey, Annie." The corner of his lips tilted and a fine spray of lines crinkled out from the corners of his unforgettably blue, thickly-lashed eyes. "It's been a long time."

Annie's stomach dipped and swayed. She wasn't sure who unnerved her more. Riley or Logan, who clearly wasn't surprised to see *her.* "A long time," she agreed faintly.

"You're a friend of my dad's," Riley accused.

"Who's your dad?"

Riley crossed her arms and stuck out her chin.

Annie started to push back her hair, realized she was still holding the dust cloth, and dropped it on the counter next to the cash register. "Logan—" even saying his name aloud felt odd "—this is m-my niece, Riley."

"Will's daughter?" Logan looked at the teen again. Assessing. "No kidding. Is he on the island, too?"

Riley rolled her eyes.

"No." Annie quickly stepped closer to her niece. She didn't entirely trust that Riley wouldn't bolt. And though Annie knew the girl couldn't get to the mainland from the island as easily as a person could hop a bus out of an ordinary town, she didn't want to take any chances. She wanted Riley to go home, not run away again somewhere she couldn't be found at all. "He and Noelle still live in Washington state," she told him.

Then she looked at Riley, speaking quickly before whatever was forming on her niece's lips could emerge. "This is Logan Drake. He might be an old friend of your dad's, but he's also Sara's *brother.* I...I'm sure he's here to see her and Dr. Hugo. He's from Turnabout. Isn't that right, Logan?"

His half smile didn't waver. "I grew up here," he confirmed.

"Bet you couldn't wait to leave it. There's hardly anything to do here, you know, even if it *is* part of California. There's, like, only five cars on the entire island. It's boring as hell."

"Riley!" She sent Logan an awkward smile. It was true that Turnabout was not a large island. Situated well off the coast of California, it was barely eleven miles long and less than half that wide, with a single road almost exactly bisecting the island down the length. Annie didn't own a car. Most people on the island didn't and instead walked, rode bicycles, or occasionally zipped around in golf carts.

"Sara's in San Diego for the week, I'm afraid," Annie finally said. "She, uh, she didn't say she was expecting you home." Truth be told, Sara rarely talked about Logan anymore, and when she did it was to speculate over the source of the money he seemed to have—evidenced by the generous checks he'd occasionally send Sara's way—or, more commonly, to bemoan his long absence.

That half smile of his, little more than a quirk at the corner of his lips really, hadn't moved. For some reason, it made her uncommonly nervous.

"She didn't know I was coming to visit," he said.

She understood his clarification. He wasn't *home.* He had no intention of staying. Though why he felt the need to clarify himself escaped her. It wasn't as if he was there to see her. She knew good and well what his opinion had been of her. There were some things that were not in her memory banks from sixteen years ago, but his opinion of her wasn't one of them.

Before she could stop the nervous gesture, she'd run her fingers through her hair. "Well, like I said, Sara is away. Riley and I were just heading over to Maisy's Place for lunch. You're welcome to join us."

He looked at her thoughtfully and she swallowed. What was she doing? She didn't ask men out to lunch, or to anything else, for that matter. Not anymore. Not even one on whom she'd once had an unrequited crush the size of the Cascade Mountains. Not even one who was the brother of her best friend.

"Oh." Her brain belatedly kicked into gear with an explanation for that look of his. "Of course you'll be wanting to see your dad, probably. I saw Dr. Hugo this morning when we came in to the shop. His office—well, of course you'd know where his office is." She was babbling and felt like an idiot.

"Actually, lunch sounds good."

For a moment, her heart seemed to stop beating. It had always been like that when Logan was around. Even back when she was only seventeen years old to his twenty-three. "Okay," she said faintly.

Riley huffed, a sound halfway between a snort and a groan. Annie ignored it. She was only Riley's aunt; pretending that she had a right to correct the girl's atrocious manners was—

She broke off the thought, recognizing the words that had been silently streaking through her mind. Words that Lucia had used, too often, to describe Annie's behavior, Annie's attitude, Annie's habits.

Nothing Riley did was *atrocious*, she reminded herself. The girl was a teenager, troubled enough to seek out an aunt she barely knew. The only thing Annie could do for her was to convince her voluntarily to go back home to her parents. As quickly as possible. Considering Riley's statement just now that the island was boring, perhaps she should focus on that angle with the girl—

She realized both Riley and Logan were staring at her. Obviously waiting. Probably wondering what was wrong with her. She smiled weakly. "Right. Lunch." She hurried into the back to get her wallet and grabbed the shop door keys as she came back out.

Logan and Riley were watching each other. It was a toss-up who looked more wary of the other. And now, because of her big mouth, they'd get to sit at a lunch table together. Joy, oh joy. She reached for the door only to find Logan's hand beating her to it. She jumped a little and felt her face flush at the nervous reaction.

Riley glared at her.

Logan looked satanically amused.

She hurriedly locked the door and set off across the bumpy road. What she wouldn't give for some of the mindless bravado she'd once had. She would have had a response for Riley's smart-aleck attitude, and she'd have looked Logan right back in those ungodly blue eyes of his without having some desire to collapse in a puddle.

She sneaked a look over her shoulder at him.

He looked right at her. Her heart squeezed and she hurriedly looked forward again. Who was she kidding? Even at seventeen, *particularly* at seventeen, she'd been a puddle where he was concerned.

Riley was already nearly Annie's own height. She easily caught up with her. "I don't care whose brother he is," she whispered, not altogether quietly. "I'll bet you a million bucks that my dad sent him to drag me home." A low roll of thunder underscored her words.

Annie looked up at the sky, half expecting lightning to strike right down from the roiling black clouds to the earth at her feet. Such an event would have been about as ordinary as having Riley and then Logan show up on Turnabout. She was acutely aware of the occasional scrape of his boot on the road as he walked right behind them.

She shivered. "You don't have a million dollars."

Riley made that impatient sound again.

"Well, maybe he is here because of your dad," she acknowledged softly. Coincidences did happen in life, but for him to show up now? It was stretching it.

"I won't go," Riley said flatly.

Yes, you will, Annie answered silently. Thunder rolled again. The air seemed far too still and full of energy, lying in wait for some perfect moment to flash.

"Storm coming," Logan said behind them.

Annie quickened her step, heading down the road to Maisy Fielding's inn. As far as she was concerned, the storm had already arrived.

Chapter 2

"As I live and breathe. Is that my very own nephew, Logan Drake?" Maisy Fielding, all five-feet-nothing of her, stood in the middle of the entry to Maisy's Place, her hands on her hips.

Despite himself, Logan felt amusement tug at his lips. Maisy Fielding was an aunt of sorts—her deceased husband having been his mom's cousin—and she looked the same as she had the last time he'd seen her. The same corkscrew red curls, the same migraine-inspiring colorful clothes, the same hefty attitude screaming from the pores of her diminutive person. "That's what my driver's license says."

She laughed heartily, then tugged his shoulders until he had to bend over her. She wrapped her skinny arms around him for a surprisingly strong hug. "Still have a smart mouth, I see," she said, patting his back. "Running away from Turnabout didn't change that a lick." She let go of him, and peered up into his face, her expression shrewd.

He wondered what she saw. Whatever it was, she waved her arm toward one side after a moment, encompassing the lush landscaping that surrounded the main inn. "Surprised you haven't managed to lose your license somewhere along the way. It took nearly ten years for the trees over at the corner to recover after you plowed that darned fool car of yours into them."

Behind him, Logan heard Riley stifle a snort. Of laughter or disgust, he couldn't tell. "Didn't expect the brakes to go out, Maisy," he said easily. "I managed not to take out the side of the inn at least."

She laughed again, a sure sign that time could heal some wounds. Twenty-three years ago when he'd been a brand-new sixteen-year-old behind the wheel of a rattletrap car his father had forbidden him to buy, Maisy had been plenty mad about him mowing down her trees. She'd meted out her punishment over an entire summer of drudgery. He'd done everything from scraping paint off her kitchen cabinets to babysitting her precocious daughter. Back then, he'd preferred dealing with the paint to dealing with Tessa. She'd been a pain in the ass.

And he still felt badly that he hadn't been around years later when she'd died. He'd only learned the news from Sara when one of her scarce letters had caught up to him.

"Well, if you're here for lunch, come on in," Maisy said, her eyes taking in Annie and Riley as well. If she saw anything unusual in Logan accompanying them, she kept it to herself, and Logan was glad. Maisy wasn't known for keeping her mouth shut when she figured something was her business. "Grapevine must have a branch missing that I didn't hear about you before seeing you." She turned toward the building. "Hugo didn't mention a word that you were coming."

Logan held open the door for the females, ignoring Maisy's reference to his father. "Business must be good. I remember you used to offer only breakfast."

"More tourists coming to Turnabout. They needed to eat somewhere." She walked straight through to an open-air dining area where at least two dozen other people were already seated at the round tables dotting the saltillo-tiled floor. "Sit anywhere you like. If it starts to rain, I'll find you a spot inside. Somewhere." She patted Logan's arm and scurried back inside.

"Have a preference?" He looked at Riley, who ignored him, and Annie, who shook her head slightly. He headed to the table farthest from the other patrons. Seeing Maisy was one thing, but he had no particular desire to run into anyone else he might know. He was only there to clear his conscience, not renew old acquaintances.

He held out Annie's seat, then habit had him sitting with his back to what passed for a wall in the dining area—a redwood trellis congested with climbing bougainvillea. A teenaged waitress he didn't recognize brought them glasses of water with lemon slices in them and they ordered after she'd recited the day's menu.

When she was gone, silence settled, broken only by the murmur of voices from the other diners. Logan looked around. The middle-aged couple with sunburned faces and crispy-new vacation clothes at the table nearest them were having a softly hissed argument. To their right was a smaller table, occupied by a lone young woman. She was reading a paperback book, occasionally looking up and studying the other diners as she toyed with her soup bowl. It was obvious to Logan that she was more interested in the people around her than the contents of her bowl. Beyond her was a young couple. Honeymooners, if he was any judge. They couldn't keep their hands apart long enough to eat their sandwiches, and beneath the iron-and-glass table, the woman was running her toes up and down the man's ankle. Logan half expected to see her slide over into her partner's lap.

He looked back at Annie. She was sitting quietly, her expression closed. Riley was studying her fingernails—painted such an ungodly black that it looked as if her hands had been caught beneath a ton of bricks.

The school picture that Will had shown him the day before had indicated how much she took after him, but in person the resemblance seemed less marked. Her expression tightened when she noticed him looking at her and she shifted in her chair, crossing her arms.

Classic defensiveness.

"I guess I don't need to ask if you and Sara kept in touch after you two graduated from Bendlemaier." Logan turned his attention back to Annie. He was perfectly aware of Riley's increased defensiveness when he mentioned the school. Another thing that Will had clued him into.

He and Noelle wanted to send their daughter to the exclusive boarding school. But it was apparent that Riley liked the idea even less than Annie once had.

Annie's smile looked forced. "I, um, I didn't graduate from Bendlemaier. But we kept in touch when she went off to college. We'd talked often enough about wanting our own shop, and when the opportunity arose, we went for it."

For some reason, Logan had assumed Annie had been in college with Sara. Showed how much he knew about his sister. He wondered if Sara had changed as much as Annie. Even though it hadn't been in his plans—which were to do what needed doing and get out of there as quickly as possible—he had more than a fleeting desire to see his kid sister.

He'd talked to her a few times in the past ten years on the phone, but he hadn't seen her in person in longer than that. He still remembered her expression the last time they'd seen each other. Confused. Hurt. It had felt like his skin was being peeled away to know he'd never come back to Turnabout to be any sort of brother that mattered. Instead, he called when the need to do so grew too great and sent her money to salve his conscience. After enough years, he could almost convince himself his system worked.

But he wasn't there to deal with *his* family issues. So he studied Annie for a moment. He'd fully expected to see her, since Will had told him that his daughter was staying with her, but he hadn't expected any of the feelings that had hit him when he did. "Your hair used to be longer, didn't it?" He knew good and well how long it had been. Thick and shining, its wild white-blond curls had reached down to the small of her back. All those years ago, she'd used that mane like a weapon against any male in her vicinity.

"Yes." She poked her fork into her water glass, spearing the lemon, which she squeezed back into the water. Her cheeks looked vaguely red. "You look pretty much the same to me." She glanced at Riley, making him wonder what she was thinking. "A little older, but aren't we all?"

"All this reminiscing makes me want to gag," you don't ruin our lunches," Logan suggested mildly.

"Then face the other way before you do, Riley, so you don't ruin our lunches," Logan suggested mildly.

She glared at him. It made him want to smile. She was very much like her aunt had once been. Full of attitude. The style of clothing had changed some in the past decade and a half, but she wore hers just as tightly and flauntingly as Annie had ever done.

He watched Annie's down-turned head for a moment. There was nothing flaunting about Annie's appearance, now. She had on a sleeveless khaki jumper that nearly reached her ankles over a short-sleeved white T-shirt. The dress was shapeless and the neckline of the shirt didn't even reveal the base of her slender throat.

She wore a plain watch with a thin black band on her left wrist and no other visible jewelry. Gone were the jangling metal bracelets, the chains around her neck, the multiple sets of dangling earrings. Her brown lashes looked soft and naked and if she wore a hint of makeup, she'd done it too subtly for him to tell. When she'd been seventeen she'd seemed to pile on the stuff with a trowel.

"Geez. Take a picture, why don't you?" Riley rolled her eyes and shook her head at him, her disgust obvious.

Annie looked up, her gaze flicking from her niece to Logan's face. Then her cheeks flushed again. She moistened her lips and seemed about to say something, but the waitress returned, arms laden with their orders, leaving Logan to wonder what had caused that flush—if it had to do with the past.

She'd never seemed the blushing type before.

The last time he'd seen her had been at her parents' palatial Seattle home, where he, along with the rest of the wedding party, had spent the night following Will's wedding. He'd been pretty damned angry with her.

But even angrier with himself. Her youth could explain her actions. He'd had no such excuse.

"Pass the ketchup, please."

He handed Riley the bottle, vaguely surprised by her politeness. But then again, attitude or not, she *was* Will and Noelle's daughter. He watched her dump it over her French fries. "Like to have one French fry with your ketchup?"

She made a face then nodded. He took the bottle when she was finished, doing the same thing with his own plate. "Me, too."

It earned him a studiously bored look.

Annie had ordered a salad. She stabbed her fork into it, moving lettuce and chunky vegetables from side to side, but not seeming to eat any of it.

"So, what did happen when you left Bendlemaier?" She didn't look up from her salad. "Not a lot."

"How come you don't still live on Turnabout, if you came from here?" Riley dredged a fry back and forth through her pool of ketchup.

"I had a job that took me elsewhere." It was true enough, though hardly the entire truth. He had the sense that Riley had only posed the question to keep him from asking more questions of his own to her aunt.

It struck him as oddly protective.

"What kinda job?"

"Riley, it's none of our business."

He shook his head at Annie's protest. "I became a spy."

"Yeah, right." Riley rolled her eyes and scooped up her dripping French fry, licking her fingers afterward.

"Okay, I'm a consultant," he said dryly. The lie had always been more palatable for people than the truth—even if he'd dared to share the truth with anybody who mattered. Even his associates had a hard time stomaching it. There were a lot of agents who worked for Coleman Black, the head of Hollins-Winword, in many capacities. But there was need for only one clean-up man.

"Consultant for what? Who?"

"Did you pick up that questioning technique from your dad? I always figured if he hadn't wanted to be a lawyer, he'd have made a good cop."

The teen wasn't fooled. "That's not an answer."

"What happened with *your* law degree?" Annie finally spoke.

"I stuck it in a closet where it's gathered a lot of dust." He smiled grimly. He did practice law. Just in a manner most people didn't want to be aware of. He'd felt that way himself many times. Until recently, though, he'd always been able to shake it, and get on with the job at hand.

A young woman with a white towel wrapped around her hips stopped by their table. "Anything else I can bring you?"

Logan shook his head. Riley sat back, her arms crossed. She'd eaten her ketchup-drenched fries and half her hamburger. Annie—who hadn't eaten even half of the salad, smiled up at the waitress. "I think we're fine, Janie. Thanks."

The waitress moved away. She hadn't been the one to serve them their meal.

"Who's the girl?" he asked, watching after her. "She looks familiar."

Annie followed his gaze toward the departing waitress. "Janie Vega. She helps Maisy out when things are busy. She's actually a stained-glass artist, though. Has her own studio on the island."

"Vega?"

Annie nodded. "I suppose you knew Sam Vega? She's his younger sister."

"I went to school with Sam." Janie had been a baby back then.

"He's sheriff now."

Logan shook his head, truly surprised at that. "When we were young, Sam wanted off the island worse than I did."

Annie toyed with her water glass. "When Sara said she hardly ever heard from you she wasn't joking. Otherwise you'd have known he was the sheriff."

Riley huffed again. "This is too old for words. I'm outta here."

"Where are you going?"

"I'll go back to your house or something."

Logan watched Annie's face. A dozen expressions seemed to cross it. Everything from alarm to reluctance to resignation. She passed her keys to her niece. "You can watch the shop until I get there."

Riley slowly took the keys. "You trust me?"

"You're not planning to go anywhere else, are you?"

Anywhere else like running away again, Logan interpreted.

"No." She turned on her heel and strode out of the dining area. Logan watched her go, calculating how likely it would be for her to get off the island if she'd been set on doing so. He'd already talked to Diego Montoya who—as he'd suspected—still ran the old man was already on the watch for Riley Hess. If the girl were to try to leave, she wouldn't be able to do so on Diego's boat. And fortunately for Logan's current purposes, the other residents of the island seemed to have held to the strange tradition of not owning any kind of watercraft more sophisticated than a dinghy. Only a fool would attempt the crossing in that small a craft.

When Riley was gone, Logan looked back to find Annie watching him. She set down her fork and pushed aside the salad with an air of finality. Her expression was unreadable. "Riley was right. Will *did* send you. I wasn't aware that you two were even in touch anymore."

"I was in Olympia and happened to look him up. He told me Riley had run away."

She raised her eyebrows. *"Happened?* Quite a coincidence. And how perfectly convenient that your consulting job allows you to head off to little-known islands whenever it suits you."

"I'm between assignments right now." It wasn't often he found himself feeling defensive, and he'd be damned if he knew why he did now. His answer was true enough, though. Except he didn't know how he could stomach another assignment after the last FUBAR. He'd told Cole that he'd needed a break, which was how

Logan came to be helping out on what should have been a straightforward runaway case. Except that Will hadn't been the one to ask him to help out. It had been Cole. Turns out his boss and Will had some dealings with each other. Dealings he hadn't known about until now.

Despite that, however, Logan didn't necessarily trust his boss to leave Logan to his task if his particular talents suddenly became necessary again. Cole's priorities were simple. Hollins-Winword—and all that it stood for, all that it protected—came first.

Annie's lips were pressed together. "Your job—whatever it is—doesn't really matter, anyway. Will should have come after Riley himself?"

Logan didn't necessarily disagree. Another argument he'd had with Cole and Will. "Your brother didn't want Riley doing something even more drastic."

"She threatened to run again if he came after her."

"I heard."

"But she needs to go home."

The fine line of her jaw looked tight. In fact, everything about Annie looked tight. *Uptight.* It wasn't a demeanor he'd have expected her to wear. "Is she causing you difficulties?"

"No. No, of course she isn't." She looked like she wanted to say more, but didn't.

"Has she told you why she left home?"

"Riley doesn't confide in me."

He frowned. "Come on, Annie. Riley didn't just run away and disappear. Fortunately. She came to *you.*"

Annie shook her head. She fiddled with her fork and spoon, neatly aligning them. "She's just curious about her black-sheep aunt who is odd enough to live on a small island."

Black sheep? She currently looked more like Bo-Peep to him. "Will and Noelle want to send Riley to Bendlemaier."

"It's a fine school."

Logan watched her for a long moment. "You hated it there."

"The academic program is——"

"You called it a prison."

"——unparalleled. Riley is very——"

"You did everything you could to get out of there."

"——bright. She'll excel there."

"Obviously you succeeded in getting out, since you've admitted you didn't graduate from Bendlemaier." He recognized her face. But the resemblance to the Annie of old was nil. "That's probably what your parents said when they sent you there. That you'd excel."

She stiffened. "You never did think much of me, Logan. But are you *really* comparing me to George and Lucia Hess?"

Impatience rolled through him. He leaned toward her across the small round table. "What the hell's happened to you, Annie?"

"I grew up," she said evenly. "What happened to you? You're the one who pretty much disappeared after Will and Noelle's wedding."

If she knew, she'd keep him miles away from Riley. "This isn't about me."

"Nor is it about me. This is about Riley and the fact that you're here to take her home because her father, my brother, couldn't be bothered to come after her himself."

"You know his reasons. He and Noelle are being cautious, given what Riley has threatened."

"Do you really think that Riley doesn't want her parents' attention despite what she says to the contrary?" She sat back, seeming to realize that her voice had risen. "Okay, so fine. You're doing your old friend a favor by retrieving his daughter. Actually, I'm surprised Will waited even a day to retrieve her, considering the unhealthy influence I'm bound to have on her."

Her tone was even. Neither defensive nor sarcastic, but factual. She could have been reciting geographic statistics from an encyclopedia for all the emotion she showed.

It bugged the hell out of him.

Years ago, there had probably been a portrait of Annie in the dictionary beside the word *precocious*, but she hadn't been a danger to anyone other than herself. "How long has it been since you've seen Will in person?" All Will had said during that very brief meeting they'd had—the only time they'd seen each other in more than fifteen years, in fact—was that Annie occasionally visited for Christmas, flying in and out just as quickly.

She lifted her shoulder. "Why does it matter?"

Because Logan already suspected that Will knew *this* Annie about as well as Logan did. Before he could get into that, however, he noticed someone entering the dining area.

He stiffened. Dammit.

"Maisy told me you were here," Hugo Drake said, stopping beside their table. "I had to see it with my own eyes, though. I guess they must be building igloos in hell 'bout now since you were pretty clear that particular place had to freeze over before you'd ever step foot on the island again."

He looked up at his father, a man he'd loathed for so many years he could barely remember feeling anything else for him. Hugo Drake was still a robust man, though the years had left their mark in the white hair, the fading eyes. But the old man still had an unlit cigar sticking out of the pocket on his shirt.

Annie had risen and was dropping bills on the table. "Where are you going?" He ignored his father.

"Back to the shop."

Her gaze darted between him and Hugo. He wondered what she was thinking. And he wondered why it mattered. He didn't care who knew about his feelings where his father was concerned. The guy had made his mother's life a misery. She'd downed a bottle of pills rather than stay married to him. Rather than hang around to finish raising her son and daughter.

Logan hadn't hated living on Turnabout so much as he'd hated being Dr. Hugo Drake's son.

He doubted all that many things had changed in the twenty years since he'd been to Turnabout, and he knew that particular thing had changed least of all.

He stood, picked up Annie's money and handed it back to her. Right or wrong, he paid his own way in life. "I'll see you later at the shop."

Her lips parted softly. But he'd already put enough cash on the table to pay the check and was walking away.

He was on Turnabout for one specific reason. Because his boss had ordered it. And that reason didn't include playing the prodigal son to the man he held responsible for his mother's death.

Chapter 3

Logan wasn't at the shop when Annie got there. Which surprised her and relieved her—and disappointed her—though she hardly wanted to dwell on that point. Given what little she knew about him now, and what she remembered of the man she'd once briefly known, she figured he wouldn't stay away for long. He'd come to the island for a purpose. She couldn't see him not fulfilling it.

Since they wanted the same thing—Riley to return home—she decided to blame any disappointment over his absence on that aspect.

Riley, though, *was* in the shop, sitting on top of the counter by the register, blowing pink bubbles in her chewing gum and watching her boots as she swung her feet in small circles.

"Has anyone come into the shop?" Annie put her wallet back in the cupboard.

"Nope."

"Any phone calls?"

"Nope."

"Any gorillas prancing down the street wearing pink tutus?"

"Yup."

Riley looked up, her latest bubble deflating around her small mouth. She plucked the sticky stuff from her lips and popped the wad of gum back in her mouth. "Yup."

Annie smiled faintly. She tugged at her ear, rubbed her hands down her arms. "Riley—"

"Huh-uh." Her niece hopped off the counter. "I don't wanna talk about it. I'm not going back."

"I wasn't—okay, I was." She studied the girl. "I haven't pressed you about anything since you arrived, Riley." She hadn't known what to do. Had been nearly paralyzed from taking any actions—sensible or otherwise. But Logan's arrival had spurred something. "Maybe if you'd just give Bendlemaier a chance, you'd—"

"Like you gave it a chance? I heard you tell that old dude you didn't even stay long enough to graduate."

She almost laughed. Logan was definitely not old. He was a mouthwateringly fit man in his prime. Which was not at all what she needed to be thinking about. Ever. But Logan had always had that effect on her. Even when he was scathingly telling her to grow up. "His name is Logan, he's hardly old, and I did go to Bendlemaier for three years, whether I graduated from there or not. But this isn't about me."

Riley shook her head, and walked over to the display

nearest the door. She picked up a bottle. Studied the label. Put it back and picked up another. "How come you never got married, Auntie Annie?" She ran the phrase together like it was one long word—anteeanee.

"Nobody ever asked me," Annie answered, lost for something more appropriate. It was the last question she might have expected.

"You think women have to wait to be asked? My mom asked Dad to marry her, you know."

Annie hadn't known that. But it seemed like something Noelle would be capable of doing. She wasn't a woman to wait around for someone else to speak when there was something in her sights. Annie could appreciate that trait now, though she hadn't back then. Not when she'd believed that beautiful, accomplished Noelle Reed was marrying Will and thereby taking away the only semblance of family that Annie cared about.

"No, I don't think women have to wait to be asked," she told Riley. "But as it happens, there's nobody that I've ever wanted to ask anyway." She'd have to allow herself into a relationship of some sort, first.

"Do you have a boyfriend? A lover?"

Good grief, the girl was persistent. "No. I don't sleep with men I don't love." She didn't sleep with anyone.

"Why not?"

"Logan was right. You've learned your questioning technique from Will. Do you have a boyfriend?" Maybe it was more than just the issue of Bendlemaier that had driven Riley to run away from home.

"No."

Relief dribbled through her.

"Mom and Dad wouldn't let me date, anyway," Riley

added. "They'd just think I was out trying to have sex or something."

"Sex! You've barely turned fifteen."

"So? There's a girl in my class at school—my *real* school, not that stupid Bendleboring—who is pregnant out to here." Riley's hands stuck straight out in front of her. "It's disgusting. She's stupid. I mean, hasn't she ever heard of the pill? They sell condoms in machines in the bathrooms everywhere." She dropped her hands and worked them into the pockets of her tight jeans, casting Annie a sidelong look. "Logan'd be your boyfriend if you wanted."

"Your conversation is making me dizzy," Annie murmured. From condoms to Logan? "Logan is not here to stay, obviously, and he's not interested in me."

"He stared at you all through lunch."

Only because he couldn't figure out what had happened to the wild Annie he'd known. And she hadn't felt inclined to tell him that she'd buried her alive in an inescapable crypt. "Riley—"

"Was he your boyfriend before?"

"No!" She swallowed and lowered her voice. "He was your *dad's* friend, Riley."

Riley didn't comment on that. Merely blew another enormous bubble that popped with a soft snap when she stuck it inside her mouth and bit down on it.

Annie let out her breath, feeling as chewed-up as the deflated bubble. "What if I talk to your dad about you not going to Bendlemaier? Will you go home, then?"

Riley, it's the middle of the school year. You're missing classes." And unlike Annie had been, her niece was a stellar student. Another reason why her appearance on Annie's doorstep seemed so shocking.

"So, I'll go to school here."

God. "That's not what I—"

"That *is* a school we pass going into town from your house, isn't it?"

Riley knew good and well that it was. It wasn't large, but the brick building was obviously a school. "Yes, but it's for the kids who *live* here."

"You just want to get rid of me, too."

She exhaled, exasperated. "Riley, nobody wants to get rid of you. But your home is with your parents. Whatever problem there is can be worked out."

"Dad says you haven't talked to Grandma and Grandpa Hess in more 'n ten years."

Your dad talks too much, Annie said silently. "Will and Noelle are nothing like George and Lucia." Thank heavens.

"Well, why can't whatever problem you've got be worked out with *them?*"

She had no parental instincts inside her. She didn't know how to deal with a young girl who—from Noelle's reports—had been captain of last year's debate team at her school. "Riley—"

"Never mind. If you don't want me here, I'll go." She suited her words with deed and pushed out the door.

Annie followed her out. Fat drops of rain had just begun to fall. The air was redolent with the scent of an impending rainstorm—wet, dusty, earthy. She hurried across the narrow sidewalk onto the bumpy road. "That's not what I said!"

Riley looked over her shoulder, continuing to walk away from Annie. "I just thought you'd care. But nobody cares. Not really." She looked ahead, her boots picking up the pace.

Annie's heart tore. She could actually feel the pain of it ripping through her. How many times had she felt exactly the same way? Only their situations were decidedly different. Her parents *hadn't* cared, Riley's did.

She swiped a raindrop from her cheek, darting after her niece, grabbing her by the shoulders. Forcing her to stop. "Everyone cares, Riley. Your parents were beside themselves with worry when I talked to them."

"Right. That's why they're pounding down the door of your beach house." Riley's eyes were stormier than the sky.

And Annie knew, for once, that her instincts had been right on the mark. Riley had run away, but, despite her threats, she'd expected her parents to follow after her. A show of love. A grand gesture. Something to prove she mattered to them.

Déjà vu, she thought wearily and prayed that this would be the only incident of it.

"You scared them, Riley. They believed your threats." She chose her words carefully. Not wanting to worsen the situation, which—when it came to family matters—was what Annie had generally done exceptionally well. "But make no mistake. They want you back home. Where you belong."

Riley just shook her head. Her blond hair was darkening from the rain, clinging wetly to her cheeks, making her look impossibly young. Vulnerable. "Why? They're never around, anyway. Dad's campaigning for work and Mom's traveling for work." Then she pulled out of Annie's hold and kept walking.

"Where are you going?" Panic raised Annie's voice. Riley's arms lifted then fell back to her sides. She never looked back.

"She won't go far. Diego's not going anywhere with this weather churning up the way it is."

She jumped, startled at the deep voice. "Where'd you come from?"

Logan smiled faintly and lifted his chin toward the building not ten feet away from where they stood in the middle of the road. "Stopped in at the sheriff's office to say hello to Sam. Couldn't help but notice you and Riley out here." He opened up the black umbrella he held and lifted it over her head.

Annie's gaze followed Riley whose posture—even at the increasing distance—screamed dejection. "I need to go after her."

"Take the umbrella, and get inside soon. Sam said the weather service thinks there's gonna be a bad blow. Storms usually miss Turnabout, but better to be safe."

She hesitated for only a moment. He was there to retrieve Riley, of that she had no doubt. So why was he allowing even a moment of time before doing so?

"Go, Annie," he said quietly. "I'll lock up the shop for you."

She swallowed, turned and went.

It was raining in earnest when Annie reached her house about twenty minutes later. As she let herself inside, her heart was in her throat, nearly choking her. Then she heard the shower running in the single bathroom.

Uncaring of the rainwater dripping from her onto the ceramic-tile floor, she pressed her back against the wall in the hallway and listened to the blessed sound of the bathroom shower. She was shivering. Not just from the chill caused by the rain, but from the past that seemed to loom up in her face no matter how many times she tried to push it behind her.

She slowly slid down until she was sitting on the floor and pressed her wet head back against the wall. Through it she could hear the hiss of the shower even more clearly, as well as the diminishing drum of raindrops on the roof. They grew more sporadic as she listened. Maybe the storm would pass by Turnabout, after all.

The thought was hopeful, but brief, being cut off by a long, crackling rumble of thunder.

From inside the bathroom came the squeak of pipes, the cessation of water, the metallic jangle of shower-curtain rings. By the time the door creaked open several minutes later, Annie was in the kitchen, a clean bath towel slung around her neck, her wet jumper replaced by a sweatshirt and baggy jeans. Riley finally came into the room, her expression wary as Annie pushed a chunky white mug across the breakfast bar toward her.

"What is it?" Riley's voice was suspicious. "Not that weird tea you make out of weeds, I hope."

Annie had quickly found that chamomile tea was *not* a hit with Riley. "Hot chocolate."

"With marshmallows?"

"Is there any other way to drink it?"

Riley crossed to the bar and picked up the mug. She lifted it carefully. Annie thought she might be smelling it. She took a sip. Followed by a longer one.

"It's *good*."

"Don't sound so surprised."

"Mom's hot chocolate is awful. No caffeine, no fat, no nothing."

Annie lifted her own mug, her smile growing. Noelle was beautiful and model-thin. There'd been a time or two on Annie's rare visits to their home when she'd heard Will admit to sneaking out for a cholesterol-laden steak and loaded baked potato behind his wife's diet-conscious back.

Riley slipped onto one of the barstools and hunched over the breakfast bar, cradling the mug. "Mom says marshmallows are all sugar."

"When we were kids, your dad wouldn't drink hot chocolate unless the cup was nearly overflowing with marshmallows."

"I'm a lot like him." Riley made the announcement as if it were a sentence being pronounced. "Mom says that all the time. I'm just like *him*." Her lips twisted as she peered into her mug.

"He's a good person," Annie said quietly. "You could do worse than be like Will." Far better that than to be like Annie.

"How come you don't have kids?"

Annie lifted her hot chocolate again and managed to singe her tongue drinking too deeply. It was early afternoon, yet the kitchen was darkening. She flipped on the light. "Some people aren't cut out to be parents," she finally said. "Fortunately, Will and Noelle are."

Riley's expression closed. She turned away from the counter, bare feet stomping across the tile. A moment later, Annie heard the slam of the bedroom door.

She cursed herself for pushing too far. Sighing, she put her mug on the counter next to Riley's. Neither one of them had finished.

The sliding glass door that led out to the small deck drew her and she moved away from the counter. Outside, the ocean beyond the narrow strip of beach looked gray and forbidding. She opened the door anyway and went out onto the deck. The rain had stopped, but the wind had picked up. Heavy, dark clouds skidded overhead.

The chaise that had seen Annie through more sleepless nights than she cared to count was wet. She pulled the towel from her neck to dry it off, then threw herself down on the seat. The wind tugged at her hair, flinging it around her shoulders. The temperature felt as if it had dropped twenty degrees since that morning. She wished she'd thought to put on socks.

"I told you to get inside."

Her head jerked. Logan had appeared around the side of the small house. He stepped around the elevated frame of her ancient water cistern. When her heart drifted back down from her throat, she chanced speech.

"Which explains why you're sneaking around outside my house." Once again, she found herself wishing that he'd do what he'd come to do and go. It would be painful—like the worst kind of bandage being ripped off her skin. But at least it would be quick.

He came toward her, looking even taller from her half-prone position. The wind was doing a number on his hair, too. Blowing through the short, thick strands of dark brown to reveal a few strands of silver. He was as darkly tanned as she remembered. The contrast made his blue eyes seem even brighter. Logan—in the flesh—made her feel as edgy as he ever had.

The sooner he left, the better.

"Riley is inside. You should take her now. You wouldn't want to get stuck on the island if the weather goes even more sour."

"In a hurry to see her go, Annie?" His expression

was considering. "Having a teenager around cramping your style?"

She swung her legs off the chaise and rose. "There's no style to cramp. She doesn't belong here with me. She belongs at home with Will and Noelle. Nothing's going to be solved by her remaining here. Everybody, including you, knows that."

"Maybe she just needs a breather. Don't you remember needing a breather when you were her age?"

"When I was her age, I'd already been at Bendlemaier for months. And the last place I wanted to be was at home with George and Lucia."

His lips twisted. He gave her a sidelong look that tightened her stomach. "Liar."

She stiffened. "What?"

He moved, catching her chin in his big palm, tilting it toward him. She went stock-still, her senses going way beyond alert at the close, windblown warmth of him.

"You heard me," he challenged softly. "When you were Riley's age, you wanted nothing more than to live at home, to have normal parents who cared more about you than their careers, to go to the same public high school that Will had gone to."

"I never told you that," she said stiffly.

His thumb gently tapped her chin. "You didn't have to tell me everything. It was obvious, Annie. And that night at the boathouse, you said—"

"I said a lot of things." She felt exposed with her face firmly tilted up to his gaze. "And I was drunk," she finished flatly.

"Nearly," he allowed. "On champagne you had no business drinking."

"Well, you were the only one who noticed."

"That pissed you off, too, didn't it?"

She stepped back, deliberately lifting her chin away from his hold. "It was a long time ago and has nothing whatsoever to do with the reason you're here."

"Are you so certain about that?"

Her knees felt weak. She refused to sit, though she wanted to. Badly. "Yes, I'm certain."

The corner of his lips lifted in that saturnine expression of his that visited her too often in her sleep. Ridiculous, really. And maybe it was only because she simply didn't get involved with men—hadn't for more years than she could count on her fingers—that she was beset with memories of this one man in particular.

She'd humiliated herself with him at Will's wedding reception, after all. Her youthfully inflated ego had convinced her that he must surely have had the hots for her, mostly because she hadn't been able to look at him without feeling as if her nerve endings were on fire.

Well, he'd corrected her on that score.

He could have taken advantage of an impetuous and spoiled teenager intent on playing with fire, but he hadn't. So, regardless of the wicked cast of his lips, Annie knew that Logan, like Will, was a straight arrow. Despite his devil-dark looks, he'd probably never even crossed the street against the light.

"Aren't you curious, Annie?"

She snatched at the towel when a gust of wind picked it up off the chaise. She twisted the terry cloth in her hands. "About what? Riley's real reasons for running away from home? It's hard to believe it would just be Bendlemaier. Noelle says that Riley has made a small career out of negotiating things she wants or doesn't want in life."

"That's all you're curious about? Only Riley?" He stepped closer again.

Beyond them, a colorful beach ball hurtled over the sand, followed by a scrap of paper that hung on the wind. For some reason, the sight of them made Annie even more aware of the solitude of her house. Her nearest neighbors were more than a mile away.

She swallowed. "That's all I can afford to be curious about."

"Sounds awfully cautious for the Annie I knew."

Her eyes burned. She blamed it on something in the blowing wind because she didn't cry. Not anymore. "The Annie you knew no longer exists." Her words were barely audible. "She learned her lessons the hard way."

"What lessons?" He jerked his head up before his lips finished forming the question.

An awful buzzing whine had rent the air. Piercing. Loud. Annie nearly jumped out of her skin and covered her ears. "What is that?" She had to yell to be heard above the alarm, above the awful thunder that was suddenly crashing overhead, sounding as if mountains were collapsing.

His hand was on her arm, pushing her through the glass door he slid open. "That's the emergency siren. A hangover from the Second World War. Get Riley."

Annie had lived on Turnabout for five years. She hadn't even known there *was* an emergency siren. She ran to the second bedroom and threw the door wide, calling Riley's name.

But the room was empty.

Chapter 4

Annie's heart stopped.

Riley wasn't in her bedroom.

Before she thought about the idiocy of it, she darted into the room, looking under the bed when she knew perfectly well the only things that fitted under there were the shallow plastic storage boxes that contained a lifetime of photographs. She also yanked open the closet door. But all that was inside were her vacuum cleaner and clothing she never wore.

"Riley?" She stumbled around the twin-sized bed to peer out the window that overlooked the front of the house, only to jump back with a cry when a palm branch slammed against it, then screeched along the side of the house as the wind carried it.

Logan was there, arm sliding about her waist, bodily

lifting her away from the shuddering windowpane. "Stay away from the glass."

She was beyond listening, twisting away from him, nearly falling over the foot of the bed again as she ran into the hall, calling Riley's name again, barely able to hear her own voice over the wail of the emergency siren.

Darkness seemed to have fallen in the span of minutes, broken by the hideous strobe of lightning that seemed too close and far too dangerous. "She's not in the house." Panic choking her, she headed toward the door, only to find Logan blocking her way. "I have to find her!"

"You don't even have on shoes. I'll go." He reached for the door himself. It blew out of his grasp when he opened it, slamming back against the wall behind it before he caught it again. "Stay here. Inside. She can't be far."

He'd barely disappeared out the door before Annie ran into her bedroom. She shoved her feet into her tennis shoes and followed him.

Her sweatshirt was immediately soaked, her hair whipping around her head, nearly blinding her as she ran around the side of the house. The wind tore Riley's name from her throat, and the siren wailed on and on and on, threatening to madden her.

Where was Riley?

Logan had headed up the path that passed for a road in the front of the house. Annie took the beach behind the house instead. Squinting against the sand that managed to blow despite the deluge of water pounding down on it, she ran past the black, cold fire pit, all the way down to the frothing, roiling edge of water. Peered right and left, staring hard between flashes of light, her heart beating so viciously she felt ill. "Riley!"

But the only thing she saw was an empty ribbon of beach.

Keeping a tenuous grip on common sense, she ran back toward the house. A sob broke out of her throat when her foot caught on a piece of driftwood and she pitched forward in the sand.

She pushed up to her knees, bowing her head against the rain that seemed to blow horizontally, right into her face.

Please, God, let us find Riley safe and sound and I'll take her right back to Will and Noelle. I promise.

Her canvas tennis shoes were full of sand, heavy with water as she unsteadily gained her feet and trudged onward, more carefully this time. Around the side of her small house, sand giving way to gravel, gravel to grass that was drowning in the water that fell too rapidly for the earth to absorb. Her rubber soles slid in the pools of water and she fell again, words coming from her mouth that she had banished from her vocabulary a decade and a half earlier.

She righted herself, shading her eyes with her hands from the storm as she bent against the weight of wind, battling her way to the front of the house, calling Riley's name until her throat ached.

And then she saw Logan in the center of the road.

He was alone, and her stomach dove.

She ran toward him. "I didn't see her on the beach! I don't think she'd have gone toward the water." Riley knew how to swim. Annie had photographs of her as a little girl, wearing a pink polka-dot swimsuit, being coaxed into a swimming pool by Noelle. But surely Riley would know better than to go near the water now.

Logan caught her arm, pulling her closer to him, seeming to shield her from the brunt of the storm. "I told you to stay inside."

"We have to find her, Logan."

He looked grim. "We will."

Lightning streaked overhead, filling the air with an odd scent. He swore and practically lifted her off her feet as he hauled her farther up the road, away from the palm tree that suddenly burst into flame. She watched, horrified, as it split in half and tumbled to the ground where they'd been standing.

The rain quickly doused the fire.

Annie covered her mouth, staring wildly around them. She didn't have time to be nauseous. Riley was out in this. Alone.

"She can't have made it to town. It'd take too long. Which means, if she's smart, she tried to find some shelter on the way."

Annie shuddered, nodding. "I'm going with you."

He grimaced, but kept hold of her as they headed toward the main road. She was grateful for the support. She'd never felt such wind in her life. Every few steps they managed, it seemed as if the rain switched directions. Blowing straight into their backs one moment. Straight into their faces the next.

Evening was hours off yet, but the clouds were so dense, so heavy, it felt as if night had already fallen. The constant, racking thunder made a mockery of her attempts to call out Riley's name.

"Dammit," Logan cursed, when a river of water

coursed toward them, nearly knocking her off her feet as it washed away the gravel.

"I'm sorry!" She scrambled to maintain her balance. She'd never realized the path was a natural wash before, because it had never rained this much.

He wasn't looking at her. Water streamed off his arm as he lifted it, pointing. "There."

She looked. On the other side of the wash stood an open-sided shack. Sara had told her once that the people who'd built the house where Annie now lived had sold produce at the stand.

"Stay here." Logan's voice was hard. "I'll check it out."

Annie swallowed. In the past decade she'd come to depend only on herself, and this went against every instinct she'd garnered. But she nodded.

He moved away and she realized immediately just how much his tall, broad body *had* shielded her from the storm. The wind plowed into her with such force she felt bruised by it. She slipped and slid her way to the edge of the wash and wedged herself against the boulders that were clustered there.

The water was up to Logan's knees as he crossed against the flood. His progress was slow, but it was steady. Then he made it to the shack.

The wind tore half the roof off and she cried out, watching it head toward him. He lifted his arm across his face, ducking. The wood glanced off him and bounced, end over end, until it slammed into a tree and splintered apart. He didn't stop, though, and disappeared into the shack only to reappear a moment later.

He carried Riley in his arms, running flat out toward Annie, splashing through the torrent.

"She's all right." His deep voice cut through the bellowing storm. "Get back to the house."

Too relieved to argue that she wanted to run her hands over Riley to feel for herself that she was okay, Annie slid away from the boulders and ran. Impossibly, the storm seemed to pick up strength with every step she took. Before she knew it, Logan had grabbed her arm and, still carrying Riley in one arm, nearly carried Annie as well. Beyond the danger of the swelling wash. Past the destroyed palm tree that blocked the lane.

She could hear his harsh breath, and knew hers sounded worse. They nearly skidded across the grass, and Annie darted forward, shoving open the door. It took a death grip to hold it against the wind, as Logan carried Riley inside and set the girl on her feet. Annie surrendered the door to Logan and grabbed her niece in her arms, pulling her close.

"Thank God," she whispered, breathless. "Thank you, God."

"We've gotta find a more secure—" Logan broke off, swearing, when the door blew open again.

Annie let go of Riley long enough to lend her weight against the door. Her wet hands fumbled with the heavy dead bolt that she'd never had cause to use before. It finally slammed home, but still the door rattled and jumped, and she had serious doubts the lock would hold against the punishing wind.

Thinking ahead of her, Logan had grabbed one end of her couch and shoved it up against the door the moment she moved out of the way. "That'll hold it for a while," he muttered. "Only time I remember them setting off the siren was when I was ten years old. Scared the living hell out of me. Everybody went to the school then. Stayed in the basement there."

A thunderous clap shuddered through the house. Windows vibrated. Lord, she didn't want to go back out in that. Fortunately, the road that had become awash didn't head straight toward her house, but they'd still have to cross it to get to town. "We can't make it to the school—" She broke off with a gasp when something crashed against the back side of her house. The glass doors shuddered.

"The bathroom," Logan said abruptly.

She could feel Riley shivering. She rushed the girl back down the short hallway and into the small bathroom, yanking folded towels off the shelf next to the sink as she moved. "Wrap these around you," she told Riley.

"Into the tub."

Annie didn't question Logan. She climbed into the tub. Riley followed, back to Annie, sitting between her legs. Logan flipped the light switch, but the power was definitely gone.

Around them, the house groaned and creaked. The emergency siren ceased as abruptly as it had begun. She contrarily wished it had continued wailing.

"Got candles? Flashlight?"

Annie continued tugging the oversized towels around Riley's shoulders and forced herself to think through her panic. Riley was in front of her, shivering, but safe. That's all that mattered.

"There's a flashlight in the kitchen somewhere," she said shakily. "Maybe the bottom drawer next to the stove. And, um, there are a few candles in my bedroom on the dresser."

He left.

Riley shivered violently. Annie hugged her arms around her niece. She had a strong desire to screech *what were you thinking* but she battled it down. "It'll be okay," she whispered instead.

The girl sniffled. "This is supposed to be an island paradise."

Annie hadn't been seeking paradise when she'd come to Turnabout. Only peace.

She pressed her forehead against the top of Riley's dripping head. Will would never forgive her if something happened to the girl.

She'd never forgive herself.

"Are you hurt anywhere?"

She felt Riley shake her head.

Logan was back in seconds. He handed Annie the flashlight and told Riley to set the candles in the tub in front of her. He also carried a gallon jug of water that Annie had left on the kitchen counter earlier that week. It hadn't fitted in her refrigerator because she was storing Island Botanica products there. He set the jug on the floor then left again.

"He's coming back, isn't he?" Riley asked a moment later. Her voice was very small.

Annie closed her eyes, wincing with every crack of thunder that shuddered through her little house. "Logan won't leave us," she promised faintly. Where would he go? Back out into the storm?

He returned quickly, bearing the blanket from Annie's bed as well as several sweaters that he dumped on the ledge beside the tub. Then he muscled the mattress from the guest room's bed into the bathroom.

She wasn't sure what shocked her more. That he'd

gone through her drawers to find dry clothing, or that he'd managed to fit a twin mattress into what she'd always considered a frightfully small bathroom.

Logan gestured at Annie and she quickly slid forward, urgency nudging out the shock when he worked his big body into the tub behind her, and pulled the mattress close until it leaned lengthwise against the edge of the tub.

Then he exhaled roughly, and managed to yank his wet shirt over his head. He tossed it beyond the mattress and it fell on the floor with a wet slap.

"Okay, this is getting seriously weird," Riley muttered. She was crunched forward, her legs bent to allow room for the two adults behind her. Her boots thumped against the porcelain. "Don't take anything else off, or I'm outta here."

"Riley, he's as wet as you are."

She huffed, but fell silent.

Logan grabbed the blanket and began working it around Annie's shoulders much the way Annie had wrapped Riley in towels.

"No, wait," Annie tried to hold him off. "You must be cold, too."

Riley huffed again, then yanked one of the towels from her own shoulders and held it back to Annie, who gave it to Logan. "What's with the bed?"

"So we can pull it over our heads if necessary," Logan's voice was matter-of-fact.

"Are you *kidding* me?" Riley's voice rose. "Auntie Annie, is the house going to blow away or something? This is *Turnabout*, not the freakin' *Wizard of Oz!*"

Annie closed her arms around her niece, enfolding

her in the blanket, too. Riley was shaking like a leaf. So was she.

Then Logan closed his arms around her and for a moment, just a brief moment, relief swept through her, calming her own panic just enough that she could sink her claws back into it and keep it under control.

Logan had found Riley.

They were all safe.

"Three men in a boat," Logan muttered. As far as Annie could tell, his breathing was already back to normal, while she still sounded—and felt—as though she'd just run a marathon.

And there they sat while the earth shuddered and the sky seemed to fall down around them. Annie realized she was peering into the hallway, watching the flash of lightning, holding her breath as she felt the steady drum of Logan's heartbeat against her back.

"Turn on the flashlight again," Riley finally begged. "Can we at least turn on a light?"

Annie flipped on the flashlight. Her own panic was starting to weasel out of her hold on it. She couldn't lose it again. There was no time.

No space!

She focused on what was physical. Logan, a reassuringly solid presence, his warmth steaming through their soaked clothing. Riley, a soft, trembling weight leaning back against *her*, for comfort.

They'd get through this. It had been a long time since Annie had had *any* storms in her life—this one just happened to be a physical storm, rather than an emotional one. And she'd survived the emotional ones. More or less.

She tilted her head to look up at Logan, only to

find the dark cast of his eyes watching her through the gloomy light.

Annie was suddenly aware of the intimacy of their positions. Of the fact that—beyond the clinging wetness of her sweatshirt and the increasingly damp blanket—his chest was pressed against her back. Hard, wide and feeling damnably perfect.

The kind of chest that could shelter her from a storm.

And had. The thought was tinged with hysteria.

And then, just then, the storm went silent. As if it, too, were holding its breath.

His long fingers skimmed over her cheek and her mouth went dry. She shuddered and the warmth of him against her wasn't merely a barrier against the fear of the storm outside, but something else, entirely.

She felt his chest lift in a deep, long breath.

His fingertips, warm, steady, glided along her jaw. Fleetingly touched the corner of her lips.

She stopped breathing.

Impossible memories of his warm touch, his rough sighs, slipped into her mind. Impossible, because he'd turned her away all those years ago. Impossible, because what they'd shared had lived only in her dreams.

Then he broke the taut moment. "Storm's here," he said, his tone arid. His hand fell away from her face, wrapping instead in the fold of the blanket around Annie's shoulder.

Her breathing kicked in, leaving her feeling dizzy. Or maybe it was only the effect of the uneven strobe of lightning that filtered into the bathroom from the rest of the house.

Riley made a choked sound. Annie had barely realized it was nervous laughter, when the house heaved a great, wrenching moan.

Logan swore, pushing down on both Annie and Riley as he dragged the mattress over their heads.

Chapter 5

"Oh...my...God."

Annie stared around at what remained of her house. Horror made her dizzy.

They'd stayed cramped in the bathtub, huddled under the suffocating, steamy warmth and protection of the mattress for what had seemed hours. But now, through the gaping hole in her roof, she could see the hint of sunlight trying to break through the clouds, and knew it couldn't have been all that long, after all.

Not until the boisterous racket of the storm ended had Logan pushed aside the mattress, along with an appalling amount of debris and allowed them to unfold their cramped bodies. The worst of the storm seemed to have passed, leaving behind a gentle, misting rainfall.

A rainfall that came right through her house, since there was a good portion of roof missing.

"Geez," Riley muttered, staring at the mess—wallboard, shingles, palm fronds—that had pummeled the mattress and littered the bathroom and hallway. "Serious bummer. Good thing you thought of the mattress," she said. "Otherwise that stuff would've landed on us, huh."

If it weren't for Logan's steadying hand warming the back of her neck, Annie thought she might well pass out. "We don't have tornadoes here," she protested faintly.

"It was probably a downburst or a microburst," he said. His hand left her neck and she blinked, trying to make sense of everything as he grabbed one of the dry sweaters he'd gotten from her room and pushed it into her hands. He looked prepared to dress her in it, as if she were incapable of doing so herself.

She probably was. She went into her room and quickly changed, slipping the limp sweatshirt she wore off and pulling the dry sweater on in its place. It felt heavenly.

But there was nothing to be done about Logan's wet clothes. She had nothing handy that would remotely fit his wide shoulders, and pants were even more out of the question. His shirt still lay in a wet heap on the floor of the bathroom underneath the debris.

But he'd pulled on his leather jacket by the time she rejoined them, and Annie managed to keep her eyes averted from the wedge of hard brown chest that showed above the half-fastened zipper.

"We learned about microbursts in science," Riley was saying. She'd already changed into drier clothes, having escaped the confines of the tub the moment Logan gave the okay. "They can do as much damage as a tornado, but they don't, you know, twist." She whirled her hand. "The force just comes straight down and blows out at the base." She shrugged, suddenly looking uncomfortable at providing them with the science lesson.

Logan nodded as he surveyed the damaged roof. "We're going to need to cover that roof up before the rain does even more damage inside."

"With what? The only wood I have around here is for burning in the fire pit out on the beach." Annie picked her way through the debris in the short hallway, fearing what she'd find in the main portion of the house. She couldn't bring herself even to wonder about the fields that supplied Island Botanica.

Without their plants, they'd have nothing. Without products, they'd have nothing. *She'd* have nothing. Again.

She deliberately pushed away the dismal thought and focused on the immediate. The glass door off the living room looked undamaged. The window in the kitchen was broken to pieces. Annie's chaise from the deck poked halfway through it, leaning drunkenly into the sink below the window. One of her cupboards hung half off the wall, the door opened to display the broken glass and dishes inside it.

"Toto, I don't think we're in Kansas anymore," Riley said, joining Annie by the breakfast counter. "All we need are some flying monkeys and the wicked witch and it'd be like we're living inside the *Wizard of Oz* movie. How are you going to get all this fixed again?"

"I always hated those flying-monkey things," Annie murmured instead of answering something she had no answer for. "They gave me nightmares." The two half-full mugs of chocolate still sat on the counter, twin sentries oblivious to the tempest that had occurred around them. The marshmallows had melted into the liquid.

She went around the counter, picked up the mugs and reaching through the legs of the chaise, dumped the cold cocoa down the sink. When she turned away, Logan was watching her, his expression strangely gentle as he set the gallon jug of water that he'd rescued on the countertop. "Try to make that last," he suggested. "I'm going to town to see if I can find something to cover the holes in the roof."

Annie nodded and moved around the counter to look through the unscathed glass door. If she tried to speak, she feared she would burst into tears. She hadn't cried in years and she had no intention of starting up again.

"Want to come with me?"

She turned around, only to realize that Logan had offered the invitation to Riley.

"Why? So you can drag me off the island?"

He just looked at the teen and finally she made a face and shrugged. "Whatever."

Logan moved the couch away from the front door, positioning it back where it belonged. It had done the job, at least, of keeping the door from flying open. He stopped to pick up a potted fern that had tipped over, spilling soil onto the tile.

"We won't be long. Don't try to pick up anything that's not stable." As if his words were prophetic, the loose cabinet in the kitchen gave a squeal of splitting wood and plunged to the floor, bouncing off the counter along the way.

Shattered glassware and dishes flew.

Annie choked back a shocked yelp and turned her gaze from the sight.

Riley was the first to break the thick silence. "Well that sucks. Hope that wasn't the family china or something."

Annie shook her head. "I think I'll go with you, too," she said. "There may be houses hit worse than mine. People who might need help."

The thought was somber and the three of them left the house in silence. Outside, it was still drizzling, and Annie ran back inside long enough to grab her umbrella from its hook in the coat closet as well as a bright yellow slicker. She told Riley to put on the slicker, then opened the umbrella and Logan held it over all three of them.

The water that had flooded the narrow road had already narrowed to a trickle. The sun was beginning to set, bathing the thick ribbons of clouds and everything below them with an otherworldly cast of red and orange.

Annie's feet dragged as she stepped over the felled palm tree. The vivid sky seemed all the more remarkable because of the rainbow that glittered, looking close enough to touch.

Rainbows were supposed to be a sign of hope, weren't they? But as she watched, the wondrous arch faded, leaving only the sunset behind.

Logan stopped, too. "Turnabout always did have unbelievable sunsets. The best view was from the Castillo House, though, at the point of the island. Old place probably doesn't even exist anymore."

"Yes, it does." Annie had a particular interest in the abandoned Mission-style house, but she was more concerned with Riley, who'd walked on ahead of them, only to stop and wait near the very boulders that had kept Annie from blowing away earlier. She put thoughts of rainbows—and hope—right out of her mind as reaction set in, making her shake at the awful "what ifs."

"She thinks she's too cool to walk underneath the umbrella," he said.

"I should have marched her right back to Will and Noelle," she said. "The day she showed up. Instead of *calling* my brother, I should have taken her back myself."

"She's okay, Annie. She's not hurt. She's probably feeling pretty foolish for leaving the house, too."

"She's okay only because you were there and knew what to do. You found her. Brought her back to the house. It never would have occurred to me to use a bathtub and a mattress for protection."

"You'd have found her if I hadn't. You'd have thought of something."

She was beyond listening, though, as she sloshed through the water and hurried up the gravel. "Riley should never be in danger. Ever. She's just a girl, a baby. Completely innocent and undeserving of——"

"Hey." He closed his hand around her shoulder and halted her. "No kid deserves to be in danger. But this was a storm. A freakish one. You didn't wiggle your pretty nose and summon it. And it's not like you can protect your niece from *life.*"

Why not? Annie barely kept from crying out the words as they heard a vehicle and the distinctive crunch of tires on gravel. In seconds, the sheriff's truck appeared and Sam Vega stuck his head out the window. "Yo, Annie. Everybody okay at your place?"

Avoiding Logan's eyes, Annie jogged over to the olive-drab vehicle. "We're not hurt," she assured shakily. "What about in town?"

Sam looked grim. "We've got a dozen or so injuries, so far, the least of which is Janie. She was trying to save some of her special glass and ended up breaking her wrist, instead. I'll know more once I've made it across the isle to check on everybody. A lot of windows broke in the winds, but most of the buildings are okay. Your shop'll need some boarding up. Got a report that Diego's dock is history, though. I haven't been by your fields yet."

"The dock?" Dismay settled like a stone inside her. Her fields overlooked the dock. "What about Diego's boats?" She struggled to keep her voice steady.

"Out of commission for a while," Sam said. His gaze went past her to Logan. "If somebody *has* to get on or off the island, it'll be by Coast Guard."

She could feel the edges of her sanity unraveling. "What about a plane? A charter? When Dr. Trahern and his wife took April Fielding off for surgery last year, they did it in a plane that landed on the main road." Her brother had connections and plenty of money. He could arrange a plane or a helicopter for Riley's sake. Cell phones didn't work out on the island, and the phone lines were undoubtedly down along with the electricity, but surely if the sheriff could reach the Coast Guard, they could manage a way to contact her brother.

"And that plane tore the hell out of the road, which wasn't in great shape to begin with. Even a chopper would have to be an emergency, Annie. The coastline is socked in from Mexico on up. We'll be lucky if this——" Sam's gesture encompassed the destruction that had already occurred "—is all we have to contend with. Before we lost communications, the weather service was warning that several storm systems were on a collision course with each other. The weather's bad here. It's worse on the mainland. They've got straight winds that are tearing the hell out of San Diego."

And Sara was in San Diego. Annie pressed her hand to her mouth, struggling for composure.

"She wants to get Riley home to her parents," Logan said.

Sam shook his head. "Riley is physically unharmed. On a scale of priorities for getting to the mainland, that means she's not going to be at the top. I'm sorry, Annie, but that's just the way it is. Hugo can do a lot with those who are injured, but his clinic is small and underequipped. Anybody needing more serious medical attention will be the first to go. My suggestion to you is to try to board up the windows at your shop—"

"And her roof at home," Logan added.

"—whatever needs doing," Sam's gaze took in Logan also, "and hunker down. At best, we've got a few days of cleanup. At worst..." He shook his head, obviously not wanting to elaborate. "So, if you guys are okay, I've gotta head on. I'll come back when I can and we'll get that palm dragged off the road."

Annie nodded and stepped away from the truck. She heard Logan offer his assistance should Sam need it, then he, too, stepped back. Sam reversed his truck up the gravel, passing by Riley who'd perched herself on the boulders to wait, and headed off into the shadows.

The light from the truck's headlights bounced over the scrubby bushes lining the hillside, seeming to reflect back on the truck because of the wall of mist shrouding the landscape.

Annie swept back her damp hair and headed toward Riley. "I need to see how bad the fields are." She didn't wait to see if Logan followed.

Of course, he did.

Riley slid off the boulder when they reached her. She said nothing, but apparently it was dark enough to quell her worry over appearing cool, for she fell into step alongside Annie underneath the protection of the umbrella that Logan still held.

The fields were in the opposite direction to the town and it was dark by the time they got there. With no moonlight to guide them, it was impossible to see what sort of damage they'd sustained. She closed her eyes against what she couldn't see and battled back fear of the worst.

Logan's hand touched her shoulder. "We'll come back when it's light."

Annie's eyes burned. She moved. His hand fell away.

They turned toward town, walking down the center of the roughly paved road that would lead them straight into the heart of Turnabout. When they reached it, people were walking up and down in front of the storefronts, circles of illumination from their flashlights bobbing along as they checked businesses and property.

She wished again that she'd thought to bring the flashlight, but she'd forgotten it in the tub when Logan had pushed back the mattress.

"What are they doing over there?" Riley pointed toward the community center across the street from them. Affectionately dubbed the "biggest building on Turnabout" by the residents even though it really was no such thing, the center had its doors opened wide. A fire burned in the domed iron fireplace outside the building and in the light from that, Annie recognized several people carrying boxes of every size through the doors.

"Taking supplies to a central point," Logan said.

"Riley, why don't you go on over there," Annie suggested. "The community center has a generator of its own. I don't imagine it will take long for someone to get it going. And there's no point in you freezing out here while I check the shop."

Riley hesitated. But a group of teenagers huddled around the heat of the fire, and after a moment, she headed toward them.

Annie watched long enough to see her niece approach the group, then, just as easily get swallowed into it. Relieved, she turned away, glancing at Logan as they set off for her shop near the other end of the string of businesses. "I'm glad she's not shy. It's debilitating."

"You were never shy a day in your life." Logan caught her arm when her shoe caught on a bump in the dark sidewalk.

"Yes, I was. Painfully." She hurried her step, mostly to get away from Logan's hand since her imagination was telling her that her arm was tingling beneath her thick sweater.

"You were born to be the life of the party."

She crossed her arms, surreptitiously rubbing that spot on her elbow. Apparently, her imagination was really in fine form. "I learned to *act* the life of the party," she corrected wearily. "It was easier to do that than let anyone see what I was really like."

"And it got George and Lucia's attention more effectively?"

Annie lifted her shoulder, neither agreeing nor disagreeing. She didn't like talking about her parents. She'd been an enormous disappointment to them. She cast a look his way, wanting to get the subject off herself. She'd been foolish for even touching on her past.

"What were you like as a teenager?"

"When I wasn't running down Maisy's trees at the inn, you mean? I'd have thought Sara would have filled you in chapter and verse."

"Like we had nothing more interesting to talk about than you?"

"I'm wounded." He pressed his hand to his chest. But she'd caught the gleam of his teeth and heard the smile in his voice.

It charmed her.

And she didn't want to be charmed. Particularly by a man who would be leaving Turnabout as quickly as possible. "You don't have to come with me to the shop. I'm capable of screwing in some planks of plywood over my windows if need be."

"And where are you going to get the sheets of wood?"

"I have some in my workroom, if you must know. And even if I didn't, I'm sure someone else would have some. Turns help each other out when it's called for."

"You weren't born on Turnabout. Therefore, you're not officially a Turn," he said smoothly. "You might consider yourself an islander now," but that doesn't change facts and make you a Turn."

"No, but your sister is a Turn, and she's my business partner. Courtesies get extended to me as a result."

He snorted softly. "Honey, you're dreaming if you think the die-hards of this place will ever truly accept you. They have too much respect for the Turnabout curse that says Turns and outsiders don't mix. That curse has been around a helluva lot longer than you have."

"Spoken with all the sureness of being a Turn yourself," Annie scoffed, even though she secretly feared there was a grain of truth in his words. Though she felt a part of the community, there still remained a lingering sense that she was not entirely accepted. Trusted.

"I wasn't born on Turnabout," Logan said. "I'm no more a Turn than you are."

Her toe caught another buckle in the sidewalk right in front of the broken plateglass window of her shop. She barely kept herself from pitching forward onto her nose, and was grateful when she didn't. She already felt as if she'd been hit by a truck. "But Dr. Hugo is a Turn, and so is your sister."

"So?"

"Well, where were you born, then?"

"Oregon."

She didn't remember Sara ever mentioning Oregon. "Your family must have lived there before Sara was born, I guess."

"My parents were separated for a while. They reunited after I was born," he said flatly. "Now, do you want to show me where this plywood of yours is, or should I head through the shop window like a bull and find it myself?"

Feeling well and truly put in her place by his tone, Annie unlocked the door. Though Logan had been right; they could just as easily have walked in through the window that no longer existed. Despite the darkness, she found her way across the retail front, and was relieved that the racks and cases seemed to be where they belonged.

In the workroom, she took a candle from the stock shelves and felt through the jumble atop the desk for one of the lighters that Sara was forever stealing from her father. Annie had always wondered why Sara bothered, considering that Hugo never did use his lighters for his cigars. But for now, she was glad of it when she found one and used it to light the candle.

She set it on the desk then lit a few more, until there was a soft, warm glow inside the workroom. She pointed to the pallets in the farthest corner of the room, beyond the oven they often used to help dry herbs.

"Plywood," she said. "Sara and I had it shipped here a few months ago. We're planning to build more shelves back here for the stock, but we haven't gotten to it, yet."

He moved toward the pallets, ducking to keep from knocking his head into the bundles hanging by string from the frame that hung suspended from the high ceiling. "Handy for us," he said.

Annie found the toolbox and brought it out to the front while Logan carried a sheet of wood. She winced anew at the crunch of glass beneath their shoes. "What a mess. And," she lifted a forestalling hand, "I know. It could be a whole lot worse. I have no reason to complain." Of course, she hadn't seen her fields, yet, either.

"I didn't say anything."

"You didn't have to." She held the door so he could carry the wood outside, then knelt down to open up the toolbox. "I can hear the judgment in your voice." She pulled out her cordless drill and handed it to him, then poked through the contents of the box until she found the jar of screws. She also found a tiny metal flashlight and flipped it on, but the batteries were dead. She tossed it back into the toolbox.

His shoulder held the plywood against the building as he took the jar and flipped off the lid. "Believe me, I'm in no position to judge anyone." Finding a few screws that satisfied him, he set the jar on the ground, then lifted the wood into place. In seconds, he'd secured it. Then he went back inside for another sheet, came out, and repeated the process. Soon, there were three large sheets of wood covering the gaping hole.

"Might as well wait until it's light to clean up the glass inside," he said as she came out with a push broom to clean off the sidewalk as best she could. He reached for it, but she didn't let go.

"I'm perfectly capable of sweeping up the mess."

"And apparently, you're capable of building your own stock shelves," he said, and deftly slipped the broom handle from her grasp. "I noticed you didn't say that you and Sara planned to have shelves *built*, but that you planned to *build* them." He shook his head a little. "Who would've thought?"

Annie crossed her arms and leaned back against the covered window, watching him work. She enjoyed it a little more than was comfortable.

Logan Drake had always been impossibly good-looking. Now, in dark jeans and a leather jacket, with his hair messy, his jaw bristled, and his hands capably dealing with wood and power tools, he was lethal.

"You're a chauvinist," she observed faintly.

His laugh was short. "If that means I think men have a duty to protect women, then I s'pose I am."

She looked away from the way his jacket gaped

against his chest. "But women aren't capable of protecting men?"

"Didn't say that."

"Or that men can't protect men? Or women protect women? And I'm not talking about personal relationships, here."

He paused, lifting his head to watch her through the darkness. "Neither am I. And believe me, Annie, there are men who'll protect men at *all* costs."

Disquiet sneaked through her, displacing her unsettling preoccupation with his physical appeal. There was something decidedly dark in his tone. "Speaking from experience?"

She thought he wouldn't answer. He began pushing the broom again. Then finally his motions ceased. Just for a moment. He looked at her, and she felt as if that look seeped into her very pores, filling her right down to her toes with a strange sense of sorrow.

"Yes," he said quietly. "I speak from experience."

Chapter 6

"Heard you were back, Logan."

"Good to see you back, Logan."

"Finally came home, eh, Logan?"

How many times had Logan heard variations of that particular comment? And how many times had he shaken his head and assured the greeter that he was only visiting?

Too damned many.

It was well after midnight and the community center—a hive of activity for hours—was now nearly silent. A dozen lanterns had been placed around the large interior to help save the load on the generator that would have to last for who knew how many days. Now, the lanterns were dimmed as low as they could go without being extinguished, and in the faint glow they emitted, Logan looked around.

Victims of the storm were settled in on cots, borrowed sleeping bags and donated bedrolls. There were no crying babies at the moment and no more gales of laughter that more often than not had verged on the edge of hysteria.

Outside the still-open community center doors, the fireplace was dark. Despite the protective dome, the flame hadn't been able to sustain itself when the rain went beyond mist to drops, to deluge. He could still hear the rain, but now there was no damaging wind, no lightning strikes.

At least he'd managed to get the sheet plastic down in time over the holes in Annie's roof, though it'd been close. He'd managed only because Maisy had sent her handyman, Leo Vega, along in a golf cart to help him soon after he'd finished up with the boards over Island Botanica's window.

While Annie and Riley stayed in town and continued helping out where they could, Logan, Leo and a half dozen other men from around town had made the rounds, including Annie's place. They'd covered windows and roofs, using up even Annie's leftover plywood on the worst, but some places had been damaged beyond repair.

And despite the work that had required all of their energy, there had still been plenty of talking going on.

Some things about Turnabout didn't change at all. The grapevine was one of them. Without trying—and he had definitely *not* been trying—he'd heard about Dante Vega being up for parole again, about Diego's latest bass-fishing trip and about the looker who'd arrived barely a week ago to stay at Maisy's Place who seemed extraordinarily curious about the people and places on the dinky island.

And once they'd gotten on the subject of females, the talk really took off. From Darla Towers who'd just gotten a divorce because she was bedding any guy who'd smile her way, to Annie Hess who'd freeze out any guy stupid enough to look her way.

With a little pressure, Logan learned from Leo that he'd been working on getting Annie to go out with him for more than a year, with no success.

Even though he knew Leo—several years younger than his brother, Sam—from way back, Logan had wanted to nudge the guy off the roof they'd been covering. He'd satisfied himself with the egging comments Leo had gotten from some of the other guys that maybe Annie Hess's refusals of Leo had more to do with her good taste than with a lack of passion.

Logan rubbed his hand down his face, brushing away the thoughts. It seemed a helluva lot longer than twenty-four hours since he'd been in Will Hess's office, thinking he'd been given a convenient opportunity to make up for a long-ago sin by retrieving Will's runaway daughter.

Annie sat down beside him with a rustle of her baggy denim jeans. She let out a long sigh, then tilted her head to look at him.

The wetter it had gotten outside, and the drier inside, the wavier her hair had become. Now, in the lantern glow, it looked as shining as moonlight, as soft as spiraled cotton.

Little more than twenty-four hours, he thought, and he had sinning on his mind all over again.

"You okay?" Her voice was barely a whisper.

He was a damned fool, is what he was. "Yeah." She stretched out her legs, then a moment later drew them back up. Nervous energy radiated from her, and she betrayed it further with the hand she brushed through her hair, causing the curls to spring even more fully to life.

Her hair had been incredible. He still remembered the way it had felt winding around his fingers when he'd sunk his hands into it. As if it were yesterday instead of more than a dozen years ago.

He quietly thumped his head against the wall behind him.

"I can't believe the storm nearly leveled the Seaspray Inn." Her soft voice pulled at him. "It's a miracle there weren't more injuries. I heard the man who had a heart attack during the storm is doing well, though, at your dad's clinic. Dr. Hugo's been working nonstop."

"A real saint," Logan drawled.

Her gaze glided over him, snagging when it met his. She moistened her lips, and pushed her hand through her hair again, looking away.

"Maisy had some vacancies," Logan told her. He knew he was keeping the conversation going only because he wanted her to look at him again, so he could see the soft, pink sheen of her lips. "The guests displaced from the Seaspray have filled her cottages to the top. Some of the residents took in people, too."

"I heard. I don't know why, but I always have to remind myself that you and Sara are related to Maisy Fielding."

"By marriage." He held a lot more fondness for Maisy than he did for his own father, that was for damned sure.

She'd closed her arms around her up-drawn knees and she rested her cheek on top of them. Her hair drifted over her shoulders. "She and your father are an item, you know. They have been for some time now."

"I've heard." It had been yet another topic for gossip during that evening.

"What do you think about it?" If possible, her voice was even softer.

"I thought she had better taste."

"What's the problem between you and your dad, anyway?"

He looked at her.

"Well, you pretty much know what the problem was between me and *my* parents." She was matter-of-fact. "I was a total screwup where they were concerned."

"Sitting on the floor in the big building in the middle of the night must make you feel chatty."

Her lips twitched. She turned her head, looking around. "The cots and bedrolls are all used up."

"I saw Riley with some other teenagers watching a few toddlers."

"Yes. She asked if she could stay here, keep helping with the children tomorrow while the parents continue the cleanup. She seemed genuinely interested in helping. I figured it was okay."

He frowned, wondering if it was his imagination, or if Annie really thought she needed to justify her decision. "She seems like a good kid." Despite worrying her entire family and the devil-take-you attitude. The few kids he'd ever had cause to have dealings with had definitely *not* been of the "good" variety. And having Riley in the middle of several dozen Turns was about as safe a place as she could be.

"She *is* good. And maybe if she feels useful, she won't try anything foolish again." She fell silent for a long moment, then abruptly rolled to her feet. "Well, I'm out of here." She pushed back her hair again. Lifted her lips in a bad imitation of a smile and started to leave.

He rose, grimacing at the stiffness in his joints from sitting on the floor. He caught up with her near the still-opened doors, stopping her short with a hand on her arm.

Her wary gaze skipped over him, taking in the room beyond them. "Is there s-something you need?"

"A bed."

"Well, all the cots are used, I think, but maybe there's a—"

"Spare bed at your place," he interrupted her. "If Riley's here tonight that means you've got a spare."

Her curls shimmered in the pale-gold light as she shook her head. "No. Absolutely not. I appreciate everything you've done today, but...*no*."

He saw several heads rise up from sleeping bags and cots to look their way. He waited long enough for them to settle back down before he spoke again, keeping his voice low. "There's no floor space left to sleep here, and your house is in better shape than some." He had no desire to sleep on the floor in the community center, though he'd slept in worse places. But tonight, he was determined, and it had a lot more to do with Annie than with finding a softer place to rest his old bones. "It's the least you can do after today, don't you think?"

"Sleep at Sara's place."

"According to the manly gossip-session I was blessed to hear, Sara doesn't own a bed. She sleeps in a hammock. And how the hell Leo Vega knows that is something we'll have to have a talk about later."

"No."

"You're going to turn away an old friend, Annie? The brother of your best friend?"

She gave a little start, and took a step back. "We're not friends, we're hardly acquaintances. And if anybody else said that, they'd sound like they were whining."

He almost laughed at that. They both knew he wasn't whining. And they both knew he wouldn't be dissuaded. Lastly, he wasn't going to get into an argument about "what" they were.

Annie Hess was not going home alone tonight. They had unfinished business, and he wanted that rectified before he took Riley back where she belonged. "I'm coming with you, so pocket the outrage for now—unless you want to stand here and keep whispering as if we're ten-year-olds cheating during a math test. I want a bed. You've got one." And he'd be smarter this time around. Which was maybe why he *was* so determined. To prove he could be stronger, smarter, than he had been before.

She jerked her arm out of his hold and spun on her heel. Her tennis shoes squeaked loudly against the hard floor as she hurried through the doorway, which drew another round of lifted heads and curious eyes.

She was standing by the cold fireplace when he followed. He pushed the doors nearly closed, then held up a small key ring. "Leo's golf cart." He started toward the vehicle.

"Did he lend the keys to you, or did you browbeat him into it?" She hurried after him, her voice an angry whisper above the soft scuff of their shoes on the wet, grass-sprigged gravel.

"Does it matter?" He slid into the cart and turned the key. The motor turned over with a faint whine. "Get in. You're getting soaked again from the rain." He felt around on the dark panel in front of him for some sort of light, but apparently the old cart didn't come equipped with one.

"I suppose this is another example of how you protect women?"

"It's a fact that I intend to sleep on a reasonably comfortable, reasonably dry mattress tonight," he said.

She finally huffed, then moved around to the driver's side. "Move over," she said flatly. "I don't want you driving off a cliff, and you won't be able to see the road at all considering how dark it is."

"I doubt the road has changed in the past fifty years," Logan countered, but he moved to the passenger seat. She climbed in the driver's seat, setting the cart into motion with a jerk. Then she twisted the wheel, veering around a bicycle lying on the gravel.

"When's the last time *you* drove?"

"Shut up."

His lips twitched with a jolt of amusement. That was more like the Annie he knew. She'd been a firebrand. Set on having her way, no matter what obstacles she might encounter. Including him.

His comment notwithstanding, however, she did drive capably, unerringly, despite the bumps and potholes, the mud puddles and storm debris. And she didn't say a word to him. It was as if she were pretending he wasn't beside her, their thighs and shoulders brushing whenever she hit a bump in the road.

Shortly after she turned down the gravel lane toward her little beach house, she veered around the palm tree blocking it, took a short cut to her front door via the patch of waterlogged lawn, and stopped so abruptly he figured she lost a foot of turf under the wheels because of it. She slipped from behind the wheel. He heard, more than saw her disappear inside the house. The latch of the closing door was barely audible above the beat of rain, and he wished that she'd just slammed the door instead.

The Annie of old would have done that.

This Annie, the one who lived the quiet existence he'd heard about again and again that evening, was something—someone—he didn't have a handle on yet.

Logan ran his hand down his face. Slicked back his wet hair. Sighed.

Then he followed her inside.

She'd already lit a few candles—probably the same ones he'd taken from her dresser earlier that day—and they sat on the breakfast bar, casting a small glow that danced off the modest furniture to birth a dozen shadows. He headed down the hall, stopping short when she stepped out of the bathroom, the flashlight in her hand. She turned it on and aimed it at his face.

"How much did Will pay you to come get Riley? Whatever it is, I'll pay you double. If you'll just go away. As soon as the ferry is running again, I'll make sure she gets home myself."

"Thought you didn't want to force Riley into going where she didn't want to go." Will had told him that.

"Yes, well, obviously I was wrong. She'll be safer at home. So…how much?"

He narrowed his eyes against the glare of light. "I

didn't take anything from Will. My time is not for sale." Which wasn't strictly accurate. "And even if it was, you couldn't afford it." Which was definitely accurate.

She made a scoffing sound, and he grabbed her hand, intending to redirect the beam of light away from his eyes.

But he felt her hand shake.

He gentled his movement, sliding his fingers around hers, slipping away the flashlight with his other hand and turning the beam toward the floor.

"Are you cold?" It was dry inside the house, and chilly, but not nearly as bad as it was outside. "Too bad you don't have a fireplace."

"I'm not cold."

He tightened his hand around hers. "You're shivering."

"Fine, then. I'm cold." Her tone was short. She tugged her hand away from his, and turning sideways slid past him toward the smaller of the two bedrooms.

He heard a thump, a muffled oath, the squeak of a drawer. He directed the flashlight through the doorway to see her dump something bulky on the box spring. A quilt, he guessed.

"You'll need to get the top mattress out of the bathroom," she said, and moved past him again. "Since I have no idea how you fitted it in there in the first place. And I doubt it'll be very comfortable anyway. The side that was up during the storm is filthy."

She was all business.

Except that she'd been shivering. Trembling.

And her hand had not been cold.

"I'll manage," he murmured. She'd headed back to the candlelit kitchen. He watched her crouch down on the floor next to the fallen cupboard and ruined dishes. She didn't go for a broom, didn't reach out to rescue any salvageable items. Just sat there, hunkered down on her heels, strands of her hair gleaming in the dim candle glow, her arms wrapped around herself.

Not to hold the cold at bay, but to hold in the trembling?

"These dishes were one of the first things I bought when I was on my own," she said after a moment, obviously aware that he was watching her. "My apartment was a tiny studio. No bedrooms. I didn't have furniture; just two folding chairs, a card table. An air mattress. One of those blow-up things that people use for camping. I'd stick it in the closet during the day. It wasn't much, but it was a home of my own creating. And I bought this set of dishes." She shook her head a little. "Silly, isn't it? Riley hoped they weren't the family china."

"These mattered to you more."

"Yes." Her voice was painfully soft. "Goodness knows, my mother would never have trusted me with her china."

"Your mother was a bitch."

He heard her suck in a breath. Slowly let it out. Then she pushed to her feet, stepping away from the mess in the kitchen. She stopped in front of him, keeping a good foot of distance between them. "If Will isn't paying you to retrieve Riley, then why are you doing it, Logan? You don't strike me as a man who owes anyone favors. So why are you really here?"

"You have to ask?" Yeah, Cole had asked him to take this on, but Logan could have refused to come to Turnabout if he'd wanted to.

He hadn't.

He still didn't know why. Curiosity? Stupidity? Or more likely that he had never fully gotten Annie out of his head.

She crossed her arms. Uncrossed them. "Apparently, I do have to ask." She crossed them yet again. "Is it your family? Sara's doing fine, you know. She misses you, I think, but she's in a good place in her life. And Dr. Hugo—"

"I'm not here because of them."

"Then why? Why get involved in another Hess mess?" She hesitated for a moment, looking pained. "I may have thrown myself at you *years* ago, but I have no desire to repeat that."

"Really?" He could practically sense the fine hair on her arms standing at attention because of the tension passing between them. She'd been too young all those years ago. But that couldn't be said now. And there was no pretending the chemistry wasn't alive and well between them.

"I don't go around asking for second helpings of humiliation," she said flatly. "One was more than enough."

His laugh was short on humor. "Humiliation? You? Come on, Annie, I'm the one who couldn't—"

"Stop!" She lifted her hand.

Exactly, he thought grimly. He hadn't stopped. And he damned well should have.

But she was talking again, looking vaguely desperate and entirely exhausted. "Let's just forget about it, okay? It was a long time ago. I'd just as soon forget it ever happened."

"Believe me, darlin', so would I. Unfortunately, I

haven't quite mastered it." The memory of that night had dogged him ever since.

"Good grief. It was a long time ago, Logan. I was seventeen years old and I threw myself at you shamelessly. But you're the original good guy. You weren't interested. You'd never do anything unsavory." She shook her head, her lips turning down at the corners. "If you weren't, we'd have been lovers sixteen years ago." She thrust back her hair and turned away from him. She picked up a candle and headed down the hall.

He stood there in her quiet kitchen, listening to the faint sounds of her moving around in her bedroom, the soft whoosh of the ocean beyond her back door.

She didn't remember.

The night that had haunted him for sixteen long years simply didn't exist for her.

Chapter 7

Her heart thudded. Her skin felt too tight. For hours—days—she'd wanted to taste his kiss. To feel his body against hers. To touch him. He was different than anyone else. Especially Drago. And now was her chance.

She pushed herself up on her elbow and leaned over his prone body. There. She slid her fingers through his thick hair, carefully drawing it off his forehead. "Kiss me," she whispered.

He didn't reply.

Then she would kiss him. She leaned over him, hesitating for a breathless moment as her breasts pressed against his chest. Then she slid upward, nearly crying in delight at the feel of his chest hair—crisp yet soft—against her tight nipples. Feeling dizzy, she quickly pressed her mouth to his.

His lips were soft. Pliable. She felt his chest lift in a

deep breath. She curved her body more closely against his. Nothing had ever felt as good, as strong, as steady as he did. She kissed him, aching for him to lift his hands, to hold her. Tell her that he felt the same, that he cared.

But he stubbornly remained silent.

She drew her leg up his, catching her breath at the sensation. Roughened by hair, and oh, so very warm. Her head swam. Before she backed out, she quickly shifted, slipping over him.

Oh. She weakly dropped her head forward, resting against his chest. Knowing what to expect in theory was a whole lot different in reality.

A whole lot better.

He made a low sound and caught her hips in his hands, pressing up against her. Yes. He was just as she'd imagined. Better. Hard where she was soft. Strong where she was not.

Before she could chicken out, she slid her hand down his side, his hip, where his skin felt impossibly smooth. She reveled in the varied textures of his body for a breathless eon. Then she shifted, reached between their bodies. Found him.

He felt hot. Hard.

For her.

She exhaled, truly shaken with want. For the first time in her life. "Now, Logan. Now, please."

He turned her, suddenly. Colors spun in her head. And then he was over her, his mouth on hers, his hands fisting in her hair—

Annie opened her eyes with a start, sitting bolt upright in the middle of her bed.

Her fingers dug into the mattress beneath her. She

was on Turnabout. In her own room. In her own house that smelled—impossibly—of coffee.

She was alone.

She exhaled shakily and slowly relaxed her grip. Her eyes felt gritty and dry from too little sleep. Weak sunlight filtered through the unadorned window beside her bed, and she automatically reached over to turn on the small lamp sitting on the bedside table.

The bulb remained dark.

The electricity was still out.

She fell back against the pillows, bending her arm over her eyes. Could half a night of dreams as tangled as the bedding that twisted about her legs cause the imagined smell of coffee?

Somehow, she doubted it.

Which meant that Logan was out there finding some creative way of brewing coffee that smelled heavenly. She usually preferred the herbal teas she and Sara produced, but right now, her nerves were crying for a solid jolt of caffeine.

She groaned softly and turned her face into her pillow. If only the previous day had been as unreal as the dream. She'd long ago accepted that the dream was a defense against a reality that so shamed her she couldn't bring herself to recall it. But this time, the dream had been particularly...lifelike.

It's just because you knew that Logan was sleeping on the other side of the wall behind your bed. Just because you were exhausted after lying awake most of the night.

Right. All the excuses in the world couldn't make her forget that, even now, her body hummed.

She was torn between wanting to stay in bed with

her head buried like an ostrich in the sand and a need to put herself as far away from the bed and dreams of Logan as possible. She knew from experience that the ostrich approach would accomplish nothing. And the dreams were nothing more than a defense.

The day before had happened. The week before had happened. The mistakes of her past had come back to haunt her.

So she pushed aside the sunny yellow blanket that she'd retrieved from the bathroom tub-shelter when she'd left Logan standing in her living room the night before. She untwisted the white sheet from her legs and forced herself out of the bed.

Unfortunately, every movement she made awakened a host of aches from head to toe. And alerted her to the fact that it was freezing.

She replaced her flannel pajamas with thick sweatpants and sweatshirt. Then added another sweatshirt over the first. She pushed her feet into rubber-soled socks and padded out of her room, stopping briefly in the plastic-roofed bathroom. One glimpse of herself in the mirror over the sink was enough to shock her back to her ostrich position in her bed, but she resisted the urge.

She wrangled her hair into a clip at the back of her head, and warily tried the faucet. Water spat from it, then eventually ran in a thin, clear trickle.

Hallelujah. She'd never felt more thankful for her antiquated water cistern.

Still, she didn't waste a drop as she quickly brushed her teeth and washed her face. Feeling somewhat more alert, she went in search of the fragrant coffee with a silent, fervent assurance to herself that she did not care if Logan thought she looked as bad as she knew she did.

That assurance fizzled the moment his shocking-blue gaze looked at her over the mug he had lifted to his mouth. He lowered the mug, revealing the amused tilt of his lips. "Morning, sleeping beauty."

She briefly considered baring her teeth. Why was it that men like Logan actually improved—a feat in itself—under circumstances like these? He hadn't shaved, his clothes looked as if he'd slept in them—which he probably had. And he still looked like fantasy-fodder.

Or dream-dweller.

She focused on the green metal camp stove sitting on top of the real stove. A blackened coffee pot sat on one burner, and a large saucepan on the other. The cupboard and mess of broken dishes had been cleared away.

Obviously Logan's doing.

She walked past him and looked into the pan on the camp stove. It contained water that was just coming to a boil. "You've been to town?" Obviously he had, since she didn't own a camp stove.

She should have awakened earlier. Gone to town herself. Checked on Riley.

Checked on a way to get Riley home as quickly as possible.

"Yeah. I went by your fields, too. I'm no master gardener, but I didn't see much damage that a few days of sun won't cure. The town's a mess, though. Looks even worse in the daylight."

Her knees felt weak. "Thanks for checking the fields. Did you see Riley when you were in town?"

"Yeah. Maisy's put her and some other kids to work,

keeping April and some of her friends out of mischief while their folks start putting things back to order."

She blindly reached for a mug and concentrated on pouring coffee into it as Logan spoke. April was Maisy's granddaughter, and after a lifetime of poor health that had been reversed thanks to an operation earlier that year, was becoming quite a handful. She figured Riley—who'd been resourceful enough to find her way alone from Olympia to the island—was probably equal to the task. "What about the, um, the ferry?"

"Two of Diego's boats sank. The third needs major repairs. The Coast Guard has already been out; picked up the heart-attack victim and a couple other injuries to transport them to the mainland."

"Then we could get another charter out here."

He shook his head. "The coastline is fogged in. Flights are grounded. The guard will be back with some supplies when they can, but they're dealing with other problems that are considerably more their domain. Why are you so anxious to get rid of Riley?"

Coffee sloshed over the side of her mug. "You came to the island to get her."

"That's not an answer."

Annie ripped a paper towel from the roll and sopped up the spill. "She's safer with Will and Noelle."

"Are you so sure about that?"

The towel crumpled in her fist. "You've been here less than twenty-four hours, Logan. And look at all that's happened in that time."

He leaned his elbows on the breakfast counter and his shoulders strained against the wrinkled fabric of his shirt. His expression was unreadable. "I'll be as happy to get off this rock as anyone. But there's been a storm.

Nobody's fault but nature's. Riley is fine. And nobody is any closer to knowing the real reason she ran away. So what's the hurry?"

She dropped the balled paper in the trash as she took a sip of the coffee. It nearly scorched through the roof of her mouth.

"It's hot," Logan offered blandly.

She let out an exasperated breath. "Gee. Thanks for the warning."

The corner of his lips tilted. "Anytime."

Her stomach was in knots and thanks to her tumbles the previous day, her body ached nearly everywhere. Yet she found herself struggling not to smile at him.

She didn't want to like Logan Drake. She'd liked him years ago. Too much. But that period of her life was so full of painful memories that anyone from it—including him—seemed tainted with it.

All of which was moot. The only thing that mattered right now was getting Riley back home—away from Annie—before something even worse happened. That was the hurry, she silently reminded herself.

She gingerly sipped the coffee, hoping it would dissolve the pained lump in her throat. All she succeeded in doing was burning her tongue.

"Annie."

She glanced at Logan. It was all she dared. Then she looked back down into the strong black coffee steaming inside the mug. Still too hot to drink, but at least holding the mug warmed her cold hands. "I don't think it's ever been this cold since I've lived here."

"It's in the low forties, probably. Thanks to the generator, everybody in the big building was warm, though. Including Riley. Sam doesn't have a clue when the power will be restored. Half the plant's fried. Looked like it took a hit of lightning."

She nodded. Tried to drink a little more, but contented herself more with inhaling the heated aroma. "I'm glad she was warm there, then."

"Thanks for the bed last night."

Her cheeks warmed, right along with her palms around the mug. "I, um, you're welcome."

"Not that I gave you much choice."

"True." She chanced another look at him, only to find herself unable to look away when his gaze captured hers. He still had that thin black ring surrounding his irises, making the blue seem even bluer.

"I was interested."

"Excuse me?"

"Last night. You said I wasn't interested. I was. And you knew it."

Her mouth ran dry.

"When you were seventeen." He pushed off the barstool. "And now."

Her spine bumped the refrigerator when he rounded the counter, seeming to take up all the space in her minute kitchen. Panic and something else—something she desperately feared was longing—streaked through her veins.

Longing? She didn't long for anything. She didn't allow herself that luxury.

"Stop!" She put out her arm, splaying her fingers against his chest. "I, um, I don't do this."

He raised an eyebrow. "Ever?"

"Never. And I don't believe you about...about before."

His lips twisted. "Right." He covered her fingers

with his, pressing them over the heavy beat of his heart. "Feel that? Nothing's changed."

She swallowed. She couldn't have spoken just then to save her soul.

Despite the blur of beard, his jaw looked tight. "I thought I could clear my conscience. About this, at least."

His conscience? "I don't...Logan, I—"

"Hell," he whispered. Then covered her mouth with his.

Her mind went blank. Her nerves came alive.

A dream was one thing.

Reality another.

Not hell, she thought vaguely. Heaven.

Flavored with the heady taste of dark coffee. Textured with the soft rasp of an unshaven cheek against the palm of her hand. Protected by shoulders that she knew were wide enough to hold the world at bay.

Just that easily, that rapidly, she wanted to drown in it. Drown in his kiss. In his touch. But she couldn't. Oh, she couldn't. She'd shut off that part of her, hadn't she? Cut it out of her existence, because it was so much safer.

His arm slid behind her back, pulling her closer, keeping her upright when her knees dissolved, setting her coffee mug aside when she was in danger of dropping it. She shivered, a trembling that had nothing to do with the temperature and everything to do with his fingertips, slipping beneath her layers of fleece, grazing her spine. "Logan—"

"Sshh." He tightened his arms around her, and she sucked in a harsh breath as he lifted her and settled her on the counter, stepping between her legs, capturing her face gently between his hands, turning her lips up to his yet again.

Her head swam. Was this another dream? So exquisitely vivid waking from it was almost painful? She dragged her mouth from his, pressing her forehead against his jaw.

This is real. He is real.

She wasn't hallucinating. She wasn't losing her mind.

She brushed her fingertips over his cheek and her fingers tingled. Then she pulled back from him. "No."

Her breath was ragged. "Riley…I have to think about my…Riley."

His hands swept down her back, then up again, curving over her shoulders. "I told you. Maisy's keeping her busy. Believe me, if anyone can keep your niece in hand, it's her."

"No." She suddenly wriggled out of his hold, nearly scrambling off the counter. If she didn't move away from him now, she feared she wouldn't do so at all. "I can't. I won't. I'm not like that. I'm not…not Easy A anymore."

His eyes narrowed. "You were never easy."

She'd tried so hard, for so many years to erase that part of her life. And she'd thought she'd succeeded. Except for those sly dreams that still tormented her sleep when she least expected it. Dreams of a night that had never happened. Not with him. Not with anyone she wanted to remember. They were only a defense against a reality she hated.

She pushed at her hair, realizing it had come loose from the clip.

"I…have to clean up. Have to, uh, start getting things

back in order." Order is what she wanted. What she craved.

Logan shoved his hands in his pockets rather than reach for her when Annie sidled away from him, panic glazing her eyes from mossy to emerald. She looked like some fey creature seeking escape.

He shouldn't have kissed her. He knew it. But he sure in hell hadn't expected a reaction like this. "We will," he said cautiously. "The hot water on the camp stove is for you."

She was visibly trembling. "G-good." But she didn't move toward it, and he figured it was just as well, given the state she was in.

"I'll move it for you."

Her brows drew together. "What?"

"There's not enough for a real bath, but you can wash up with it. I'll pour it in the sink in the bathroom. You can add a little cold water to it so you don't burn yourself."

He watched her watch him as he suited his calm, steady words with action. And her wariness made something inside him hurt.

"Thank you." Her words were nearly silent when he'd dumped the boiling water into the sink. The steam from it billowed up, clouding the mirror above it. Then she quietly closed the bathroom door, leaving him standing in the narrow hallway with an oversized pan clenched in his hand.

He let out a long breath and stared at the smooth-paneled door. The door wasn't substantial. But he couldn't hear a single sound from inside. Not the splash of water, not the shifting of a rubber-soled sock or the rustle of too-large clothing designed to hide a slender, female body.

Too easily, he pictured her standing there in front of the sink, her eyes shadowed and turned inward, her body braced against the shudders that wracked it.

He knew what it was like to have demons in your mind. He recognized the signs. He'd battled his own— sometimes winning, too often losing.

But what demons were keeping company with Annie Hess?

He was beginning to suspect what they were. And the suspicion that somebody, somewhere along the line, had hurt Annie in ways no person deserved made him feel murderous.

He drew in a long breath. Exhaled in even longer, measured beats. But the feeling didn't pass.

It scared the hell out of him.

Chapter 8

"What do you know about Annie?"

Logan was working alongside Sam Vega as they cleared the southern end of the main road of the trees that had fallen across it.

At the question, Sam straightened and ran his arm across his sweaty brow. He shrugged. "What's there to know? She keeps to herself and she's in business with your sister, man."

But Logan couldn't reach Sara, since the phone lines were still down. It was bad enough that he'd hadn't spoken with her in years. Then to pump her for information about Annie?

He frowned and swung the ax again, biting into another tree branch. "Turnabout is as bloody backward as it ever was," he muttered. "Not one single person has a chain saw." He'd seen a house with a satellite dish, but did anyone have a chain saw? Hell no.

They couldn't even use Sam's truck at this point to drag the trees, because they were caught awkwardly between the fence that strangled the road. Using the truck now would probably pull down the iron fence as well. And God knew nobody could touch the fence that cordoned off the property of the Castillo house.

The place was a sacred—albeit barren—cow to the Turns.

He glared at the fence. The trees. The rundown dwelling that sat beyond it on a cliff. "Backward."

Sam grinned faintly. "Place is still a couple decades behind the times in some ways. There *are* folks who like it that way."

Logan grimaced and kept chopping. He wasn't one of them. "You must. You came back."

"Not to take a step backward in time or technology."

The branch finally groaned, tilting away from the main trunk. He kicked his boot against it, finishing the job, then dragged it away from the fence. Straightening, he tilted his head back, looking up at the sky. Over the course of the afternoon, it had cleared, and was as pristine blue as he ever remembered seeing it during his childhood. "Fickle weather."

Sam snorted softly. "Almost as bad as a woman. But in this instance—" he cast his gaze around "—I'm glad for the respite. We don't have the resources to get through one disaster, much less having another storm on top of it. Help me here. I think we've cut enough."

He gestured at the heavy tree trunk.

Logan added his muscle, and, between the two of them, they managed to drag it—roots protruding up in the air like some maniacal hand out of a horror flick—beyond the iron fence. When they'd cleared the fence, Sam used the winch on his truck to finish the job, dragging the tree clear of the road. Which left only two more trees to go.

Logan picked up the ax again and approached the next tree. The afternoon air was cold, crisp and smelled of fresh-cut wood. It was a combination completely out of place for Turnabout. If anything, it reminded him of Washington state. About the time of year that Will had been getting hitched.

He swung the ax, cutting off that particular thought. Beside him, Sam swung also. Wood chips flew as they fell into a rhythm and they steadily hacked their way through the next tree, then started on the last.

Logan's back began to ache. They'd both shrugged off their jackets despite the brisk temperature. Sam had long sent his brother Leo off for a saw, but the guy had yet to return. Obviously, Leo had taken to heart the Turns' typically fluid definition of *time*.

"I hate this," Logan muttered. The last tree was enormous. Had probably stood as a sentinel to the southern end of the island for over a hundred years. "It'd be easier to swim to the mainland and get a chainsaw." He looked at Sam. "Why'd you come back here?"

Sam grimaced, leaving the ax-head buried in the wood. "Why did you?"

"I'm not back."

Sam smiled faintly and uncapped the jug of water he'd brought, along with the miserably insufficient axes. The jug was nearly empty. "But you're here," he pointed out, slanting a look his way.

"Stuck here. For now."

Sam just shook his head and finished off the water. "That's what we all say."

"There's nothing on this island for me." Logan looked around at the landscape. Some of it was wild. Unkempt. With treacherous cliffs and barren ground. And then, a half mile up the road, a person could stand in the checkerboard of Annie and Sara's fields. They currently looked bedraggled, but even he could tell they were ordinarily lush with good health.

"Ask not what the island has for you but what you have for the island."

He wished he had a chain saw is what he wished. "You getting philosophical in your old age?"

Sam grunted, his grin fading. "Watch it. I'll throw you in the tank. You got something going with Annie? That why you're asking about her?"

"No." The only thing he had going with Annie was a long-ago night that should never have occurred and newly acquired suspicions that would be just one more thing to keep him awake at night.

"Heard you spent the night at her place."

"People around here always were too nosy."

"Small towns," Sam said. "Nothing more interesting to speculate over than what the neighbors are doing behind closed doors."

"And you came back to it."

Sam tossed the empty jug beyond the fence and it sailed into the back of his truck. "There are worse things."

For a long time, Logan had doubted that. Until he began dwelling in the worst the world had to offer. He flexed his back. Then his hands. Grabbed the long handle again and continued chopping.

The irony of his task didn't escape him. Once again, he was cleaning up a mess. This one just happened to be caused by the destruction of nature, rather than the destruction of man.

Just once, he thought, he'd like to make something new.

"Whoa. Wicked trees."

Both men looked up from their task at the young voice.

Logan absorbed the sight of Annie followed by Riley move slowly toward the tree. Annie had changed into jeans since that morning, but still looked as if she were drowning in layers of knit sweaters. Her niece was similarly dressed. It was almost like having double vision.

"Hey, Annie," Sam called out easily. "Don't think even your talents can save these babies."

Annie and Riley stopped on the other side of the last tree wedged between the road and the fence. Even lying on the ground the branches soared over their heads. Her gaze on the tree, Annie set down the bucket she was carrying and slowly settled her palm on a thick, gnarled branch. "What a shame." She didn't look Logan's way.

He watched her hand. Her thumb stroked gently against the bark.

"Oh, man. People really carve their initials into trees?" Riley had scrambled into the thick of the branches and was peering at the trunk. "With hearts and everything. That is *so* corny."

Logan deliberately looked away from Annie's gentle caress of the uprooted tree. Despite Riley's bored tone, she was avidly studying the etchings that marred the tree trunk. "Some of those carvings are pretty old," he said. "When corny was *in*."

"Logan's probably got an initial or two on there," Sam said. "He was always bringing girls up here to——"

"Watch the sunsets," Logan inserted.

Sam's lips twitched. "Right."

"And I usually ran into you and your flavor of the day when I got here," Logan reminded the other man, amused at the memory. He'd almost forgotten that there had been some decent times on Turnabout.

"That's just gross."

"Glad you think so," Annie smoothly told Riley. "Then I don't have to worry about you and your new friend from Denver watching any *sunsets*, do I?"

Logan caught the look between the two females.

"Friend?"

"Yeah, a friend." Riley's voice was defensive.

"Kenny Hobbes," Annie said. "His family are guests at Maisy's. They seemed to have…hit it off." Her expression was anything but delighted.

Riley huffed and deliberately pushed aside a branch. "Nobody carved their whole name. There are only initials. Look at this one."

Logan waited, wondering if Annie would pursue the issue. But after a moment her shoulders relaxed and she moved over beside Riley, slipping between two branches to see. "HD and CC. The heart around them is really elaborate." She touched the bulging bark surrounding the carved sentiment. "Look at the way the tree's healed around it."

"I bet this one's been here longer." Riley poked at another carving, higher up the trunk. It was far more faded. "Looks like ES and…what is that? Something, then a C."

"Probably an L," Sam said. "Luis Castillo. He was

the son of the people who built this old place. Supposedly, the Turnabout curse started because Luis was betrayed by his fiancée, Elena, when she fell in love with a friend of his he'd brought to the island after the First World War."

Riley snorted. "A curse? What kind of idiot believes in curses?"

An island of them, Logan thought. He studied the HD and CC for a moment.

"Sara believes it," Annie said. "Maisy believes it. Neither of them are *idiots*."

"They'd be better off if they didn't believe," Logan said flatly. "Riley's right. Superstitious nonsense is what it is."

Annie's eyes—looking as green now as the leaves still clinging to the tree branches surrounding her—looked at him. "Your father says the same thing. But a person *does* wonder."

Being in agreement with Hugo was nothing Logan strove to obtain. "Do you even know what the curse claims? Turns hardly used to talk about it, because they were too freaked it'd mar their lives." He doubted things on that score had changed much.

"Sara told me."

"She did?" Sam looked surprised.

"Well...what is it?" Riley looked impatient.

"It's garbage," Logan said.

Annie's chin lifted a little. "What are you worried about, Logan? You told me yourself you're not a Turn and we all know you can't wait to leave the island again."

"Doesn't matter what my plans are," Logan countered. "Somebody should either restore Castillo House or tear it down."

Annie blinked a little, and looked at her niece.

Riley just lifted her eyebrows. "I said the same thing when she—" her chin jerked toward her aunt "—said we were coming out here to rescue some of her plants. The place is a dump."

"Well, anyway," Annie said hurried, "Luis Castillo's fiancée married his friend, Jonathan, who was a stranger to the island. Luis was brokenhearted, and as a result, his mother cast a curse that people born on the island would only find happiness with someone else born on the island, apparently to prevent something like what Elena had done—marrying an outsider."

Riley made a face. "Weird."

"Actually, what I think is interesting is that *since* then, supposedly, nothing grows in the ground around Castillo House. Sara says it was the price the Castillo family paid in return for the curse." Annie glanced beyond Logan to the property surrounding the decaying house. "The trees were the only living things left, but they stood here at the edge of the property next to the fence. That's why I tried planting near them."

"There used to be an iron gate that blocked off the road," Sam said. "But I finally removed it because it was getting too dangerous for the kids who came out here and played on it. If the gate were still here, the trees would actually have been on the outside of it."

"Are those your plants?" Riley pointed at a sparse row along the fence line. The stems were barely strong enough to hold a leaf. "*That's* what we are supposed to save?"

Annie nodded. "There's no physical reason why plants shouldn't thrive here. It's, well, it is *weird*."

"It's probably some Turn who dumped something toxic around the place to prove their point that the curse existed," Logan countered. "And the trees are so old, the root systems were too deep to be affected."

Her gaze slanted his way, amused. "Skeptic."

"Realist."

"Well, as it happens, I've had the soil tested and it's perfectly fine. A little acidic, but not unusually so."

"So, why does it matter to you whether or not you can get plants to grow out here?"

"Oh, I will," she said, her voice determined. "I can grow plants anywhere. But this space is perfect to expand our fields for Island Botanica. Sara and I need more land to produce more crops to keep up with our mail-order business. The thing that makes our products unique is that everything is derived from plants grown here on Turnabout. We're totally organic, totally pure. And we don't want to have to obtain supplies off island."

She was serious.

He looked over his shoulder at the barren expanse surrounding the house that—as far as he was concerned—was pretty much an eyesore. "Is the property even available?" The last member of the Castillo family had left the island when he was a baby. He figured he'd have heard by now—given the grapevine—if a Castillo had ever returned. That would have been major news for Turnabout.

"Sara's been looking into it. That's one of the reasons she's in San Diego this past week. Doing some title research on the land. The last owner of record was

Caroline Castillo, but we haven't been able to locate her, yet. She left Turnabout nearly forty years ago. We're not even sure she's still alive. It'd be easier if we could afford an investigator to do research, but we're getting there. Slowly," she added with a wry shrug.

Logan picked up the ax and moved around to the top of the tree, away from where Annie and Riley stood.

"Isn't there some way we could at least save the tree trunk?" Annie's voice stopped him midswing.

"For what?"

"I don't know. Posterity. These old carvings meant something to people." She gestured toward the other trees. "Look at all that. It's not as if you need *this* one for firewood."

"If we don't get the power restored soon, we might," Sam said. He looked back at the tree. "Where would we put it?"

"I don't know. The community center or something. The town council could decide, right? I'll keep the trunk in my workshop if nobody else wants it. Think about it, Sam. This tree was probably the oldest living thing on Turnabout."

Sam shrugged and looked at Logan, his expression not at all convinced. "We'll see. For now, let's just get it out of the road." He caught Riley's arm and helped her climb over the trunk, then handed her the shovel she'd been carrying.

Annie followed but stopped short, wincing. "Hold on, Riley, I'm—ouch!—caught." She twisted, reaching behind her.

Logan stepped through the branches toward her. "Stop moving." He worked his way around behind her. "Your sweater is hung up on a branch." He reached for the broken branch that snagged her, and felt a fine shiver dance down her spine as he worked the sweater free.

"No." She looked up at him, then away. "Yes. But it's okay." Her soft lips pressed together.

Heat blasted through him.

If she moved an inch, she'd be pressed up against him. He wedged his arm between Annie and the branches, giving them both more breathing room. The last thing he needed was to send her back into a panic, and finding out he was hard just from looking at her face would probably do just that. "Be careful."

Her gaze skidded over his face, lingering on his mouth. "I will. Um...thanks."

"Talk to Hugo."

"What? It's just a scratch, Logan. I hardly need a doctor's opinion. I have my own remedies, anyway. Aloe vera is very—"

"About Caroline Castillo."

"Oh." She blinked. "Right. Your dad would have known her, of course. He hasn't said anything special to Sara, though."

She shifted and despite multiple layers of knit, he felt the soft push of her breasts against his side. "I'm not surprised. Sara doesn't know."

"Know what?"

He tapped the inscription on the trunk once. "Caroline Castillo left Turnabout when her affair with my father came to light. Wouldn't surprise me if Hugo kept track of her." It's what his mother had always believed. Her suspicions had dogged her into misery for most of Logan's childhood. Every time Hugo had left the island, she'd ranted that he'd gone to see his lover. As far as Logan knew, Hugo had never denied it.

Her eyes were soft, her expression shocked. "I'm sorry."

"It's old news."

"Sometimes it's hard to acknowledge that your parents aren't perfect. But Logan, that was a *long* time ago. If that's what's causing the distance between the two of you, then—"

"Hey." Riley waved the shovel handle through the branches and they rustled, leaves cascading everywhere. "You better not be looking for any *sunsets* in there."

Amusement tugged at him. The girl really was protective of her aunt. He wondered if either one of them noticed it.

Annie's cheeks had flushed. "Thanks for the, uh, the rescue. Yet another one. And for helping save the tree trunk. You're a good guy, Logan Drake."

His amusement died.

Logan could detest his father for his mother's unhappiness all he wanted. But Hugo had still done some decent things. He'd been the only doctor the island possessed.

The truth of it was that Hugo was closer to being a "good guy" than Logan was.

"No," he said so softly she'd never hear as she worked her way from the clinging branches. "I'm not."

Chapter 9

Logan sat in the sheriff's office. Even after darkness fell, he didn't light the utilitarian lantern sitting on Sam's desk as he thumbed the mike to the emergency radio that Sam had managed to procure. "Any more letters?"

For a moment, his only answer was static. Then Will's voice came on again. "Not for a week now. I can send a charter out for you and Riley."

Logan stared at the microphone. There was no reason for Will not to do exactly that. But there was an itch at the base of his spine that told him to wait.

How many times had he sat in some filth-encrusted location, his finger hovering on a trigger, his eye on a scope, as that same itch told him to wait. Wait.

When he'd been in Will's office that day, the other man had shown him a file of letters containing oblique threats to the effect that if he didn't back out of the special election for attorney general, he'd regret it. The letters hadn't been directly threatening, but they'd been worrying enough that Will hadn't been as anxious as he might otherwise have been to get Riley back under his roof.

Will hadn't liked the idea of his daughter seeking out Annie, but until he had a finger on the source of the threatening letters, he'd also figured she was just as safe *away* from Olympia.

Logan's thoughts raced, ranging from the meeting he'd had with Will and Cole when he'd been asked to come after Riley, to keep watch over her, to bring her home when they all deemed it safe, to Annie.

He thumbed the mike. "Wait."

Static met him again.

Though it had been sixteen years since they'd been in the same place at the same time, Logan knew Will was worried about Riley. The man was in an untenable situation.

Wanting his daughter back.

Wanting her safe, even more.

His old friend was undoubtedly going to be the next attorney general for Washington state. He could have depended on any number of more traditional means for retrieving his daughter since he, himself, was embroiled in the middle of a special election. But he hadn't. And Logan still had trouble adjusting his cynicism enough to believe that Will's decision hadn't been affected—at least in part—by the adverse effect on the polls if it came to public awareness that his only daughter had run away from home.

So Will had prevailed upon his connection with

Coleman Black, who in turn, had put Logan on the task. The only one of the three men who hadn't seemed surprised by the pairing had been Cole. Which probably meant his boss had an ulterior motive in bringing two guys who'd lost touch over the years back in contact.

He finally received a static-laden answer. "Check in tomorrow."

Logan let go of the mike and sat back in Sam's desk chair, scrubbing his hands down his face.

He knew his reasons for putting Will off were more selfish than not, despite that faint itch of his. But he wasn't ready to haul Riley back home, not without somebody figuring out what the hell had motivated her to run away in the first place. And he wasn't ready to leave Annie just yet, either. Not until..until *what?*

He shoved back the chair.

Cole would have a laugh if he saw Logan now. His cold-blooded cleanup man, troubled by people from a past that he'd long ago cut from his life.

Eventually, Logan left Sam's office and went to the community center where nearly the entire town was gathered, pooling food for dinner and anxiously awaiting a progress report on utilities and supplies. And again, he went through the ritual of responding to the "nice to see you back" comments that followed his progress before he spotted Annie sitting at a long table.

She was turned away from him, talking to someone at the next table. He watched her profile for a long moment. And when her glance turned his way and her eyes widened a little and the corners of her soft lips lifted in a faint smile, his heart stopped.

Hell.

He shook it off and walked over to her. "I got a message to Will that everyone here is okay." He set his bowl of chili on the long narrow table and sat down beside her. "Where's Riley?"

Her faint smile died. "I suppose Will said to get her home. Pronto."

"Nobody on the isle is going anywhere for the time being."

She chewed the corner of her lip for a moment, then seemed to accept his words. "She's at Maisy's again. She's pretty fascinated with April, apparently. And she, um, she's already eaten, so I didn't see the harm in it."

He'd only wondered where the girl was, not why Annie felt justified in letting the kid do what she wanted.

Hell, they *were* stuck on an island.

He began eating.

"Hi, Logan. Annie."

At the too-cheerful greeting, he sighed and looked up as Darla Towers slid into the empty seat across from them.

"This is such a nightmare, isn't it?" Darla crossed her arms on the table and leaned forward. "I'm going to die if I can't get a bottle of your lavender cream, Annie." Her words were for Annie but the woman's dark eyes were on him.

"We have plenty of cream at the shop, Darla. I'll get some to you."

"Thanks. Now if I could just find someone to help me put it on my back." She giggled.

"Try Leo," he suggested blandly.

Darla's lips tightened and she stood from the chair so quickly it nearly tipped over before she walked away.

"You could have been nicer, you know," Annie said a moment later.

Logan shrugged. He wasn't interested in Darla Towers. He wasn't interested in any woman on the island, save one. There had been plenty of women in his life, but not a one who'd kept him awake at night. Not like the memory of Annie Hess. He continued eating, perfectly aware that Annie was doing more toying with her spoon than using it to eat the soup that filled her bowl.

The community center was noisy with chatter. Several people stopped by to ask Annie about her shop, or to offer assistance with the fields if she needed it. The only person who hadn't stopped by was Hugo. He was there, all right, over in the corner of the community center with his medical bag and a table of first-aid supplies. Judging by the look of it, he'd been wrapping, swabbing and icing since long before Logan arrived for dinner.

And, as well as being aware of Annie's lack of appetite, he caught the surreptitious looks she cast his way, then Hugo's.

"Appearances are deceiving."

"What?"

He jerked his chin in the direction of his father. "You're sitting here wondering whether what I told you is true or not, because he looks like the saint of Turnabout over there."

"No," she said quietly, "I'm sitting here thinking how sad it is that there's such distance between the two of you."

He was amused, despite himself. "How long has it been since you talked with George and Lucia?" Her head tilted, acknowledging the irony. "The situations aren't really the same, though. I know what you said about...about Dr. Hugo, but as I've said, it was a long time ago. Caroline Castillo left the island decades ago. You said yourself that you were a baby."

"Yet the ripples of that Castillo rock falling into the Drake pond continued for a long time," he said evenly. "Eat your soup."

She looked down at the spoon she was swirling in her bowl, as if surprised that it was still there. Then he felt the whisper of her gaze lingering on him.

He finally pushed away his bowl of chili and looked right at her. "What?"

She frowned a little. "What *have* you been doing all these years, Logan?"

"I told you. Consulting."

"For whom?"

"You wouldn't have heard of them."

"Try me."

He lifted an eyebrow, giving her words an entirely different meaning than she'd intended.

The pupils of her eyes suddenly dilated, and she moistened her lips, looking away. "Is it in law? This consulting you do?" Her voice sounded a little strangled.

Their gazes tangled, breaking only when the chatter around them suddenly ceased. Annie looked away from him, her cheeks flushed.

"More or less."

She folded her hands together. "Are you *trying* to make me more curious about you, Logan? Or is this just all part of that hardness that you hide underneath a veil of civility?"

It was Sam, now standing on a small riser, who had garnered everyone's attention.

Logan listened with half an ear as the sheriff read off a brief series of announcements that met with an equal number of groans from the residents. Most of his attention, however, was on Annie's assessment of him.

Coming from anyone else, it would have rolled off his back. From her, though, it didn't.

He heard Annie sigh when Sam was finished speaking. "I don't know how to live without electricity," she murmured.

The ironies continued. "Fortunately," he said, "I do."

Annie's curiosity where Logan was concerned was still unquenched when she tracked down her niece after dinner and steered her back to the beach house.

Logan hadn't accompanied them. She'd told herself she was glad. Once home, she lit several candles and started boiling water on the camp stove. If it took her all night, she was going to boil enough water to provide Riley and herself with decent baths.

She learned a few hours later, however, that the fuel for the stove only went so far. Riley got her bath.

Annie did not.

Which meant that she had yet to fully wash away the grime from their efforts earlier that day on the Castillo property. With Riley's help, she'd removed two flats of the small plants that had been beaten down by the rain so badly they'd barely clung to the soil. The flats now sat on the floor next to Annie's couch.

When the sun came up in the morning, she'd move them next to the glass door, to catch the light. Right now, they were warmer away from the window.

Riley shuffled into the room, her hair hidden beneath a towel. "The candle in the bathroom's going out. It's burned down to nothing."

"Logan said he'd get more candles when he gets the batteries for your Walkman." He'd disappeared after the community potluck dinner, saying only that he'd bring some supplies back to her house later.

She wondered if that meant he intended to sleep here again.

She wondered what she'd tell him if he did.

"If there are any batteries and stuff *left*." Riley's glum voice interrupted Annie's unnerving thoughts. "Everything's getting used up so fast."

"Well, I can't help with batteries. But I'm not worried about candles. We'll pull them from the stock at the shop if necessary." She studied Riley for a moment. "Guess you didn't count on having to play frontier woman when you came here."

Riley snorted. "Just 'cause I wish we had the electricity back doesn't mean I want to go home." She crouched down next to the plants, pushing up the sleeves of the sweatshirt Annie had given her to wear; the supply of clothes she'd carried with her in her backpack had been meager.

Since Annie wore her clothing too large in the first place, her niece was practically swimming in the garment. Without her customary globs of eyeliner and mascara and in the too-large sweatshirt, Riley looked just as young as she really was.

Which was way too young to have made her way, alone, from Washington state to Turnabout. It was a miracle that she'd managed it without encountering any trouble.

Annie swallowed down the panic over those awful what-ifs. "The Coast Guard will be coming by in the next day or two, Riley. The sheriff thinks he can arrange it for you and Logan to go with them to the mainland." She moistened her lips. She hadn't told Logan about her conversation with Sam, but he'd surely agree.

"I think you should go."

"Fine. I'll go to the mainland."

She pressed her hand against her midriff, willing away a surge of dizziness before it occurred to her—just as rapidly—that Riley's answer had come entirely too easily. She narrowed her eyes, studying her niece's stiff shoulders. "To the mainland—but not *home*."

Riley didn't reply.

Annie shoved her hair more securely into the clip at the back of her head. She sat down beside her niece, casting about for something helpful to say, some magic words to make everything right. "You know, Riley, there's nothing you...can't tell your parents...that you can't tell me." Maybe if she'd had someone in her life who'd seemed interested in listening to her, things for Annie might have turned out differently.

Riley shot to her feet. "I'm going to bed."

Annie sighed. "Good night."

But the girl had already left the room. A moment later, she heard the bedroom door close.

Feeling older than she ought to, Annie slowly stood. She went into the kitchen. Checked the phone even though she knew it was futile.

Nothing but silence filled her house.

Annie wasn't one to constantly need the noise of a television or a radio around her. But still, the utter silence was unnerving, possibly because there was nothing to blot out the voices in her head.

She finally grabbed one of the pots she'd used to boil water for Riley's bath and stuck it under the tap, filling it again. She grabbed a towel and washcloth and a bottle of Island Botanica shampoo, and let herself out the rear door.

Ahh, yes. The sound of the ocean, quiet though it was, filled the air. For a long moment she stood there on her deck and absorbed the peaceful sound, before carrying everything down to the fire pit. She made another trip back to the house, sorting through the wood pile for the driest pieces, which she also carried back to the pit. It took a few attempts, but she finally managed to get a flame going, and once the fire caught and burned brightly, she set the pot of water on the blackened grill that was suspended over one edge.

She left the water to heat, and traipsed back up to the house. She filled the empty water jug, grabbed another towel and her robe, stuck some toiletries in the robe's pocket, then stopped by Riley's bedroom door. She knocked softly and when there was no answer, her heart jerked in her chest. Riley had been exhausted, she assured herself. She wouldn't have sneaked out again.

Still, Annie opened the door and peeked inside. Her niece was sprawled on the bed, face turned away from the door.

Annie pressed her forehead against the door for a long moment, waiting for her heart to climb down from her throat. Then she started to close the door once more, but stopped. She set the water jug on the floor and went inside the room to carefully draw the quilt over Riley.

The sleeping girl didn't stir and Annie quietly left

the room again. She picked up the water and headed back outside.

Only when she stopped shaking a long while later did she get around to the task of bathing. She spread one towel on the wide concrete edge surrounding the pit and slid out of her clothes, working in shifts, because it was simply too cold to completely disrobe all at once.

She wasn't afraid of being seen. There were only stars to see whatever she did on this little stretch of beach and she knew she could dance naked under the moon if she chose without anyone knowing. A bath was her only intention, though, and she made quick work of it.

The water in the pot was too hot and the water in the jug was too cold for the process to be enjoyable. Within minutes, she had her damp body wrapped in her robe and she set about the task of washing her hair. By the time she poured the last of the jug's contents over her head to finish rinsing her hair, she was shivering so badly she ached from it.

She wrapped her head in the towel and left everything but the bottle of her lavender cream right there on the sand as she jogged back toward the house, leaving the glowing embers of the flame to burn themselves out.

But the glow of another ember stopped her in her tracks as she made it to the deck. "Logan? Is that you?"

"Sorry. Didn't mean to startle you." He sat on the edge of the deck, and he leaned forward into the thin gleam of moonlight to snuff out his cigarette in the sand.

Embarrassment joined her shivering, increasing her

discomfort tenfold. She'd expected him to take longer, if he'd return that night at all.

How long had he been sitting there?

It didn't matter how long, she assured herself. The fire pit was too far from the house to see anything. Even if he'd been in the house, or on the deck, he couldn't have seen her hasty, hunched-against-the-cold nudity.

Are you sure, Annie? Or had you hoped he would? You knew he'd eventually come back to the house. He'd promised to bring by more supplies. You're still the same as you always were, aren't you?

The voice in her head had always been colored with her mother's judgmental tone.

"Annie?" Logan's voice seemed to come at her through a fog. "Are you okay?"

Chapter 10

Logan started to stand. Annie looked as if she was ready to collapse. But she blinked. Waved her hand a little and tugged the lapels of her robe closer together. "I'm fine. You just...surprised me. I, um, I didn't know you smoked."

"I try not to." Smoking was one of those things that tended to give away your presence.

"Oh. Well. I was just washing my hair."

"So I see."

She stepped up on the deck and edged closer to the door, wiping sand from her feet as she did so.

"I brought the candles and batteries."

"Good." Her response was a little too quick. "Riley will be relieved. She has one of those portable CD players."

"I know. She told me earlier."

"Right." She smiled weakly and tugged on her belt again.

She was obviously uncomfortable.

"I also brought more fuel for the stove," he said. "The store's nearly out; you'll probably want to save it for necessities."

"Which probably doesn't include using it all to heat water so Riley can have a warm bath."

"Probably not," he agreed, knowing full well that was what she'd already done. "I would have brought you a lantern, but there aren't any mantles left in the store. I would've gotten you a gas grill for cooking, but propane's all sold out, too."

"How much did you spend? I'll pay you——"

"Forget about it. You're shivering. Go inside."

She reached for the door and slid it open. "Are you... where are you...Riley's asleep in her room. I think she's dead to the world for once."

"Glad to hear it. Chasing after her yesterday was more than enough for me."

Annie still didn't go inside. "What I meant is that her bedroom isn't available tonight. But the couch is. If you need a place to sleep that is. It's pretty comfortable. I'm not sure it's long enough for you. And you'd probably be warmer over at the community center. Or there might be someone else's house where you'd prefer to stay." She pressed her lips together, seeming to realize she was babbling.

"Are you trying to talk me into or out of using your couch?"

"Good question." She hesitated for a moment. "I, um, I don't want a repeat of what happened this morning."

It was an unpalatable nugget, but not an unexpected one. "Neither do I." He didn't think he could stand seeing her scramble away from him again the way she had.

"Okay then. Well, it's up to you. About the couch, I mean." She went inside and closed the door. She didn't lock it, though.

He let out a rough breath and pulled another cigarette from the pack he'd picked up along with the candles, the batteries, the fuel.

He bent his head against the breeze to light it, then sat there on the edge of the deck, his feet planted in the sand. Behind him, the plastic covering the window over her sink rippled, shifting and sighing with the wind.

In front of him, not quite out of his line of sight, was the glow from Annie's dying fire and beyond that, miles of night-dark ocean. Always there. Never silent. Never the same, yet never different.

He'd been on the island for two days. Long enough for the expected urge to leave it again to grab hold of him.

Yet behind him, inside a small beach cottage that had been built so long ago he remembered it from his own childhood, lived a woman who had got under his skin as easily as she ever had.

It wasn't the island that was causing his restlessness now, he knew. It was Annie.

Maybe—as unlikely as it might seem to him—she *didn't* remember what had happened between them all those years ago. But he sure as hell did. And of all the things he'd done in his life that he regretted, that night was the worst.

He sat there until his cigarette burned down into one long ash, until clouds rolled in and obliterated the thin moonlight, until the only noise coming from the house behind him was the hissing ripple of thick plastic.

Sam had offered him a bed for as long as he needed it. Given Annie's obvious discomfort and his own state of mind, taking him up on the offer was the wise choice.

He snuffed and stripped the cigarette out of habit, then pushed to his feet and silently slid open the glass door.

"I wasn't putting on a show out there at the fire pit for you." Her voice came out of the darkness the moment he stepped inside, and he went still.

"I thought you'd be in bed by now."

"Obviously, I'm not." He heard the scrape of a match, then watched her light the candle sitting on the coffee table in front of her. "I don't know what you saw, or think you saw, but I thought I was alone," she said. "So, if you want someone to strip for you, I suggest you look elsewhere."

Even in the minimal light cast by the candle, he could see the stiffness in her posture. The protective way she clutched her robe around her.

The fact was, he'd seen every furtive movement she'd made down there by the fire pit. He'd seen the way sparks had danced up from the fire when she'd stoked it. He'd seen the way she'd revealed one leg, then the other in the orange fire glow. Washing. Drying. Quickly. He'd seen the graceful arch of her back when she'd tugged off her sweater.

There'd been nothing seductive in her actions. Only simple practicality against the conditions in which they'd found themselves.

The sight had nevertheless grabbed him by the throat and yanked all the way down to his gut.

"Well?" Tension vibrated in her voice.

"I didn't see a thing," he lied.

The release of her tension was palpable. She cleared her throat. "Well...that's good. I, um, I'll get you a sheet and blanket for the couch, then. You...*are* planning to sleep here?"

"Yeah."

She quickly left the room. Returned a moment later with a neatly folded stack of bedding. "I hope you'll be warm enough."

"I don't think that'll be a problem." Fortunately, his self-directed irony escaped her.

"Okay."

She hovered close enough that he could smell the soft scent of her. And Annie seemed to have no clue as she stood there, unknowingly driving nails into his coffin of want. "Well. Good night, Logan."

If she didn't leave he was going to touch her, regardless of what they'd both said.

"I plan to wash up, myself, Annie," he said evenly. "With hot water. Right there in the kitchen next to the stove. So unless you want to see something *you don't want to see*, I suggest you stay in your room once you go there."

Her lips parted. She ran her hand down the hair she'd obviously braided while he'd sat out on the deck, as if she were actually contemplating his words.

She was killing him.

"Annie—"

She fled.

Another storm hit the island before morning.

An awesome crack of thunder jerked Annie upright

in her bed. Before the second round finished rattling the windows, she'd thrown back the covers and left her room at a run.

Riley was sitting up in her bed when Annie darted into her room. "Great." The girl flopped back down. "I thought I was dreaming."

"Maybe it won't be as severe," Annie said hopefully. The window next to Riley's bed had no curtains. Lightning flickered outside, but not long enough to really illuminate anything.

"Good, 'cause I don't want to sleep in the bathtub." Riley yanked the quilt over her head.

"The resilience of youth."

Annie whirled around at Logan's soft comment. He stood near the door. A flash of lightning revealed enough of him to assure he hadn't been caught midbath. She knew that he'd had plenty of time to accomplish his ablutions, but that hadn't kept her from lying awake in her bed for the past few hours thinking about it.

"More resilient than I am," she murmured, moving past him into the hallway. He started to pull Riley's door closed, but she touched his arm, staying his movement.

He looked at her and she snatched back her hand. Curled her fingers safely against her palm. "I think we should leave it open."

"Not if you're gonna stand there talking about it all night." Riley's voice was muffled by the quilt, but still clear.

It was too dark to see for certain, but Annie felt sure that Logan smiled. She headed back to the kitchen where she felt around—aided by the flickering lightning—for the matches she'd left near the candle. But

Logan's hand covered the book of matches first and she heard the soft scrape, saw the bright flare, and in the glow of it found his gaze on her face.

She swallowed. In a blink, the moment passed. He lit the candle. Another crack of thunder had her wincing.

"I know it's the lightning that causes the damage, but I really *hate* that thunder." She kept her voice low, striving for normalcy. "Do you think we should stay here?"

"I don't particularly want to walk to town in the rain unless we have to."

"Too bad you gave back Leo's golf cart." Annie rubbed her arms. She'd jumped from bed too rapidly to think about grabbing her robe to cover her thick flannel pajamas, and she was excruciatingly aware of the fact that he wore only a pair of dark jeans.

She moved to the glass door and peered out. "It doesn't seem as windy, at least."

"Small mercies."

She looked back to see him moving to the couch, flexing his arm, as if it pained him. She'd jumped from bed too rapidly to cover her thick flannel out with a deep sigh. "Go back to sleep, Annie. I'll wake you up if the storm gets worse."

"I wasn't asleep."

"Go to bed anyway."

Still, she hesitated. "Your arm is hurting, isn't it? From that piece of roof that hit you from the shack."

"I'll live."

"Did the skin break?"

"It's fine, Annie. Go to bed."

"But I have some ointment that might help." It bothered her that she hadn't thought to ask before now. If it hadn't been for her and Riley, he would never have been near that decrepit shack in the first place. He wasn't indestructible. Of course he could have gotten hurt. "I just need to know if the skin is broken or not. Some remedies—"

"If I agree to use your goop will you go to bed?" He sounded exasperated.

"Yes."

"Fine." He hardly sounded agreeable.

Annie hurried into the bathroom and fumbled around in the dark cupboard beneath the sink until she found her plastic box of first-aid supplies. She carried it, along with a washcloth she wet under the faucet, out to the living room and sat down on the hassock in front of the couch, then flipped off the lid. "Sit up."

"I can do it."

She looked at him, the tube in her hand. "You took the hit on the back side of your shoulder."

"You still like to get your way, don't you?" He sat up and twisted around so she could reach the spot where he'd taken the brunt of the blow from the shack's roof.

She squirted out the ointment on her fingers and carefully spread it over his arm and the hard bulge of his shoulder. It heated gently as she worked it in, and she heard him sigh.

"Feel better?"

"That you're probably spreading pig placenta all over me?"

"Eye of newt," she corrected blandly.

He turned his head and looked at her.

"Cayenne," she relented. "And a few other things, but trust me. You don't want to get it near your eyes, or use this on broken skin. It'd burn like fury."

"Pepper." He shook his head. "Damnedest thing."

"It'll help, though. I promise. I could also make you

an herbal tea. Healing from the inside is as critical—more so—than healing from the outside. A little valerian and passion flower, or maybe black willow and—"

"No thanks. Do you do chants, too? Maybe under your soft skin you're a Turn, after all. The original Castillos were supposedly into voodoo."

"Ergo, the curse."

"Right."

"Western medicine is the new kid on the block, Logan. Natural remedies have been around far longer."

"Well, my herbalist friend, for tonight we'll make do with the pepper goop on my arm." Amusement had replaced his exasperation.

It was ridiculous. Their conditions were not quite miserable, but another few days without utilities or the ability to reach the mainland, and they would be. Yet, Annie found herself smiling.

Mostly because Logan was smiling. A true smile. One that wasn't underlaid with that sense of grimness he carried around with him.

She capped the ointment tube and wiped her fingers on the damp washcloth. Then she rose and left everything on the breakfast counter.

She still doubted that she'd sleep. But she *had* agreed. "Good night, Logan."

"Good night, Annie."

She padded down the dark hall to her room and climbed back into bed. Outside, thunder still crackled. She pulled the blankets up to her neck and closed her eyes.

And finally slept.

Chapter 11

Three days on the island.

Logan stood in the road and eyed the colorful house. It had been converted into an office for Dr. Hugo Drake so long ago that he couldn't remember it ever being used *as* a house. The place hardly looked professional. Wind chimes hung from the eaves on the porch. How they'd managed to survive the storm, he didn't know. But then maybe his old man kept a bushel of wind chimes stored inside and he just hung up more of the infernal things when he wanted.

The front door was wide open. He went up the steps, ducking under the chimes, and went inside.

His father was with a patient.

Logan didn't learn that from the receptionist who sat at the battered desk in the front room. He knew it because he could hear the murmur of voices through the thin walls. Logan headed for a chair in the hall near Hugo's examining rooms. An upturned barrel was beside the chair. The barrel had sat there as long as he could remember, too.

There'd been a time when he'd sat on Hugo's knee while they played solitaire on top of the barrel.

He shoved his hands in his pockets and looked out the door that was open at the rear of the building. He could see the rooftop of Maisy's Place, the tall spires of palm trees clustered around it. And beyond that, the glitter of water.

His gaze went back to the barrel. So many things were just the way he remembered, the way he expected.

Unexpected, though, was the small, inexpertly carved box that sat on top of the barrel.

The carvings on the sides and top weren't perfect. But the wood was smooth as he ran his thumb back and forth over it, and the lid—when he pushed experimentally on it—still fitted securely.

He'd made the thing in the sixth grade. During wood shop. Back when his mother was still alive. He lifted the lid. A thumb-worn deck of playing cards was stored inside.

He closed the box and left it on the barrel, and then headed back to the reception area.

Hugo stood near the now-vacant desk in conversation with his patient. Other than a glance, he gave no indication what he thought about Logan's appearance, until his business was concluded and he had been paid by his elderly female patient with a batch of her homemade plum preserves. He sat the jars of preserves on the desk, then studied his cold cigar for a moment before tucking it between his teeth. "Hear you've taken up with young Annie."

Logan stepped more fully into the waiting area.

"She's past the age of consent," He was damned if he'd let the old man make him feel defensive. "What happened to Caroline?"

Hugo looked blank for a fraction of a second. Then his eyes narrowed. "Why are *you* interested? Now?"

"Sara and Annie want the Castillo House."

"They want the land around Castillo House," Hugo countered.

"Since you know that, why not help your daughter acquire it?"

"Lend her money?" Hugo's lips twisted as he picked up one of the jars sitting on the desk. "S'pose I could start selling off Mabel Bellanova's plum preserves." He set the jar down with a soft thump.

Logan wasn't amused. "By telling her how to reach Caroline."

Hugo looked weary. He sat down on the top of the desk. "She left the isle long before Sara was born. You were an infant. It's the last I saw of her."

"She was the love of your life."

Hugo's gaze met Logan's. "You telling or asking?"

"Stating a fact," Logan said flatly.

"A fact according to your mother."

"Well, I guess she'd have known."

Hugo's lips twisted. He said nothing.

"Where did she go after she left Turnabout?"

"I don't know."

"I don't believe you."

"And I can't help that, any more than I could ever change what your mother thought."

"What she *knew*."

"You're as pigheaded as she was," Hugo said after a moment. "Why the hell didn't you give her a divorce? Let her go?"

"She knew the truth about you. About you and Caroline. Why the hell didn't you give her a better reason."

"You think your mother would still be alive if I had." It wasn't a question. And Logan didn't like the pitying look he saw in his father's eyes. "You don't know the truth, Logan, because you've never wanted to see it. It was easier to blame your old man. You hated this island, and you hated me. Wouldn't even take a dime from me when you went off to college."

"Like you had any dimes to spare?" Logan laughed humorlessly. But Hugo was right. Even if the old man had been able to provide financial assistance, Logan would have refused it. Instead, he'd found himself in a deal with a man who some called a saint and some called a devil.

Even Logan wasn't sure which term more aptly suited his boss.

"I don't give a damn if you're still involved with Caroline, if you haven't seen her in five years, or in fifteen. All I want to know is where she was last, or at the very least where she headed when she left the island for good."

"And I'm telling you that I don't know." Hugo's voice was tight as he rose and stepped toward Logan. "Do you think I didn't wonder? The only family she had were her parents, and she gave up her own existence to care for them until they died. She was a young woman. She'd rarely been off Turnabout."

Keep on believing what you want. You hated this island, and you hated me. Wouldn't even take a dime from me when you went off to college."

"So you took advantage of her."

"I gave her a job here," he said evenly.

"And you drove my mother away because of Caroline."

"Your mother left *me*, Logan. Well before I hired Caroline. I didn't even know she was pregnant with you when she left. I had to hire a private investigator to find her and it took nearly a year, at that. You were six months old by then."

The story was hardly a news flash. "And you dragged us both back to Turnabout where you kept Caroline right under my mother's nose. Did you think she was an idiot? That she wouldn't figure out what you and your little receptionist were doing back in exam room one?"

Hugo eyed him, his face expressionless. "Why did you come back to Turnabout?"

There was a pain deep inside his head and his jaw ached. His father was as tall as he. They stood eye to eye. Similar. Completely different.

"Because I try to make up for my mistakes," he said after a moment.

Then he walked away.

Three days without power.

Annie looked over at the boxes stacked neatly near the rear door of the workshop. All orders that needed to be shipped.

Only there currently was no way to ship them.

"This stuff smells disgusting."

She looked over at Riley, stifling a sigh. The girl had already made it quite clear she'd rather have been over at Maisy's Place than helping Annie at Island Botanica. However, Annie knew the main appeal at the inn wasn't helping Maisy, but hanging with Kenny Hobbes of the stranded Denver Hobbeses, and she'd deliberately kept her niece occupied well into the afternoon in hopes of staving off another episode of finding her niece and the boy locking lips. She'd already caught them at it once. "Fortunately, the people who buy those herbal teas don't think so."

Riley made a face, but she continued slipping the small packages of dried herbs into the dark green envelopes with the silver script. She had already filled a large basket with finished envelopes. "Smells like licorice. Black licorice. I hate licorice."

Annie stretched a piece of packing tape across the last box. "Then I'll try not to force it on you at dinner today," she assured.

Riley fell quiet.

The only sounds were the rustle of the special envelopes, the crinkle of the raffia that Annie was using on the gift basket she was preparing, and the drip of water falling on the tin roof.

Even with the irritation that seemed to roll off Riley's shoulders in waves, Annie found the work as peaceful as she usually did.

The peace continued for all of ten minutes. Until Kenny-of-Denver stuck his head through the rear door. "Hey, whoa, I found you." His face seemed to hold a perpetually cocky sneer, and it was typically evident as he looked around the interior of the workroom. "Got some crazy-ass looking stuff hanging from your ceiling. Anything illegal up there?"

Annie eyed him. "No, but it'd be pretty easy for me to poison someone."

His eyes flickered, then he grinned, certain she was joking. "Cool. So, Riley, you gotta keep doing the work thing, or is there any chance of parole?"

Riley looked at her hopefully. "Can I?"

And the fact that she *asked* made Annie weaken. "No sunsets," she warned, knowing perfectly well that Riley would know what she meant.

Riley's cheeks colored. She nodded.

"And be at the community center by dinnertime," Annie called as the two teenagers headed out the door. They barely waved at her, ducking and laughing as they dodged the water that dripped from the eaves.

"Sounding like the voice of mothers everywhere."

Logan stepped into the doorway.

She jerked. The roll of raffia escaped her grasp and fell on the floor.

"Didn't mean to startle you." He caught the roll as it bounced across the floor toward him. "Here." He walked over to the workbench and set it beside her.

"Thanks." She wasn't going to ask what he'd been doing all day. He'd been gone that morning when she woke, leaving behind a pot of coffee warm on the stove and the bedding folded at one end of the couch. She realized he'd shaved. Maybe he'd done it last night and she hadn't noticed. He was also wearing fresh clothes. Blue jeans that were faded nearly white, and a UCLA T-shirt that strained a little across his shoulders. And his face was positively grim. "You all right?"

His brows drew together for a moment. "Same as ever." Then he looked around at the pile of boxes ready to ship. "You've been busy."

She could take a hint. He didn't want to talk. Not about himself, at any rate. What else was new? "Those were the last of the mail orders we'd received before the storm hit." She looked over at the oven that she couldn't use to aid the drying process. "Instead of playing catch-up on order processing like we usually do, Sara and I will be playing catch-up on production once things get back to normal."

"Except you'll probably find out there are orders you've received in the past few days that you don't even know about yet."

That was true enough. She quickly finished tying the raffia around the basket and placed it inside the shipping box she'd already made for it. She deftly added packing material to protect the basket and its variety of contents, slipped the paperwork on top, then sealed the box and stuck the label on it. "Ready to go." She carried the box over to the pile.

She looked around the workshop, brushing her hands down her apron as she sorted through her mind for some task to keep herself busy. But her mind seemed far too empty of ideas and her workroom far too full of Logan's presence. "How does your arm feel today?" She picked up the large basket of teas that Riley had finished, only to have Logan pluck it away from her.

"Where?"

She pointed at the empty spot on the storage shelves.

"It feels fine." He easily positioned the basket in place. "How's the scratch on your back?"

She'd had Riley spread aloe on it that morning. "It's fine." The polite exchange made her head throb. "Any news on the phone lines or the electricity?"

"No." He picked up a sprig of rosemary and sniffed it. "You don't look particularly bothered by that." She drew off her apron and hung it on a wall hook.

"I'm a patient man."

She lifted her eyebrows, unwillingly amused. "If you say so." She retrieved a bottle of lotion from the shelf and stuck it in an Island Botanica gift bag, then picked up her keys and headed to the rear door. There had been no need to unlock the front entrance at all.

"Where are you headed now?"

She lifted the gift bag. "Drop this off to Darla Towers. Then go to the fields."

"They're wet."

"They often are." She closed the door after him and locked it.

"When I lived here, nobody had to lock anything."

She dropped the keys in the side pocket of her jumper. "I thought you didn't like Turnabout." She glanced up and down the alley. For the moment, the drizzle had ceased.

"I don't." He fell into step beside her as she walked.

"Yet you just sounded like you miss it."

"I miss the days when people didn't have to lock their doors."

"Well, I lock the shop because of the cash register and the computer and the inventory. There are just more tourists on Turnabout these days—even when they're not stuck here like they are right now. Town's had a few break-ins, and they are almost always committed by someone from off-island. But the only thing I've locked my door at home against was the storm. All things considered, I find it pretty comforting." They rounded the side of her building and came out on the road in front of it. Darla lived in one of the bungalows that lined up straight as soldiers before the road curved and headed down to Maisy's Place. "Where do *you* live?" she asked.

"Nowhere in particular."

She stopped in the road and looked up at him. The man was too cagey by far. "You know, Logan, if you don't think it's any of my business, just say so."

"I'm serious."

She clucked skeptically. "I don't believe you're homeless."

"Didn't say I was."

She lifted her hands. Dropped them. Shook her head. "Fine. Whatever." She would not indulge her curiosity where this man was concerned. She'd already indulged more than was safe for her peace of mind. He was only there in the first place at her brother's request.

She started walking again, steps brisk.

He fell in step beside her, shortening his pace to match hers. "Do you always deliver personally?"

"No, but I don't think there's any point in opening the shop these days. If somebody needs something, they'll let me know. Like Darla did."

"The only reason Darla stopped by the table last night was to flash her implants at me."

Annie glared at him. "She's a perfectly nice woman, Logan. Just because she's having a hard time right now—"

"Hey, okay. Didn't know you were now the champion of the lost-and-seeking."

She huffed. "Would you prefer I was still good ol' Easy A?"

"You probably started that nickname yourself to piss off your parents."

She wasn't altogether certain that he was wrong.

"It was all an act, anyway. You told me so yourself," he added when she shot him a look. "And I think you're more interesting now."

That comment thoroughly disconcerted her. "I'm not *trying* to be interesting to anyone."

"Some things can't be helped."

"Well, there's interesting as in 'oh, look at that fascinating bug with five legs,' and there's interesting as in 'wonder if she's good in bed.'" Her face went hot. She clamped her lips together, but her runaway tongue had already done the damage.

His lips twitched. He deliberately looked at her legs. Her tan jumper nearly reached her ankles, and she wore short white socks with her canvas shoes. Hardly seductive trappings.

She still felt scorched by the time he looked up at her face again.

"I only see two," he murmured.

Studiously ignoring him, she hurriedly walked on to Darla's place, made her delivery, collected her cash and continued down the road.

"Your fields are the opposite direction, Annie."

"We're almost to Maisy's Place, and I'm pretty sure that's where Riley is. I should check on her. Make sure she's okay."

"That kid she was with reminds me of someone."

Ivan Mondrago, Annie thought before she could stop herself. Trouble with a capital T.

"I'm not sure you should let her hang around with him."

She stopped dead in the road. "I am not Riley's parent, Logan. I don't know the first thing about being a good one. It would be stupid to pretend otherwise."

He looked impatient. "You're the closest thing she's got to a parent right now. That kid is a creep. You should be locking her away from him."

"The only thing that's accomplished by *locking* a kid away from something is turning that very kid into a picklock."

"I guess you'd know."

Her stomach suddenly felt tight. She knew nothing about Logan's life, now. Which was probably just as well, since nothing would be served with her increasing fascination. But he'd once been Will's friend until life had apparently taken them in separate directions. He'd known all about the troublesome antics from which her brother had faithfully plucked her.

"I guess I would," she agreed. She started walking again, only to stop a moment later and look up at him. "Adults aren't the only ones who face hard choices, Logan. Kids, teenagers. They face them, too."

"You're bending over backward to trust Riley because your parents never trusted you."

"My parents trusted me to screw up. And I did. Over and over again, so in that, they were correct. It's not Riley I don't trust. It's—" *Drago*, her mind whispered. "—Kenny," she finished carefully.

"The only thing your parents were correct about was what fork to use for the shrimp course."

Despite herself, she laughed. But nothing about the situation—her past or Riley running away—was laughable. "I'm going to Maisy's. Are you...are you coming?"

"I'll pass."

She knew why. He didn't want to run into Dr. Hugo who was often at Maisy's Place. It was sad. She didn't speak with her own parents for a number of reasons. But she'd never heard Dr. Hugo speak badly of his son.

"All right. Well, I guess I'll see you at dinner."

"I'll be there."

It was a promise. It was a curse.

Her stomach felt that odd little curl in it as his gaze held hers.

And just then, the drizzling rain started to fall again. His lips tilted. The breathless moment passed.

She shook her head and lifted her hands to feel the moisture collect on her palms. "Somebody up there must really think Turnabout needs a good, *long* bath."

"Maybe so." Moisture gleamed like diamonds in his thick, dark hair. "But whatever the reason, you do look good in raindrops."

She went stock-still as he leaned down and brushed his lips over hers. Then, with a faint smile, he strode away.

Her fingers touched her lips.

"Annie?"

At the voice, she whirled around to see Sara standing on the raised porch of Maisy's Place. "Sara! How did you get here?"

Sara slowly came down the steps. "Never mind that. Was that my *brother* you were kissing?"

Chapter 12

Dinner at the community center was over.

Now that the initial shock of the storm had worn off, the islanders were obviously heading right back into fine form. The generator was humming, the fireplace in the domed pit was burning brightly. There was even a group of people dancing to the enthusiastic—if not professional quality—music being played by some impromptu band.

And there was a smile on Riley's face. "It's like a party," she said. "You're gonna let me stay here tonight, right? There's nothing to do at your house."

"You're gonna stay *here*, right?" Annie eyed Riley right back. "I'm not going to find you and Kenny together the way I did before we had dinner, am I?" She'd found the teens in yet another clinch that had only served to underscore her unease where the boy was concerned.

"He's staying at Maisy's Place with his parents," Riley reminded. "I told you that before."

She had.

Annie pinched the pain hovering beneath the bridge of her nose. She had to stop equating Riley with herself. The girl was nothing like her; she wasn't a magnet for trouble the way Annie had been. "All right. Fine. If they have a place for you to sleep tonight, then you can stay."

Riley immediately turned, leaving Annie to follow. They worked their way through the room, stepping around cots that were shoved together in some haphazard manner that probably made sense to someone, and found the school principal who—according to one of Sam's announcements at dinner—had been appointed to keep order at the center. Assured that Riley was indeed welcome to stay—they could always use another pair of hands when it came to snuggling with the little ones who were having a hard time adjusting to the odd circumstances—Riley barely looked at Annie before heading away into the fray.

She sighed faintly, watching her niece get swallowed among the throng. She was no closer to understanding what was driving Riley than she had been when the girl had appeared on her doorstep days earlier. And Annie was getting entirely too accustomed to having her there on Turnabout, despite the circumstances.

Annie finally turned away, only to stop short at the sight of Logan standing behind her.

"Oh. Hi." Her heart danced a nervous jig and it annoyed her no end. Despite his assurance earlier that he'd see her at dinner, he'd been noticeably absent. And she'd be darned if she'd ask what had kept him. "Sara's on the island, you know." Her friend had thoroughly grilled Annie over the kiss she'd seen. Annie dearly loved her partner—considered her to be the sister she'd never had—but she'd never told her about Logan, about the intense dream that had been her companion for way too many years. Trying to explain what Logan was doing on the island, what he was doing with Annie, had about exhausted her. Following up that event with finding Riley and Kenny in a clinch had just added another dimension of discomfiture.

"Yeah," he said. "I heard about the way she finagled her way across. She'd have been smarter to stay on the mainland."

Obviously, there was *no* surprising him. "Well, Sara knew what the situation was and wanted to come home anyway. Some people actually *like* being in their homes."

"And some people are lucky enough to *have* homes." He closed his hand over her arm, keeping her from slipping away among the dancing bodies when she tried to leave. "What's wrong?"

"Nothing." She pulled at her arm. "Since you know she's on the island, why don't you go *see* her? She's thrilled that you deigned to visit, or do you plan to avoid her the same way you do your father?"

When it rains, it pours, Logan thought. "If that's what's got you upset, don't bother. I've already seen my sister. *And* my father." His voice was even.

"I am *not* upset."

Her eyes were glassy, her cheeks flushed. She was either upset or drunk, and the latter was unlikely. According to the grapevine, Annie was a teetotaler. "Is it

Riley?" He could see the teen from where they stood. She actually had a smile on her face as she twirled in circles holding hands with April. "She looks like she's having a good time, for once."

"She is. That's why she's staying here for the night again."

Logan's gaze slanted back to Annie. She looked stiff. Completely uncomfortable among the boisterous revelry. He knew it wasn't because she felt out of place among the islanders. He'd seen her interact with them too many times over the past few days to believe that. Which meant it was a reaction to him, or to Riley. Or both.

He slid his hand down her arm, latching his fingers around hers. "Come on."

"I'm not going anywhere with you. I'm going home."

"Fine. I'll scare up a golf cart and drive you."

"I don't need a ride. I've been walking all over this island for five years now. And I'll still be doing it when you're gone."

"I'm not gone yet."

"More's the pity. If you'd taken Riley back right away, then——"

"She could well have run away again." He kept his voice low as he hustled her toward the door, knowing she'd be unlikely to resist and draw more attention to herself. "Which you know better than anyone." He didn't let go of her until they were outside. "Now what's the real reason you've got your knickers in a twist?"

She yanked at the sleeves of her blue jacket, neatening them around her slender wrists. "You said you'd be there for dinner." She looked shocked, as if the words were unwelcome.

"I had something I needed to do."

"Fine." Her shoulder lifted. "Whatever. It's no business of mine. Sara—"

"Sara already gave me her opinion." The sister that he remembered as a schoolgirl—bookish and quiet—had grown into a leggy, raven-haired woman who was no more quiet when it came to voicing what she thought than Hugo was.

And what Sara thought was that he'd better not plan on doing anything more than kiss her best friend unless he intended to stick around awhile.

He could have told Sara that he'd sooner turn monk than hurt Annie more than she'd already been hurt, but he hadn't.

The fact was, he wanted Annie. He wanted her bad. And only some whisper-thin sense of decency he was surprised to find still living inside him kept him from taking exactly what he wanted.

"I'll drive you home."

"I don't need you to."

"Maybe *I* do."

Annie went still as his words sank into her. She looked up at him. There were shadows under his eyes. A muscle flexed in his jaw. She didn't *know* this man. And yet, even as she reminded herself of that inescapable fact, she *did*.

As much as she wanted—needed—to maintain her distance from anyone who shook the secure little world she'd created for herself, she couldn't bring herself to refuse him.

She swallowed. Nodded.

Tension seemed to leave his face.

Logan commandeered Leo's golf cart again. But this time, Annie didn't insist on driving.

The moonlight was a thin wash across the uneven road. She kept a firm hold of the metal bar next to the seat cushion, maintaining as much distance between them as she could as they left behind the noise of the community center and headed straight into the quiet night.

Maybe I do. Logan's quiet statement circled in Annie's mind.

She'd spent a long time, years, molding her life into something she could manage. Something she could respect. She'd put nearly all her efforts into Island Botanica. She'd made friends, she'd walked the straight and narrow path of responsibility. She'd been so diligent, so focused, as if she could completely eradicate the person she'd once been.

She could manage a business; she could cultivate plants where others had failed; she could finally make her own way in life without fear of harming what she'd loved most.

Yet in the span of three days, she felt as if all of that was unraveling.

She didn't know if it was the storm. Or Riley. Or Logan.

Perhaps, it was all three.

Logan turned off the road and headed down her steep little path. The motor hummed softly as he pulled to a stop right in front of her house.

She could hear her pulse beating in her ears.

There was no practical reason anymore for him to stay at her place. He wouldn't sleep under his father's roof, but he'd have no such reservations where his sister was concerned.

Yet Annie knew, if she looked at him, she would beg him to stay.

So she kept her eyes on her front door as she slid from her seat. She'd barely closed herself in the house when she heard the distinctive whine of the golf cart heading up the road.

He'd seen no reason to stay.

It was so dark inside that she could barely tell whether her burning eyes were opened or closed. Despite the flashlight tucked in her pocket, she carefully crossed through the living room, and went into Riley's bedroom.

She slid off the crinkling jacket, dropping it on the mattress, and knelt to reach beneath the bed. Her fingers easily closed over the hard plastic box stored there. Drawing it out, she carried it to the living room. She started to set it on the breakfast counter, but the silence of the house pressed in on her. Instead, she slid open the sliding glass door, and went out onto the deck.

She dragged the chaise to the edge of the deck because the moonlight was brighter there, and flipped back the lid of the plastic box. She lifted out the three albums inside and dropped the box on the deck. Her hands shook as she arranged the thick books on her lap, the most recent on top.

A young girl's lifetime, captured on film.

She flipped open the cover.

She made it halfway through the first album before the tears completely blinded her.

"Annie?" Logan was there, crouched down beside her. His hand cupped her cheek. "I knocked."

She could only stare at him, her chest aching. Without volition, she pressed her cheek against the warmth of his hard hand, closing her eyes. "I heard you leave."

"I came back." He moved the heavy albums from her lap and tucked them beneath the chair. "Let's get you inside."

"It's too quiet. Too empty." She pressed her fist against her mouth, stifling a hiccupping sob.

He exhaled roughly. "Ah, Annie." He sat on the edge of the chaise, lifting her, as if she were a child, right onto his lap. "Don't." His hands stroked through her hair. "It'll be all right."

She shook back her head, looking into his face. She'd left tears and childhood long behind. "No," she whispered. He didn't know what had happened; he didn't know what she'd done. If he did, he'd hate her as much as she'd hated herself. "No," she said again, and leaning into him, she pressed her mouth against his.

His lips felt cool, like the night. She felt the way his hands tightened in her hair, then deliberately loosened and fell away. "Annie—"

"Kiss me."

He made a low sound.

Her lips skimmed over his. Her heart raced. Her stomach felt tight. Ever since the last time, she'd wanted to taste him again. To feel him again.

She wanted his hands on her. Then, maybe, she could forget.

"Logan, kiss me." She twisted in his arms, sliding her hands up his soft jacket, over his shoulders.

He caught them, stilling, as they reached his neck. "I want more than a kiss, Annie. You're not—"

She moved her lips over his again. Nibbling. Tasting. He wouldn't let go of her hands so she curled her fingers down over his, holding him in return. "I want more," she whispered. Her lips tingled against the soft scrape as she drew them along his jaw. She reached his throat, right beneath his ear. "Everything."

He suddenly let go of her hands and grasped her head between his two hands, forcing her back so he could look into her face. His eyes were dark shadows in the night, no less intense because of it. "Are you sure?"

He'd sheltered her from a storm.

If only he could shelter her from herself.

"Yes."

He inhaled sharply. She waited, her breath stalled in her throat, for his kiss. For him to devour her, the way his eyes said he wanted to do. Instead, his touch was slow. Achingly gentle, as he brushed his thumb over her lips.

No. She didn't want gentle. She wanted a raging flood that would block out all thought. She twisted her head, restless. "Logan—"

"Sshh." His hand crept behind her head, cradling it while his other thumb continued gliding back and forth against her lip. Then up her cheek, drying the trail of tears.

Pinpricks burned behind her eyes.

He tilted her head and kissed the corner of her lips. The corner of her eyes. His gentleness was like some exquisite pain squeezing her soul.

She exhaled, truly shaken.

Then he stood, drawing her up with him.

Her legs shook. Her breath stumbled.

"I won't hurt you."

She would have laughed had she possessed the

strength. She could only seem to stand there, quivering as his fingertips slowly explored the shape of her face, the curve of her neck. He slipped those tantalizing fingertips beneath the neckline of her T-shirt, grazing the hollow of her throat, then back up again, sliding along her jaw, slipping into her hair.

"You are so beautiful." His voice seemed to come from somewhere deep inside him. "More now than ever."

An image of that long-ago incident at the wedding reception sidled into her mind. He'd called her beautiful then, too. A beautiful *child* too foolish and selfish for her own good.

"Not the past," she was barely aware of speaking the words. "Don't think of the past."

"Sshh. It's okay." His lips touched hers. "It's gone. It's over."

Her eyes felt heavy. Her body ached from an eon of loneliness. "Make love with me, Logan." She slid her hand around his neck, tugging his head closer. The more boneless she felt, the more tensely he held himself. She could feel it in his corded neck, in his tight jaw when she kissed it. "Now."

She pulled at the wide strap of her jumper until it came off her shoulder. Then the other side. The dress was so loose, it fell straight down her hips, piling in folds of khaki around her feet.

He muttered a soft oath and sat down again on the edge of the chaise. His arm was like an iron brace around her back, yet she didn't feel trapped, only treasured as he pressed his mouth against her abdomen, his warm breath stealing through the tight weave of her T-shirt.

Her hands twisted in the shirt he wore, pressing against the unyielding breadth of his shoulders. Her knees would have buckled if not for his hold on her when his mouth ran up the center of her shirt, kissed the valley between her breasts, then closed, open-mouthed over one tight crest, then the other. But it wasn't enough. She wanted—needed—his mouth on her skin. She wanted his *skin* on her skin.

She scrabbled at his shirt, tugging and pulling until she managed to break his hold on her long enough to drag the shirt over his head. She tossed it to the deck, and reached for her own, but his hands beat her to it. With agonizing slowness, he drew it upward, letting her pull her arms free, then tugged it completely away.

Her hair tumbled around her shoulders and for a painfully exposed moment she wished for the days when her hair had been able to blanket her to the waist.

Her skin pebbled in the chill night air, yet beneath the surface, she felt hot. As if her skin had shrunk a size beneath the heat of his hooded gaze.

Then his hands covered her. Shaped her, plumped her to his lips.

And her knees did give way.

He caught her easily and rose, lifting her right off her feet. She had a fleeting thought that she must look silly in only her panties and short white socks and canvas shoes, but there was nothing in his gaze that told her so.

If anything, he looked…he looked…fierce.

Male to her female.

His mouth covered hers as he carried her inside. She toed off her shoes and gave them no further thought as liquid heat stole through her. He carried her unerringly through to her bedroom, despite the pitch dark. Slowly lowered her legs until she stood in front of him. His jeans felt coarse against her, and she was hazily grateful for that pitch dark for it hid the way her mouth opened in a soundless gasp when she felt his hands slide down her hips. Her thighs.

He lifted her ankle and drew off one little sock.

He kissed her knee.

Drew off the other sock.

Kissed her thigh.

And he kissed the heart of her, right through the utterly conventional, thoroughly unimaginative white cotton panties she wore.

Her hands tangled in his hair and her gasp found voice. "Logan, I don't, I can't—"

His lips moved to her belly. Her hips. "Shh," he soothed. "We'll go as slow as you want, Annie. Whatever you need."

What she'd needed was an end to the pain of the past. What she'd gotten was a writhing ache inside her that only he could quench. "I need you." She slid down to her knees on the sisal rug, hissing as her breasts grazed the hair whirling over his chest. Without conscious thought, she arched into him, swaying against the delicious friction.

He made a sound, a growl, that sent shivers skittering along her spine, and he kissed her again.

Hard.

Her head fell back, pushing against the side of the mattress that she hadn't even realized was so near. His tongue swept inside, taunting her. Tempting her.

"Come out, come out, come out to play."

The tune dangled in her mind and she found herself

smiling against him, her heart leaping in some foolishly hopeful dance that she couldn't even put a name to.

She felt his lips curve, too, and the sensation was alternately unique and seductive. And when he finally lifted his head, their harsh breaths were audible in the utter silence, a song that she knew would remain with her the rest of her days.

She went still, caught in a web of need so deep she wasn't sure she'd ever emerge. Or if she wanted to.

"We can still stop."

His voice was husky.

She frowned. Stop? The darkness made her bold. She ran her hands down his chest until she found the waistband of his jeans. She brushed her knuckles over the rigid length of him that no amount of stonewashed denim could disguise. "Can we?"

He grunted and grabbed her hand, pressing it back against the mattress beside her head. "Yes." But his voice sounded strained. "If you're not ready for this, I can stop."

"Then you're stronger than I am." He wouldn't release her hand, but she had the rest of her body at her disposal, and she arched against him, fitting herself against him. "Because I can't."

He let go of her hand and suddenly lifted her until she sat on the edge of the bed. Some portion of her mind thought he must have eyes like a cat to be able to make out anything at all in the night-blackened room. She heard a rustling, sensed that he'd risen and was pulling off his jeans.

Then his hands slid over her thighs, between them, and she stopped thinking altogether.

She felt his kiss on her knee. Her thigh. Her shoulder. Her breast.

Never expected, a random delight.

She dug her fingers into the bedding beneath her. Her head fell back like an overblown bloom; a moan rose in her throat. Where his lips fell, his hands teased elsewhere. Sliding down her spine, seeming to feel out every vertebrae, grazing soothingly over the still-tender scratch, then pressing against her throat, as if to absorb the feel of the gasping moan she couldn't seem to contain. Skimming over her panties again, slowly urging them away from the moisture where they clung.

And his rough exhalation when his hand covered her. Her stomach clenched, hard.

Her thighs instinctively closed and he made that soft shushing sound again, stilling until she relaxed once more.

And then she felt his fingers draw through that moisture, sift through that down. She sank back against the bed, pulling at him, certain that their heartbeats were as loud as their uneven breathing.

She wasn't a virgin, there was no point in pretending she was. But this was still new to her.

New and—oh, please—so excruciatingly wondrous.

His hand rocked against her. "Yes?"

Her head twisted. She pressed her heels against the mattress. *"Yes."*

Then his mouth was on her, and everything she thought she knew ceased to exist. There was only him. His loving.

She cried out, and the bed squeaked ever so softly as she convulsed, only his hands on her to keep her from flying apart.

Shudders still quaked through her when he finally—*finally*—moved up onto the bed beside her. She was barely aware of the hot tears that had streaked out from her eyes, but he seemed to know they were there, and he brushed them away, murmuring nothing as he tucked her head against his chest, and held her while her world tried to right itself.

A futile endeavor.

There was his heart, thundering beneath her cheek. His abdomen rigid beneath her palm as she slowly stroked down his torso.

He caught her hand before she could reach him. "Wait."

She could no more wait now than she could have stopped earlier. But he didn't go anywhere. Just leaned away for a moment. Then she heard a soft tear, and the bed gave that little squeak.

Realization nudged through the desire that shrouded her. "I'll bet you were an Eagle Scout," she whispered.

"Always prepared." He tipped her back and her thighs eagerly welcomed the weight of him.

And then there were no more words. Nothing but her soft cries and his long, low groan, as he pressed into her tight body. Again. And again. And when she started trembling wildly, his hard palms slid against hers, his fingers threading through hers.

He could protect her from herself. But as they hurtled into the abyss, and his head fell to her shoulder, her body a cradle for his, she had the fleeting thought that, perhaps, she could protect him, too.

Annie's eyes came open with a start. She propped herself up on her arm and Logan's hand slid through her hair.

"You okay?" His voice was husky with sleep.

She listened, not sure what had wakened her. But the house was silent. No storm raged outside. The glimmer of dawn had broken through the window, bathing her bed in hazy silhouette.

"I don't know. Yes."

She looked down at him, and, no matter that she still felt weak from his lovemaking, her blood suddenly ran streaking through her veins.

His hair looked darker than ever against her white pillow and his shoulder where her hand rested looked like bronzed satin. But it wasn't his darkly handsome looks that made her nerves sing. It was the way his gaze touched her face, the way his eyes looked into hers, intensely intimate. Sunlight unfurling her petals.

Helpless in the grip of it, she leaned over him, her lips a hairbreadth from his. She slowly drew her leg up his, and reveled in the way he inhaled, his chest pressing against her breasts. His hands skimmed down her spine, then curled around her hips as she slid over him, and with agonizing slowness, began taking him in.

He groaned. His fingers flexed against her hips, and she cried out, her senses racing as he thrust upward, then twisted over, dragging her beneath him. Stealing all coherent thought but one.

Reality was better than the dream.

Chapter 13

He'd filled the bath for her. And the water was warm enough to actually steam the air in the chilly bathroom.

While she'd slept, he'd heated gallon after gallon of water.

She was still scrambling for composure against the thoroughly unexpected gesture when the door creaked and he joined her.

A practical man who could be impractical.

She leaned up, sliding her arms around his shoulders.

"Hey." He hastily set down the pot of hot water he carried. "If I'd known all it took was warm water—" She laughed softly and pushed away, tilting her head away from him to dash at a tear. She slipped off her robe and quickly stepped into the water.

It felt heavenly. She slowly sat and leaned back. Even

though she was anxious to get to the community center and check on Riley, she sighed deeply. How much could a little time hurt? "Ohhhh, yes."

He made a strangled sound.

She looked up at him through her lashes. "Come on in, Logan. The water's perfect."

"I heated the water for *you*." He moved the pot of clean water until it was within her reach.

She slid down until the bathwater lapped her chin.

Her hand lazily drifted through the water. "We already know there's room for two. I'll wash your back," she added.

"And what will you let me wash?"

"Whatever you can reach," she said, and bit her lip at her own bravado.

He dropped his jeans. "Scoot forward."

Annie swallowed at the sight of him, bravado fading. No moonlight shadows to hide behind, no tangle of bedding. Only...him. Mercy. She let out a little breath and sat forward, the water sloshing.

He stepped into the water. As he slid down, the water level rose dangerously high. Then his arm scooped her back against him, and a small wave lapped over the side of the tub. He reached for the oval cake of soap sitting in the abalone shell she used as a soap dish and held it up between his fingers. "Island Botanica?"

"Of course."

He dipped the cake in the water, then rubbed it between his hands until they were slippery with a velvet-soft froth. "Smells like you." His deep voice vibrated through her back.

She plucked the soap from his hand and—sacrificing another splash of water over the side—slid around until her back was against the other end of the tub. If he touched her with those soapy hands of his, she'd be lost.

"I want to get to Riley this morning."

"Before the Denver delinquent gets to her first?" He caught her ankle and lifted it out of the water, soaping his way from her toes toward her ankles and beyond. "Relax. It's early yet. You wake up at the crack of dawn. It'll be a while yet before anyone's stirring over at the community center."

Relax? His hands were slipping over the sensitive skin behind her knees. "On an *ordinary* day, I work in the fields before we open the shop. Whoa." She jerked her leg back. "Enough of that."

He slanted a knowing look at her, then captured the cake of soap from the water that was turning milky. His legs bumped hers. "Never enough of *that*."

He was wicked, that's what he was. She curled her legs closer to her side of the tub and finished washing them.

He laughed softly.

And she had a long moment's qualm over her ability to keep this in perspective.

They traded the soap back and forth. Cursing under his breath, he used her razor to shave, then—despite her embarrassment—watched avidly as she quickly dashed it over her legs.

Perhaps bathing with a man was ordinary fare for other women, but it wasn't for her. She'd never felt more exposed, or more disgustingly gleeful.

Ordinary. Ordinary. Pretend this was ordinary. "What's an ordinary day like for you?" She quickly tilted her head back into the water, poured shampoo in her hand and started working it through her hair. The water was cooling all too quickly. "When you're not stuck on islands you hate while trying to retrieve your friends' runaway kids, that is."

Her tone was light, her half smile teasing. But the words only served to remind Logan that his days on Turnabout were numbered.

"That's more ordinary than you'd think." The irony tasted bitter. He reached out for the pot of clean water and handed it to her to rinse the shampoo from her hair. While she did so, he stood. Water sluiced down his body and he very nearly scooped her out of the water despite everything when her green gaze widened and lingered on him.

That vaguely shocked, utterly fascinated look of hers was enough to melt an iceberg. He stepped out of the tub into a good inch of water on the floor. "There's another pan of water on the stove." If it hadn't boiled dry by now. He left the room, snatching a towel off the rack as he went.

He wrapped it around his waist. His wet feet slapped against the tile as he headed into the kitchen. The water hadn't boiled down to nothing, but the flame had gone out.

The fuel can was empty. Only one full can remained.

He sighed. Damage to Turnabout wasn't extensive enough to warrant federal assistance, and—to Sam's well-earned disgust—the town council had already assured other emergency channels that they were handling their own recovery efforts perfectly well.

Yet they hadn't managed to get power restored; they hadn't done anything to bring necessities *to* Turnabout. They had only ensured that the severest injuries had made it *off* Turnabout.

He didn't doubt his ability to get off the island. He'd never doubted it. He wouldn't have come to Turnabout without being entirely certain about leaving it again and the storm hadn't changed that.

So what the *hell* was bugging him about it now?

He exhaled, shoving his hand through his hair.

With no effort at all he could go back into that dinky bathroom, scoop Annie against him and stave off coherent thought for a considerable length of time.

But reality—his reality—would still be waiting.

He slowly unscrewed the fuel can, threw it in the trash with vicious aim and turned away.

Annie stood there wrapped in a towel, her eyes wide. "You're upset."

Aggravated, annoyed and generally frustrated didn't begin to cover it. "No."

Her gaze slipped to the narrow trash can. She sucked in her lower lip for a moment. "You can talk to me, you know."

Could he? They'd climbed inside each other's skin until they were inseparable. But had they really talked?

"I'm not angry," he said.

Her lashes swept down. She gave an acquiescent little nod that made him feel as if he'd kicked her. "I should get to Riley."

"That's it? No argument from you, no debate, no challenging what I say? You just accept it and head on down the road for another day?"

She winced. Kicked again. "What do you want from me, Logan?"

He hadn't wanted anything from her. "I want you to stop acting as though life is going to punish you if you don't toe some line of perfection that your head has drawn in the sand."

Her eyes looked like bruised gems, but at least they contained a spark. "Life's already punished me, Logan. And frankly, I like myself a lot more *now* than I ever used to. Can you say the same?" She shook her head after a moment. "Of course, you *won't say* anything. You can come here, play hero where Riley is concerned, get a little action from good ol' Annie, who's more like *poor* little Annie nowadays, and head on out again feeling like you've done us all a service."

"I didn't—"

"You ought to look in a mirror, Logan. You need help just as much as the rest of us human beings. Do you even let anyone know who you are? Let anyone inside?"

"I let you inside," he said flatly.

She looked startled. Then sad. The corners of her lips curved downward. "I think we both know there's little truth in that statement. Despite what…what we've done together, there are too many things we don't know. Too much we hide." She looked down and tucked the folds of the towel more securely around her. "We're a lot alike, Logan. You and me. I don't think I realized that before."

"You're nothing like me." She planted, nurtured, harvested, and repeated the process.

He destroyed. Once and for all. End of story.

"You let someone in—me—only as far as you deem comfortable. But the rest of you, you hold off. You'll chance yourself only so far. Because you don't want to get hurt."

"I don't get hurt."

Her eyes went soft. "I think you've been hurting longer than any of us, Logan Drake."

He deliberately eyed her. "The only thing hurting me is caused by wanting what that towel covers."

She swallowed. He watched the motion all down the long line of her throat. Then her fingers flicked the knot holding the towel and the thick, soft terry cloth plunged to the floor, piling around her feet.

She had a beautiful body.

But what grabbed him by the throat was the sight of her pulse throbbing at the base of her neck.

She lifted one foot clear of the towel. Then the other. Until she stood right in front of him, a feast of slender, soft skin and lush female curves. And he had no clear idea of how he'd come to have his backside against the counter, and her tight nipples pressed against his bare chest.

"What's hurting you, Logan, isn't here." Her hand skimmed over the front of his towel, so lightly he wasn't sure he hadn't imagined it. "It's here." Her palm settled on his chest, over his heart. And even though her touch was still light, still little more than a hint of contact, he felt the burn of it as if she'd pressed a hot poker to him.

Then she turned and walked away, gracefully bending down without slowing to pick up the towel. A moment later, he heard the soft, definitive click of her bedroom door latch.

After a long while, he forced himself to move. To pull on another set of borrowed clothes.

He was waiting outside when Annie finally let herself out the front door. If she was surprised to see him still there, she didn't voice it. Nor did she make any comment when they silently walked to Leo's golf cart that sat on the side of the road where he'd left it the night before.

Was she glad he'd turned that cart back?

Or was she sorry?

The sun was warm in the sky as it cleared the horizon; there was only the faintest of breezes and not a cloud in sight. A perfect Turnabout day, hinting at nothing but the coming spring.

The irony felt black and heavy.

They went straight to the community center.

A column of smoke rose from the fireplace in front. Someone had set up several long tables outside the double doors. They were laden with large plastic bins containing fruit—oranges, grapes, apricots. A wide basket held muffins, and steam billowed up from a tray of scrambled eggs.

At least the generator was powered by gas and Diego had a good supply of that down at the dock.

Maisy—looking small next to the two men with her—seemed to be directing operations. She spotted Logan, and waved him over. "Perfect timing. Come help me move these tables. We need more room."

Logan had no interest in seeing Hugo again. But he wasn't going to ignore Maisy just because she stood next to him.

Annie looked from him to Hugo. With a murmured "good morning," she headed inside the building.

Maisy pulled him by the arm and gestured where she wanted everything arranged. "George is cooking up breakfast here. Kitchen's useless at the inn. Perishables have to be used up or thrown out." She gestured at her cook—a lumbering man with a tattoo that seemed to shimmy covering his entire right arm as he whisked a huge bowl of eggs. "Might as well use the generator here for something. Everyone from the inn will be working their way up here soon."

"Along with everyone else on this rock when they smell bacon cooking," Hugo said. He studied his cigar for a moment, then stuck it between his teeth and grabbed the other end of the heavy iron table. The legs scraped against the flagstones as they dragged it where Maisy wanted.

Annie returned. "Logan, Riley's not here." Her face was pale. "She didn't sleep here at all."

Maisy looked up from the box of cooking utensils she was rummaging in. "Saw her this morning, Annie. Just a little while ago. On the beach. She was with that Hobbes boy—"

"Kenny." Her voice was tight. Gravel crunched as she spun away on her heel.

Logan caught up to her in her in half a stride.

"This is my fault." Her hands raked her hair back. "I should have kept her at the house with me." She broke into a jog, her smooth-soled shoes skidding as she hit the hill that led down toward the beach.

She had barely rounded the old stone sea wall when she broke into a run. *"No! Get away from her!"*

Logan swore and vaulted over the wall, prepared for anything.

Annie had darted between the teens, pushing Kenny away from her niece with a none-too-gentle shove. Riley was crying. Her shoulders quaking.

Logan had barely taken in the fact that—aside from the tears—she looked unharmed, when Annie turned on Kenny, grabbing him by the shirt. "What did you do to her?"

The boy looked shocked. Several inches taller than Annie, he still stumbled back. "Whoa, hey—"

She followed, looking fit to kill. "Damn you, Drago. What did you do?"

Logan scooped his arm around her waist, hauling her back from Kenny. "He's not Drago," he whispered against her ear. He ached down to his gut. "He's not Drago, baby."

He slanted a look toward Kenny when the boy started sidling away. "Don't move." His voice was deadly quiet as he contained Annie's struggle to free herself. He didn't like the kid, but he didn't want Annie looking up the nose of an assault charge, either.

Then he looked at Riley.

She was staring at her aunt, openmouthed.

"Are you all right?" he asked.

Her expression turned mutinous, and she started to look away. But she didn't.

She finally nodded.

"Who the hell's Drago?" Kenny's subdued state had unfortunately been brief.

Annie wasn't listening to any of it. She scrabbled at Logan's arm. "If you so much as breathed on her, I'll take you apart."

Logan shifted his grip on her and stifled an oath when her foot connected with his shin. "Cut it out, I'm trying to help you, here."

"Then let me go!"

"We were just talking!" Riley's voice rose over Kenny's grumbled, "Man, she is crazy."

"Talking! You were crying, Riley."

The girl's eyes suddenly looked like wet sapphires. "Yes, talking! At least he wants to listen to me. You just want to send me back home so you can watch *sunsets* with him." She gestured at Logan.

Annie's struggles abruptly ceased.

"No." She finally spoke after a long, taut moment. "Riley, that's not—"

"I saw you together," Riley's voice shook. "I came back 'cause I was finally ready to...to tell you that I knew...but you were with *him*."

"You came back. To the house?"

Logan felt dismay rocket through Annie, along with every other emotion that seemed to pour from her shaking limbs. "When?" he asked.

Riley's gaze cut to him. "You left your clothes on the deck." Her voice was flat. "You were in her room. It doesn't take a genius." Her lips twisted and she glared at her aunt again. "No wonder you said I could stay at the community center. You wanted me out of the way, more than anybody else ever did!"

"I never wanted you out of my way," Annie's voice was hoarse.

Riley took a step back and the sand shifted under her foot. She struggled to keep from falling. "Don't lie to me! I'm sick of everybody lying to me!"

Logan felt Annie leaning out to the girl, prepared to catch her, but she sagged back against Logan at the accusation. "Nobody's lying." Her voice was thick.

"Riley, baby—"

"Everybody's been lying to me. My whole life! Nobody wants me around. You want me off the island. My *parents* want to send me off to some school so they can act like I don't exist."

"Riley, you have to know that's not true. They love you. They—"

"They love their jobs," Riley spat. "William Hess. Destined to be the new attorney general. Everybody's always telling me what a great man he is. If he were *great*, he'd know that our home isn't even a home any-more. He always said we were more important than anything, but he lied. Our house is like campaign cen-tral."

"It takes people to run an election."

"Yeah, well *he's* never there. Mom's always off get-ting some client sprung from jail. We don't even…even see each other some days." Her voice rocked. "Even when I warned him that he'd regret it, he didn't care. He just goes around with his big campaign slogan…Truth rises. Well, I know better!"

Realization settled. "You sent the letters," Logan said. "Didn't you, Riley?"

Annie's voice was faint. "What letters?"

Riley looked at him. "And weren't *they* effective," she said sarcastically. The effect was ruined by the tears thickening her voice. "There I was right under his nose and they still didn't notice. I used the stationery Mom keeps in their office at home. Cut the letters out of *his* magazines. Real observant, wouldn't you say?"

"He didn't consider his own daughter a suspect," Logan pointed out.

"Suspect?" Bewilderment joined the other shadows in Annie's eyes.

"*I'm not his daughter!*" Riley's voice rang out over the quiet beach. Then her eyes focused on Annie. Tears crawled down her young cheek. "I'm hers."

Chapter 14

Annie's legs nearly gave way.

Riley knew.

Dear Lord, she knew.

She moved, vaguely aware that Logan had finally released his hold on her, and reached out to her niece.

The daughter she could no longer claim.

But Riley backed away again, and Annie's fingers curled against her palm. Useless. "Oh, Riley."

"See? You lied." Her face twisted. "They lied. Everybody lied."

How could she deny words that were true? They had lied. By omission at the very least. Annie closed her arms around herself. "How did you find out?"

"Grandma Hess. She wanted to take me out for lunch for my fifteenth birthday, but my mom said no. So she came to my school, instead." Riley's head tilted. "Wasn't that nice of her?"

Lucia Hess had never done an unselfish thing in her entire, miserable life. It would be just like her to use righteousness for truth as a cloak for simple cruelty. She couldn't lash out at Annie any longer for her transgressions, so she'd chosen the next best thing. The daughter she'd forbade Annie to even bear. Annie had never wanted to see her mother again, but just then she'd gladly have sought her out, just so she could find some way to hurt her the way she'd hurt Riley. "What did she tell you?" Her voice was careful.

"Everything." Riley looked over at Kenny, who was watching them all with the wary fascination of a bystander who had happened across a train wreck. "You want to know who Drago is?"

Nausea suddenly rocked through Annie. No. No. No.

"He's my father," she told him. "Grandma Hess thought I ought to know he was finally getting out of prison for dealing drugs."

Annie covered her mouth as Kenny tucked his arm over Riley's shoulders and drew her away. She stumbled after them, but Logan stepped in her path. "Let her go."

"But he's——"

"Not Drago." She turned to him to talk. "I don't like the kid, either, but he's the only one she's not upset with right now."

"How could my mother do that? Hurt Riley? She never did anything to my parents, never embarrassed them, she was nothing but an innocent child! How?" She dropped to her knees in the sand, struggling not to retch. "Why?"

Logan sat beside her, his bent knee behind her

back. He didn't try touching her, and for that Annie was grateful. He just seemed to surround her, keeping her from the ocean breeze. But there was really no protecting her now.

Not anymore.

"Riley can't continue blaming Will and Noelle. No matter what Riley thinks, Logan, they love her." She caught her lip between her teeth, and her eyes burned. "It's the only thing that's kept me going sometimes. Believing that."

"Riley's smart," he said quietly. "She's hurting. But when she found out the truth, she came here to you."

"And I failed her again."

"How? By not reading her mind? Come on, Annie."

"I knew there was something else. Something beyond her not wanting to go to Bendlemaier."

"She probably wanted to judge you for herself. If she'd believed whatever tripe Lucia fed her, she'd never have come here the way she did."

"And instead of disproving my mother's words, Riley only found the truth of them."

"What she found were facts," Logan said. "She doesn't know anything about the truth. The circumstances surrounding the facts."

Annie thrust her shaking hands through her hair and pushed to her feet. A quartet of people rounded the seawall and headed toward the water's edge, where the sand was hard-packed, and began jogging. Logan rose, also, but Annie couldn't bring herself to look at him.

What was the truth? He'd been with them only a few days. Already he'd gotten into her pores. But he would leave, and she'd be left with a loneliness she'd only realized because of his presence. She had been surviving the position she held in her daughter's life for years. Maybe not well, but she'd done it, because she'd known Riley was okay. Only now it felt as though the veneer she'd managed to acquire had been wrenched away by a storm bearing Logan's face.

"The *truth* is that Will and Noelle adopted Riley when she was two years old. They couldn't love her any more than if she'd been born to them."

"Why not tell her, though? Where was the harm in letting her know you're her birth mother? She could have understood that you were little more than a kid yourself when you had her." He moved around until he could see her face. "Eighteen?"

His eyes had always seen too much. "And I was twenty when I finally admitted *the truth*." Her voice was harsh. "That I was incapable of providing Riley with the kind of care she deserved. She got sick, Logan. Really sick. She had a respiratory virus that she could have died from, but I was too broke to afford a doctor for her and too proud to ask for public assistance. If it hadn't been for Will and Noelle—" She pressed her lips together, unable to continue as the awful memories surged in her throat.

"And your parents didn't help?"

"Are you kidding me?" She pulled out of his grasp. "They tried to force me into having an abortion when they found out I was pregnant. They didn't want to pollute the Hess bloodline with Drago's. And when I refused, they kicked me out."

She sank down on the edge of the seawall because she wasn't sure her legs would hold her any longer. "I had no job. No money. I'm sure they thought I'd cave in and do whatever they said."

"But you didn't."

She looked down at her hands. "I'd always lived down to their expectations, Logan. But for once, there was something that mattered more. I was pregnant. There was going to be a baby. A completely innocent baby." Her hands lifted, then fell. "Yes, I know I was young. But my...behavior...caused that, and I had to be old enough to deal with the consequences. I refused to crawl back to them. The last thing my, my *mother*, said to me was that I was so useless that I would be incapable of caring for a baby."

He made a rough sound. "What *did* you do?"

It had been so long since she'd spoken of that time. But it was as clear as yesterday. "Will called in some favors and helped me get into a studio apartment without having to pay all the deposits and such. He and Noelle paid my rent for the first few months. I refused to depend on their charity forever, though. I was going to be a mom. Maybe we'd be poor, but I'd never be the kind of mother Lucia was. I tried to get a decent job. But nothing panned out. I had no high-school diploma because I'd finally managed to get myself kicked out of that infernal school. They didn't want pregnant students on their campus. I had no references. So I...lied about my age and got in as a cocktail waitress at a bar near the university where the manager was more interested in how well you filled out the uniform than how well your job application checked out. I had to quit when my pregnancy started to show, of course, but by then I'd saved enough of my tips to pay the rent on my own. And I found another job where a sexy waistline didn't matter."

"Sara knew all this was going on?"

"Sara was…great." Annie bit her lip. "I went into labor when she was supposed to be taking a final exam. But she'd promised to stay with me, and she didn't budge from my side. Not until after Riley was born."

"Loyal Sara." His voice was tight.

"Riley was such a perfect baby, Logan. She did everything early. Walking. Talking." Her throat ached. "I knew she deserved more than I could give her, but I just…couldn't do that. I couldn't give her up. I was too selfish."

"There's not a selfish bone in your body."

She shook her head in denial. "I was. And then she got sick. And Will and Noelle were there, just as they'd always been. I was so jealous of Noelle when she married Will. Well, you remember."

He made a faint noise of assent.

"I thought she was going to take away what little family I had. But I was wrong. She was decent. And nicer to me than I deserved. And I finally got it…how much Will loved her. She, um, she babysat for me sometimes when I had to work. She was trying to pass the bar exam, and you know how hard that is. But she was always willing to help with Riley no matter how busy she was."

"Yeah, they're all saints." Logan's voice was short. He felt a strong desire to choke the life out of George and Lucia Hess, and…when it came to that, Will and Noelle weren't so far behind. "Why didn't they just help you *keep* Riley? Or at the very least, tell her the truth before she could find out the way she did? There's no shame in adoption. She deserved to know."

"But I'm the one who begged them to take her!" She leaned forward and buried her face in her hands.

"I hadn't realized how dangerously ill she was." Her voice was muffled. "Not until it was nearly too late. She wasn't safe with me! Everything my parents had warned about had come true. The only truly decent thing I did as a parent was to give Riley to people who *were* capable of caring for her. Noelle took one look at Riley and drove us both straight to the hospital. *She knew how to be a mother.*"

"What about Drago?"

She hunched, looking nauseous. "He was in jail. I... never told him. I never spoke to him again after that day. After Will's wedding. Not even when we were both arrested the next day."

Logan's world suddenly narrowed down to a pin-point—Annie. Her head was lowered, her silky waves parting over the vulnerable skin at her nape. "You didn't see Ivan Mondrago. Ever?"

"He tried coming to the house a few days later. After he'd gotten released on bond. But my father had hired a guard to prevent that very thing. That, and to keep me in. I'm not sure if they were ever convinced that I hadn't been in league with Drago's drug ring." She lifted her head. "Please, Logan, can we drop it? Surely you can see why we didn't want Riley to know I was her mother. The next question she would have asked was who her natural father was. It was better that she never knew any of it, than to learn that he was a criminal."

He looked out over the ocean, but all his mind saw was Annie. Long rippling hair trailing over their bodies. Sleek, shapely legs sliding over his.

And her gasp. The way she'd stiffened when he'd breached her tight body.

He'd been certain she was a virgin.

But if she'd been a virgin until that night, and she hadn't seen Drago after the wedding, then how could she claim that Drago was Riley's father?

The bed that Annie had slept in that night hadn't been anyone's but Logan's.

And that was something that Annie didn't even remember.

"I have to go find her," Annie said. She pushed to her feet. "Talk to her, tell her—"

"What?"

Her eyes were heavy, full of sorrow that ran deep, without hope of ceasing. "I don't know. But I can't let her continue believing that she doesn't matter to her parents, Logan. That's what I believed. And look what happened."

He watched her go.

Then he sat down on the cold hard edge of the stone sea wall and stared blindly at the glimmering water.

The truth?

Even Annie didn't know the entire truth.

But he did.

Riley was not only Annie's daughter.

She was Logan's.

And if Annie thought Drago was a bad prospect for a father, what would she think if she knew the truth about *him?*

"Hey, there." Seemingly out of nowhere, Sara sat down beside him. "You look like you lost your best friend."

"I don't have friends." Only people he'd hurt. Some more knowingly than others.

She tsked. Tucked her arm through his and leaned

her dark head against his shoulder. "I remember we used to sit on this wall before you left the island."

"You were just a kid."

"So? I *still* remember." She lifted her long legs out in front of her, flexed her feet, then lowered them again. "We'd sit here and throw crumbs out for the birds. We had good times."

"Did we?" He barely remembered anything but his mother's misery. And her biscuits had been inedible. More suited for bird feed than breakfast. "Why did you come back here, Sara? You graduated from college with honors. You could have gone anywhere you wanted."

She sighed a little and he saw her blue gaze rove over the seascape. A gaze nearly the same color as the glittering blue water. The same color as Riley's.

As his.

How could he not have seen it? Now that he knew, there were a multitude of resemblances he could see. Her bouncing hair and ivory skin were all Annie's. But the level brows, the sharp chin, the eyes.

They were Drake, all the way.

"Turnabout is an interesting place," Sara finally said, her voice contemplative. She smiled a little. "Some things are so backward. But if we were *really* backward, we'd have been more prepared to live without power. Instead of depending on an ancient plant that isn't even equipped to handle the load we *do* need, we'd have had alternative means. More generators, maybe. Solar power. Or even windmills. We'd have used the gifts this place does have, and the constant breeze is one of them. We'd have a decent emergency plan, instead of just depending on Sam to scramble around doing what he can."

"*You* need to be on the town council," Logan said. Maybe there'd be some hope of the place moving into the current century.

"It's not all bad, Logan. There's a...oh, I don't know. A sort of healing mystique." She shrugged. "Sometimes miracles happen here. It's hard to resist. And for me, it's home."

Healing? Not in his experience. "You ought to be married with kids by now."

At that, her eyes rolled. "*Now*, you sound like Dad."

"Great?"

"And we could say the same about you," she pointed out. "But I suppose you're too busy leading your mysterious life to have stopped and made time for a wife and kids. Unless you're hiding them away somewhere for fear they'll fall in love with the island home you hate."

He closed his eyes for a moment. God.

Sara was silent for a long while. "Dad misses you, you know."

Logan doubted it. But his thoughts weren't on Hugo. Or Turnabout. Or even his little sister, for that matter. "Riley knows Annie is her natural mother," he said abruptly.

Sara sucked in her breath. A long moment ticked by. "Oh," she said on an exhale, "my. I'd be lying if I said it's completely unexpected. Sooner or later, Riley was bound to find out something."

"She did." He told her what Lucia had done.

"That woman should never have had children. Only then there wouldn't be Annie or Will. You know Annie told me once that Lucia told her she'd been a mistake. That she'd never wanted another child after Will." Her eyebrows lifted delicately. "And Annie told you about Riley?"

The rising sun glinted against the sand. It was a sight he'd known as long as he could remember. "Not intentionally." He slanted a look at her. "You've been a good friend to her."

Sara's lips curved, and for a moment she looked sad. "It hasn't been a one-way street, you know. She's been a good friend to me, too." She caught his narrow look and the cast of her lips turned upward. "Don't worry. Nothing like what Annie went through."

"Good." He wasn't up to hearing what sort of situations remained after that "nothing like" of hers.

She looked vaguely amused, then. "Do I need to ask you what your intentions are toward Annie?"

"You've already posted your warning." Which he'd ignored.

"That's not an answer, Logan."

"It's the only one you're going to get." He pulled her head close and kissed the top of it. "Go find Annie. She needs a friend."

Her head tilted back, looking up at him as he stood. "What about you? What do you need?"

The same thing he'd needed for sixteen years. Redemption.

Instead of finding a piece of it by coming to Turnabout, he'd succeeded only in pushing it further from his grasp.

"Breakfast," he said smoothly, and looked up the hill to where a crowd had been steadily growing by the community center. "I need breakfast."

His sister's lips smiled faintly, but her eyes did not.

It might have been years since they'd seen one another, but her expression exposed his lie for what it was. "Well, it's up there waiting, Logan. All you have to do is put out your hand and ask. You'll get your fill."

She pushed off the wall and headed down the beach.

Logan shoved his hands in his pockets, and stared out at the water.

Reach out and ask?

Easy enough to say.

Impossible to do.

Chapter 15

The sky above the lattice roof was blue. All hint of the storm gone.

What she was facing now was worse than any storm.

Annie looked away from the blue expanse as she paused at the entrance to Maisy's open-aired dining room. It wasn't hard to spot Riley.

She was the only person there. Everyone else had gone to the community center for a hot breakfast.

She slowly crossed to the small round table where the girl sat. It was the same table where the three of them—Annie, Riley and Logan—had sat the day he had showed up at the shop.

How could a person's life change in a matter of days?

The question was futile, though.

Her saner self already knew the answer. Lives did

change. In the blink of an eye. And in the passage of decades. In her case, the days had been numbered.

Truth rises.

Will had always believed that. Had told it to Annie time and again when he'd helped her out of some foolish stunt she'd pulled to gain her parents' attention.

"Truth rises, Annie," he'd say. "Stop trying to find it the hard way."

And there was nothing harder for Annie now than crossing that room, watching Riley eye her with such a tangle of distrust and pain that it caused a physical ache inside her.

She stopped shy of the table. It didn't matter how hard Annie found this. Riley mattered more.

She always had.

"We should have told you."

Riley's eyes reddened. "Yeah." She looked down at the orange she held. She didn't say anything else. Nor did she shove back from the table and leave.

Annie cautiously pulled out the opposite chair and sat. "I'm sorry I accused Kenny of hurting you."

"Just because he has a pierced lip doesn't mean he's bad."

"I know." She struggled for words. Something, anything to make this better. "I'm sorry."

"Did you love him?"

She moistened her lips. "Drago?"

"Not him. Logan. You're sleeping with him. You told me that you didn't sleep with men you didn't love. Or was that just another big lie of yours?"

She tucked her hands in her lap, her hands twisting together. "Yes."

Riley's jaw cocked to one side. "A big lie."

"Yes, I love him." Her throat closed. The truth of it couldn't be escaped. She'd loved him in her dreams for sixteen long, lonely years. She loved him beyond the surface to see what was beneath, even when that meant calling her to task for throwing herself at him. She loved that he made her smile when she least expected, that he braved storms, heated water and made something withered inside her bloom when he touched her.

And she'd love him when he left, which he would surely do. "But Logan's not part of this, Riley." She watched Riley's fingers turn the orange. "When you were a baby, you loved anything, as long as it was orange. Orange-tasting. Orange-colored. It didn't matter."

"I painted a wall in my room orange. Mom hates it."

"Is that why you did it?"

Riley didn't respond.

Annie exhaled. "You know that I used to do everything under the sun if I thought there was a good chance of upsetting my parents."

"Is that why you got pregnant with me? To piss them off?"

She winced, but for once she didn't hear her mother's screeching voice in her head accusing her of that very thing. "No. No, you were totally unexpected."

"A punishment."

Annie's hands immediately lifted above the table. She settled her fingers on the revolving orange. "No, Riley. A gift. Always, *always* a gift." Her voice went hoarse.

A tear slid down Riley's cheek. "Then why'd you give me away?"

The hardest question of all. "Because I loved you

that much. And I couldn't take care of you the way you deserved."

"You could have gotten rid of me before I was born. Grandma and Grandpa would never even have known."

Annie could barely stand to hear Riley speak of George and Lucia. But she had no intention of burdening Riley with the knowledge that they had been the ones to demand her pregnancy be terminated. Nor was she going to get into a debate over the right or wrong of abortion.

She stopped the orange again, waiting until Riley finally looked at her. "There was never a day that I regretted being pregnant with you." Riley's very existence had forced her to stop seeking what she'd never find from her parents. Love. Acceptance. "Not one single day. Not before you were born. Not after. I loved you all the while." Her head ached with unshed tears. "And so did Will and Noelle. We should have just told you the truth long ago, Riley, but *please* don't believe that it was ever because any of us didn't love you. Or that we didn't want what's best for you."

"Mom can't have kids, you know. She told me that when she started in on sending me to Bendlemaier. That I was the only child she'd ever have and she wanted me to have the best." Riley's voice broke.

Annie nodded, even though she *hadn't* known. But it made sense. Noelle was cultured, beautiful and excruciatingly intelligent. An attorney. Yet she'd never made any secret of her adoration of Riley. If she'd been able, she'd have probably filled Will's house with children.

"How come you hardly visit us? And you want me to leave Turnabout so badly?"

Why didn't you love me enough?

It was her own voice she heard in her head this time. The endless cry she'd never cried, that she'd finally realized would never be answered. Not by George and Lucia.

"Because it hurt too much to see you," she said, and the honesty stripped her raw. "And to have to leave you again. And when you came here, I said I wanted you to go...because my heart..." she pressed her hand against her chest, her voice nearly soundless "...only wants you to stay. But no matter what I feel, your home is with... your parents. They've raised you. They've loved you."

She tried to draw in a breath, but it rattled with tears. She exhaled. Swallowed. Steadied her voice. "And no matter how mad you are about Will's campaign or your mom's job, or about the garbage your grandmother dumped on you along with the facts, you love your parents, too. Or you wouldn't be so hurt now."

Riley's silence lengthened. Then slowly, she let go of the orange and it rolled off the table. She touched her fingertips to Annie's. "Can I come back and visit?" Her voice was very small.

Annie nodded.

Then she opened her arms when Riley rounded the table and sat on her lap, her young arms a crushing grip around Annie.

And Annie wondered, yet again, how many times a person's heart could break.

"She's ready to go home." Annie didn't move from the couch when Logan let himself into her house later that afternoon. "Whenever you can arrange it. She won't be running away again."

He pushed the door closed behind him with his foot

and set the small heater and heavy electrical cord he carried on the floor. She'd be able to hook it up to the small generator he'd finally scrounged up in Diego's mess of equipment at the dock. "Are you okay?"

"No." Her voice sounded raw. As if she had a cold. Or she'd been crying. "But I'll survive," she went on. "It's what I do best."

"Nice try," he murmured. "You may be a survivor, but there are other things you excel at more."

"Like wanting impossible things?" She sighed and finally looked at him. "Sam brought this message by for you." She held out a scrap of paper. It vibrated with a fine shimmer. "Apparently it came in this afternoon over that radio he got."

He took the sheet and shoved it in his pocket.

"You're not going to read it?"

He shook his head.

"It said *two days*. That's all. Just *two days*."

He wasn't interested in the message. "Where is she?" She didn't need to ask who he meant. "Still at Maisy's. She, um, she wanted to help out with the kids again over there. Mostly, I think she wanted some distance to...to digest everything."

"You talked to her, then."

"Yes." Her expression was too still.

"And about Drago. That you think you were with Ivan Mondrago. That *he* is Riley's natural father."

Her hands curled into fists. "Who else could it be?"

Logan's chest ached. "And you told Riley that?"

"She didn't ask about Drago, and I didn't tell. God knows what exactly Lucia told her, seeing how I'd done such a whiz-bang job of earning their disgust."

"Stop blaming yourself for their failings."

"Habit." She finally pushed off the couch and noticed the heater. "What's that for?"

"It'll keep you warm at night. I scared up a generator for you. It's out front."

Her lashes lowered, hiding her expression. "You could keep me warmer." She laughed humorlessly a moment later and waved her hand in dismissal. "Thanks. I know it would be easier if I just stayed at the community center, but—"

"You want to be in your own home." Because it was one of her own creating.

She nodded. "I, um, I need to thank you. For keeping me from doing something awful to that poor boy. I don't know where my mind went. Well, no," she added after a moment. "I do know. And I didn't want that to happen to Riley." She ran her hands down the sides of her pale-blue jumper, looking so brittle that he was afraid even to reach out for her, lest she shatter.

"You didn't want *what* to happen to her?"

"I never told Drago I'd sleep with them. I never told anyone I'd sleep with them. They just looked at the way I dressed, and the way I behaved, and always thought... assumed...and it infuriated my parents, so I fostered the impression. For their benefit. The guys—I never promised any of them anything."

"I know."

But she was beyond hearing. "I told Drago over and over again that I had no intention of sleeping with him. We'd had a deal. He wanted an in at Bendlemaier and I believed riding on his reputation would get me out of Bendlemaier. When I learned he was dealing drugs, I told him the deal was off. I wasn't going to be part of that scene. But he wouldn't believe me. He'd bought my act too well." She pushed her hands through her hair, shaking her head. "I was such an idiot, such a fool. I deserved whatever happened to me. I all but asked for it."

"It." It was all he could do not to grab her. "What *it?*"

"There was so much champagne left over. My parents were furious with me, accusing me of inviting Drago."

Forget control. Logan closed his hands over her shoulders, turning her around to face him. "You sneaked more champagne, even after what happened between you and me by the boathouse?" He'd already realized that's what she must have done.

"Yes, I—," She frowned. "I took a bottle to my room. I drank it all, I think. I don't remember." She pushed at her forehead. "I...it's all messed up with my dream, you see. But I woke up in my bed in the morning and I was...naked...and my—I felt sore—" She shook her head. "Before I could even get out of bed, the police had arrived. They'd found Drago hiding in the wine cellar. And they came in and arrested me, too."

Her eyes were wet. "He was in the house that night. And...while I was drunk...he, we...God." She pressed her face into her hands, her shoulders shaking. "What's worse? Willingly sleeping with someone I despised, or being so drunk that I can't even remember him forcing me? Lucia, of course, assured me that she saw Drago leaving my room before dawn."

Logan hauled her into his arms. No matter what his life was, he couldn't let her continue believing what she thought. "Maybe Drago was in your room that night. But you weren't. You weren't with Drago. He didn't force you. And you didn't choose him."

"You don't know that. I don't know that! I spent years in therapy, and the therapist doesn't know that!"

"I *do* know that." He caught her face between his hands and carefully made her look at him. Her lashes were spiky from tears. "I know, because you were with *me* that night. In the guest room. I carried you back to your room in the morning."

Her softly arched brows drew together. Her lips parted. "What? No, that's not right. You didn't want me. You told me so at the wedding reception. You'd never have——"

"I did." There was no mitigating the truth. "You came to my room late that night. I woke up and found you in bed beside me." And even after realizing the warm, enticing female wasn't the bridesmaid who'd been coming on to him throughout the wedding festivities, but his best friend's impetuous little sister, Logan hadn't done what he should have done. Instead of bundling her off to her own bed without so much as touching a hair on her head, he'd kissed her mouth, tasted the champagne she'd consumed on her tongue and had dragged her beneath him.

He'd broken the trust of his friendship with Will that night, and he'd taken advantage of Annie's inebriated innocence. He'd thought he'd never regret anything more. Until now. Until realizing what Annie had believed all these years about that night.

His hands were shaking as he brushed them down her hair. Him. The man whose hands never shook. Who never missed. Who went in and cleaned up situations where there was no other recourse. "I didn't realize you couldn't remember."

"It was real?" She was staring at him as if she'd

never seen him before. "All these years, it's the… dream…that's been real."

"What dream?"

"About you. And me. Making love." She stumbled back from him, covering her mouth. Her eyes looked dazed.

"You dream about that night?" God knows it had haunted him ever since. Now he had even more to add to the repertoire of transgressions.

"My therapist said it was my subconscious defense against what had really happened with Drago. And I knew he'd been in my room. Not just because Lucia said so but because he'd left his jacket there. A Harley jacket. He wore it a lot. Was wearing it at the boathouse when you—" she broke off, her throat working.

He'd never been big on therapy. There were times it was required through his work, and he'd always hated it. "It was a memory of us, Annie. Not a dream. Drago hadn't assaulted you before the wedding. You were never in your bedroom with him. He damn sure didn't do it afterward when he was locked up in jail."

She inhaled sharply. "Riley. Dear God." Her skin went white and she sank onto the couch as if her legs had suddenly given out.

"Yeah." He knew exactly what her mind had finally wrapped itself around. "Riley is *my* daughter."

There was an odd buzzing inside Annie's head. Riley was Logan's daughter. Not Drago's. She blinked, trying to focus on that fact, but it kept spinning away from her. What was wrong with her? She should have seen the resemblance. She should have remembered that night!

"Don't faint." Logan sat beside her, nudging her head forward.

"I don't faint." She grabbed his hand on the back of her neck and pulled it away. "You knew." It was like a tumbler falling into place on a lock. "You'd already figured out that you were her father." She shoved away from him. She wanted to scream but couldn't. "God. The secrets just keep rolling out, don't they? And when were *you* planning to say something? Or were you just going to go on your merry way as if none of it mattered?"

He looked weary. "What would you have had me say, Annie?"

"I don't know. Something! Anything. These past few days, all these years, you've known."

"What I knew all these years was that I'd slept with you when I never should have. These past few days, I should have stopped, but I didn't. I don't even have the excuse that I *couldn't* stop. And you passed out afterward. I carried you back to your bed the next morning and left."

"I remember I half expected you to show up at the police station with Will. He said you'd already left because of some job thing."

"Yeah. As for the past few days, I started to think maybe you'd been assaulted."

"Seeing as how I'm such a model for perfect mental health."

"I recognize the signs. And there's nothing wrong with your mental health."

"Except I got some kid from Denver confused with Drago!"

"Stress. Riley running away, the storm. Me. It was

a matter of time before the pot boiled. It doesn't mean you're crazy or that you're a danger to anyone."

Annie paced across the room. Stared out the glass door. The surf had risen again. Clouds scuttled across the sky, destroying the blank expanse of blue. "We have to tell her."

"She's not going to want to know that I'm her father."

Her fingers curled against her palms. "Why not? Because you don't want to be tied down by being one?"

Her lips twisted over the words as she retraced her steps to him. "Riley *has* a father. A man who—regardless of what Riley currently thinks—is devoted to her. You can't tell me that she has a right to know who I am, and honestly think she doesn't have a right to know about you! We can't just sit here and pick and choose what pieces of the truth to reveal, Logan. For God's sake! Look at what thinking that Drago was her father did to *me*."

"Drago's a two-bit hood who's incapable of making a life outside of prison. What he *is* is never gonna touch Riley's life."

"*Why?* You think Lucia isn't as capable of contacting him about his supposed daughter as she was about telling Riley about me?"

"Lucia never said a word before. What would she gain by doing so now?"

Annie wanted to tear out her hair. "I don't know! I don't know what possessed her to do what she did now!" She'd probably never know. "I gave up trying to understand my parents a long time ago. But I won't let her hurt Riley again, Logan, and the only way to prevent that is if she knows the truth. That *you* were the one I was with that night."

"No." His voice was flat.

She stared at him, wishing she understood him. Wishing she had a single clue about what caused the shadows deep in his eyes. "What is it you're afraid of, Logan? That Riley will blame you or something?"

"Leave it alone, Annie."

She crouched in front of him, her hands on his knees. She didn't think it possible for her heart to ache more than it had, yet it did. "I can't. Not anymore. I left things alone way too long, because I thought I was doing the right thing and I was wrong. *Wrong*."

He deliberately set aside her hands and pushed to his feet, moving away from her. "There are things you don't know."

"Only because you won't say." She slid up on the seat, hugging her arms around herself. "You're not a consultant."

"No."

Her lips pressed together. "Hmm. I've never met a spy before." The paltry attempt at humor fell short.

"You said you were one that very first day. Guess we should have believed you."

"Not really. Spying's not my specialty."

"What is?" She lifted her hands. "Come on, Logan. Give me a reason, one good enough to make me believe that you're right. That Riley is better off not knowing about you. Because, frankly, unless you're some cutthroat murderer, I can't see——"

"I am."

Her hands lowered. "What?"

Logan had to make her understand. "I wanted to be a lawyer," he said. "And scholarships and grants only went so far."

She frowned, looking confused. "I know. But what—"

"Hear me out."

She subsided.

"I was approached by an organization. They would finance the rest of my schooling, pay off the loans I'd already taken out. In exchange, I'd work for them for a set period of time once I passed the bar exam."

"That doesn't sound so unusual. Don't some law firms make similar arrangements with promising students?"

"What was unusual was what the organization did."

She looked uneasy. "Organization. Like...the mob?"

He laughed shortly. "No. Hollins-Winword isn't the mob. They're...peacekeepers mostly. On an international scale."

Her shoulders had relaxed only a little. Now, she pressed her fingertips to her forehead. "I don't understand."

"You don't have to. It's better that you don't." Cole preferred it that way. Helping to keep justice in a world where justice was increasingly rare was more easily accomplished on a need-to-know basis.

"Do you have a, um, a specialty?"

"Cleanup," he said. There was only one situation that he'd left in a true mess. And she was across the room from him.

He knew people who'd broken under less trauma than she'd endured in the past few days.

But not Annie.

"Somehow, I don't think you mean cleaning with a dustpan and broom."

"No."

"Okay, fine. But that still doesn't mean that Riley can't know about you."

He'd thought he was making headway with her.

"Dammit, Annie, no."

She pushed to her feet. "Riley's not going to want a job résumé from you, Logan. You're a decent man—"

"I'm a sharpshooter," he said. "They send me in when a situation can't be rectified by any other means."

Her eyes narrowed. He could see her brain mulling that over. What it implied.

"For...personal gain? Because you love it?" She shook her head. "I don't believe that. Your expression says otherwise."

"Well, you should believe it. I'm paid well," he said flatly. And for a lot of years the life had been just what he wanted. Until one day he'd realized it was likely to be the only life he was suited for. If he'd come to hate the life he led, how could anyone else not feel the same?

"Just because you hate yourself for something doesn't mean that Riley will. If you don't like what you do, then you're the one with the power to change it."

There were very few individuals who successfully left H-W behind. "Pretty words."

She watched him for a long moment. "Maybe. True words, at least. They were your words, Logan. That night at the boathouse. It took me a while, but I finally listened to them. So why can't you?"

She moved away from him and picked up the sweater and umbrella sitting on the counter. "I'm going to the shop."

"The shop's not going anywhere, Annie. It's been a hard day for—"

"For me? For you? For Riley?" Her gaze flickered

for a moment. "Sometimes work is all we have. That message Sam passed on for you is proof of that, isn't it? But as it happens, I'm going to the shop to see my friend. Your sister." Her jaw tightened. "Riley's *aunt*."

She went out the door and pulled it shut behind her.

Logan just stood there. The paper in his pocket wasn't even noticeable, but just then, it seemed to weigh a ton.

Chapter 16

Four days without power.

Annie sighed and ran her dust rag over the display shelves. Habit had her glancing toward the big glass window at the front of the shop, but her gaze encountered the muted tone of the plywood instead.

She sighed again and turned away. She'd propped open the front door to let in some light and the bell over it jingled softly in the breeze. It was a softly peaceful, gently cheerful sound in utter contrast to her state of mind as well as the dreary, rainy day.

"Here." Riley came out from the workroom and set a mug on the countertop. Steam billowed up from the mug's contents. "Hot chocolate."

Annie smiled faintly and picked up the mug. A few small marshmallows floated on the rich, chocolaty drink. "You and Sara obviously got a fire to burn out back, despite the rain."

"I'm handy that way." Sara sailed into the room, carrying her own mug. She dashed raindrops off her hair. "Comes from dating Eagle Scouts. Learned how to build fires under all sorts of conditions." She winked at Riley, who rolled her eyes. Good-naturedly, though. The two had an obvious ease with each other.

Annie buried yet another sigh, this time in the depths of hot chocolate. She hadn't seen Logan since the previous day. Hadn't seen him, heard from him or heard of him. Considering the size of the island, it could only mean that he was off somewhere avoiding everyone, including her.

And Riley.

She watched the teen and Sara a moment longer. But all too quickly she felt a warning prickle behind her eyes. "I'm going to take this stuff down to Maisy's." She set down the mug and picked up the box of candles she'd packed earlier.

"We'll help you."

Annie waved off her partner's offer. "No point in all of us getting rained on. I'll be back in a jiffy." She wasn't going to bust into tears in front of them. But then she saw Riley's face. "Unless…you really want to come."

The frown cleared and Riley nodded. "I'll get an umbrella." She hurried into the workroom.

Annie swallowed. Then Sara touched her arm. "Hang in there," she said softly. Encouragingly.

Sara didn't know the half of it.

But the threat of tears passed, moved hurriedly along by a surge of anger. At Logan, for making it impossible

for Annie to let Sara know the full truth. At the sende
of that message for Logan. Two days. Now one. Sh
didn't have to be a genius to figure out that the mes
sage meant he'd soon be leaving.

Knowing in her head that he would certainly leav
the island and knowing it for a fact, however, wer
proving to be two very different things.

Riley returned, and the three set off. Sara was taller
and she held the oversized umbrella. Annie and Rile
carried the carton between them.

In minutes, they'd made it down to Maisy's Plac
where Annie left her protest unvoiced when Riley wen
in search of Kenny while Annie and Sara took the car
dles inside to Maisy's office.

The sight of Logan sitting in front of Maisy's desk
his long legs stretched across the minuscule office, wa
a surprise. But the sight of Hugo Drake leaning over hi
son with a suture needle in hand was a complete shock

Annie stood stock-still in the hallway, staring.

Sara took the sight in stride more easily. She slippe
around her father's bulk to peer at the wound Hugo wa
stitching together. "Good grief, Logan. Do you hav
a death wish or something? Another few inches an
that slice would be on your neck instead of your jaw."

A gasp slid past Annie's lips. Logan's head turne
and he looked at her.

"Dammit, son, hold still. You're gonna have a butt
ugly scar as it is."

Annie felt her vision narrowing.

"How'd you cut yourself like that?" Sara's voic
seemed to come from inside a tunnel.

"Doing something stupid, no doubt," Hugo said.

"Maisy, I told you not to call Hugo," Logan said.

"Rather leave your jawbone hanging out for the birds to peck at than have me touch you?" Hugo harrumphed, and kept working. "Should have gone to my office, but no. Stubborn cuss."

"Like someone else we know and love," Maisy said, her gaze pointedly on Hugo. "Stop grumbling and fix him."

"All I wanted was a bandage."

"I told you not to move. That includes talking," Hugo snapped. "Or do you want to lose even more blood?"

"I still want to know what happened," Sara complained. "You look like you've been in a knife fight, for heaven's sake! Do I need to get the sheriff?"

Annie silently crumpled.

Logan jerked, pushing past his father, who cursed colorfully, and caught Annie a spare moment before her head hit the hardwood floor.

"Good Lord." Maisy swept by him, pushing at him. "Let your father finish."

"But—"

She glared at him, but her touch was gentle as she sat down beside Annie, chafing her hands. "Get."

Sara crouched down, too. Her eyes were sharp as she looked from him to Annie and back again. "You're dripping blood on her." She handed him one of the gauze pads Hugo had brought.

He pressed it to his jaw and carefully thumbed away a drop from Annie's arm.

"She's exhausted."

"And you're not?" Sara raised her eyebrows. "Let Dad finish, Logan."

Annie was already stirring. Her lashes slowly lifted

and she stared up at him. "What…oh, God." Color suffused her cheeks. "I'm sorry." He smoothed her hair back from her forehead.

Her fingers lifted toward him. "What happened?"

"A piece of wire snapped. Caught me wrong."

"And I'm gonna pump you full of antibiotics because of it," Hugo said above them. "Now get up here."

"Let him finish." Annie's urging was soft. "Please?"

He exhaled roughly. Then resumed his seat inside the doorway of Maisy's office. Hugo snapped on a fresh pair of gloves and leaned over him again. "If she asks you to stay on the island in that sweet voice, you going to agree to that, too?" His voice was soft, meant only for Logan.

Logan closed his eyes. "Stitch and shut up." His voice was as low as Hugo's.

"You're a cold bastard."

"Take after my father."

A strong hand closed over Logan's shoulder. He looked up into Maisy's face. Her hair practically vibrated with the anger that lit her eyes. "I ought to lock the two of you alone in here until you can be civil with each other."

"Our cold dead bodies would be discovered eventually," Hugo's voice was dry.

Maisy threw up her hands. She made no attempt at keeping her voice quiet this time. "Idiots. Both of you. You," she pointed at Hugo, "never told your children that their mother was clinically depressed and made your life hell when she wouldn't take her medication. And you," she pointed at Logan, "never saw that your father was suffering more than any of you. Your mother didn't commit suicide because of him, she did it despite him. And you're both a pair of idiots."

"He gave her plenty cause to be depressed." Logan looked at his father.

Maisy stomped her foot. Hard. "Stop. Right now. I won't have it."

Hugo was staring at Maisy as if he'd never seen her before. "Woman, you had no right to tell them about Madeline."

Maisy's eyebrows shot up into her corkscrew bangs. "Oh, really. Really? Sara practically grew up with no mother at all. You think she didn't have a right to know why?"

Her gaze took in both Logan and Sara—who looked shocked as she sat next to Annie on the floor. "Madeline was ill *years* before either one of you children came along. Just because Madeline was too proud to admit it publicly didn't mean that people didn't know, Hugo. But she was a Turn and Lord knows Turns *always* watch out for each other, even if that meant covering for her illness. What purpose does it serve to honor her *secret* after all these years, particularly when it only hurts the people she left behind?"

Hugo rapidly tied off another stitch. The last one. Then he jabbed a hypodermic syringe into Logan's arm, seeming to relish the task as he gave the antibiotic, before he tossed everything back into his case, peeled off the gloves and tossed them in also. He picked the bag off the desk, stuck his cigar between his teeth and towered over Maisy. "You are an annoying old woman."

She glared right back. "You are an annoying old man."

Hugo exhaled noisily. He turned on his heel and,

stepping over both Sara and Annie, stomped away down the hall.

Maisy's shoulders drooped. Sara pushed to her feet and quickly hugged her. "Don't worry. Dad will get over his mad."

Maisy patted Sara's shoulder. "I know." Then she stepped back, straightened her dress and shoved her hands into the patch pockets on the front of it. "Sara, put a dressing on your brother's jaw. Annie, go to the kitchen and tell George to give you a few of the muffins he made up at the community center yesterday morning. You need to eat."

Then she turned on her heel and hurried down the hall.

"I don't have the nerve not to obey," Sara muttered. She picked up one of the wrapped packets Hugo had left on the desk and, peeling it open, stuck the dressing across Logan's jaw. Then she brushed her hands down her thighs. Looked between Annie and Logan a moment longer, then hurried in the same direction Maisy had taken.

Annie started to push to her feet.

Logan was out of his chair in a flash, helping.

If he hadn't touched her, there might have been some hope that she wouldn't start shaking. But he did. And she did.

"Does it hurt?" Her fingers skimmed the edge of the self-adhesive bandage.

"Not as much as the javelin he shoved in my arm."

"What were you doing to cut yourself with wire?"

"It doesn't matter."

"In other words, it's none of my business."

He looked like a man at the end of his tether.

"Where's Riley?"

"With Kenny, most likely."

"Then let's go find her."

Annie's head swam a little, and it had nothing to do with feeling faint. "Logan?"

"We'll tell her together."

She pressed her palms against the sudden churning in her stomach. And then what? The question cried inside her head.

She didn't voice it. She already knew the answer.

Two days. Now one.

Logan would leave.

Riley would go back home.

Annie would stay on Turnabout, with her herbs and her potions.

Nobody would be together.

But they'd all know the truth.

Just then, the value of that seemed almost out of her understanding. Almost.

"Okay," she said. "We'll go find her."

In the end, Riley took hearing the news better than Logan and Annie took delivering it. She stared at Logan across the little round table in the dining area that seemed to be their unspoken place for gut-wrenching moments when it came to the three of them. "You're the reason I have blue eyes, then."

Annie closed her hands together in her lap as Logan nodded.

The young set of blue eyes turned toward Annie. "Thought you said he wasn't your boyfriend. Not now. Not before."

"He wasn't. We—"

"We never had time to be boyfriend and girlfriend,
Logan cut her off. His gaze met hers. "But we wer
friends." He barely hesitated over the statement.

"Then how come you didn't know Auntie Annie wa
pregnant with me?"

Words failed her.

"Because I let her down," Logan said in a voice a
stark as the white bandage covering his jaw. "And I'n
sorry."

He spoke to Riley, but Annie knew the words wer
for her.

"I don't need another dad, you know." Riley's voic
was gruff. Defensive. "I don't need another mom, ei
ther."

Annie's eyes burned. Not from what Riley said. Sh
understood perfectly where Riley stood.

Logan nodded after a moment. "I know. You alread
have parents."

"Makes it easy on you, huh?"

"Riley—"

"Well?" Riley shot Annie a look. "He never had to
do anything hard about any of this. He just slept wit
you and walked. He didn't even come to Turnabout o
his own. He came 'cause my dad hired him to com
and get me. Dad doesn't know about you, I'll bet. Oth
erwise he'd have hired somebody else."

"You're probably right." A deep voice came from
across the room.

Annie twisted in her chair to look. Riley jumped ou
of her chair so fast it tipped over behind her.

Logan stood, too. More slowly. He eyed the mar

across the room. Contained the urge to strangle him. "Hello, Will."

Annie's voice was hushed. "Riley, you can go and find Kenny again. I'm sure he's still waiting for you."

"But—"

"Please."

Riley subsided. She stuffed her fingers in her pockets and walked over to her dad. "I'm still mad at you," she said.

"Figured as much."

"Where's Mom?"

"At home. Waiting for us."

Riley absorbed that. Then she sidestepped around Will and headed to the doorway, only to look back. "I'm warning you, Daddy. Be nice."

The adults waited until the sound of Riley's boots against the tile faded to nothing.

Annie had turned around to face the table again, her elbows bent, head propped in her hands. "How much did you hear?"

She posed the question far more calmly than Logan might have. He watched the other man loosen his tie several more inches as he walked closer to the table. "Enough." He warily watched Logan as he bent down and righted Riley's toppled chair and sat.

After a long moment, Logan sat, too.

Finally, Will broke the silence. "Who would think there was this much coincidence in the world?"

"Not me," Logan said flatly. His boss's handiwork was all over this, and it infuriated him that he hadn't seen it sooner. "Why'd you go to Cole?"

"They recruited you while we were in school?"

"That's not an answer."

Will's lips twisted. "No. It always bugged me that you disappeared the way you did. But I wasn't inclined to do anything about it. Noelle married me, but she'd dated you first."

Annie lifted her head, her face shocked. "What? I never heard about that."

"Yeah, we dated," Logan said evenly. "Then she met your fair-haired brother and never looked back." He'd been fine with it then, he was fine with it now. And he still had the strong feeling that they'd all been manipulated. "How'd you meet Cole?"

"You're not the only person H-W talked to when we were in school."

Logan's eyes narrowed. Then he sat back, laughing softly. "No damn way. You're too public, Will. They'd never use you."

"No. They didn't. But they kept tabs. Cole would call now and then. We traded favors occasionally. The guy's only a few years older than we are, but—" Will broke off, shaking his head. "When Riley ran away, I automatically thought of him."

"You told him that Riley was adopted."

Will nodded. "I thought he was coming down here, himself. I wanted him prepared. I didn't know what mother had done. What she'd told Riley. I only knew I was getting threatening letters, and I wanted my daughter safe."

"But Cole didn't come himself. He dragged me into it."

"Delegation seems to be his style."

A twisted sense of humor was more like it. "Every one of Cole's crew undergoes analysis. Mandatory.

More often, even, during the first few years after going in."

"So?"

"So it was in my record from the start." Logan's teeth were clenched. "Logan Drake's weaknesses. Namely the betrayal he committed by sleeping with his best friend's little sister."

Annie's hands spread across the small table, one on each of the men's tense arms. "Stop. This isn't getting anywhere." She sent Logan a pleading look. "You didn't betray anyone. Tell him, Will. He didn't."

"If he tells me that he didn't seduce you because I got Noelle."

Annie's hands drew back. She seemed to shrink into herself. "Well. Everyone's always wanted Noelle most. My brother. My...daughter. And you." Her gaze slid to Logan.

Then she pushed back her chair and strode from the room, not hesitating a single step, even when Logan called her name.

"Are you going to contest it?"

"What?" Logan stared at Will.

"Our custody of Riley. You can, you know. It's only fair to tell you. You have grounds." Will looked grim.

"I'll fight you, though."

"Did you even notice Annie just now?"

"She left. It's what she does. Leaves when things get too tough for her."

Logan's fists curled. "You know, Will, Annie's been insisting all along that Riley belongs with you and No-elle. That you're the best parents she could have. I never doubted that before. Until now."

***

He ran into Riley before he found Annie. She was bounding up the stairs outside Maisy's Place as he was racing down them.

She took one look at him. "You and my dad aren't friends so much anymore."

His life was not pretty and he never wanted any of it to touch this girl. This unexpected child. "Not so much at the moment," he agreed. "It doesn't have to be that way forever."

Her chin lifted, but her blue eyes were swimming. "I shouldn't have come to Turnabout. Nobody would be mad at anybody, then. 'Cept Grandma Hess. I think she's mad at everyone in the universe."

"You're probably right on target where Lucia's concerned. But it's not your fault that everyone is upset right now. We're the adults. Not you. You were only trying to get answers."

"Auntie Annie says it's okay for me to love all of them. Guess that probably includes you."

Logan's chest ached. "You don't have to love me, Riley. There's no requirements here. You don't even know me."

"*She* loves you, though. She told me she did."

The words cut deep.

"Dad's not going to leave Turnabout without me, you know. He thinks Auntie Annie is a flake."

"He's wrong."

"I know. But I don't like leaving her alone."

There was that protective vein again. And she was watching Logan, obviously expecting him to assure her that Annie *wouldn't* be alone. "Annie wouldn't want you worrying." He had to push the words past the unreasonable instinct to grab this girl, grab Annie and run. To find a place where nothing and no one could hurt either of them.

Which was impossible.

His life was ruled by a world that required such organizations as Hollins-Winword, such people as Coleman Black. That world and this one here—Annie's world—weren't made to mesh.

Riley's lips pressed together for a long moment. "I better go see my dad before he splits an artery or something." But her boots didn't move toward the door.

"Don't pierce your lip like Kenny did," Logan said after a moment. "And stay on Will's case about spending too much time on the campaign trail. And don't go to bloody Bendlemaier unless *you* want to."

A tear slipped down Riley's smooth young cheek. His hand shook as he dashed it away. "And don't ever forget that you're as beautiful as both your mothers are."

Riley sucked her lip. She nodded and started to back toward the door.

Then she took Logan's breath when she reversed her steps and hugged him. Tightly. Briefly.

He caught a flash of tears when she quickly turned away and slipped through the door of Maisy's Place.

He let out a long breath and sat down right there on the step. He couldn't have moved just then if his life depended on it.

He propped his elbows on his knees and stared at his hands.

Annie wasn't a flake.

She was stronger than all of them combined.

Eventually, he heard the distinctive whine of a golf

cart motor and looked up when the wheels crunched to a stop in the gravel a few feet from him.

"Maisy seemed to think you might want a ride to Annie's."

"So?"

Hugo shrugged. Studied his cigar for a moment. "She's a bossy woman," he said after a moment. "You getting in, or not?"

Logan got in. Hugo set off with a lurch.

"You're a grandfather."

Hugo didn't seem surprised. "Sara told me how things were. About damned time. About the grand-child part, I mean. You're no spring chicken."

Logan shook his head. "You're annoying as hell."

"So I've been told." His gaze slid Logan's way for a moment and there was the faintest of smiles playing about his lips. "Runs in the family."

Logan barely waited for Hugo to stop the cart when they got to Annie's place. He jumped out and headed straight inside.

She was sitting on the couch, the photo albums she'd cried over stacked beside her. She didn't so much as jump or turn a hair when he went inside. "Go away, Logan."

Not yet. He rounded the couch and sat down in front of her. "I didn't care when Noelle fell for your brother," he said bluntly.

She lifted a shoulder. "It was a long time ago. It doesn't matter."

He reached for her hands. They were cold. "It does matter. You don't really think Riley is *choosing* her over you."

"No. Yes." Her fingers flexed. "No. They're the only parents she's really known. And I'm not fit—"

"Don't."

"It's true." Her throat worked. "I failed my own child in the worst possible way."

"You were little more than a child, yourself, then. You're not a child now."

"And it's too late."

"Is it?"

Her gaze flew to his. Her lips parted for a moment. "Say the word, Annie. I'll help you fight them."

"And if we won custody of her? What then? What would you do?"

"I'd—"

"Still leave," she challenged huskily. "Tell me I'm wrong."

But he couldn't.

He lowered his head. "I'll make sure building supplies and food are delivered. Get Diego a bloody boat that isn't forty years old and leaking like a sieve." He'd never used his connections for anything but the job, but he would now.

"The town council is taking care of all that."

Irritation tightened inside him. "The town council would pretend that Turnabout doesn't belong to anything but itself—not California, not the United States— if they could get away with it. It's been that way for at least fifty years and it'll be that way for fifty more. If you wait on them to do something productive, you'd better plan on growing more than lavender and marigolds in those fields of yours or you'll be going hungry." There was an old orange grove on the island that still produced fruit, but it was hardly in prime condition.

"I think you're exaggerating."

He lifted his head, his eyebrow cocked. "Yeah?"

"Well. Maybe not." She moistened her lips. "I'm sorry about your mother. About all that Maisy said."

"Me, too." He thought about that carved box sitting on the barrel outside Hugo's clinic. "Nothing's the way it seemed. Not with my family. Not with yours." He looked at her. "What if you're pregnant again?"

She paled. "We used protection."

The first time he had. But not the last. Not when they'd wakened at dawn and she'd slid over him.

He'd been as careless then as he had all those years ago when he'd wakened in a guest room at George and Lucia Hess's palatial estate to find their wayward daughter naked in bed with him, her mouth on his mouth, her innocently awkward fingers circling his erection.

"What would you do, though?"

"Nothing. It's not—"

"If you were. What would you do?"

"I'm not interested in being a single parent and somehow I can't see you coming home in time for dinner and homework."

"Annie—"

"I'd do a better job than I did the first time!" Her voice rose. "Are you satisfied now?"

"You did a good job already. You loved Riley enough to do what you knew needed to be done. So stop blaming yourself for it."

"Well, it's the wrong time of the month, anyway." Her face was drawn. "So stop worrying."

Was he worrying? Or looking for an excuse?

He heard a sudden roar overhead. Saw by Annie's

face the moment the sound registered. "Was that a heli-copter? He's taking her away right now, isn't he? With-out even letting her say goodbye." She scrambled off the couch and out the door, running out in front of her house. She craned her head back, shading her eyes with her hands. "Is it already gone?"

Logan knew the chopper would circle again. "Will didn't come by helicopter, Annie."

"But—" She straightened, and realization settled on her face. "It's for you."

"Yeah." The helicopter bulleted across the sky again. It was circling. Looking for a clearing. He didn't have to guess where the chopper would land. There was only one clearing large enough. The old Castillo estate.

His remaining day had just shrunk down to min-utes. Despite Cole's obvious manipulation in putting Logan in the same place as Annie and their daughter, business called too urgently to be ignored. He looked back at her little beach cottage. Less than a week, yet it felt like the only home he'd known in way too long. He went inside long enough to grab his leather jacket and shrugged into it. It, too, had been through a storm and it looked it. Then he grabbed one of the albums and flipped back the cover. Baby pictures. He exhaled roughly and shoved the album under his arm.

Annie was watching him, her expression still as he stepped out onto the small porch. She obviously noted the album, but said nothing.

"Diego will deliver enough gas every day for the generator I found for you until the plant's going again. And Sara's got an electric cooktop she's going to bring over for you. Maisy said she's getting Leo to move one of her ranges over to the community center. The generator there's bigger. She said use it whenever you need to dry your herbs——"

Her lashes drifted down. "I always knew you'd leave. That nothing mattered here enough for you. I just didn't expect it to be so soon."

He left the porch and caught her face in his hands, pressing his mouth to hers for an aching, long moment.

"You do matter, Annie Hess."

"Because now you know we share a daughter who will never be ours?"

"You matter just because of you."

"But not enough to make you stay."

The chopper circled again. He cast a look up, watching the Huey scream through the sky. Damn Cole for taking away even the grace of a day. "Enough to know the life I lead is not good enough for you."

Then he set Annie away from him and jogged up the narrow, gravel path toward the main road. Heading back toward an inescapable life he'd chosen long ago and had hated himself for ever since.

Leaving behind a woman he shouldn't have loved, but couldn't regret.

Chapter 17

Seventy-two days without Riley.

Seventy-five without Logan.

Annie turned off the stove beneath her hot chocolate and looked out the window over her sink at the ocean shimmering beyond the sand.

She'd made it through every day. At first counting off minutes. If she made it through five minutes, then she could make it through five hours. Then five days. Maybe in five months…five years…the emptiness inside her would abate.

She filled a tall mug with the cocoa, dropped in a handful of tiny marshmallows and fit the lid on top. It was the beginning of May and entirely too warm for the hot drink. But that didn't stop her from making it every single day.

She grabbed her wide-brimmed hat off the counter

and put it on. She was planting rosemary today. The flat of cuttings she'd taken from the main fields had rooted, and sat on the floor by the door, scenting her house with their distinctively woody fragrance.

The phone rang before she reached the door and she automatically grabbed it as she pulled a fresh pair of gardening gloves out of the drawer.

"Annie!"

"We won, of course."

Riley's voice greeted her and Annie's heart tugged the way she'd accepted it always would. She smiled and tucked the phone in her shoulder. "How'd the debate go?"

"I told you that you would." She lifted the flat and carried it out the front door to the small pickup parked there, and slid it into the truck bed. The truck had arrived within days of Logan's departure. Along with a veritable barrage of other supplies. "Never doubted it." She took the phone in her hand and leaned back against the side of the vehicle. "How's everything else going?"

"Mom quit her job, but she probably told you that already. We're taking piano lessons together. She wants to play duets. How old-fashioned is that?" Riley's voice sounded bored, but Annie heard beyond the surface. Not all of Riley's family issues had been solved. But her running away had been the wake-up call they'd all needed.

"When they bring you out to visit this summer, you can play them on the piano at the community center."

Riley snorted. "Not likely. Listen, I gotta go. Just wanted to tell you about the debate. You know, Bendlemaier's team has been state champions for four years running. My school is gonna stomp their butts next year. Just watch us. Oh. And I got a letter from Logan the other day, too."

Annie's smile froze. The tug was more like a yank, this time. And it held on, good and tight, until she pressed her hand to her heart. As if that would be any real help. "That's nice. What'd he say?"

"Not much. He's been traveling a lot. The stamp was from Germany. He asked if I still talked to Kenny Hobbes. *As if.* The guy's a total dweeb. I'd write Logan back and tell him that, but there was no return address."

There never was. Annie knew that Logan had written Riley several times over the past weeks. Never saying much more than that he was thinking about her. And the actions seemed to be enough for Riley, who had adjusted to the news of him—and not Drago—being her father with far less trauma than learning about Annie being her mother.

But then, Lucia hadn't had anything to do with imparting the information about Logan.

Since then, Annie had gone to Olympia twice for long weekends, and Riley was already planning to spend a month with Annie that summer.

It wasn't always easy. Riley wasn't always sweetness and light. She was a Hess, after all. But it was better than Annie had ever thought it could be. And, thanks to Noelle's calming influence, Will had stopped ranting with concern that Logan would challenge them over Riley's custody.

So, maybe Annie owed Lucia her thanks after all.

She'd ripped off a bandage with intent to harm.

Instead, the festering wound had finally started to heal.

"Oh, gotta go. Mom's honking. Piano lesson, you

know." Riley's voice was rushed. But it was the natural rush of teenagers everywhere.

The phone clicked.

"Love you, too," Annie murmured.

She tilted her head back, looking up at the sky. The sun shone warmly on her face. Finally, she sighed a little. She took the phone back inside, retrieved the gardening gloves and her hot chocolate and went out to the truck.

But her gaze lingered on the tree stump from the Castillo estate that sat in her front yard. So far, the town council hadn't been able to agree what to do with the thing. Until then, Sam had assured Annie the trunk would stay in her yard.

But it wasn't really the stump that she looked at. It was the fresh carving there.

Then she shook herself a little. She spent too much time looking at the darned thing. Her foot hit the gas pedal and the truck revved neatly up her path. She turned south at the road, making the drive to Castillo House in mere minutes. Which was good, considering that Sara was expecting her at the shop in a short while. It was the middle of spring and tourism was ripening. So was business at Island Botanica.

She pulled up as close to the house as she could, and walked around the truck bed, her gaze on the plants. She'd given up trying to cultivate the land near the fence and had moved closer to the crumbling house. So far, a leggy vine of bougainvillea was all that grew.

But it was more than ever had grown before.

She lifted the rosemary out of the truck and carried the wooden crate toward the house. She'd plant on the southwest side, she thought.

"Like the hat."

She stopped. Her hands loosened.

The flat fell straight to the ground. It hit with a thud, and fine soil burst out from beneath it.

"I looked for you at the shop."

"I'm not there," she said inanely. Her eyes roved over him. His hair was a little longer. His bronzed face lean and hard, the scar along his jaw nearly white. And his eyes were bluer than the ocean. "What are you doing here, Logan?"

He stepped forward, away from the weathered house. He wore a white shirt and khaki pants and she thought he'd never looked so good.

He nodded toward the vine that clung gamely to the roughly textured wall. "You were right. You can grow plants anywhere."

"Logan—"

"See you got the truck. It's working out for you?"

He walked over to the vehicle and circled it.

"Kick the tires, why don't you?"

He slanted a look her way, dark. Amused.

She crossed her arms. "The truck has been helpful. Thank you. The windows were perfect, the new roof is better than the entire cottage deserved. What are you doing here?"

"I wanted you to have what you needed."

"Well, your conscience can be clear," she said evenly. "I'm the envy of half the island." And hers was one of very few houses—along with Sara's, Maisy's and Hugo's—that now possessed a generator of its own that could probably power them through the next millennium if need be. He could dislike his father all he wanted. He'd still had a generator delivered and installed, and that was no cheap feat. "So far we haven't had to use the generators," she added. "But you never know when a freakish storm might blow in."

"So, you've got everything you need, then." He walked toward her and her and her mouth dried a little. But he merely knelt down and picked up the flat of rosemary. "Where do you want it?"

She pressed her lips together and pointed.

He deposited it at the spot.

She blindly reached into the truck bed and grabbed the bucket that carried her tools. She knelt down beside the flat and pushed her shaking hands into the gloves. If he wanted to act as if his presence was not extraordinary, then so be it.

Just because he'd carved their names into that infernal tree didn't mean that she'd been waiting for him for seventy-five endless days.

She grabbed the short-handled shovel from the bucket and pushed it into the earth. She'd barely turned over the second shovel of soil when he crouched beside her. He took a spade from the bucket and neatly fitted a cutting into the row she was digging.

"Don't look so surprised," he murmured. "You don't think Sara was the only one who learned a little about gardening growing up on this rock, do you?"

She tossed down the shovel and sat back. "I don't know what to think, frankly. What are you *doing* here, Logan?"

He sat back, too. Crooked his wrist over his bent knee and pointed the tip of the spade at the bougainvillea. "How'd you get that thing to root?"

"I told you. There's nothing wrong with the soil here."

"Yeah, but you're the only one to come along in forty years or so who believed it enough to prove it." He turned his head, surveying the land behind them. "I used to come out here when I was a kid."

"Yes, I remember. To watch the *sunsets*, you said."

"Before that." His smile flashed, far too briefly. "When I was little. Scared the devil out of my mom. She was always afraid of somebody going off the cliff behind the house."

"Aren't you just full of reminiscences." She didn't care if she sounded peevish. She was. He'd left her. He'd stayed away. Eighteen hundred long, endless hours.

"You and Sara haven't found the current owner yet?"

"No."

He nodded. Reached over and neatly planted several more cuttings, then sat back again. "I quit."

"Well, I didn't ask you to help me plant in the first place. I didn't ask anything of you." Her tongue didn't stop. "Didn't expect anything. You leave behind that tree trunk for me to find and then you just show up here and act as if everything is hunky-dory! For all you know, I could have been pregnant when you left here, regardless of what I said the day you left." She hadn't been. She'd been relieved. And saddened.

Logan's gaze drifted down her body. Slender, curvy. Wearing a pair of dark green shorts that displayed impossibly beautiful legs. The shorts were modest, but they were not the camouflaging dresses she'd worn.

"You weren't pregnant. I called Sara a few times. I know you wouldn't have kept that a secret from her and she'd have told me."

"You send letters to Riley. You call your sister." Her

jaw tightened. She leaned forward again to turn the shovel.

"Yes," he admitted. "But I came back to you." Her green eyes turned glacial. "Don't toy with me, Logan."

"I'll help you find the owner."

She blinked at his sudden change of tack, but she recovered quickly. "Another little trick you can pull from your bag along with trucks and roofs and generators?"

"I know people," he said. There was no point in pretending he didn't have connections across the globe. And maybe he was uncertain enough about what he was doing here that he wanted her to know he came with *some* sort of ability.

"Bully for you." She leaned forward, stabbing the shovel into the dirt. "Don't do me any favors, Logan. I can manage on my own. I should have sent all that stuff back when it started arriving. The truck, everything."

"Why didn't you?"

"It was all from you."

He absorbed that. "You found the tree trunk?"

Her expression tightened. The muscles in her lightly tanned arms flexed as she settled plants in the soil. "Sam made sure of it. You didn't admit that the cut on your jaw happened while the two of you were moving the tree trunk." Only the faintest shimmer in her voice gave the slightest clue to her emotions as she glanced at him. "Looks like it healed up all right, though."

"I meant what I carved."

"Really." She looked unconvinced. "Logan loves Annie.' Was it supposed to be my consolation prize or something?"

He deserved that. He changed tack again. "How's Riley?"

"Call her yourself and find out." She sighed a little. "Rising above *all* of her parents' imperfections. Including yours. Now is that all the information *you* need? Because I need to get these in the ground and get to the shop. Sara's expecting me."

"I quit my job."

Her shoulders bowed for a moment. Then she kept digging. "Why? You believed you *were* your job."

"I wanted to make something rather than destroy it." Cole had countered that Logan wasn't destroying anything, but salvaging a bad situation caused by worse circumstances. "But there aren't many who quit Coleman. When he picks you, he picks you to stay."

She paused. "He sounds dangerous."

He supposed Cole was. But the real danger was in a world that had created a need for such men. For clandestine agencies that operated in the murkiness that guarded the boundaries of decency. "He was…" he searched for a description, "…peeved." Despite his own hand in the situation.

She suddenly looked at him. "Did he hurt you?"

Logan laughed softly and caught her hands in his. He drew off her gloves and tossed them aside. "Would you go for his throat if you thought he did?"

Her fingers flexed. Then slowly tangled with his. "Maybe."

Probably. She wanted to protect what she had. Because of the decisions she'd had to make.

"There's no person I respect more than you, Annie."

"Respect." Her lips turned down.

Her fingers started to slide from his. He tightened

his grip. "But there's not a lot of reason for you to respect me."

Her mouth rounded. "How can you say that?"

"The facts pretty much speak for themselves, Annie. I've left you alone. Twice."

"Facts." Her gaze went beyond him. She drew off her hat and her hair, longer than it had been during the storm, tumbled past her shoulders in a wealth of white-gold waves. "Facts don't necessarily tell the truth, Logan. You told me that yourself. When I was seventeen, I wanted what I wanted, when I wanted it. And you were what I wanted. So I took, even though you'd tried to stop me."

"But I didn't stop."

"I know you didn't. And that night is still little more than a dream to me, Logan. But I wouldn't change it, because we created something beyond measure."

She moistened her lips. And her gaze wasn't glacial. It was softer than spring dew. Her eyes were the eyes of a girl he'd never been able to forget; of a woman he didn't want to forget.

"Every one of us could have made different choices somewhere along the way, Logan. Maybe better choices, even. Ones less hurtful. But I believe that Riley is exactly where she was intended to be. Not because it's the easiest thing to believe—the least painful for me. But because it is *right*. I believe that coming to Turnabout and opening up Island Botanica with Sara is exactly where I was intended to be. I may not be an official Turn, but this is *my* island, too. It's my home, and I love it."

"Are you willing to share it?"

She went still. "That depends. On whether you meant what you carved on the tree trunk."

"I do."

"For how long?"

"As long as you'll have me."

"Why?"

"Because I heard you can make things grow anywhere. I'm not sure if I've got anything worthwhile that'll take root, but maybe given a century or two, you might have some luck."

She leaned toward him. "Sometimes a person needs a challenge in their life."

He held her off. "I didn't want the darkness of the world I lived in crossing paths with the sunlight in yours. But when I left, it was like your light came with me. I couldn't shake it. Couldn't shake you. And I didn't want to. I hated what I was doing, what it was making me. You'd turned your life around into what you needed it to be for you. So I came back. There was nothing about this place that I couldn't live without before. Until I found you here. I swear to God, Annie, leaving you after just those few days was like leaving behind an entire lifetime. Sam said something that day we were out here clearing the trees about not looking at what the island would give me but what I could give to it."

He looked at the Castillo house. Half crumbling. Not barren, after all. "And I want to give it back this place."

"Restore it or get rid of it?"

"I'm done in the 'getting rid of' business. I love you, Annie. You're the first woman I've said that to. And you'll be the last."

She was silent for a long while. Then a shudder worked through her shoulders. And when she finally looked at him there were tears in her eyes. And such naked love on her face that it rocked him.

He'd come back, and he'd hoped. But until that very moment, he'd not truly let himself believe.

"The last?" She slid her arms around his neck. Threaded her fingers through his hair. "I hope not. The Castillo house is a large house, Logan. If we're really going to do this, I'm going to want to fill a bedroom or two; maybe with a miniature woman who's going to want to hear 'I love you' from her daddy."

She'd unmanned him. His hands circled her back. "You're willing to do that? After everything that's happened, you'd still want——"

"Everything. I still want everything. With you, Logan Drake. Only with you."

Then she pressed her mouth to his.

And it was the easiest choice of all.

* * * * *

We hope you enjoyed reading

THE RETURN OF CAINE O'HALLORAN

by *New York Times* bestselling author
JoANN ROSS and **HARD CHOICES** by *USA TODAY* bestselling author **ALLISON LEIGH**.

Both were originally
Harlequin® series stories!

Discover more heartfelt tales of family, friendship and love from the Harlequin® Special Edition series. Romance is for life and these stories show that every chapter in a relationship has its challenges and delights, and that love can be renewed with each turn of the page.

*Discover A WEAVER VOW,
a new tale of love, loss and second chances from the
Harlequin® Special Edition series and
USA TODAY bestselling author Allison Leigh.*

***

Murphy, please don't get into more trouble.

Whatever had made her think she could be a better parent to Murphy than his other options? He needed a man around, not just a woman he could barely tolerate.

He needed his father.

And now all they had was each other.

Isabella Lockhart couldn't bear to think about it.

"It was an accident!" Murphy yelled. "Dude! That's my bat! You can't just take my bat!"

"I just did, *dude*," the man returned flatly. He closed his hand over Murphy's thin shoulder and forcibly moved him away from Isabella.

Isabella rounded on the man, gaping at him. He was wearing a faded brown ball cap and aviator sunglasses that hid his eyes. "Take your hand off him! Who do you think you are?"

"The man your boy decided to aim at with his blasted baseball." His jaw was sharp and shadowed by brown stubble and his lips were thinned.

"I did not!" Murphy screamed right into Isabella's ear. She winced, then pointed. *"Go sit down."*

She drew in a calming breath and turned her head into the breeze that she'd begun to suspect never died here in Weaver, Wyoming, before facing the man again.

"I'm Isabella Lockhart," she began.

"I know who you are."

She'd been in Weaver only a few weeks, but it really was a small town if people she'd never met already knew who she was.

"I'm sure we can resolve whatever's happened here, Mr.…—?"

"Erik Clay."

Focusing on the woman in front of him was a lot safer than focusing on the skinny black-haired hellion sprawled on Ruby's bench.

She tucked her white-blond hair behind her ear with a visibly shaking hand. Bleached blond, he figured, considering the eyes that she turned toward the back of his truck were such a dark brown they were nearly black.

Even angry as he was, he wasn't blind to the whole effect. Weaver's newcomer was a serious looker.

***

Enjoy A WEAVER VOW
by USA TODAY bestselling author Allison Leigh.

Available April 23, 2013, from
Harlequin® Special Edition, wherever books are sold.

NYTEXP0413

❤HARLEQUIN®

SPECIAL EDITION

Life, Love and Family

Save $1.00 on the purchase of

A WEAVER VOW

by *USA TODAY* bestselling author

Allison Leigh,

available April 23, 2013

or on any other Harlequin® Special Edition book.

Available wherever books are sold, including most bookstores, supermarkets, drugstores and discount stores.

Save $1.00

on the purchase of
A WEAVER VOW
by *USA TODAY*
bestselling author Allison Leigh,
available April 23, 2013

or on any other Harlequin® Special Edition book.

Coupon valid until July 22, 2013. Redeemable at participating retail outlets in the U.S. and Canada only. Limit one coupon per customer.

Canadian Retailers: Harlequin Enterprises Limited will pay the face value of this coupon plus 10.25¢ if submitted by customer for this product only. Any other use constitutes fraud. Coupon is nonassignable. Void if taxed, prohibited or restricted by law. Consumer must pay any government taxes. Void if copied. Nielsen Clearing House ("NCH") customers submit coupons and proof of sales to Harlequin Enterprises Limited, P.O. Box 3000, Saint John, NB E2L 4L3, Canada. Non-NCH retailer—for reimbursement submit coupons and proof of sales directly to Harlequin Enterprises Limited, Retail Marketing Department, 225 Duncan Mill Rd., Don Mills, Ontario M3B 3K9, Canada.

U.S. Retailers: Harlequin Enterprises Limited will pay the face value of this coupon plus 8¢ if submitted by customer for this product only. Any other use constitutes fraud. Coupon is nonassignable. Void if taxed, prohibited or restricted by law. Consumer must pay any government taxes. Void if copied. For reimbursement submit coupons and proof of sales directly to Harlequin Enterprises Limited, P.O. Box 880478, El Paso, TX 88588-0478, U.S.A. Cash value 1/100 cents.

5 26107 16

5 65373 00076 2   (8100)0 11832

NYTCOUPC

REQUEST YOUR FREE BOOKS!

2 FREE NOVELS FROM THE ROMANCE COLLECTION PLUS 2 FREE GIFTS!

YES! Please send me 2 FREE novels from the Romance Collection and my 2 FREE gifts (gifts are worth about $10). After receiving them, if I don't wish to receive any more books, I can return the shipping statement marked "cancel." If I don't cancel, I will receive 4 brand-new novels every month and be billed just $5.99 per book in the U.S. or $6.49 per book in Canada. That's a savings of at least 25% off the cover price. It's quite a bargain! Shipping and handling is just 50¢ per book in the U.S. and 75¢ per book in Canada.* I understand that accepting the 2 free books and gifts places me under no obligation to buy anything. I can always return a shipment and cancel at any time. Even if I never buy another book, the two free books and gifts are mine to keep forever.

194/394 MDN FVUR

Name _____

(PLEASE PRINT)

Address _____ Apt. # _____

City _____ State/Prov. _____ Zip/Postal Code _____

Signature (if under 18, a parent or guardian must sign) _____

Mail to the Harlequin® Reader Service:
IN U.S.A.: P.O. Box 1867, Buffalo, NY 14240-1867
IN CANADA: P.O. Box 609, Fort Erie, Ontario L2A 5X3

Want to try two free books from another line?
Call 1-800-873-8635 or visit www.ReaderService.com.

* Terms and prices subject to change without notice. Prices do not include applicable taxes. Sales tax applicable in N.Y. Canadian residents will be charged applicable taxes. Offer not valid in Quebec. This offer is limited to one order per household. Not valid for current subscribers to the Romance Collection or the Romance/Suspense Collection. All orders subject to credit approval. Credit or debit balances in a customer's account(s) may be offset by any other outstanding balance owed by or to the customer. Please allow 4 to 6 weeks for delivery. Offer available while quantities last.

Your Privacy—The Harlequin® Reader Service is committed to protecting your privacy. Our Privacy Policy is available online at www.ReaderService.com or upon request from the Harlequin Reader Service.

We make a portion of our mailing list available to reputable third parties that offer products we believe may interest you. If you prefer that we not exchange your name with third parties, or if you wish to clarify or modify your communication preferences, please visit us at www.ReaderService.com/consumerschoice or write to us at Harlequin Reader Service Preference Service, P.O. Box 9062, Buffalo, NY 14269. Include your complete name and address.

ROM11

HARLEQUIN®

A Romance FOR EVERY MOOD™

Love the Harlequin book you just read?

Your opinion matters.

Review this book on your favorite book site, review site, blog or your own social media properties and share your opinion with other readers!

Be sure to connect with us at:
Harlequin.com/Newsletters
Facebook.com/HarlequinBooks
Twitter.com/HarlequinBooks

HARLEQUIN ®

TM

A Romance FOR EVERY MOO[D]

Stay up-to-date on all your romance-reading news with the *Harlequin Shopping Guide*, featuring bestselling authors, exciting new miniseries, books to watch and more!

The newest issue will be delivered right to you with our compliments! There are 4 each year.

Signing up is easy.

EMAIL

ShoppingGuide@Harlequin.ca

WRITE TO US

HARLEQUIN BOOKS
Attention: Customer Service Department
P.O. Box 9057, Buffalo, NY 14269-9057

OR PHONE

1-800-873-8635 in the United States
1-888-343-9777 in Canada

Please allow 4-6 weeks for delivery of the first issue by mail.

HSGSIGNU[P]